THE POACHER

THE POACHER

Captain Frederick Marryat

WILDSIDE PRESS

INTRODUCTION

FOR reasons probably connected with his own love for an outdoor life and a career of adventure, Captain Marryat was as fond of poachers as he was of pirates and smugglers. We are told that he had a theory that the worst poacher made the best gamekeeper, probably on the well-known principles that a thief should be set to catch a thief, and that reformed rakes make the best husbands. At all events, in the novel before us, Captain Marryat chooses to have as his hero a boy who was trained to defy the Game Laws, who inherited from his father a woodland craft of illegitimately snaring pheasants and hares, and who ultimately proved to be not only a young man of excellent moral fibre, but on the whole a singular favourite of fortune. Such misfortunes as he encountered were, in reality, the consequence of his own boyish virtue. Joseph Rushbrook, when quite a child, deliberately takes upon himself all the terrible consequences of a paternal crime, and because his father had committed murder, lives for years under the suspicion of an act of guilt quite sufficient, were it not for his tender years, to bring him to the scaffold. In somewhat tardy fashion—as a matter of fact in the very last page of his book—the author feels that his theme may be condemned by moral purists as not conforming to any well-established code of ethics. "In this story," he says, "we have shown how a young lad who commenced his career with poaching, ultimately became a gentleman of £7000 a year; but we must remind our youthful readers, that it does not follow that every one who commences with poaching is to have the same good fortune. We advise them, therefore, not to attempt it, as they may find that instead of £7000 a year, they may stand a chance of going to where our hero very narrowly escaped from being sent : that is, to a certain portion of her Majesty's dominions beyond the seas, latterly termed Australia, but more generally known by the appellation of Botany Bay." The construction of these characteristic sentences is perhaps hardly so praiseworthy as their obviously good intention.

The date of the publication of "The Poacher" is 1841, and it is noticeable that at this period Captain Marryat had the opportunity of defending himself from a not unfamiliar form of literary attack. The story was brought out in weekly numbers in the *Era,* and the critic fell foul of the author for choosing so unworthy a method of appealing to the public. An article appeared in *Fraser* commenting on this "hebdomadal habit" as being more likely to ruin Marryat's fame than even the monthly instalments of Mr. Ainsworth's productions. Here is a sentence of this slashing critic which seems to indicate a certain amount of personal spite : "That which is venial in a miserable starveling of Grub Street is *perfectly disgusting* in the extravagantly paid novelists of these days—the *caressed* of generous booksellers. Mr. Ainsworth and Captain Marryat ought to disdain such *pitiful peddling.* Let them eschew it without delay." Our author's answer was partly humorous, partly serious. He pointed out that if the rarity or frequency of an author's productions were the sole standard of merit, "My Lady-Anybody" who produces one novel a year is twice as great a writer as the novelist who produces two, and twelve times as great as the *Fraser* man whose production is monthly. But the real defence of the mode of publication which Marryat had adopted lies in his belief that he is doing some good to the lower classes, "who until lately—and the chief credit of the alteration is due to Mr. Dickens—had hardly an idea of such recreation."* The democracy, in point of fact, was, he thought, to be weaned from such exciting and demoralising writing as was to be found in the *Weekly Dispatch,* in the columns of which demagogues and Chartists, *et hoc genus omne,* find encouragement, and disaffection and ill-will towards the Government is recklessly promoted. Captain Marryat believes that in writing for the amusement and instruction of the poor man he is serving his country, a task not unworthy of the proudest

* See " Captain Marryat," by David Hannay (Walter Scott), p. 129.

INTRODUCTION

Englishman. Possibly if he had lived in our days he might have been a little more sceptical of the effects of good literature upon the people, and at all events hesitated to declare his belief that the poor man, if given his option, would always prefer the better to the worse.

As a matter of fact, however, "The Poacher" is hardly good literature, even in the most tolerant conception of that somewhat elastic term. About this period of his life Captain Marryat was involved in some personal misfortunes and difficulties, which made it necessary for him to get money at all hazards. His health was not particularly good, his pecuniary position was not a flourishing one. The result was that he drove his pen at a reckless rate of speed, which materially interfered with the success of his creations. "The Poacher" bears many marks of the pressure of necessity—*parce qu'il faut vivre.* It is not so bad a novel as its successor "Percival Keene," but it is too evidently composed at breakneck haste, without much regard for probability, and with no particular care in the delineation of character. None of the personages live in the memory, except possibly the bumboat woman, Mrs. Chopper; while the eccentric characters are manifestly deficient in plausibility. Captain O'Donahue and Major M'Shane, to whom may be added the tinker, Mr. Spikeman, are instances in point, doing impossible things in a highly ingenious but scarcely convincing fashion. O'Donahue, an out-at-elbows Irishman, marries a Polish lady, Princess Czartorinski; Mr. Spikeman unites himself with a sentimental young lady, Miss Melissa Mathews, in bold defiance of all conventional laws; while the Princess is not prevented by any considerations of social rank from becoming an intimate friend of Mrs. M'Shane, who was the keeper of an eating-house. Startling coincidences abound in these pages; the proper persons required for the solution of the problem turn up exactly where and when they are needed, with delightful promptitude; and the author seems to care not at all for *vraisemblance,* so long as he succeeds in knitting his story together somehow. When O'Donahue goes to Russia to find his titled wife, he has no difficulty whatever in getting the highest recommendations, as well as most useful introductions, from His Royal Highness the Commander of the Forces. If the author were not obviously serious in the evolution of his plot, one might almost have suspected that he was trying to parody certain popular contemporary romances of intrigue and adventure.

The style is the one with which all readers of Marryat are familiar—excessively careless and slipshod, sometimes ungrammatical; but the author is always lively, spirited, and good-tempered, full of animal spirits, and never at a loss for novel complications to arrest the inevitable conclusion. Now and again Captain Marryat desires to be meditative and philosophical, and thereby reveals the poverty of the land. He can tell his story, and prove to his own satisfaction that a murderer, even when he escapes the immediate consequences of his crime, leads a profoundly gloomy and conscience-tortured life; he can prove how a meritorious boy, starting under the gravest disadvantages, can, because he is self-sacrificing and chivalrous, end by a position of luxury and affluence. But he cannot moralise except in trivial fashion, and when he meditates he is lost. There is a curious passage at the commencement of Chapter xl., which may serve as an illustration. The subject is the difference between man and woman, and the reason why man has got the upper hand; but the explanation given is not one which is likely to appeal to later students of the relations between the sexes. The complexity of the female mind as compared with the single-ness and simplicity of the masculine intellect, despite the novelty of the argument, is not a point which has commended itself in any large measure to modern observers.

W. L. C.

October 1897.

CONTENTS

ix

CONTENTS

CONTENTS

CHAPTER XVIII

PAGE

CHAPTER XIX

CHAPTER XX

CHAPTER XXI

CHAPTER XXII

CHAPTER XXIII

CHAPTER XXIV

CHAPTER XXV

CHAPTER XXVI

CONTENTS

CHAPTER XXVII

CONTENTS

CONTENTS

THE POACHER

CHAPTER I

In which there is more ale than argument.

IT was on a blusterous windy night in the early part of
November, 1812, that three men were on the highroad near
to the little village of Grassford, in the south of Devonshire.
The moon was nearly at the full, but the wild scud, and occasionally the more opaque clouds, passed over in such rapid
succession, that it was rarely, and but for a moment or two,
that the landscape was thrown into light and shadow; and
the wind, which was keen and piercing, bent and waved the
leafless branches of the trees which were ranged along the
hedgerows, between which the road had been formed.

The three individuals to whom we have referred appeared
all of them to have been indulging too freely in the ale
which was sold at the public-house about half a mile from
the village, and from which they had just departed. Two
of them, however, comparatively speaking sober, were assisting home, by their joint efforts, the third, who, supported
between them, could with difficulty use his legs. Thus did
they continue on; the two swayed first on the one side of
the road, and then on the other, by the weight of the third,
whom they almost carried between them. At last they
arrived at a bridge built over one of those impetuous streams
so common in the county, when, as if by mutual under-
standing, for it was without speaking, the two more sober
deposited the body of the third against the parapet of the
bridge, and then for some time were silently occupied in
recovering their breath. One of the two who remained

1   A

leaning on the parapet by the side of their almost lifeless companion, was a man of about forty years of age, tall and slender, dressed in a worn-out black coat, and a pair of trousers much too short for him, the original colour of which it would have been difficult to have surmised; a sort of clerical hat, equally the worse for wear, was on his head. Although his habiliments were mean, still there was something about his appearance which told of better days, and of having moved in a different sphere in society; and such had been the case. Some years before he had been the head of a grammar-school, with a comfortable income; but a habit of drinking had been his ruin, and he was now the preceptor of the village of Grassford, and gained his livelihood by instructing the children of the cottagers for the small modicum of twopence a head per week. This unfortunate propensity to liquor remained with him; and he no sooner received his weekly stipend than he hastened to drown his cares, and the recollection of his former position, at the ale-house which they had just quitted. The second personage whom we shall introduce was not of a corresponding height with the other: he was broad, square-chested, and short—dressed in knee-breeches, leggings, and laced boots—his coat being of a thick fustian, and cut short like a shooting-jacket: his profession was that of a pedlar.

"It's odd to me," said the pedlar, at last breaking silence, as he looked down upon the drunken man who lay at his feet, "why ale should take a man off his legs; they say that liquor gets into the head, not the feet."

"Well," replied the schoolmaster, who was much more inebriated than the pedlar, "there's argument even in that; and, you see, the perpendicular deviation must arise from the head being too heavy, that's clear; and then, you see, the feet, from the centre of gravity being destroyed, become too light; and if you put that and that together, why, a man can't stand. You understand my demonstration?"

"It *was* heavy wet, that ale, and so I suppose it's all right," replied the pedlar; "but still ale a'n't poured into the head or into the feet of a man, but into the internals, which are right in the middle of a man; so, how do you make out your case, Mr. Furness?"

"Why, Byres, you talk of the residuum."

2

THE POACHER

"Never said a word about it; and, as I stand here, **never** even heard the word before."

"Perhaps not: the residuum is, you see, Byres, what is left."

"If that's residgium, I didn't mean to say a word about it; there was none left, for you drained the pot."

"Good, Byres; you have never been to college, that's clear. Now, observe, when a man pours down into his stomach a certain quantity of liquor, the spirituous or lighter part ascends to his head, and that makes his head heavy. Do you understand?"

"No; what's light can't make things heavy."

"Can't it?—you know nothing about the matter. Have you not a proof before you?" replied the schoolmaster, reeling, and catching hold of the parapet for support; "look at that unfortunate man, who has yielded to excess."

"Very true; I see that he's drunk, but I want to know how it is that he got drunk?"

"By drinking."

"That I knew before."

"Then why ask any more questions? Had we not better proceed, and take him home to his expectant and unhappy wife? 'Tis a sad, sad thing, that a man should 'put an enemy into his mouth to steal away his brains.'"

"Half a pint will do that with Rushbrook," replied the pedlar; "they say that he was wounded on his head, and that half his brains are gone already, and that's why he has a pension."

"Yes, seventeen pounds a year; paid quarterly, without deduction, and only to walk four miles to get it," replied Furness; "yet how misplaced is the liberality on the part of the government. Does he work? No; he does nothing but drink and lie in bed all day, while I must be up early and remain late, teaching the young idea at twopence per week. Friend Byres, 'mercy is not itself which oft looks so.' Now, it is my opinion that it would be a kindness to this poor wretch if we were to toss him, as he now is, over the bridge into the rushing stream; it would end all his troubles."

"And save us the trouble of getting him home," replied Byres, who determined to humour his more inebriated companion. "Well, Mr. Furness, I've no objection. Why should he live? Is he not a sinecurist—one of the locusts who fatten on the sweat and blood of the people, as the Sunday paper says? Don't you remember my reading it this morning?"

"Very true, Master Byres."

"What d'ye say, then?—shall we over with him?"

"We must think a little," replied the schoolmaster, who put his hand up to his chin, and remained silent for a minute or two. "No," resumed he, at last; "on second thoughts I cannot do it. He halves his beer with me. No pension—no beer; that's a self-evident proposition and conclusion. It were ingratitude on my part, and I cannot consent to your proposal," continued the schoolmaster; "nay, more, I will defend him against your murderous intentions to the very last."

"Why, Master Furness, you must be somewhat the worse for liquor yourself: it was your proposal to throw him over the bridge, not mine."

"Take care what you say," replied the schoolmaster; "would you accuse me of murder, or intent to murder?"

"No, not by no means—only you proposed heaving him over the bridge : I will say that."

"Friend Byres, it's my opinion you'll say anything but your prayers; but in your present state I overlook it. Let us go on, or I shall have two men to carry home instead of one. Come now, take one of his arms, while I take the other, and raise him up. It is but a quarter of a mile to the cottage."

Byres, who, as we observed, was by far the more sober of the two, did not think it worth his while to reply to the pedagogue. After a few staggers on the part of the latter, their comrade was raised up and led away between them.

The drunken man appeared to be so far aware of what was going on that he moved his legs mechanically, and in a short time they arrived at the cottage door, which the pedagogue struck with his fist so as to make it rattle on its hinges. The door was opened by a tall, handsome woman, holding a candle in her hand.

"I thought so," said she, shaking her head. "The old story : now he will be ill all night, and not get up till noon. What a weary life it is with a drunken husband. Bring him in, and thank you kindly for your trouble."

4

"It has been hard work and hot work," observed the schoolmaster, sitting down in a chair, after they had placed their comrade on the bed.

"Indeed, and it must be," replied the wife. "Will you have a drop of small beer, Mr. Furness?"

"Yes, if you please, and so will Mr. Byres, too. What a pity it is your good man will not keep to small beer."

"Yes, indeed," replied the wife, who went into the back premises, and soon returned with a quart mug of beer.

The schoolmaster emptied half the mug, and then handed it to the pedlar.

"And my little friend Joey, fast asleep, I'll warrant!"

"Yes, poor child, and so should I have been by this time; the clock has gone twelve."

"Well, Mrs. Rushbrook, I wish you a good night. Come, Mr. Byres, Mrs. Rushbrook must want to be in bed."

"Good night, Mr. Furness, and good night, sir, and many thanks."

The schoolmaster and pedlar quitted the cottage. Mrs. Rushbrook, after having watched them for a minute, carefully closed the door.

"They're gone now," said she, as she turned to her husband.

What would have created much astonishment could anybody else have witnessed it, as soon as his wife had spoken, Rushbrook immediately sprang upon his feet, a fine-looking man, six feet in height, very erect in his bearing, and proved to be perfectly sober.

"Jane, my dear," said he, "there never was such a night: but I must be quick, and lose no time. Is my gun ready?"

"Everything's ready; Joey is lying down on his bed, but all ready dressed, and he awakes in a minute."

"Call him, then, for there is no time to lose. That drunken fool, Furness, proposed throwing me over the bridge. It was lucky for them that they did not try it, or I should have been obliged to settle them both, that they might tell no tales. Where's Mum?"

"In the wash-house. I'll bring him and Joey directly."

The wife left the room, while Rushbrook took down his gun and ammunition, and prepared himself for his expedition. In a minute or two a shepherd's dog, which had been released from the wash-house, made his appearance, and quietly lay down close to his master's feet; it was soon followed by Mrs. R., accompanied by Joey, a thin, meagre-looking boy, of about twelve years old, very small for his age, but apparently as active as a cat, and with energy corresponding. No one would have thought he had been roused from his sleep; there was no yawning or weariness of motion—on the contrary, his large eye was as bright as an eagle's, as he quietly, although quickly, provided himself with a sack, which he threw over his shoulders, and a coil of line, which he held in his hand, waiting until his father was ready to start. The wife put out the lights, softly opened the cottage door, looked well round, and then returned to her husband, who, giving a low whistle, as a summons to Joey and the dog, walked out of the door. Not a word was spoken; the door was softly shut to; and the trio crept stealthily away.

CHAPTER II

In which the hero of the tale is formally introduced.

BEFORE we proceed with our narrative, perhaps it will be better to explain what may appear very strange to the reader. Joseph Rushbrook, who has just left the cottage with his son and his dog, was born in the village in which he was then residing. During his younger days, some forty years previous to his present introduction to the reader, the law was not so severe, or the measures taken against poachers so strong as they were at the period of which we write. In his youth he had been very fond of carrying a gun—as his father had been before him—but he never was discovered; and after having poached for many years, and gained a perfect knowledge of the country for miles round, he was persuaded, in a fit of semi-intoxication at a neighbouring fair, to enlist in a marching regiment. He had not been more than three months at the depot when he was ordered out to India, where he remained eleven years before he was recalled. He had scarcely been six months in England, when the exigency of the war demanded the services of the regiment in the Mediterranean, where he remained for twelve years, and

6

having received a severe wound in the head, he was then
pensioned off and discharged. He resolved to return to his
native village, and settle down quietly, hoping by moderate
labour, and his pension, to gain a comfortable living. On
his return he was hardly known; many had emigrated to
a foreign clime ; many had been transported for offences
against the laws, particularly for the offence of poaching :
and as most of his former allies had been so employed, he
found himself almost a stranger where he expected to meet
with friends. The property also about the village had
changed hands. People recollected Squire So-and-So, and
the Baronet, but now their lands were held by wealthy
manufacturers or retired merchants. All was new to Joe
Rushbrook, and he felt himself anywhere but at home. Jane
Ashley, a very beautiful young woman, who was in service
at the Hall, the mansion appertaining to the adjacent property, and the daughter of one of his earliest friends, who
had been transported for poaching, was almost the only one
who could talk to him after his absence of twenty-four years ;
not that she knew the people at the time, for she was then
an infant, but she had grown up with them after Joe had left,
and could narrate anecdotes of them, and what had been
their eventual destinies. Jane having been the daughter of
a man who had been transported for poaching, was to Joe
a sort of recommendation, and it ended in his taking her for
his wife. They had not been long settled in their cottage
before Joe's former propensities returned ; in fact, he could
not be idle, he had carried a musket too long, and had lived
such a life of excitement in the service of his country, that
he found it impossible to exist without shooting at something. All his former love of poaching came strong upon
him, and his wife, so far from checking him, encouraged
him in his feelings. The consequence was, that two years
after his marriage, Joe Rushbrook was the most determined
poacher in the county. Although often suspected, he had
never been detected ; one great cause of this was his appear-
ing to be such a drunkard, a plan hit upon by his wife, who
had observed that drunken men were not suspected of being
poachers. This scheme had therefore been hit upon, and
very successfully ; for proving before a magistrate that a man
was carried home dead drunk and speechless at midnight,

7

was quite as good an *alibi* as could be brought forward. Joe Rushbrook had, therefore, the credit of being a worthless drunken fellow, who lived upon his pension and what his wife could earn; but no one had an idea that he was not only earning his livelihood, but laying by money from his successful night labours. Not that Joe did not like a drop occasionally—on the contrary, he would sometimes drink freely; but, generally speaking, the wounds in his head were complained of, and he would, if the wind was fresh and set in the right quarter, contrive to be carried home on the night in which he had most work to do. Such was the case, as we have represented in the first chapter.

Little Joey, who, as the reader may anticipate, will be our future hero, was born the first year after marriage, and was their only child. He was a quiet, thoughtful, reflective boy for his years, and had imbibed his father's love of walking out on a dark night to an extraordinary degree: it was strange to see how much prudence there was, mingled with the love of adventure, in this lad. True it is, his father had trained him early, first to examine the snares and conceal the game, which a little shrimp like Joey could do, without being suspected to be otherwise employed than in picking blackberries. Before he was seven years old, Joey could set a springe as well as his father, and was well versed in all the mystery and art of unlawful taking of game. Indeed, he was very valuable to his father, and could do what his father could not have ventured upon without exciting suspicion. It was, perhaps, from his constant vigils, that the little boy was so small in size; at all events, his diminutive size was the cause of there being no suspicion attached to him. Joey went very regularly to the day-school of Mr. Furness; and although often up the best part of the night, he was one of the best and most diligent of the scholars. No one could have supposed that the little fair-haired, quiet-looking boy, who was so busy with his books or his writing, could have been out half the night on a perilous excursion, for such it was at the time we are speaking of. It need hardly be observed that Joey had learned one important lesson, which was to be *silent;* not even *Mum*, the dog, who could not speak, was more secret or more faithful.

It is astonishing how much the nature and disposition of

8

a child may be altered by early tuition. Let a child be always with its nurse, even under the guidance of a mother, regularly brought up as children usually are, and it will continue to be a child, and even childish, after childhood is gone. But take the same child, put it by degrees in situations of peril, requiring thought and observation beyond its years, accustom it to nightly vigils, and to watching, and to hold its tongue, and it is astonishing how the mind of that child, however much its body may suffer, will develop itself so as to meet the demand upon it. Thus it is with lads that are sent early to sea, and thus it was with little Joey. He was a man in some points, although a child in others. He would play with his companions, laugh as loudly as the others, but still he would never breathe a hint of what was his father's employment. He went to church every Sunday, as did his father and mother; for they considered that poaching was no crime, although punished as such by the laws; and he, of course, considered it no crime, as he only did what his father and mother wished. Let it not be thought, therefore, that the morals of our little hero were affected by his father's profession, for such was not the case.

Having entered into this necessary explanation, we will now proceed. No band of North American Indians could have observed a better trail than that kept by our little party. Rushbrook walked first, followed by our hero and the dog Mum. Not a word was spoken; they continued their route over grass-lands and ploughed fields, keeping in the shade of the hedgerows: if Rushbrook stopped for a while to reconnoitre, so did Joey, and so did Mum, at their relative distances, until the march was resumed. For three miles and a half did they thus continue, until they arrived at a thick cover. The wind whistled through the branches of the bare trees, chiefly oak and ash; the cold, damp fog was now stationary, and shrouded them as they proceeded cautiously by the beaten track in the cover, until they had passed through it, and arrived on the other side, where the cottage of a gamekeeper was situated. A feeble light was burning, and shone through the diamond-paned windows.

Rushbrook walked out clear of the cover, and held up his hand to ascertain precisely the direction of the wind. Having satisfied himself, he retreated into the cover, in a

9

direction so as to be exactly to leeward of the keeper's house, that the noise of the report of his gun might not be heard. Having cleared the hedge, he lowered his gun, so as to bring the barrel within two or three inches of the ground, and walked slowly and cautiously through the brushwood, followed, as before, by Joey and Mum. After about a quarter of a mile's walk, a rattling of metal was heard, and they stopped short; it was the barrel of the fowling-piece which had brushed one of the wires attached to a spring-gun, set for the benefit of poachers. Rushbrook lifted up his left hand, as a sign to Joey not to move; and following the wire, by continually rattling his barrel against it, he eventually arrived at the gun itself, opened the pan, threw out all the priming, leaving it with the pan open, so that it could not go off, in case they fell in with another of the wires. Rushbrook then proceeded to business, for he well knew that the gun would be set where the pheasants were most accustomed to roost; he put a small charge of powder in his fowling-piece, that, being so near, he might not shatter the birds, and because the noise of the report would be much less; walking under an oak-tree he soon discovered the round black masses which the bodies of the roosting pheasants presented between him and the sky, and raising his piece, he fired. A heavy bound on the earth near his feet followed the discharge; Joey then slipped forward and put the pheasant into his bag; another and another shot, and every shot brought an increase to Joey's load. Seventeen were already in it when Mum gave a low growl. This was the signal for people being near. Rushbrook snapped his finger; the dog came forward to his side, and stood motionless, with ears and tail erect. In a minute's time was heard the rustling of branches as the party forced their way through the under-wood. Rushbrook stood still, waiting the signal from Mum, for the dog had been taught, if the parties advancing had another dog with them, always to raise his fore-feet up to Rushbrook's knees, but not otherwise; Mum made no such sign, and then Rushbrook lay down in the brushwood, his motions being closely followed by his son and his dog.

Voices in whispers were now heard, and the forms of two men with guns were to be seen not four yards from where they were lying. "Somewhere about here, I'll swear," said

10

one. "Yes, I think so; but it may be further on—the wind has brought down the sound."—"Very true, let's follow them, and they may fall back upon the spring-gun." The parties then advanced into the cover, and were soon out of sight; after a time Rushbrook held his ear to the wind, and, satisfied that all was safe, moved homewards, and arrived without further adventure, having relieved Joey of the heavy sack as soon as they were in the open fields.

At three o'clock in the morning he tapped at the back door of the cottage. Jane opened it, and the spoils of the night having been put away in a secret place, they were all soon in bed and fast asleep.

CHAPTER III

Train a child in the way he should go, and he will not depart from it.

IT is an old saying, that "if there were no receivers there would be no thieves," and it would have been of very little use for Rushbrook to take the game if he had not had the means of disposing of it. In this point, Byres, the pedlar, was a valuable accessory. Byres was a radical knave, who did not admire hard work. At first he took up the profession of bricklayer's labourer, one, that is, of a nature only affording occasional work and moderate wages. He did this that he might apply to the parish for relief, and do nothing for the major portion of the year. But even a few months' work would not suit him, and subsequently he gained his sustenance by carrying on his head a large basket of crockery, and disposing of his wares among the cottagers. At last he took out a pedlar's licence—perhaps one of the most dangerous permits ever allowed by a government, and which has been the cause of much of the ill-will and discontent fomented among the lower classes. Latterly, the cheapness of printing and easiness of circulation have rendered the profession of less consequence: twenty years ago the village ale-houses were not provided with newspapers; it was an expense never thought of; the men went to drink their beer and talk over

11

the news of the vicinity, and if there was a disturbance in any other portion of the United Kingdom, the fact was only gained by rumour, and that vaguely and long after it had taken place. But when the pedlar Byres made his appearance, which he at last did, weekly or oftener, as it might happen, there was a great change; he was the party who supplied information, and, in consequence, he was always welcome, and looked upon as an oracle; the best seat near the fire was reserved for him, and having deposited his pack upon the table or in a corner, he would then produce the *Propeller*, or some other publication full of treason and blasphemy, and read it aloud for the benefit of the labourers assembled. A few months were more than sufficient to produce the most serious effects: men who had worked cheerfully through the day, and retired to bed satisfied with their lot, and thankful that work was to be obtained, now remained at the public-house, canvassing the conduct of government, and leaving their resort satisfied in their own minds that they were ill-used, harshly treated, and in bitter bondage. If they met their superiors, those very parties to whom they were indebted for employment, there was no respect shown to them as formerly—or, if so, it was sullen and forced acknowledgment. The church was gradually deserted—the appearance of the pastor was no longer a signal for every hat to be lifted from the head; on the contrary, boys of sixteen or seventeen years of age would lean against the church, or the walls of the churchyard, with their hands in both pockets, and a sort of leer upon their faces, as though they defied the pastor on his appearance—and there would they remain outside during the service, meeting, unquailed and without blushing, his eyes, cast upon them as he came out again. Such was the state of things in the village of Grassford in one year after the pedlar had added it to his continual rounds —and Byres was a great favourite, for he procured for the women what they commissioned him to obtain, supplied the girls with ribbons and gewgaws, and trusted to a considerable extent. His reappearance was always anxiously looked for; he lived scot-free at the public-house, for he brought so much custom, and was the occasion of the drinking of so much ale, that the landlord considered his coming as a godsend. His box of ware was well supplied in the summer months, for the

12

fine weather was the time for the wearing of gay ribbons; but in the winter he travelled more to receive orders, or to carry away the game supplied to him by the poachers with whom he was in league. Had his box been examined during the shooting season, it would have been found loaded with pheasants, not with trinkets and ribbons. It need hardly be observed after this that Byres was the party who took off the hands of Rushbrook all the game which he procured, and which he had notice to call for before daylight, generally the *second* morning after it had been obtained; for Rushbrook was too cautious to trust Byres with his secret, that of never going out of a night without having previously pretended intoxication, and having suffered himself to be led or carried home.

Our readers will acknowledge that little Joey was placed in a very dangerous position; it is true that he was not aware that he was doing wrong in assisting his father; nevertheless, being a reflective boy, it did sometimes occur to him that it was odd that what was right should be done so secretly; and he attempted to make out how it was that the birds that flew about everywhere, and appeared to belong to every one, might not be shot in the open day. He knew that the laws forbade it; but he inquired of himself why such laws should be. Joey had heard but one side of the question, and was therefore puzzled. It was fortunate for him that the pastor of the parish, although he did not reside in it, did at least once a week call in at Mr. F.'s school, and examine the boys. Mr. Furness, who was always sober during the school hours, was very proud of these visits, and used to point out little Joey as his most promising scholar. This induced the pastor to take more immediate notice of our hero, and the commendation which he received, and the advice that was bestowed upon him, was probably the great cause why Joey did attend assiduously to his lessons, which his otherwise vagrant life would have disinclined him to do; and also kept a character for honesty and good principle, which he really deserved. Indeed, his father and mother, setting aside poaching, and the secrecy resorted to in consequence, were by no means bad examples in the ordinary course of life; they did to their neighbours as they would be done by, were fair and honest in their dealings, and invariably inculcated probity and a regard to truth on their son. This may appear

13

anomalous to many of our readers, but there are many strange anomalies in this world. It may therefore be stated in a very few words, that although our little hero had every chance of eventually following the road to ruin, yet, up to the present time, he had not entered it.

Such was the life led by little Joey for three years subsequent to our introduction of him to the reader; every day he became more useful to his father; latterly he had not attended school but in the forenoon, for, as we have before observed, Joey could, from his diminutive size and unsuspicious appearance, do much that his father would not have ventured to attempt. He was as well versed in the art of snaring as his father, and sauntering like a child about the fields and hedgerows, would examine his nooses, take out the game, and hide it till he could bring it home. Sometimes he would go out at night attended only by Mum, and the dog would invariably give him mute notice, by simply standing with his ears and tail erect, when the keepers had discovered the snares, and were lying in wait for the poacher, to lay hold of him when he came to ascertain his success. Even in such a case, Joey very often would not retreat, but, crawling on his stomach, would arrive at the snare, and take out the animal without the keepers perceiving him; for their eyes were invariably directed to the horizon, watching the appearance of some stout figure of a man, while Joey crawled along, bearing away the prize unseen. At other times, Joey would reap a rich harvest in the broad day, by means of his favourite game-cock. Having put on the animal his steel spurs, he would plunge into the thickest of the cover, and, selecting some small spot of cleared ground for the combat, he would throw down his gallant bird, and conceal himself in the brushwood; the game-cock would immediately crow, and his challenge was immediately answered by the pugnacious male pheasant, who flew down to meet him : the combat was short, for the pheasant was soon pierced by the sharp steel of his adversary; and as one antagonist fell dead, again would the game-cock crow, and his challenge be accepted by another. In an hour or two the small arena was a field of blood; Joey would creep forward, put his victorious cock into his bag together with many dead adversaries, and watch an opportunity for a safe retreat.

Such was the employment of our hero; and although suspicion had often been attached to his father, none had an idea that there had been a violation of the laws on the part of the son, when an event took place which changed our hero's destiny.

CHAPTER IV

In which the author has endeavoured, with all his power, to suit the present taste of the public.

W E have said that Byres was the receiver of the game obtained by Rushbrook. It so happened, that in these accounts Byres had not adhered to his duty towards his neighbour; in fact, he attempted to overreach, but without success, and from that time Byres became Rushbrook's determined but secret enemy. Some months had passed since their disagreement, and there was a mutual mistrust (as both men were equally revengeful in their tempers), when they happened to meet late on a Saturday night at the ale-house which was their usual resort. Furness the schoolmaster was there; he and many others had already drunk too much; all were boisterous and noisy. A few of the wives of those drinking were waiting patiently and sorrowfully outside, their arms folded in their aprons as a defence against the cold, watching for their husbands to come out, that they might coax them home before the major part of the week's earnings had been spent in liquor. Byres had the paper in his hand—he had taken it from the schoolmaster, who was too far gone to read it, and was declaiming loudly against all governments, monarchy, and laws—when a stranger entered the tap-room where they were all assembled. Rushbrook was at the time sitting down, intending quietly to take a pint and walk home, as he had too much respect for the Sabbath to follow his profession of poacher on the morning of that day: he did not intend, therefore, to resort to his usual custom of pretending to be intoxicated; but when the stranger came in, to his great surprise he observed a glance of recognition between him and Byres, after which they appeared as if they were perfect strangers. Rushbrook watched them carefully, but so as not

15

to let them perceive he was so doing, when a beckon from the stranger to Byres was again made. Byres continued to read the paper and to harangue, but at the same time took an opportunity of making a signal in reply. There was something in the stranger's appearance which told Rushbrook that he was employed as a keeper, or something in that way, for we often single out our enemies by instinct. That there was mischief in the wind Rushbrook felt sure, and his heart misgave him—the more so, as occasionally the eyes of both were turned towards him. After a little reflection, Rushbrook determined to feign intoxication, as he had so often done before : he called for another pint, for some time talked very loud, and at last laid his head on the table ; after a time he lifted it up again, drank more, and then fell back on the bench. By degrees the company thinned, until there was no one left but the schoolmaster, the pedlar, and the stranger. The schoolmaster, as usual, offered to assist the pedlar in helping Rushbrook to his cottage ; but Byres replied that he was busy, and that he need not wait for Rushbrook ; the friend he had with him would assist him in taking home the drunken man. The schoolmaster reeled home, leaving the two together. They sat down on the bench, not far from Rushbrook, who appeared to them to be in the last stage of inebriety. Their conversation was easily overheard. The pedlar stated that he had watched several nights, but never could find when Rushbrook left his cottage, but he had traced the boy more than once ; that R. had promised to have game ready for him on Tuesday, and would go out on Monday night for it. In short, Rushbrook discovered that Byres was about to betray him to the man, whom, in the course of their conversation, he found out to be a gamekeeper newly hired by the lord of the manor. After a while they broke up, Byres having promised to join the keeper in his expedition, and to assist in securing his former ally. Having made these arrangements, they then took hold of Rushbrook by the arms, and, shaking him to rouse him as much as they could, they led him home to the cottage, and left him in charge of his wife. As soon as the door was closed, Rushbrook's long-repressed anger could no longer be restrained : he started on his feet, and striking his fist on the table so as to terrify his wife, swore that the pedlar should pay dear for his peaching. Upon his wife's demanding an explanation, Rushbrook, in a few hurried sentences, explained the whole. Jane, however she might agree with him in his indignation, like all women, shuddered at the thought of shedding blood. She persuaded her husband to go to bed. He consented; but he slept not: he had but one feeling, which was vengeance towards the traitor. When revenge enters into the breast of a man who has lived peaceably at home, fiercely as he may be impelled by the passion, he stops short at the idea of shedding blood. But when a man who had, like Rushbrook, served so long in the army, witnessed such scenes of carnage, and so often passed his bayonet through his adversary's body, is roused up by this fatal passion, the death of a fellow-creature becomes a matter of indifference, provided he can gratify his feelings. Thus it was with Rushbrook, who, before he rose on the morning of that Sabbath in which, had he gone to church, he could have so often requested his trespasses might be forgiven, as he "forgave them who trespassed against him," had made up his mind that nothing short of the pedlar's death would satisfy him. At breakfast he appeared to listen to his wife's entreaties, and promised to do the pedlar no harm; and told her that, instead of going out on the Monday night, as he had promised, he should go out on that very night, and by that means evade the snare laid for him. Jane persuaded him not to go out at all; but this Rushbrook would not consent to. He told her that he was determined to show them that he was not to be driven off his beat, and would make Byres believe on Tuesday night that he had been out on the Monday night. Rushbrook's object was to have a meeting with Byres, if possible, alone, to tax him with his treachery, and then to take summary vengeance.

Aware that Byres slept at the ale-house, he went down there a little before dark, and told him that he intended going out on that night; that it would be better if, instead of coming on Tuesday, he were to meet him at the corner of one of the covers, which he described, at an hour agreed upon, when he would make over to him the game which he might have procured. Byres, who saw in this an excellent method of trapping Rushbrook, consented to it, intending to inform the keeper, so that he should meet Rushbrook. The

17　　　　　　　　　　　B

time of meeting was arranged for two o'clock in the morning. Rushbrook was certain that Byres would leave the ale-house an hour or two before the time proposed, which would be more than sufficient for his giving information to the keeper. He therefore remained quietly at home till twelve o'clock, when he loaded his gun, and went out without Joey or the dog. His wife perceiving this, was convinced that he had not gone out with the intention to poach, but was pursuing his scheme of revenge. She watched him after he left the cottage, and observed that he had gone down in the direction of the ale-house; and she was afraid that there would be mischief between him and Byres, and she wakened Joey, desiring him to follow and watch his father, and do all he could to prevent it. Her communication was made in such a hurried manner that it was difficult for Joey to know what he was to do, except to watch his father's motions, and see what took place. This Joey perfectly understood; and he was off in an instant, followed, as usual, by Mum, and taking with him his sack. Our hero crept softly down the pathway in the direction of the ale-house. The night was dark, for the moon did not rise till two or three hours before the morning broke, and it was bitterly cold: but to darkness and cold Joey had been accustomed, and although not seen himself, there was no object could move without being scanned by his clear vision. He gained a hedge close to the ale-house. Mum wanted to go on, by which Joey knew that his father must be lurking somewhere near to him: he pressed the dog down with his hand, crouched himself, and watched. In a few minutes a dark figure was perceived by Joey to emerge from the ale-house, and walk hastily over a turnip-field behind the premises: it had gained about half over, when another form, which Joey recognised as his father's, stealthily followed after the first. Joey waited a little time, and was then, with Mum, on the steps of both; for a mile and a half each party kept at their relative distances, until they came near a furze bottom, which was about six hundred yards from the cover; then the steps of Rushbrook were quickened, and those of Joey in proportion; the consequence was, that the three parties rapidly neared each other. Byres—for it was he who had quitted the ale-house--walked along leisurely, having no suspicion that he

18

was followed. Rushbrook was now within fifteen yards of the pedlar, and Joey at even less distance from his father, when he heard the lock of his father's gun click as he cocked it.

"Father," said Joey, not over loud, "don't——"

"Who's there?" cried the pedlar, turning round. The only reply was the flash and report of the gun; and the pedlar dropped among the furze.

"O father!—father!—what have you done?" exclaimed Joey, coming up to him.

"You here, Joey!" said Rushbrook. "Why are you here?"

"Mother sent me," replied Joey.

"To be evidence against me," replied his father, in wrath.

"Oh no! to stop you. What have you done, father?"

"What I almost wish I had not done now," replied he mournfully; "but it is done, and——"

"And what, father?"

"I am a murderer, I suppose," replied Rushbrook. "He would have peached, Joey—have had me transported, to work in chains for the rest of my days, merely for taking a few pheasants. Let us go home;" but Rushbrook did not move, although he proposed so doing.

He leant upon his gun, with his eyes fixed in the direction where Byres had fallen.

Joey stood by him—for nearly ten minutes not a word was spoken. At last Rushbrook said—

"Joey, my boy, I've killed many a man in my time, and I have thought nothing of it; I slept as sound as ever the next night. But then, you see, I was a soldier, and it was my trade, and I could look on the man I had killed without feeling sorrow or shame; but I can't look upon this man, Joey. He was my enemy; but—I've murdered him—I feel it now. Go up to him, boy—you are not afraid to meet him—and see if he be dead."

Joey, although generally speaking fear was a stranger to him, did, however, feel afraid; his hands had often been dyed with the blood of a hare or of a bird, but he had not yet seen death in his fellow-creatures. He advanced slowly and tremulously through the dark towards the furze-bush in which the body lay; Mum followed, raising first one paw and pausing, then the other, and as they came to the body, the dog raised his head and gave such a mournful howl, that it induced our hero to start back again. After a time Joey recovered himself, and again advanced to the body. He leant over it, he could distinguish but the form; he listened, and not the slightest breathing was to be heard; he whispered the pedlar's name, but there was no reply; he put his hand upon his breast, and removed it reeking with warm blood.

"Father, he must be dead, quite dead," whispered Joey, who returned trembling. "What shall we do?"

"We must go home," replied Rushbrook; "this is a bad night's work;" and, without exchanging another word until their arrival, Rushbrook and Joey proceeded back to the cottage, followed by Mum.

CHAPTER V

The sins of the father visited upon the child.

JANE had remained in a state of great anxiety during her husband's absence, watching and listening to every sound; every five minutes raising the latch of the door, and looking out, hoping to see him return. As the time went on her alarm increased; she laid her head down on the table and wept; she could find no consolation, no alleviation of her anxiety; she dropped down on her knees and prayed.

She was still appealing to the Most High when a blow on the door announced her husband's return. There was a sullen gloom over his countenance as he entered: he threw his gun carelessly on one side, so that it fell and rattled against the paved floor; and this one act was to her ominous of evil. He sat down without speaking; falling back in the chair, and lifting his eyes up to the rafters above, he appeared to be in deep thought, and unconscious of her presence.

"What has happened?" inquired his wife, trembling as she laid her hand on his shoulder.

"Don't speak to me now," was the reply.

20

"Joey," said the frightened woman, in a whisper, "what has he done?"

Joey answered not, but raised his hand, red with the blood which was now dried upon it. .

Jane uttered a faint cry, dropped on her knees and covered her face, while Joey walked into the back kitchen, and busied himself in removing the traces of the dark deed.

A quarter of an hour had elapsed—Joey had returned, and taken his seat upon his low stool, and not a word had been exchanged.

There certainly is a foretaste of the future punishment which awaits crime; for how dreadful were the feelings of those who were now sitting down in the cottage! Rushbrook was evidently stupefied from excess of feeling; first, the strong excitement which had urged him to the deed; and now from the reaction the prostration of mental power which had succeeded it. Jane dreaded the present and the future —whichever way she turned her eyes the gibbet was before her—the clanking of chains in her ears; in her vision of the future, scorn, misery, and remorse—she felt only for her husband. Joey, poor boy, he felt for both. Even the dog showed, as he looked up into Joey's face, that he was aware that a foul deed had been done. The silence which it appeared none would venture to break, was at last dissolved by the clock of the village church solemnly striking *two*. They all started up—it was a warning—it reminded them of the bell tolling for the dead—of time and of eternity. But time present quickly effaced for the moment other ideas; yes, it was time to act; in four hours more it would be daylight, and the blood of the murdered man would appeal to his fellow-men for vengeance. The sun would light them to the deed of darkness—the body would be brought home— the magistrates would assemble—and who would be the party suspected?

"Merciful Heaven!" exclaimed Jane, "what can be done?"

"There is no proof," muttered Rushbrook.

"Yes, there is," observed Joey, "I left my bag there, when I stooped down to——"

"Silence!" cried Rushbrook. "Yes," continued he, bitterly, to his wife, "this is your doing; you must send the boy after me, and now there will be evidence against me; I shall owe my death to you."

"Oh, say not so! say not so!" replied Jane, falling down on her knees, and weeping bitterly as she buried her face in his lap. "But there is yet time," cried she, starting up; "Joey can go and fetch the bag. You will, Joey: won't you, dear? you are not afraid—you are innocent."

"Better leave it where it is, mother," replied Joey calmly. Rushbrook looked up at his son with surprise; Jane caught him by the arm; she felt convinced the boy had some reason for what he said—probably some plan that would ward off suspicion—yet how could that be, it was evidence against them, and after looking earnestly at the boy's face, she dropped his arm. "Why so, Joey?" said she, with apparent calmness.

"Because," replied Joey, "I have been thinking about it all this time; I am innocent, and therefore I do not mind if they suppose me guilty. The bag is known to be mine—the gun I must throw into a ditch two fields off. You must give me some money, if you have any; if not, I must go without it; but there is no time to be lost. I must be off and away from here in ten minutes; to-morrow ask every one if they have seen or heard of me, because I have left the house some time during the night. I shall have a good start before that; besides, they may not find the pedlar for a day or two, perhaps; at all events, not till some time after I am gone; and then, you see, mother, the bag which is found by him, and the gun in the ditch, will make them think it is me who killed him; but they will not be able to make out whether I killed him by accident, and ran away from fear, or whether I did it on purpose. So now, mother, that's my plan, for it will save father."

"And I shall never see you again, my child!" replied his mother.

"That's as may be. You may go away from here after a time, mother, when the thing has blown over. Come, mother, there is no time to lose."

"Rushbrook, what say you—what think you?" said Jane to her husband.

"Why, Jane, at all events, the boy must have left us, for, you see, I told Byres, and I've no doubt but he told the keeper, if he met him, that I should bring Joey with me. I did it to deceive him; and, as sure as I sit here, they will have that boy up as evidence against his father."

"To be sure they will," cried Joey; "and what could I do? I dare not—I don't think I could—tell a lie; and yet I would not peach upon father neither. What can I do—but be out of the way?"

"That's the truth—away with you, then, my boy, and take a father's blessing with you—a guilty father's, it is true; God forgive me. Jane, give him all the money you have; lose not a moment: quick, woman, quick." And Rushbrook appeared to be in agony.

Jane hastened to the cupboard, opened a small box, and poured the contents into the hands of Joey.

"Farewell, my boy," said Rushbrook; "your father thanks you."

"Heaven preserve you, my child!" cried Jane, embracing him, as the tears rained down her cheeks. "You will write —no! you must not—mercy!—mercy!—I shall never see him again!"—and the mother fainted on the floor.

The tears rose in our hero's eyes as he beheld the condition of his poor mother. Once more he grasped his father's hand; and then, catching up the gun, he went out at the back door, and driving back the dog, who would have followed him, made over the fields as fast as his legs would carry him.

CHAPTER VI

" The world before him, where to choose."

WE have no doubt but many of our readers have occasionally, when on a journey, come to where the road divides into two, forking out in different directions, and the road being new to them, have not known which of the two branches they ought to take. This happens, as it often does in a novel, to be our case just now. Shall we follow little Joey, or his father and mother?—that is the question. We believe that when a road does thus divide, the wider of the two branches is generally selected, as being supposed to be the

continuation of the highroad. We shall ourselves act upon
that principle; and, as the hero of the tale is of more consequence than characters accessory, we shall follow up the
fortunes of little Joey. As soon as our hero had deposited
the gun so that it might be easily discovered by any one
passing by, he darted into the highroad, and went off with
all the speed that he was capable of, and it was not yet
light when he found himself at least ten miles from his native
village. As the day dawned, he quitted the highroad, and
took to the fields, keeping a parallel course, so as to still
increase the distance; it was not until he had made fifteen
miles that, finding himself exhausted, he sat down to recover
himself.

From the time that he had left the cottage until the
present, Joey had had but one overwhelming idea in his head,
which was, to escape from pursuit, and by his absence to
save his father from suspicion; but now that he had effected
that purpose, and was in a state of quiescence, other thoughts
rushed upon his mind. First, the scenes of the last few
hours presented themselves in rapid array before him—he
thought of the dead man, and he looked at his hand to
ascertain if the bloody marks had been effaced; and then
he thought of his poor mother's state when he quitted the
cottage, and the remembrance made him weep bitterly: his
own position came next upon him,—a boy, twelve years of
age, adrift upon the world—how was he to live—what was
he to do? This reminded him that his mother had given
him money; he put his hand into his pocket, and pulled
it out to ascertain what he possessed. He had £1, 16s.; to
him a large sum, and it was all in silver. As he had become
more composed, he began to reflect upon what he had better
do; where should he go to?—London. It was a long way,
he knew, but the farther he was away from home the better.
Besides, he had heard much of London, and that every one
got employment there. Joey resolved that he would go to
London; he knew that he had taken the right road so far,
and having made up his mind, he rose up, and proceeded.
He knew that, if possible, he must not allow himself to be
seen on the road for a day or two, and he was puzzled how
he was to get food, which he already felt would be very
acceptable; and then, what account was he to give of him-

self, if questioned? Such were the cogitations of our little
hero as he wended his way till he came to a river, which
was too deep and rapid for him to attempt to ford—he was
obliged to return to the highroad to cross the bridge. He
looked around him before he climbed over the low stone
wall, and perceiving nobody, he jumped on the footpath,
and proceeded to the bridge, where he suddenly faced an
old woman with a basket of brown cakes something like
gingerbread. Taken by surprise, and hardly knowing what
to say, he inquired if a cart had passed that way.

"Yes, child, but it must be a good mile ahead of you,"
said the old woman, "and you must walk fast to overtake it."

"I have had no breakfast yet, and I am hungry; do you
sell your cakes?"

"Yes, child, what else do I make them for? three a penny,
and cheap too."

Joey felt in his pocket until he had selected a sixpence,
and pulling it out, desired the old woman to give him cakes
for it, and taking the pile in his hand, he set off as fast as he
could. As soon as he was out of sight, he again made his
way into the fields, and breakfasted upon half his store. He
then continued his journey until nearly one o'clock, when,
tired out with his exertions, as soon as he had finished the
remainder of his cakes, he lay down under a rick of corn
and fell fast asleep, having made twenty miles since he
started. In his hurry to escape pursuit, and the many
thoughts which occupied his brain, Joey had made no observation on the weather; if he had, he probably would have
looked after some more secure shelter than the lee-side of a
haystack. He slept soundly, and he had not been asleep
more than an hour, when the wind changed, and the snow
fell fast; nevertheless, Joey slept on, and probably never
would have awakened more, had it not been that a shepherd and his dog were returning home in the evening, and
happened to pass close to the haystack. By this time Joey
had been covered with a layer of snow half an inch deep,
and had it not been for the dog, who went up to where he
lay, and commenced pawing the snow off him, he would
have been passed by undiscovered by the shepherd, who,
after some trouble, succeeded in rousing our hero from his
torpor, and half dragging, half lifting him, contrived to lead

25

him across one or two fields, until they arrived at a black-smith's shop, in a small village, before Joey could have been said to have recovered his scattered senses. Two hours' more sleep, and there would have been no further history to give of our little hero.

He was dragged to the forge, the fire of which glowed under the force of the bellows, and by degrees, as the warmth reached him, he was restored to self-possession. To the inquiries made as to who he was, and from where he came, he now answered as he had before arranged in his mind. His father and mother were a long way before him; he was going to London, but having been tired, he had fallen asleep under the haystack, and he was afraid that if he went not on to London directly, he never might find his father and mother again.

"Oh, then," replied the shepherd, "they have gone on before, have they? Well, you'll catch them, no doubt."

The blacksmith's wife, who had been a party to what was going on, now brought up a little warm ale, which quite re-established Joey; and at the same time a waggon drove up to the door and stopped at the blacksmith's shop.

"I must have a shoe tacked on the old mare, my friend," said the driver. "You won't be long?"

"Not five minutes," replied the smith. "You're going to London?"

"Yes, sure."

"Here's a poor boy that has been left behind by his father and mother somehow—you wouldn't mind giving him a lift?"

"Well, I don't know; I suppose I must be paid for it in the world to come."

"And good pay too, if you earn it," observed the black-smith.

"Well, it won't make much difference to my eight horses, I expect," said the driver, looking at Joey; "so come along, youngster: you may perch yourself on top of the straw, above the goods."

"First come in with me, child," said the wife of the black-smith; "you must have some good victuals to take with you —so, while you shoe the horse, John, I'll see to the boy."

The woman put before Joey a dish in which were the

26

remains of more than one small joint, and our hero commenced his attack without delay.

"Have you any money, child?" inquired the woman.

Joey, who thought she might expect payment, replied, "Yes, ma'am, I've got a shilling;" and he pulled one out of his pocket and laid it out on the table.

"Bless the child! what do you take me for, to think that I would touch your money? You are a long way from London yet, although you have got such a chance to get there. Do you know where to go when you get there?"

"Yes, ma'am," replied Joey; "I shall get work in the stables, I believe."

"Well, I dare say that you will; but in the meantime you had better save your shilling—so we'll find something to put this meat and bread up for your journey. Are you quite warm now?"

"Yes, thank'ee, ma'am."

Joey, who had ceased eating, had another warm at the fire, and in a few minutes, having bade adieu, and giving his thanks to the humane people, he was buried in the straw below the tilt of the waggon, with his provisions deposited beside him, and the waggon went on its slow and steady pace, to the tune of its own jingling bells. Joey, who had quite recovered from his chill, nestled among the straw, congratulating himself that he should now arrive safely in London, without more questioning. And such was the case: in three days and three nights, without any further adventure, he found himself, although he was not aware of it, in Oxford Street, somewhat about eight or nine o'clock in the evening.

"Do you know your way now, boy?" said the carman.

"I can ask it," replied Joey, "as soon as I can go to the light and read the address. Good-bye, and thank you," continued he, glad at last to be clear of any more evasive replies.

The carman shook him by the hand as they passed the Boar and Castle, and bade him farewell, and our hero found himself alone in the vast metropolis.

What was he to do? He hardly knew—but one thought struck him, which was, that he must find a bed for the night. He wandered up and down Oxford Street for some time, but every one walked so quick that he was afraid to speak to them: at last a little girl, of seven or eight years of age, passed by him, and looked him earnestly in the face.

"Can you tell me where I can get a bed for the night?" said Joey.

"Have you any brads?" was the reply.

"What are those?" said Joey.

"Any money, to be sure; why, you're green—quite."

"Yes, I have a shilling."

"That will do—come along, and you shall sleep with me." Joey followed her very innocently, and very glad that he had been so fortunate. She led him to a street out of Tottenham Court Road, in which there were no lamps—the houses, however, were large, and many storeys high.

"Take my hand," said the girl, "and mind how you tread."

Guided by his new companion, Joey arrived at a door that was wide open: they entered, and, assisted by the girl, he went up a dark staircase, to the second storey. She opened a room door, when Joey found himself in company with about twenty other children, of about the same age, of both sexes. Here were several beds on the floor of the room, which was spacious. In the centre were huddled together on the floor, round a tallow candle, eight or ten of the inmates, two of them playing with a filthy pack of cards, while the others looked over them: others were lying down or asleep on the several beds. "This is my bed," said the girl; "if you are tired you can turn in at once. I shan't go to bed yet."

Joey was tired, and he went to bed; it was not very clean, but he had been used to worse lodgings lately. It need hardly be observed that Joey had got into very bad company, the whole of the inmates of the room consisting of juvenile thieves and pickpockets, who in the course of time obtain promotion in their profession, until they are ultimately sent off to Botany Bay. Attempts have been made to check these nurseries of vice: but pseudo-philanthropists have resisted such barbarous innovation: and upon the Mosaic principle, that you must not seethe the kid in the mother's milk, they are protected and allowed to arrive at full maturity, and beyond the chance of being reclaimed, until they are ripe for the penalties of the law.

Joey slept soundly, and when he awoke next morning found that his little friend was not with him. He dressed himself, and then made another discovery, which was, that every farthing of his money had been abstracted from his pockets. Of this unpleasant fact he ventured to complain to one or two boys, who were lying on other beds with their clothes on; they laughed at him, called him a greenhorn, and made use of other language, which at once let Joey know the nature of the company with whom he had been passing the night. After some altercation, three or four of them bundled him out of the room, and Joey found himself in the street without a farthing, and very much inclined to eat a good breakfast.

There is no portion of the world, small as it is in comparison with the whole, in which there is more to be found to eat and to drink, more comfortable lodgings, or accommodation and convenience of every kind, than in the metropolis of England, provided you have the means to obtain it; but notwithstanding this abundance, there is no place, probably, where you will find it more difficult to obtain a portion of it, if you happen to have an empty pocket.

Joey went into a shop here and there to ask for employment—he was turned away everywhere. He spent the first day in this manner, and at night, tired and hungry, he lay down on the stone steps of a portico and fell asleep. The next morning he awoke shivering with the cold, faint with hunger. He asked at the areas for something to eat, but no one would give him anything. At a pump he obtained a drink of water—that was all he could obtain, for it cost nothing. Another day passed without food, and the poor boy again sheltered himself for the night at a rich man's door in Berkeley Square.

CHAPTER VII

If you want employment, go to London.

THE exhausted lad awoke again, and pursued his useless task of appeals for food and employment. It was a bright day, and there was some little warmth to be collected by basking in the rays of the sun, when our hero wended his way through St. James's Park, faint, hungry, and disconsolate. There were several people seated on the benches;

and Joey, weak as he was, did not venture to go near them, but crawled along. At last, after wandering up and down, looking for pity in everybody's face as they passed, and receiving none, he felt that he could not stand much longer, and, emboldened by desperation, he approached a bench that was occupied by one person. At first he only rested on the arm of the bench, but as the person sitting down appeared not to observe him, he timidly took a seat at the farther end. The personage who occupied the other part of the bench was a man dressed in a morning suit *à la militaire*, and black stock. He had clean gloves and a small cane in his hand, with which he was describing circles on the gravel before him, evidently in deep thought. In height he was full six feet, and his proportions combined strength with symmetry. His features were remarkably handsome, his dark hair had a natural curl, and his whiskers and mustachios (for he wore those military appendages) were evidently the objects of much attention and solicitude. We may as well here observe that, although so favoured by nature, still there would have been considered something wanting in him by those who had been accustomed to move in the first circles, to make him the refined gentleman. His movements and carriage were not inelegant, but there was a certain *retenue* wanting. He bowed well, but still it was not exactly the bow of a gentleman. The nursery-maids as they passed by said, "Dear me, what a handsome gentleman!" but had the remark been made by a higher class, it would have been qualified into, "What a handsome man!" His age was apparently about five-and-thirty—it might have been something more. After a short time he left off his mechanical amusements, and turning round, perceived little Joey at the farther end. Whether from the mere inclination to talk, or that he thought it presuming in our hero to seat himself upon the same bench, he said to him—

"I hope you are comfortable, my little man; but perhaps you've forgot your message."

"I have no message, sir, for I know no one: and I am not comfortable, for I am starving," replied Joey, in a tremulous voice.

"Are you in earnest now, when you say that, boy; or is it that you're humbugging me?"

THE POACHER

Joey shook his head. "I have eaten nothing since the day before yesterday morning, and I feel faint and sick," replied he at last.

His new companion looked earnestly in our hero's face, and was satisfied that what he said was true.

"As I hope to be saved," exclaimed he, "it's my opinion that a little bread and butter would not be a bad thing for you. Here," continued he, putting his hand into his coat-pocket, "take these coppers, and go and get something into your little vitals."

"Thank you, sir, thank you, kindly. But I don't know where to go : I only came up to London two days ago."

"Then follow me as fast as your little pins can carry you," said the other. They had not far to go, for a man was standing close to Spring Garden Gate, with hot tea and bread and butter, and in a few moments Joey's hunger was considerably appeased.

"Do you feel better now, my little cock ?"

"Yes, sir, thank you."

"That's right, and now we will go back to the bench, and then you shall tell me all about yourself, just to pass away the time. Now," said he, as he took his seat, "in the first place, who is your father, if you have any ; and if you haven't any, what was he ?"

"Father and mother are both alive, but they are a long way off. Father was a soldier, and he has a pension now."

"A soldier ! Do you know in what regiment ?"

"Yes, it was the 53rd, I think."

"By the powers, my own regiment ! And what is your name, then, and his ?"

"Rushbrook," replied Joey.

"My pivot man, by all that's holy. Now haven't you nicely dropped on your feet ?"

"I don't know, sir," replied our hero.

"But I do ; your father was the best fellow I had in my company—the best forager, and always took care of his officer, as a good man should do. If there was a turkey, or a goose, or a duck, or a fowl, or a pig within ten miles of us, he would have it : he was the boy for poaching. And now tell me (and mind you tell the truth when you meet with a friend) what made you leave your father and mother ?"

31

"I was afraid of being taken up——" and here Joey stopped, for he hardly knew what to say; trust his new acquaintance with his father's secret he dare not, neither did he like to tell what was directly false; as the reader will perceive by his reply, he partly told the truth.

"Afraid of being taken up! Why, what could they take up a spalpeen like you for?"

"Poaching," replied Joey; "father poached too: they had proof against me, so I came away—with father's consent."

"Poaching! well, I'm not surprised at that, for if ever it was in the blood, it is in yours—that's truth. And what do you mean to do now?"

"Anything I can to earn my bread."

"What can you do—besides poaching, of course? Can you read and write?"

"Oh yes."

"Would you like to be a servant—clean boots, brush clothes, stand behind a cab, run messages, carry notes, and hold your tongue?"

"I could do all that, I think—I am twelve years old."

"The devil you are! Well then, for your father's sake, I'll see what I can do for you, till you can do better. I'll fit you out as a tiger, and what's more, unless I am devilish hard up, I won't sell you. So come along. What's your name?"

"Joey."

"Sure that was your father's name before you, I now recollect; and should any one take the trouble to ask you what may be the name of your master, you may reply, with a safe conscience, that it's Captain O'Donahue. Now come along. Not close after me—you may as well keep open file just now, till I've made you look a little more decent."

CHAPTER VIII

A dissertation upon Pedigree.

OUR readers will not perhaps be displeased if we introduce Captain O'Donahue more particularly to their notice: we shall therefore devote this chapter to giving some account of his birth, parentage, and subsequent career. If the father of Captain O'Donahue was to be believed, the race of the O'Donahues were kings in Ireland long before the O'Connors were ever heard of. How far this may be correct we cannot pretend to offer an opinion, further than that no man can be supposed to know so much of a family's history as the descendant himself. The documents were never laid before us, and we have only the positive assertion of the Squireen O'Donahue, who asserted not only that they were kings in Ireland before the O'Connors, whose pretensions to ancestry he treated with contempt, but further, that they were renowned for their strength, and were famous for using the longest bows in battle that were ever known or heard of. Here we have circumstantial evidence, although not proof. If strong, they might have been kings in Ireland, for there "might has been right" for many centuries; and certainly their acquirements were handed down to posterity, as no one was more famous for drawing the long-bow than the Squireen O'Donahue. Upon these points, however, we must leave our readers to form their own opinions. Perhaps some one more acquainted with the archives of the country may be able to set us right if we are wrong, or to corroborate our testimony if we are right. In his preface to "Anne of Geierstein," Sir Walter Scott observes, that "errors, however trivial, ought, in his opinion, never to be pointed out to the author without meeting with a candid and respectful acknowledgment." Following the example of so great a man, we can only say, that if any gentleman can prove or disprove the assertion of the Squireen O'Donahue, to wit, that the O'Donahues were kings of Ireland long before the O'Connors were heard of, we shall be most happy to acknowledge the favour, and insert his remarks in the next edition. We should be further obliged to the same party, or indeed, any other, if they would favour us with an idea of what was implied by a king of Ireland in those days; that is to say, whether he held a court, taxed his subjects, collected revenue, kept up a standing army, sent ambassadors to foreign countries, and did all which kings do nowadays? or whether his shillelagh was his sceptre, and his domain some furze-crowned hills and a bog, the intricacies of which were known only to himself? whether he was arrayed in jewelled robes, with a crown of gold weighing on his temples? or whether he went bare-legged and bare-armed, with his bare locks flowing in luxurious wildness to the breeze? We request an answer to this in full simplicity. We observe that even in Ireland now, a fellow six feet high, and stout in proportion, is called a "prince of a fellow," although he has not where-withal to buy a paper of tobacco to supply his dhudeen: and, arguing from this fact, we are inclined to think that a few more inches in stature, and commensurate muscular increase of power, would in former times have raised the "heir-apparent" to the dignity of the Irish throne. But these abstruse speculations have led us from our history, which we must now resume.

Whatever may once have been the importance of the house of O'Donahue, one thing is certain, that there are many ups and downs in this world; every family in it has its wheel of fortune, which revolves faster or slower as the fates decree, and the descendant of kings before the O'Connors' time was now descended into a species of viceroy, Squireen O'Donahue being the steward of certain wild estates in the county of Galway, belonging to a family who for many years had shown a decided aversion to the natural beauties of the country, and had thought proper to migrate to where, if people were not so much attached to them, they were at all events more civilised. These estates were extensive, but not lucrative. They abounded in rocks, brushwood, and woodcocks during the season; and although the Squireen O'Donahue did his best, if not for his employer, at least for himself, it was with some difficulty that he contrived to support, with anything like respectability (which in that part of the country means "dacent clothes to wear"), a very numerous family, lineally descended from the most ancient of all the kings of Ireland.

Before the squireen had obtained his employment, he had sunk his rank and travelled much—as a courier—thereby gaining much knowledge of the world. If, therefore, he had no wealth to leave his children, at all events he could impart to them that knowledge which is said to be better than worldly possessions. Having three sons and eight daughters, all of them growing up healthy and strong, with commensurate appetites, he soon found that it was necessary to get rid of them as fast as he could. His eldest, who, strange to say, for an O'Donahue, was a quiet lad, he had as a favour lent to his brother, who kept a small tobacconist and grocer's shop in Dublin, and his brother was so fond of him, that eventually O'Carroll O'Donahue was bound to him as an apprentice. It certainly was a degradation for the descendant of such ancient kings to be weighing out pennyworths of sugar, and supplying halfpenny papers of tobacco to the old apple and fish women; but still there we must leave the heir-apparent while we turn to the second son, Mr. Patrick O'Donahue, whose history we are now relating, having already made the reader acquainted with him by an introduction in St. James's Park.

CHAPTER IX

In which the advice of a father deserves peculiar attention.

IT may be supposed that, as steward of the estates, Squireen O'Donahue had some influence over the numerous tenants on the property, and this influence he took care to make the most of. His assistance in a political contest was rewarded by the offer of an ensigncy for one of his sons, in a regiment then raising in Ireland, and this offer was too good to be refused. So, one fine day, Squireen O'Donahue came home from Dublin, well bespattered with mud, and found his son Patrick also well bespattered with mud, having just returned home from a very successful expedition against the woodcocks.

"Patrick, my jewel," said the squireen, taking a seat and wiping his face, for he was rather warm with his ride, "you're a made man."

"And well made too, father, if the girls are anything of judges," replied Patrick.

"You put me out," replied the squireen; "you've more to be vain of than your figure."

"And what may that be that you're discoursing about, father?"

"Nothing more nor less, nor better nor worse, but you're an ensign in his Majesty's new regiment—the number has escaped my memory."

35

"I'd rather be a colonel, father," replied Patrick, musing.

"The colonel's to come, you spalpeen," said the squireen.

"And the fortune to make, I expect," replied Patrick.

"You've just hit it; but haven't you the whole world before you to pick and choose?"

"Well," replied Patrick, after a pause, "I've no objection."

"No objection! Why don't you jump out of your skin with delight? At all events, you might jump high enough to break in the caling."

"There's no ceiling to break," replied Patrick, looking up at the rafters.

"That's true enough; but still you might go out of your seven senses in a rational sort of a way."

"I really can't see for why, father dear. You tell me I'm to leave my poor old mother, who doats upon me; my sisters, who are fond of me; my friends here (patting the dogs), who follow me; the hills, that I love; and the woodcocks, which I shoot; to go to be shot at myself, and buried like a dead dog, without being skinned, on the field of battle."

"I tell you to go forth into the world as an officer, and make your fortune; to come back a general, and be the greatest man of your family. And don't be too unhappy about not being skinned. Before you are older or wiser, dead or alive, you'll be skinned, I'll answer for it."

"Well, father, I'll go; but I expect there'll be a good deal of ground to march over before I'm a general."

"And you've a good pair of legs."

"So I'm told every day of my life. I'll make the best use of them when I start; but it's the starting I don't like, and that's the real truth."

The reader may be surprised at the indifference shown by Patrick at the intelligence communicated by his father; but the fact was, Mr. Patrick O'Donahue was very deep in love. This cooled his national ardour; and it must be confessed that there was every excuse, for a more lovely creature than Judith M'Crae never existed. To part with her was the only difficulty, and all his family feelings were but a cloak to the real cause of his unwillingness.

"Nevertheless, you must start to-morrow, my boy," said his father.

"What must be, must," replied Patrick, "so there's an end of the matter. I'll just go out for a bit of a walk, just to stretch my legs."

"They require a deal of stretching, Pat, considering you've been twenty miles, at least, this morning, over the mountains," replied the squireen. But Patrick was out of hearing; he had leapt over a stone wall which separated his father's potato ground from Cornelius M'Crae's, and had hastened to Judith, whom he found very busy getting the dinner ready.

"Judith, my dear," said Patrick, "my heart's quite broke with the bad news I have to tell you. Sure I'm going to leave you to-morrow morning."

"Now, Patrick, you're joking, surely."

"Devil a joke in it. I'm an ensign in a regiment."

"Then I'll die, Patrick."

"More like that I will, Judith; what with grief and a bullet to help it, perhaps."

"Now, what d'ye mean to do, Patrick?"

"Mean to go, sure; because I can't help myself; and to come back again, if ever I've the luck of it. My heart's leaping out of my mouth entirely."

"And mine's dead," replied Judith, in tears.

"It's no use crying, mavourneen. I'll be back to dance at my own wedding, if so be I can."

"There'll be neither wedding for you, Patrick, nor wake either, for you'll lie on the cold ground, and be ploughed in like muck."

"That's but cold comfort from you, Judith, but we'll hope for a better ending; but I must go back now, and you'll meet me this evening beyond the shealing."

"Won't it be for the last time, Patrick?" replied Judith, with her apron up to her eyes.

"If I've any voice in the matter, I say no. Please the pigs, I'll come back a colonel."

"Then you'll be no match for Judith M'Crae," replied the sobbing girl.

"Shoot easy, my Judith, that's touching my honour; if I'm a general it will be all the same."

"O Patrick! Patrick!"

Patrick folded Judith in his arms, took one kiss, and then

hastened out of the house, saying—"Remember the shealing, Judith, dear, there we'll talk the matter over easy and
comfortable."

Patrick returned to his house, where he found his mother
and sisters in tears. They had received orders to prepare
his wardrobe, which, by-the-bye, did not give them much
trouble from its extent; they only had to mend every
individual article. His father was sitting down by the
hearth, and when he saw Patrick he said to him,—"Now
just come here, my boy, and take a stool, while you listen
to me and learn a little worldly wisdom, for I may not have
much time to talk to you when we are at Dublin."

Patrick took a seat, and was all attention.

"You'll just observe, Pat, that it's a very fine thing to
be an officer in the king's army; nobody dares to treat you
ill, although you may ill-treat others, which is no small
advantage in this world."

"There's truth in that," replied Patrick.

"You see, when you get into an enemy's country, you may
help yourself; and, if you look sharp, there's very pretty
pickings—all in a quiet way, you understand."

"That, indeed."

"You observe, Pat, that as one of his officers, the king
expects you to appear and live like a gentleman, only he for-
gets to give you the means of so doing; you must, therefore,
take all you can get from his Majesty, and other people must
make up the difference."

"That's a matter o' course," said Patrick.

"You'll soon see your way clear, and find out what you
may be permitted to do, and what you may not; for the
king expects you to keep up the character of a gentleman,
as well as the appearance."

"O' course."

"Mayhap you may be obliged to run in debt a little—a
gentleman may do that; mayhap you may not be able to pay
—that's a gentleman's case very often: if so, never go so
far as twenty pounds; first, because the law don't reach;
and secondly, because twenty pound is quite enough to make
a man suffer for the good of his country."

"There's sense in that, father."

"And, Patrick, recollect that people judge by appearances

38

in this world, especially when they've nothing else to go by.
If you talk small, your credit will be small; but if you talk
large, it will be just in proportion."

" I perceive, father."

" It's not much property we possess in this said county
of Galway, that's certain; but you must talk of this property
as if I was the squire, and not the steward; and when you
talk of the quantity of woodcocks you have bagged, you
must say on *our* property."

" I understand, father."

" And you must curse your stars at being a younger
brother; it will be an excuse for your having no money, but
will make them believe it's in the family, at all events."

" I perceive," replied Patrick.

" There's one thing more, Pat; it's an Irish regiment, so
you must get out of it as soon as possible by exchange."

" For why ? "

" This for why. You will be among those born too near
home, and who may doubt all you say, because your story
may interfere with their own. Get into an English regiment
by all means, and there you'll be beyond the reach of contradiction, which ain't pleasant."

" True enough, father."

" Treasure up all I have told you—it's worldly wisdom,
and you have your fortune to make; so now recollect, never
hold back at a forlorn hope; volunteer for everything;
volunteer to be blown from a cannon's mouth, so that they
will give you promotion for that same; volunteer to go all
over the world, into the other world, and right through that
again into the one that comes after that, if there is any, and
then one thing will be certain, either that you'll be colonel
or general, or else——"

" Else what, father ? "

" That you won't require to be made either, seeing that
you'll be past all making; but luck's all, and lucky it is, by-
the-bye, that I have a little of the squire's rent in hand to
fit you out with, or how we should have managed, the saints
only know. As it is, I must sink it on the next year's
account; but that's more easy to do than to fit you out with
no money. I must beg the tenants off, make the potato
crop fail entirely, and report twenty, by name at least, **dead**

39

of starvation. Serve him right for spending his money out of Old Ireland. It's only out of real pathriotism that I cheat him—just to spend the money in the country. And now, Patrick, I've done; now you may go and square your accounts with Judith, for I know now where the cat jumps; but I'll leave old Time alone for doing his work."

Such was the advice of the squireen to his son; and, as worldly wisdom, it was not so bad; and, certainly, when a lad is cast adrift in the world, the two best things you can bestow on him are a little worldly wisdom and a little money, for without the former, the latter and he will soon part company.

The next day they set off for Dublin, Patrick's head being in a confused jumble of primitive good feeling, Judith M'Crae, his father's advice, and visions of future greatness. He was fitted out, introduced to the officers, and then his father left him his blessing and his own way to make in the world. In a fortnight the regiment was complete, and they were shipped to Liverpool, and from Liverpool to Maidstone, where, being all newly raised men, they were to remain for a time to be disciplined. Before the year had expired, Patrick had followed his father's advice, and exchanged, receiving a difference, with an ensign of a regiment going on foreign service. He was sent to the West Indies: but the seasons were healthy, and he returned home an ensign. He volunteered abroad again after five years, and gained his lieutenant's commission, from a death vacancy, without purchase.

After a fifteen years' hard service, the desired captain's commission came at last, and O'Donahue, having been so unsuccessful in his military career, retired upon half-pay, determined, if possible, to offer his handsome person in exchange for competence. But, during the fifteen years which had passed away, a great change had come over the ingenuous and unsophisticated Patrick O'Donahue; he had mixed so long with a selfish and heartless world, that his primitive feelings had gradually worn away. Judith had, indeed, never been forgotten; but she was now at rest, for, by mistake, Patrick had been returned dead of the yellow fever, and at the intelligence she had drooped like a severed snowdrop, and died. The only tie strong enough to induce him to return to Ireland was therefore broken, his father's worldly advice had not been forgotten, and O'Donahue considered the world as his oyster. Expensive in his habits and ideas, longing for competence, while he vegetated on half-pay, he was now looking out for a matrimonial specu- lation. His generosity and his courage remained with him —two virtues not to be driven out of an Irishman—but his other good qualities lay in abeyance; and yet his better feelings were by no means extinguished; they were dormant, but by favourable circumstances were again to be brought into action. The world and his necessities made him what he was; for many were the times, for years afterwards, that he would in his reveries surmise how happy he might have been in his own wild country, where half-pay would have been competence, had his Judith been spared to him, and he could have laid his head upon her bosom.

CHAPTER X

In which Major M'Shane narrates some curious matrimonial speculations.

OUR hero was soon fitted out with the livery of a groom, and installed as the confidential servant of Captain O'Donahue, who had lodgings on the third floor in a fashionable street. He soon became expert and useful, and, as the captain breakfasted at home, and always ordered sufficient for Joey to make another cold meal of during the day, he was at little or no expense to his master.

One morning, when Captain O'Donahue was sitting in his dressing-gown at breakfast, Joey opened the door, and announced Major M'Shane.

"Is it yourself, O'Donahue?" said the major, extending his hand; "and, now, what d'ye think has brought me here this fine morning? It's to do a thing that's rather unusual with me—neither more nor less than to pay you the £20 which you lent me a matter of three years ago, and which, I dare say, you never expected to see anything but the ghost of."

"Why, M'Shane, if the truth must be told, it will be

41

something of a resurrection when it appears before me," replied O'Donahue; "I considered it dead and buried; and, like those who are dead and buried, it has been long forgotten."

"Nevertheless, here it is in four notes—one, two, three, four: four times five are twenty; there's arithmetic for you, and your money to boot, and many thanks in the bargain, by way of interest. And now, O'Donahue, where have you been, what have you been doing, what are you doing, and what do you intend to do? That's what I call a comprehensive inquiry, and a very close one too."

"I have been in London a month, I have done nothing, I am doing nothing, and I don't know what I intend to do. You may take that for a comprehensive answer."

"I'll tell you all about myself without your asking. I have been in London for nearly two years, one of which I spent in courting, and the other in matrimony."

"Why, you don't mean to say that you are married, M'Shane; if so, as you've been married a year, you can tell me am I to give you joy?"

"Why, yes, I believe you may; there's nothing so stupid, O'Donahue, as domestic happiness, that's a fact; but, altogether, I have been so large a portion of my life doubtful where I was to get a dinner, that I think that on the whole I have made a very good choice."

"And may I inquire who is the party to whom Major M'Shane has condescended to sacrifice his handsome person?"

"Is it handsome you mane? As the ugly lady said to the looking-glass, I beg no reflections—you wish to know who she is; well, then, you must be content to listen to all my adventures from the time we parted, for she is at the end of them, and I can't read backwards."

"I am at your service, so begin as you please."

"Let me see, O'Donahue, where was it that we parted?"

"If I recollect, it was at the landing made at ——, where you were reported killed."

"Very true, but that, I gave my honour, was all a lie; it was fat Sergeant Murphy that was killed, instead of me. He was a terrible fellow, that Sergeant Murphy; he got himself killed on purpose, because he never could have

42

passed his accounts; well, he fought like a devil, so peace be with him. I was knocked down, as you know, with a bullet in my thigh, and as I could not stand, I sat upon the carcase of Sergeant Murphy, bound up my leg, and meditated on sublunary affairs. I thought what a great rogue he was, that Sergeant Murphy, and how he'd gone out of the world without absolution; and then I thought it very likely that he might have some money about him, and how much better it would be that I should have it to comfort me in prison than any rascally Frenchman, so I put my hand in his pocket and borrowed his purse, which was, taking the difference of size, as well lined as himself. Well, as you had all retreated and left me to be taken prisoner, I waited very patiently till they should come and carry me to the hospital, or wherever else they pleased. They were not long coming for me: one fellow would have passed his bayonet through me, but I had my pistol cocked, so he thought it advisable to take me prisoner. I was taken into the town, not to the hospital or the prison, but quartered at the house of an old lady of high rank and plenty of money. Well, the surgeon came and very politely told me that he must cut off my leg, and I very politely told him to go to the devil; and the old lady came in and took my part, when she saw what a handsome leg it was, and sent for another doctor at her own expense, who promised to set me on my pins in less than a month. Well, the old lady fell in love with me; and although she was not quite the vision of youthful fancy, as the saying is, for she had only one tooth in her head, and that stuck out half an inch beyond her upper lip, still she had other charms for a poor devil like me; so I made up my mind to marry her, for she made cruel love to me as I lay in bed, and before I was fairly out of bed the thing was settled, and a week afterwards the day was fixed; but her relatives got wind of it, for, like an old fool, she could not help blabbing, and so one day there came a file of soldiers, with a corporal at their head, informing me that I was now quite well, and therefore, if it was all the same to me, I must go to prison. This was anything but agreeable, and contrary to rule. As an officer, I was entitled to my parole; and so I wrote to the commanding officer, who sent for

me, and then he told me I had my choice, to give up the
old lady, whose friends were powerful, and would not permit
her to make a fool of herself (a personal remark, by-the-
bye, which it was unhandsome to make to a gentleman in
my circumstances), or to be refused parole, and remain in
prison, and that he would give me an hour to decide; then
he made me a very low bow, and left me. I was twisting
the affair over in my mind, one moment thinking of her
purse and carriage and doubloons, and another of that awful
long tooth of hers, when one of her relatives came in and
said he had a proposal to make, which was, that I should
be released and sent to Gibraltar, without any conditions,
with a handsome sum of money to pay my expenses, if I
would promise to give up the old lady now and for ever.
That suited my book; I took the money, took my leave,
and a small vessel took me to Gibraltar; so after all, you see,
O'Donahue, the thing did not turn out so bad. I lost only
an old woman with a long tooth, and I gained my liberty."

"No; you got out of that affair with credit."

"And with money, which is quite as good; so when I
returned and proved myself alive, I was reinstated, and had
all my arrears paid up. What with Sergeant Murphy's purse,
and the foreign subsidy, and my arrears, I was quite flush; so
I resolved to be circumspect, and make hay while the sun
shone: notwithstanding which, I was as nearly trapped by a
cunning devil of a widow. Two days more, and I should
have made a pretty kettle of fish of it."

"What, at your age, M'Shane?"

"Ah, bother! but she was a knowing one—a widow on a
first floor, good-looking, buxom, a fine armful, and about
thirty—met her at a party—pointed out to me as without
encumbrance, and well off—made up to her, escorted her
home—begged permission to call, was graciously received—
talked of her departed husband, thought me like him—everything so comfortable—plenty of plate—good furniture—
followed her up—received notes by a little boy in sky-blue
and silver sugar-loaf buttons—sent me all her messages—
one day in the week to her banker's to cash a cheque. Would
you believe the cunning of the creature? She used to draw
out £25 every week, sending me for the money, and, as I
found out afterwards, paid it in again in fifties every fortnight,

44

and she only had £50 in all. Wasn't I regularly humbugged? Made proposals—was accepted—all settled, and left off talking about her departed. One day, and only two days before the wedding, found the street-door open, and heard a noise between her and her landlady on the top of the stairs, so I waited at the bottom. The landlady was insisting upon her rent, and having all her plate back again—my charming widow entreating for a little delay, as she was to be married —landlady came downstairs, red as a turkey-cock, so I very politely begged her to walk into the parlour, and I put a few questions, when I discovered that my intended was a widow with a pension of £80 a year, and had six children, sent out of the way until she could find another protector, which I resolved, at all events, should not be Major M'Shane; so I walked out of the door, and have never seen her since."

"By the head of St. Patrick, but that was an escape!"

"Yes, indeed, the she-devil with six children, and £80 a year; it's a wicked world this, O'Donahue. Well, I kept clear of such cunning articles, and only looked after youth and innocence in the city. At last I discovered the only daughter of a German sugar-baker in the Minories, a young thing about seventeen, but very little for her age. She went to a dancing-school, and I contrived, by bribing the maid, to carry on the affair most successfully, and she agreed to run away with me: everything was ready, the postchaise was at the corner of the street, she came with her bundle in her hand. I thrust it into the chaise, and was just tossing her in after it, when she cried out that she had forgotten something, and must go back for it; and away she went, slipping through my fingers. Well, I waited most impatiently for her appearance, and at last saw her coming; and what d'ye think she'd gone back for? By the powers, for *her doll*, which she held in her hand! And just as she came to the chaise, who should come round the corner but her father, who had walked from Mincing Lane. He caught my mincing Miss by the arm, with her doll and her bundle, and bundled her home, leaving me and the postchaise, looking like two fools. I never could see her again, or her confounded doll either."

"You have been out of luck, M'Shane."

"I'm not sure of that, as the affair has ended. Now comes another adventure, in which I turned the tables, anyhow. I

45

fell in with a very pretty girl, the daughter of a lawyer in Chancery Lane, who was said to have, and (I paid a shilling at Doctors' Commons, and read the will) it was true enough, an independent fortune from her grandmother. She was always laughing—full of mischief and practical jokes. She pretended to be pleased, the hussy, with my addresses, and at last she consented, as I thought, to run away with me. I imagined that I had clinched the business at last, when one dark night I handed her into a chaise, wrapped up in a cloak, and crying. However, I got her in, and away we went as if the devil was behind us. I coaxed her and soothed her, and promised to make her happy; but she still kept her handkerchief up to her eyes, and would not permit me a chaste salute —even pushed me away when I would put my arm round her waist; all which I ascribed to the extra shame and modesty which a woman feels when she is doing wrong. At last, when about fifteen miles from town, there was a burst of laughter, and 'I think we have gone far enough, Major M'Shane.' By all the saints in the calendar, it was her scamp of a brother that had taken her place. 'My young gentleman,' said I, 'I think you have not only gone far enough, but, as I shall prove to you, perhaps a little too far,' for I was in no fool of a passion. So I set to, beat him to a mummy, broke his nose, blackened both his eyes, and knocked half his teeth down his throat; and when he was half dead, I opened the chaise door as it whirled along, and kicked him out to take his chance of the wheels, or any other wheels which the wheel of fortune might turn up for him. So he went home and told his sister what a capital joke it was, I've no doubt. I'll be bound the young gentleman has never run away with an Irishman since that: however, I never heard any more about him, or his lovely sister."

"Now, then, for the wind-up, M'Shane."

"Courting's very expensive, especially when you order postchaises for nothing at all, and I was very nearly at the end of my rhino; so I said to myself, 'M'Shane, you must retrench.' And I did so; instead of dining at the coffeehouse, I determined to go to an eating-house, and walked into one in Holborn, where I sat down to a plate of good beef and potatoes, and a large lump of plum-pudding, paid 1s. 6d., and never was better pleased in my life; so I went there again, and became a regular customer; and the girls who waited laughed with me, and the lady who kept the house was very gracious. Now, the lady was good-looking, but she was rather too fat; there was an amiable look about her, even when she was carving beef; and by degrees we became intimate, and I found her a very worthy creature, and as simple-minded as a child, although she could look sharp after her customers. It was, and is now, a most thriving establishment—nearly two hundred people dine there every day. I don't know how it was, but I suppose I first fell in love with her beef, and then with her fair self; and finding myself well received at all times, I one day, as she was carving a beefsteak-pie which might have tempted a king for its fragrance, put the question to her, as to how she would like to marry again. She blushed, and fixed her eyes down upon the hole she had made in the pie, and then I observed that if there was a hole in my side as big as there was in the pie before her, she would see her image in my heart. This pretty simile did the business for me, and in a month we were married; and I never shall want a dinner as long as I live, either for myself or friend. I will put you on the free list, O'Donahue, if you can condescend to a cook's shop: and I can assure you that I think I have done a very wise thing, for I don't want to present any wife at court, and I have a very comfortable home."

"You have done a wise thing, in my opinion, M'Shane—you have a wife who makes money, instead of one who spends it."

"And, moreover, I have found my bargain better than I anticipated, which is seldom the case in this world of treachery and deceit. She has plenty of money, and is putting by more every year."

"Which you have the control of, at your disposition, do you mean to say?"

"Why, yes, I may say that *now;* but, O'Donahue, that is owing to my circumspection and delicacy. At first starting, I determined that she should not think that it was only her money that I wanted; so, after we were married, I continued to find myself, which, paying nothing for board and lodging and washing, I could easily do upon my half-pay; and I have done so ever since, until just now.

"I had not been married a week before I saw that she expected I would make inquiries into the state of her finances, but I would not. At last, finding that I would not enter into the business, she did, and told me that she had £17,000 Consols laid by, and that the business was worth £1000 per annum (you may fish at Cheltenham a long while, O'Donahue, before you get such a haul as that). So I told her I was very glad she was well off, and then I pretended to go fast asleep, as I never interfered with her, and never asked for money. At last she didn't like it, and offered it to me; but I told her I had enough, and did not want it; since which she has been quite annoyed at my not spending money; and when I told her this morning that there was a brother officer of mine arrived in town, to whom I had owed some money for a long while, she insisted upon my taking money to pay it, put a pile of bank-notes in my hand, and was quite mortified when she found I only wanted £20. Now you see, O'Donahue, I have done this from principle. She earns the money, and therefore she shall have the control of it as long as we are good friends; and upon my honour, I really think I love her better than I ever thought I could love any woman in the world, for she has the temper, the kindness, and the charity of an angel, although not precisely the figure; but one can't have everything in this world. And so now you have the whole of my story, and what do you think of it?"

"You must present me to your wife, M'Shane."

"That I will with pleasure. She's like her rounds of beef—it's cut and come again; but her heart is a beauty, and so is her beefsteak-pie—when you taste it."

CHAPTER XI

In which an interchange and confidence take place.

AND now, O'Donahue," said M'Shane, "if you are not yet tired of my company, I should like to hear what you have been doing since we parted: be quite as explicit, but not quite so long-winded, as myself, for I fear that I tired you."

THE POACHER

" I will be quite as explicit, my good fellow; but I have no such marvellous adventures to relate, and not such a fortunate wind-up. I have been to Bath, to Cheltenham, to Harrogate, to Brighton, and everywhere else where people meet, and people are met with, who would not meet or be met with elsewhere. I have seen many nice girls; but the nice girls were, like myself, almost penniless; and I have seen many ill-favoured, who had money: the first I could only afford to look at—the latter I have had some dealings with. I have been refused by one or two, and I might have married seven or eight; but, somehow or other, when it came near the point, the vision of a certain angel, now in heaven, has risen before me, and I have not had the heart or the heartlessness to proceed. Indeed, I may safely say that I have seen but one person since we parted who ever made the least impression on me, or whom I could fancy in any degree to replace her whom I have lost, and she, I fear, is lost also; so we may as well say no more about it. I have determined to marry for money, as you well know; but it appears to me as if there was something which invariably prevents the step being taken; and, upon my honour, fortune seems so inclined to balk me in my wishes, that I begin to snap my fingers at her, and am becoming quite indifferent. I suffer now under the evil of poverty; but it is impossible to say what other evils may be in store if I were to change my condition, as the ladies say. Come what will, in one thing I am determined—that if I marry a girl for money, I will treat her well, and not let her find it out; and as that may add to the difficulty of a man's position when he is not in love with his wife, why, all I can say is, Captain O'Donahue doesn't go cheap —that's decided."

" You're right, my jewel; there's not such a broth of a boy to be picked up every day in the week. Widows might bid for you, for without flattery, I think you a *moral* of a man, and an honour to Old Ireland. But, O'Donahue, begging your pardon, if it's not a secret, who may have been this lady who appears to have bothered your brains not a little, since she could make you forget somebody else ?"

" I met her at the Lakes of Cumberland, and being acquainted with some of the party, was invited to join them.

I was ten days in her company at Windermere, Ambleside,
Derwentwater, and other places. She was a foreigner, and
titled."

" Murder and Irish ! you don't say so ? "

" Yes ; and moreover, as I was informed by those who
were with her, has large property in Poland. She was, in
fact, everything that I could desire—handsome, witty, speaking English and several other languages, and about two or
three and twenty years old."

" And her name, if it's no offence to ask it ? "

" Princess Czartorinski."

" And a princess in the bargain ? And did you really pretend to make love to a princess ? "

" Am not I an Irishman, M'Shane ? and is a princess anything but a woman, after all ? By the powers ! I'd make
love to, and run away with the Pope himself, if he were
made of the same materials as Pope Joan is said to have
been."

" Then, upon my faith, O'Donahue, I believe you—so now
go on."

" I not only made love to her, but in making love to her, I
got most terribly singed myself, and I felt, before I quitted
her, that if I had ten thousand a year, and she was as poor
as my dear Judith was, that she should have taken her place
—that's the truth. I thought that I never could love again,
and that my heart was as flinty as a pawnbroker's ; but I
found out my mistake when it was too late."

" And did she return you the compliment ? "

" That I was not indifferent to her, I may without vanity
believe. I had a five minutes alone with her just before we
parted, and I took that opportunity of saying how much pain
it was to part with her, and for once I told the truth, for I
was almost choking when I said it. I'm convinced that
there was sincerity in my face, and that she saw that it was
there ; so she replied, ' If what you say is true, we shall
meet at St. Petersburg next winter ; good-bye, I shall expect you.' "

" Well, that was as much as to say, come, at all events."

" It was ; I stammered out my determination so to do, if
possible ; but I felt at the time that my finances rendered it
impossible—so there was an end of that affair. By my hopes

of salvation, I'd not only go to St. Petersburg, but round the whole world, and to the north pole afterwards, if I had the means only to see her once more."

"You're in a bad way, O'Donahue; your heart's gone and your money too. Upon my soul, I pity you; but it's always the case in this world. When I was a boy, the best and ripest fruit was always on the top of the wall, and out of my reach. Shall I call to-morrow, and then, if you please, I'll introduce you to Mrs. M'Shane?"

"I will be happy to see you and your good wife, M'Shane; health and happiness to you. Stop, while I ring for my little factotum to let you out."

"By-the-bye, a sharp boy that, O'Donahue, with an eye as bright as a hawk. Where did you pick him up?"

"In St. James's Park."

"Well, that's an odd place to hire a servant in."

"Do you recollect Rushbrook in my company?"

"To be sure I do—your best soldier, and a famous caterer he was at all times."

"It is his son."

"And, now I think of it, he's very like him, only somewhat better-looking."

O'Donahue then acquainted M'Shane with the circumstances attending his meeting with Joey, and they separated.

The next day, about the same time, M'Shane came to see his friend, and found O'Donahue dressed, and ready to go out with him.

"Now, O'Donahue, you mustn't be in such a hurry to see Mrs. M'Shane, for I have something to tell you which will make her look more pretty in your eyes than she otherwise might have done upon first introduction. Take your chair again, and don't be putting on your gloves yet, while you listen to a little conversation which took place between us last night, just before we dropped into the arms of Murfy. I'll pass over all the questions she asked about you, and all the compliments I paid you behind your back: because, if I didn't, it would make you blush, Irishman as you are; but this she did say,—that it was great kindness on your part to lend me that money, and that she loved you for it; upon which I replied, I was sorry you were not asy in your mind, and so very unhappy: upon which she, in course, like every

51

woman, asked me why; and then I told her merely that
it was a love-affair, and a long story, as if I wished to go to
sleep. This made her more curious, so, to oblige her, I
stayed awake, and told her just what you told me, and how
the winter was coming on and you not able to keep your
appointment. And what d'ye think the good soul said?
'Now,' says she, 'M'Shane, if you love me, and have any
gratitude to your friend for his former kindness, you will
to-morrow take him money enough, and more than enough,
to do as he wishes, and if he gains his wife he can repay
you; if not, the money is not an object.' 'That's very kind
of you, dearest,' said I; 'but then will you consent to another
thing? for this may prove a difficult affair, and he may want
me with him; and would you have any objection to that,
dearest?' for you see, O'Donahue, I took it into my head
that I might be of the greatest use to you: and, moreover,
I should like the trip, just by way of a little change.
'Couldn't he do without you?' replied she gravely. 'I'm
afraid not; and although I thought I was in barracks for
life, and never to leave you again, yet still for his sake, poor
fellow, who has been such a generous fellow to me——'
'An' how long would you be away?' said she. 'Why, it
might be two months at the most,' replied I; 'but who can
tell it to a day?' 'Well,' said she, 'I don't like that part
of the concern at all; but still, if it is necessary, as you say,
things shouldn't be done by halves,' and then she sighed,
poor soul. 'Then I won't go,' says I. 'Yes,' says she, after
a pause; 'I think it's your duty, and therefore you must.'
'I'll do just what you wish, my soul,' replied I; 'but let's
talk more about it to-morrow.' This morning she brought
up the subject, and said that she had made up her mind,
and that it should be as we had said last night; and she
went to the drawer and took out three hundred pounds in
gold and notes, and said that if it was not enough, we had
only to write for more. Now ain't she a jewel, O'Donahue?
and here's the money."

"M'Shane, she is a jewel, not because she has given
me money, but because her heart's in the right place, and
always will be. But I really do not like taking you away
with me."

"Perhaps you don't think I'd be of any use?"

"Yes; I do not doubt but that you will be, although at present I do not know how."

"But I do, for I've thought upon it, and I shall take it very unkind if you don't let me go with you. I want a little divarsion; for you see, O'Donahue, one must settle down to domestic happiness by degrees."

"Be it so, then; all I fear is, I shall occasion pain to your excellent wife."

"She has plenty to do, and that drives care away; besides, only consider the pleasure you'll occasion to her when I come back."

"I forgot that. Now, if you please, I'll call and pay my respects, and also return my grateful thanks."

"Then, come along."

Captain O'Donahue found Mrs. M'Shane very busily employed supplying her customers. She was, as M'Shane had said, a very good-looking woman, although somewhat corpulent: and there was an amiability, frankness, and kindness of disposition so expressed in her countenance, that it was impossible not to feel interested with her. They dined together. O'Donahue completely established himself in her good graces, and it was agreed that on that day week the gentlemen should embark for Hamburg, and proceed on to St. Petersburg, Joey to go with them as their little valet.

CHAPTER XII

An expedition, as of yore, across the waters for a wife.

THE first step taken by O'Donahue was to obtain a passport for himself and suite; and here there was a controversy, M'Shane having made up his mind that he would sink the officer, and travel as O'Donahue's servant, in which capacity he declared that he would not only be more useful, but also swell his friend's dignity. After a long combat on the part of O'Donahue, this was consented to, and the passport was filled up accordingly.

"But, by St. Patrick! I ought to get some letters of introduction," said O'Donahue; "and how is that to be managed? —at all events to the English ambassador. Let me see—I'll go to the Horse Guards."

O'Donahue went accordingly, and, as was always the case
there, was admitted immediately to an audience with the
Commander of the Forces. O'Donahue put his case forward,
stating that he was about to proceed on a secret mission to
Russia, and requested his Royal Highness to give him a few
letters of introduction. His Royal Highness very properly
observed, that if sent on a secret mission, he would, of course,
obtain all the necessary introductions from the proper
quarters, and then inquired of O'Donahue what his rank was,
where he had served, &c. To the latter questions O'Donahue
gave a very satisfactory reply, and convinced the Duke that
he was an officer of merit. Then came the question as to
his secret mission, which his Royal Highness had never heard
of. "May it please your Royal Highness, there's a little
mistake about this same secret mission; it's not on account
of government that I'm going, but on my own secret
service;" and O'Donahue, finding himself fairly in for it,
confessed that he was after a lady of high rank, and that
if he did not obtain letters of introduction, he should not
probably find the means of entering the society in which
she was to be found, and that as an officer who had served
faithfully, he trusted that he should not be refused.

His Royal Highness laughed at his disclosure, and, as there
was no objection to giving O'Donahue a letter or two, with
his usual good-nature he ordered them to be written, and
having given them to him, wished him every success. O'Donahue bowed to the ground, and quitted the Horse Guards,
delighted with the success of his impudent attempt.

Being thus provided, the party set off in a vessel bound
to Hamburg, where they arrived without any accident,
although very sea-sick; from Hamburg they proceeded to
Lübeck, and re-embarked at Travemünde in a brig, which
was bound for Riga; the wind was fair, and their passage
was short. On their arrival they put up at an hotel, and
finding themselves in a country where English was not
understood, O'Donahue proceeded to the house of the
English consul, informing him that he was going on a secret
mission to Petersburg, and showing, as evidences of his
respectability and the truth of his assertions, the letters
given him by his Royal Highness. These were quite sufficient
for the consul, who immediately offered his services. Not

being able to procure at Riga a courier who could speak
French or English, the consul took a great deal of trouble
to assist them in their long journey to Petersburg. He
made out a list of the posts, the number of versts, and the
money that was to be paid; he changed some of O'Donahue's
gold into Russian paper-money, and gave all the necessary
instructions. The great difficulty was to find any carriage
to carry them to the capital, but at last they found an old
cabriolet on four wheels which might answer, and, bidding
adieu to the consul, they obtained horses, and set off.

"Now, M'Shane, you must take care of the money, and
pay the driver," said O'Donahue, pulling out several pieces of
thick paper, some coloured red, some blue, and others of a
dirty white.

"Is this money?" said M'Shane, with astonishment.

"Yes, that's roubles."

"Roubles, are they? I wonder what they'd call them in
Ireland; they look like soup-tickets."

"Never mind. And now, M'Shane, there are two words
which the consul has told me to make use of: one is *Scoro*,
and when you say that, it means '*Go fast*,' and you hold up a
small bit of money at the same time."

"*Scoro!* well, that's a word I sha'n't forget."

"But then, there's another, which is *Scorae*."

"And what may be the English of that?"

"Why, that means '*Go faster*,' and with that you hold up a
larger piece of money."

"Why, then, it's no use remembering *Scoro* at all, for
Scorae will do much better; so we need not burden ourselves
with the first at all. Suppose we try the effect of that last
word upon our bear-skin friend who is driving!"

M'Shane held up a rouble, and called out to the driver—
"*Scorae!*" The fellow turned his head, smiled, and lashed
his horses until they were at the full speed, and then looked
back at them for approval.

"By the powers, that's no fool of a word! it will take us
all the way to St. Petersburg as fast as we wish."

"We do not sleep on the road, but travel night and day,"
said O'Donahue, "for there is no place worth sleeping at."

"And the 'ating, O'Donahue?"

"We must get that by signs, for we have no other means."

On that point they soon found they had no difficulty; and thus they proceeded, without speaking a word of the language, day and night, until they arrived at the capital.

At the entrance their passports were demanded, and the officer at the guard-house came out and told them that a Cossack would accompany them. A Cossack, with a spear as long as a fir-tree, and a beard not quite so long, then took them in charge, and trotted before the carriage, the driver following him at a slow pace.

"An't we prisoners?" inquired M'Shane.

"I don't know, but it looks very like it," replied O'Donahue.

This, however, was not the case. The carriage drove to a splendid street called the Neffsky Perspective, and as soon as it stopped at the entrance of an hotel, the Cossack, after speaking to the landlord, who came out, took his departure.

A journey of four hundred miles, day and night, is no joke; our travellers fell fast asleep in their spacious apartment, and it was not till the next day that they found themselves clean and comfortable, Joey being dressed in a rich livery, as a sort of page, and M'Shane doing duty as valet when others were present, and when sitting alone with O'Donahue, taking his fair share of the bottle.

Two days after their arrival, the landlord procured for O'Donahue a courier who could speak both English and French as well as Russian, and almost every other language. It was resolved by O'Donahue and M'Shane, in council, to dress him up in a splendid uniform; and a carriage having been hired for the month, O'Donahue felt that he was in a position to present his credentials to the English ambassador and the other parties for whom he had received letters of introduction.

CHAPTER XIII

In which there is some information relative to the city of St. Petersburg.

FOR 300 roubles a month, O'Donahue had procured a drosky, very handsomely fitted up; the shaft horse was a splendid trotter, and the other, a beautifully shaped animal, capered about curving his neck, until his nose almost touched his knee, and prancing, so as to be the admiration of the passers-by. His coachman, whose name was Athenasis, had the largest beard in St. Petersburg; Joey was the smallest tiger; Dimitri, one of the tallest and handsomest yägers. Altogether, Captain O'Donahue had laid out his money well; and on a fine sunny day he set off to present his letters to the English ambassador and other parties. Although the letters were very short, it was quite sufficient that they were written by so distinguished and so universally beloved a person as his Royal Highness. The ambassador, Lord St. H., immediately desired O'Donahue to consider his house open to him, requesting the pleasure of his company to dinner on the following day, and offered to present him to the emperor at the first levee. O'Donahue took his leave, delighted with his success, and then drove to the hotel of the Princess Woronzoff, Count Nesselrode, and Prince Gallitzin, where he found himself equally well received. After his visits were all paid, O'Donahue sported his handsome equipage on the English and Russian quays, and up and down the Neffsky Perspective for an hour or two, and then returned to the hotel.

"I am very sorry," said O'Donahue, after he had narrated to M'Shane all that had taken place, "that I permitted you to put yourself down on the passport as valet in the foolish way you have. You would have enjoyed yourself as much as I probably shall, and have been in your proper position in society."

"Then I'm not sorry at all, O'Donahue, and I'll tell you why. I should have enjoyed myself, I do not doubt—but I should have enjoyed myself too much; and, after dining with ambassadors, and princes, and counts, and all that thing—should I ever have gone back comfortable and contented to Mrs. M'Shane, and the cook's shop? No, no—I'm not exactly reconciled, as it is; and if I were to be drinking champagne, and 'ating French kickshaws with the Russian nobility for three or four months, dancing perhaps with princesses, and whispering in the ears of duchesses, wouldn't my nose turn up with contempt at the beefsteak pie, and poor Mrs. M'Shane, with all her kind smiles, look twice as corpulent as ever? No, no, I'm better here, and I'm a wise man, although I say it myself."

"Well, perhaps you are, M'Shane; but still I do not like that I should be spending your money in this way without your having your share of it at least."

"My share of it—now, O'Donahue, suppose I had come over here on my own account, where should I have been? I could not have mustered up the amiable impudence you did, to persuade the commander-in-chief to give me letters to the ambassador: nor could I have got up such a turn-out, nor have fitted the turn-out so well as you do. I should have been as stupid as an owl, just doing what I have done the whole of the blessed morning for want of your company— looking after one of the floating bridges across the river, and spitting into the stream, just to add my mite to the Baltic Sea."

"I'm sorry you were not better amused."

"I was amused; for I was thinking of the good-humoured face of Mrs. M'Shane, which was much better than being in high company, and forgetting her entirely. Let me alone for amusing myself after my own fashion, O'Donahue, and that's all I wish. I suppose you have heard nothing in your travels about your Powlish princess?"

"Of course not; it will require some tact to bring in her name—I must do it as if by mere accident."

"Shall I ask the courier if she is an acquaintance of his?"

"An acquaintance, M'Shane?"

"I don't mean on visiting terms; but if he knows anything about the family, or where they live?"

"No, M'Shane, I think you had better not; we do not know much of him at present. I shall dine at the ambassador's to-morrow, and there will be a large party."

During the day invitations for evening parties were brought in from the Prince Gallitzin and Princess Woronzoff.

"The plot thickens fast, as the saying is," observed M'Shane; "you'll be certain to meet your fair lady at some of these places."

"That is what I trust to do," replied O'Donahue; "if not, as soon as I'm intimate, I shall make inquiries about her; but we must first see how the land lies."

O'Donahue dined at the ambassador's, and went to the other parties, but did not meet with the object of his search. Being a good musician, he was much in request in so musical

58

a society as that of St. Petersburg. The emperor was still at his country palace, and O'Donahue had been more than a fortnight at the capital without there being an opportunity for the ambassador to present him at court.

Dimitri, the person whom O'Donahue engaged as courier, was a very clever, intelligent fellow; and as he found that O'Donahue had all the liberality of an Irishman, and was in every respect a most indulgent master, he soon had his interest at heart. Perhaps the more peculiar intimacy between O'Donahue and M'Shane, as a valet, assisted Dimitri in forming a good opinion of the former, as the hauteur and distance generally preserved by the English towards their domestics are very displeasing to the continental servants, who, if permitted to be familiar, will not only serve you more faithfully, but be satisfied with more moderate wages. Dimitri spoke English and French pretty well, German and Russian of course perfectly. He was a Russian by birth, had been brought up at the Foundling Hospital at Moscow, and therefore was not a serf. He soon became intimate with M'Shane : and as soon as the latter discovered that there was no intention on the part of Dimitri to be dishonest, he was satisfied, and treated him with cordiality.

"Tell your master this," said Dimitri, "never to give his opinion on political matters before any one while in Petersburg, or he will be reported to the government, and will be looked upon with suspicion. All the servants and couriers here, indeed every third person you meet, is an agent of police."

"Then it's not at all unlikely that you are one yourself," replied M'Shane.

"I am so," replied Dimitri coolly, "and all the better for your master. I shall be ordered to make my report in a few days, and I shall not fail to do so."

"And what will they ask you?" said M'Shane.

"They will ask me first who and what your master is? Whether I have discovered from you, if he is of family and importance in his own country? whether he has expressed any political opinions? and whether I have discovered the real business which brought him here?"

"And what will you reply to all this?" answered M'Shane.

"Why, I hardly know. I wish I knew what he wished

me to say, for he is a gentleman whom I am very fond of, and that's the truth ; perhaps you can tell me ?"

"Why, yes, I know a good deal about him, that's certain. As for his family, there's not a better in Ireland or England, for he's royal if he had his right."

"What !" exclaimed Dimitri.

"As sure as I'm sitting in this old arm-chair, didn't he bring letters from the brother of the present king? does that go for nothing in this country of yours? or do you value men by the length of their beards ?"

"Men are valued here not by their titles, but by their rank as officers. A general is a greater man than a prince," replied Dimitri.

"With all my heart, for then I'm somebody," replied M'Shane.

"You ?" replied the courier.

"I mean my master," returned M'Shane, correcting himself; "for he's an officer, and a good one, too."

"Yes, that may be; but you said yourself," replied the courier, laughing. "My good friend, a valet to any one in Petersburg is no better than one of the mujiks who work in the streets. Well, I know that our master is an officer, and of high rank; as for his political opinions, I have never heard him express any, except his admiration of the city, and of course of the emperor."

"Most decidedly ; and of the empress also," replied M'Shane.

"That is not at all necessary," continued Dimitri, laughing. "In fact, he has no business to admire the empress."

"But he admires the government and the laws," said M'Shane ; "and you may add, my good fellow—the army and the navy—by the powers, he's all admiration, all over !— you may take my word for it."

"Well, I will do so ; but then there is one other question to reply to, which is, why did he come here? what is his business?"

"To look about him, to be sure ; to spend his money like a gentleman; to give his letters of introduction ; and to amuse himself," replied M'Shane. "But this is dry talking, so, Dimitri, order a bottle of champagne, and then we'll wet our whistle before we go on."

"Champagne ! will your master stand that ?" inquired Dimitri.

"Stand it? to be sure, and he'd be very angry if he thought I did not make myself comfortable. Tell them to put it down in the bill for me; if they doubt the propriety, let them ask my master."

Dimitri went and ordered the champagne. As soon as they had a glass, Dimitri observed, "Your master is a fine liberal fellow, and I would serve him to the last day of my life; but you see that the reasons you give for your master being here are the same as are given by everybody else, whether they come as spies or secret emissaries, or to foment insurrection; that answer, therefore, is considered as no answer at all by the police (although very often a true one), and they will try to find out whether it is so or not."

"What other cause can a gentleman like him have for coming here? He is not going to dirty his hands with speculation, information, or any other botheration," replied M'Shane, tossing off his glass.

"I don't say so; but his having letters from the king's brother will be considered suspicious."

"The devil it will! Now in our country that would only create a suspicion that he was a real gentleman—that's all."

"You don't understand this country," replied Dimitri.

"No, it beats my comprehension entirely, and that's a fact; so fill up your glass. I hope it's not treason; but if it is, I can't help saying it. My good friend Dimitri——"

"Stop," said Dimitri, rising and shutting the door, "now, what is it?"

"Why, just this; I haven't seen one good-looking woman since I've been in this good-looking town of yours; now, that's the truth."

"There's more truth than treason in that," replied the courier; "but still there are some beautiful women among the higher classes."

"It's to be hoped so; for they've left no beauty for the lower, at all events."

"We have very beautiful women in Poland," said the courier.

"Why don't you bring a few here, then?"

"There are a great many Polish ladies in Petersburg at this moment."

"Then go down and order another bottle," said M'Shane, "and we'll drink their healths."

The second bottle was finished, and M'Shane, who had been drinking before, became less cautious.

"You said," observed he, "that you have many Polish ladies in Petersburg; did you ever hear of a Princess Czartowinky? —I think that's the name."

"Czartorinski, you mean," replied Dimitri; "to be sure I did; I served in the family some years ago, when the old prince was alive. But where did you see her?"

"In England, to be sure."

"Well, that's probable, for she has just returned from travelling with her uncle."

"Is she now in Petersburg, my good fellow?"

"I believe she is—but why do you wish to know?"

"Merely asked—that's all."

"Now, Macshanovich,"—for such was the familiar way in which Dimitri addressed his supposed brother-servant—"I suspect this Princess Czartorinski is some way connected with your master's coming here. Tell me the truth—is such the case? I'm sure it is."

"Then you know more than I do," replied M'Shane, correcting himself, "for I'm not exactly in my master's secrets; all that I do know is, that my master met her in England, and I thought her very handsome."

"And so did he?"

"That's as may be; between ourselves, I've an idea he was a little smitten in that quarter; but that's only my own opinion, nothing more."

"Has he ever spoken about her since you were here?" said Dimitri.

"Just once, as I handed his waistcoat to him; he said—'I wonder if all the ladies are as handsome as that Polish princess that we met in Cumberland?'"

"If I thought he wished it, or cared for her, I would make inquiry, and soon find out all about her; but otherwise, it's no use taking the trouble," replied the courier.

"Well, then, will you give me your hand, and promise to serve faithfully, if I tell you all I know about the matter?"

"By the blessed St. Nicholas, I do!" replied Dimitri; "you may trust me."

"Well, then, it's my opinion that my master's over head and ears in love with her, and has come here for no other purpose."

"Well, I'm glad you told me that; it will satisfy the police."

"The police; why murder and Irish! you're not going to inform the police, you villain?"

"Not with whom he is in love, most certainly, but that he has come here on that account; it will satisfy them, for they have no fear of a man that's in love, and he will not be watched. Depend upon it, I cannot do a better thing to serve our master."

"Well, then, perhaps you are right. I don't like this champagne—get a bottle of Burgundy, Dimitri. Don't look so hard—it's all right. The captain dines out every day, and has ordered me to drink for the honour of the house."

"He's a capital master," replied Dimitri, who had begun to feel the effects of the former bottles.

As soon as the third bottle was tapped, M'Shane continued—

"Now, Dimitri, I've given my opinion, and I can tell you, if my master has, as I suspect, come here about this young lady, and succeeds in obtaining her, it will be a blessed thing for you and me; for he's as generous as the day, and has plenty of money. Do you know who she is?"

"To be sure I do; she is an only daughter of the late Prince Czartorinski, and now a sort of ward under the protection of the emperor. She inherits all the estates, except one which was left to found an hospital at Warsaw, and is a rich heiress. It is supposed the emperor will bestow her upon one of his generals. She is at the palace, and a maid of honour to the empress."

"Whew!" whistled M'Shane; "won't there be a difficulty?"

"I should think so," replied the courier gravely.

"He must run away with her," said M'Shane, after a pause. "How will he get to see her?"

"He will not see her, so as to speak with her, in the palace; that is not the custom here; but he might meet her elsewhere."

"To be sure, at a party or a ball," said M'Shane.

"No, that would not do; ladies and gentlemen keep very apart here in general company. He might say a word or two when dancing, but that is all."

"But how is he to meet her, then, in this cursed place of yours, if men and women keep at arm's length?"

"That must depend upon her. Tell me, does she love him?"

'Well, now, that's a home question: she never told him she did, and she never told me, that's certain; but still I've an idea that she does."

"Then all I can say, Macshanovich, is, that your master had better be very careful what he is about. Of course, he knows not that you have told me anything; but as soon as he thinks proper to trust me, I then will do my utmost in his service."

"You speak like a very rational, sensible, intelligent courier," replied M'Shane, "and so now let us finish the bottle. Here's good luck to Captain O'Donahue, alive or dead: and now—please the fleas—I'll be asleep in less than ten minutes."

CHAPTER XIV

Going to court, and courting.

WHEN M'Shane awoke the next morning he tried to recall what had passed between him and Dimitri, and did not feel quite convinced that he had not trusted him too much. "I think," said he, "it was all upon an *if*. Yes, sure; *if* O'Donahue was in love, and *if* she was. Yes, I'm sure that it was all upon *ifs*. However, I must go and tell O'Donahue what has taken place."

M'Shane did so; and O'Donahue, after a little thought, replied, "Well, I don't know: perhaps it's all for the best; for you see I must have trusted somebody, and the difficulty would have been to know whom to trust, for everybody belongs to the police here, I believe: I think, myself, the fellow is honest, at all events, I can make it worth his while to be so."

"He would not have told me he belonged to the police if he wished to trap us," replied M'Shane.

"That's very true, and on the whole I think we could not do better. But we are going on too fast; who knows whether she meant anything by what she said to me when we parted; or, if she did then, whether she may not have altered her mind since?"

64

"Such things have been—that's a fact, O'Donahue."

"And will be, as long as the world lasts. However, to-morrow I am to be presented—perhaps I may see her. I'm glad that I know that I may chance to meet her, as I shall now be on my guard."

"And what shall I say to Dimitri?"

"Say that you mentioned her name, and where she was, and that I had only replied, that I should like to see her again."

"Exactly; that will leave it an open question, as the saying is," replied M'Shane.

The next day O'Donahue, in his uniform, drove to the ambassador's hotel, to accompany him to the Annishkoff palace, where he was to be presented to the emperor. O'Donahue was most graciously received,—the emperor walking up to him, as he stood in the circle, and inquiring after the health of his Royal Highness the commander-in-chief, what service he had been employed upon, &c. He then told O'Donahue that the empress would be most glad to make his acquaintance, and hoped that he would make a long stay at St. Petersburg.

It was with a quickened pulse that O'Donahue followed the ambassador into the empress's apartments. He had not waited there more than five minutes, in conversation with the ambassador, when the doors opened, and the empress, attended by her chamberlain, and followed by her ladies in waiting and maids of honour, entered the room. O'Donahue had made up his mind not to take his eyes off the empress until the presentation was over. As soon as he had kissed hands, and answered the few questions which were graciously put to him, he retired to make room for others, and then, for the first time, did he venture to cast his eyes on the group of ladies attending the empress. The first that met his view were unknown, but, behind all the rest, he at length perceived the Princess Czartorinski, talking and laughing with another lady. After a short time she turned round, and their eyes met. The princess recognised him with a start, and then turned away and put her hand up to her breast, as if the shock had taken away her breath. Once more she turned her face to O'Donahue, and this time he was fully satisfied by her looks that he was welcome.

Ten minutes after, the ambassador summoned O'Donahue, and they quitted the palace.

"I have seen her, M'Shane," said O'Donahue; "she is more beautiful, and I am more in love than ever. And now, what am I to do?"

"That's just the difficulty," replied M'Shane. "Shall I talk with Dimitri, or shall I hold my tongue, or shall I think about it while you go to dinner at the ambassador's?"

"I cannot dine out to-day, M'Shane. I will write an excuse."

"Well, now, I do believe you're in for it in good earnest. My love never spoiled my appetite; on the contrary, it was my appetite that made me fall in love."

"I wish she had not been a princess," said O'Donahue, throwing himself on the sofa.

"That's nothing at all here," replied M'Shane. "A *princess* is to be had. Now, if she had been a *general* it would have been all up with you. Military rank is everything here, as Dimitri says."

"She's an angel," replied O'Donahue, with a sigh.

"That's rank in heaven, but goes for nothing in Petersburg," replied M'Shane. "Dimitri tells me they've *civil* generals here, which I conceive are improvements on our staff, for devil a civil general I've had the pleasure of serving under."

"What shall I do?" said O'Donahue, getting up and preparing to write his note to the ambassador.

"Eat your dinner, drink a bottle of champagne, and then I'll come and talk it over with you, that's all you can do at present. Give me the note, and I'll send Dimitri off with it at once, and order up your dinner."

M'Shane's advice not being very bad, it was followed. O'Donahue had finished his dinner, and was sitting by the fire with M'Shane, when there was a knock at the door. M'Shane was summoned, and soon returned, saying, "There's a little fellow that wants to speak with you, and won't give his message. He's a queer little body, and not so bad-looking either, with a bolster on the top of his head, and himself not higher than a pillow; a pigeon could sit upon his shoulder and peck up peas out of his shoes; he struts like a grenadier, and, by the powers! a grenadier's cap would serve as an extinguisher for him. Shall I show him in?"

"Certainly," replied O'Donahue.

The reader may not be aware that there is no part of the globe where there are so many dwarfs as at St. Petersburg; there is scarcely an hotel belonging to a noble family without one or two, if not more; they are very kindly treated, and are, both in appearance and temper, very superior to the dwarfs occasionally met with elsewhere. One of this diminutive race now entered the room, dressed in a Turkish costume. He was remarkably well-made and handsome in person; he spoke sufficient French to inquire if he addressed himself to Captain O'Donahue; and on being replied to in the affirmative, he gave him a small billet, and then seated himself on the sofa with all the freedom of a petted menial. O'Donahue tore open the note; it was very short :—

"As I know you cannot communicate with me, I write to say that I was delighted at your having kept your promise. You shall hear from me again as soon as I know where I can meet you; in the meantime, be cautious. The bearer is to be trusted; he belongs to me. C."

O'Donahue pressed the paper to his lips, and then sat down to reply. We shall not trouble the reader with what he said; it is quite sufficient that the lady was content with the communication, and also at the report from her little messenger of the Captain's behaviour when he had read her billet.

Two or three days afterwards, O'Donahue received a note from a German widow lady, a Countess Erhausen, particularly requesting he would call upon her in the afternoon, at three o'clock. As he had not as yet had the pleasure of being introduced to the countess, although he had often heard her spoken of in the first society, O'Donahue did not fail in his appointment, as he considered that it was possible that the Princess Czartorinski might be connected with it; nor was he deceived, for on his entering the saloon, he found the princess sitting on the sofa with Madame Erhausen, a young and pretty woman, not more than twenty-five years of age. The princess rose, and greeted Captain O'Donahue, and then introduced the countess as her first cousin. A few minutes after his introduction, the countess retired, leaving them alone. O'Donahue did not lose this opportunity of pouring out the real feelings of his heart.

"You have come a long way to see me, Captain O'Donahue, and I ought to be grateful," replied the princess: "indeed, I have much pleasure in renewing our acquaintance."

O'Donahue, however, did not appear satisfied with this mere admission: he became eloquent in his own cause, pointed out the cruelty of having brought him over to see her again if he was not to be rewarded, and after about an hour's pleading he was sitting on the sofa by her side, with her fair hand in his, and his arm round her slender waist. They parted, but through the instrumentality of the little dwarf, they often met again at the same rendezvous. Occasionally they met in society, but before others they were obliged to appear constrained and formal; there was little pleasure in such meetings, and when O'Donahue could not see the princess his chief pleasure was to call upon Madame Erhausen and talk about her.

"You are aware, Captain O'Donahue," said the countess, one day, "that there will be a great difficulty to overcome in this affair. The princess is a sort of ward of the emperor's, and it is said that he has already, in his own mind, disposed of her hand."

"I am aware of that," replied O'Donahue; "and I know no other means than running away with her."

"That would never do," replied the countess; "you could not leave Petersburg without passports; nor could she leave the palace for more than an hour or two without being missed. You would soon be discovered, and then you would lose her for ever."

"Then what can I do, my dear madame? Shall I throw myself upon the indulgence of the emperor?"

"No, that would not answer either; she is too rich a prize to be permitted to go into foreign hands. I'll tell you what you must first do."

"I'm all attention."

"You must make love to me," replied the countess. "Nay, understand me. I mean that you must *appear* to make love to me, and the report of our marriage must be spread. The emperor will not interfere in such a case; you must do so to avoid suspicion. You have been here very often, and your equipage has been constantly seen at the door. If it is supposed you do not come on my account, it will be inquired why you do come ; and there is no keeping a secret at Petersburg. After it is supposed that it is a settled affair between us, we then may consider what next ought to be done. My regard for my cousin alone induces me to consent to this ; indeed, it is the only way she could avoid future misery."

" But is the emperor so despotic on these points ? "

" An emperor is not to be trifled with ; a ward of the emperor is considered sacred—at least, so far, that if a Russian were to wed one without permission, he probably would be sent to Siberia. With an Englishman it is different, perhaps ; and, once married, you would be safe, as you could claim the protection of your ambassador. The great point is, to let it be supposed that you are about to marry some one else ; and then, suspicion not being awakened, you may gain your wish."

" But tell me, madame,—that I may be safe from the emperor's displeasure is true—but would the princess, after he discovered it ? Could he not take her away from me, and send her to Siberia for disobedience ? "

" I hope, by the means I propose, to get you both clear of the emperor—at least, till his displeasure is softened down. Me he cannot hurt ; he can only order me out of his dominions. As for the princess, I should think that, if once married to you, she would be safe, for you could claim the protection of the ambassador for her, as your wife, as well as for yourself. Do you comprehend me now ? "

" I do, madame ; and may blessings follow you for your kindness. I shall in future act but by your directions ? "

" That is exactly what I wished you to say ; and so now, Captain O'Donahue, farewell."

CHAPTER XV

A runaway and a hard pursuit.

WELL, now," said M'Shane, after he had been informed by O'Donahue of what had passed between him and the countess,—"this is all very pretty, and looks very well ; but tell me, are we to trust that fellow Dimitri ? Can we do without him ? I should say not when it comes to the finale ;

and is it not dangerous to keep him out of our confidence, being such a sharp, keen-witted fellow? Nay, more, as he has stated his wish to serve you in any way, it is only treating him fairly. He knows the little dwarf who has been here so often; indeed, they were fellow-servants in the Czartorinski family, for he told me so. I would trust him."

"I think so, too; but we must not tell him all."

"No, that we certainly need not, for he will find it out without telling."

"Well, M'Shane, do as you please; but on second thoughts, I will speak to the countess to-morrow."

O'Donahue did so, the countess called upon the princess at the palace, and the next morning O'Donahue received a note stating that Dimitri was to be trusted. O'Donahue then sent for the courier, and told him that he was about to put confidence in him on a promise of his fidelity.

"I understand you, sir, and all you intend to do; there is no occasion to say anything more to me, until you want my assistance. I will not, in the meantime, neglect your interest, for I hope to remain with you, and that is the only reward I ask for any services I may perform. I have only one remark to make now, which is, that it will be necessary, a few days before you leave Petersburg, to let me know, that I may advertise it."

"Advertise it?"

"Yes, sir, you must advertise your departure, that you may not run away in debt. Such is the custom; and without three notices being put in the *Gazette*, the police will not give you your passport."

"I am glad that you mentioned it. Of course you are aware that I am paying attention to the Countess Erhausen, and shall leave Petersburg with her, I trust, as my wife?"

"I understand, sir, and shall take care that your intimacy there shall be known to everybody."

So saying, Dimitri left the room.

The winter now set in with unusual severity. The river was one mass of ice, the floating bridges had been removed, the Montagnes-Russes became the amusement of the day, and the sledges were galloping about in every direction. For more than a month O'Donahue continued his pretended addresses to the fair cousin of the princess, and during that time he did not once see the real object of his attachment: indeed, the dwarf never made his appearance, and all communication, except an occasional note from her to the countess, was, from prudence, given up. The widow was rich, and had often been pressed to renew her bonds, but had preferred her liberty. O'Donahue, therefore, was looked upon as a fortunate man, and congratulated upon his success. Nor did the widow deny the projected union, except in a manner so as to induce people to believe in the certainty of its being arranged. O'Donahue's equipage was always at her door, and it was expected that the marriage would immediately take place, when O'Donahue attended a levee given by the emperor on the Feast of St. Nicholas. The emperor, who had been very civil to O'Donahue, as he walked past him, said, "Well, Captain O'Donahue, so I understand that you intend to run away with one of our fairest and prettiest ladies —one of the greatest ornaments of my court?"

"I trust that I have your Majesty's permission so to do," replied O'Donahue, bowing low.

"Oh, certainly you have; and, moreover, our best wishes for your happiness."

"I humbly thank your Majesty," replied O'Donahue; "still I trust your Majesty does not think that I wish to transplant her to my own country altogether, and that I shall be permitted to reside, for the major part of the year, in your Majesty's dominions."

"Nothing will give me greater pleasure; and it will be a satisfaction to feel that I shall gain instead of losing by the intended marriage."

"By the powers! but I will remind him of this, some day or another," thought O'Donahue. "Haven't I his permission to the marriage, and to remain in the country?"

Everything was now ripe for the execution of the plot. The countess gave out that she was going to her country seat, about ten miles from St. Petersburg; and it was naturally supposed that she was desirous that the marriage should be private, and that she intended to retire there to have the ceremony performed; and O'Donahue advertised his departure in the *Gazette*.

The Princess Czartorinski produced a letter from the countess, requesting her, as a favour, to obtain leave from

71

the empress, to pass two or three days with her in the country; and the empress, as the countess was first-cousin to the princess, did not withhold her consent; on the contrary, when the princess left the palace, she put a case of jewels in her hand, saying, "These are for the bride, with the good wishes and protection of the empress, as long as she remains in this country." One hour afterwards O'Donahue was rewarded for all his long forbearance by clasping his fair one in his arms. A priest had been provided, and was sent forward to the country château, and at ten in the morning all the parties were ready. The princess and her cousin set off in the carriage, followed by O'Donahue, with M'Shane and his suite. Everything was *en règle*. The passports had been made out for Germany, to which country it was reported the countess would proceed a few days after the marriage, and the princess was to return to the palace. As soon as they arrived at the château the ceremony was performed, and O'Donahue obtained his prize; and to guard against any mishap, it was decided that they should leave the next morning, on their way to the frontier. Dimitri had been of the greatest use, had prepared against every difficulty, and had fully proved his fidelity. The parting between the countess and her cousin was tender. "How much do I owe, dear friend!" said the princess. "What risk do you incur for me! How will you brave the anger of the emperor?"

"I care little for his anger. I am a woman, and not a subject of his; but, before you go, you must both write a letter—your husband to the emperor, reminding him of his having given his consent to the marriage, and his wish that he should remain in his dominions; and let him add his sincere wish, if permitted, to be employed in his Majesty's service. You, my dear cousin, must write to the empress, reminding her of her promise of protection, and soliciting her good offices with the emperor. I shall play my own game; but, depend upon it, it will all end in a laugh."

O'Donahue and his wife both wrote their letters, and O'Donahue also wrote one to the English ambassador, informing him of what had taken place, and requesting his kind offices. As soon as they were finished, the countess bade them farewell, saying, "I shall not send these letters until you are well out of reach, depend upon it;" and, with many thanks for her kindness, O'Donahue and his bride bade her adieu, and set off on their long journey.

The carriage procured for their journey was what is called a German *bâtarde*, which is very similar to an English chariot with coach-box, fixed upon a sleigh. Inside were O'Donahue and his young bride, M'Shane preferring to ride outside on the box with Joey, that he might not be in the way, as a third person invariably is with a newly married couple. The snow was many feet deep on the ground; but the air was dry, and the sun shone bright. The bride was handed in, enveloped in a rich mantle of sable; O'Donahue followed, equally protected against the cold; while M'Shane and Joey fixed themselves on the box, so covered up in robes of wolf-skins, and wrappers of bear-skin for their feet, that you could see but the tips of their noses. On the front of the sleigh, below the box of the carriage, were seated the driver and the courier; four fiery young horses were pawing with impatience; the signal was given, and off they went at the rate of sixteen miles an hour.

"Where's the guns, Joey, and the pistols, and the ammunition?" inquired M'Shane; "we're going through a wild sort of country, I expect."

"I have put them in myself, and I can lay my hands on them immediately, sir," replied Joey; "the guns are behind us, and your pistols and the ammunition are at my feet; the captain's are in the carriage."

"That's all right, then; I like to know where to lay my hands upon my tools. Just have the goodness to look at my nose now and then, Joey; and if you see a white spot on the tip of it, you'll be pleased to tell me, and I'll do the same for you. Mrs. M'Shane would be anything but pleased if I came home with only half a handle to my face."

The journey was continued at the same rapid pace until the close of the day, when they arrived at the post-house; there they stopped, M'Shane and Joey, with the assistance of the courier, preparing their supper from the stores which they brought with them. After supper they retired, O'Donahue and his wife sleeping in the carriage, which was arranged so as to form a bed if required; while M'Shane and Joey made it out how they could upon the cloaks and what little straw they could procure, on the floor of the post-house, where, as

73

M'Shane said the next morning, they " had more bed-fellows than were agreeable, although he contrived to get a few hours' sleep in spite of the jumping vagabonds." When they rose the next morning, they found that the snow had just begun to fall fast. As soon as they had breakfasted they set out, nevertheless, and proceeded at the same pace, M'Shane telling Joey, who was, as well as himself, almost embedded in it before the day was half over, that it was " better than rain, at all events ;" to be sure that was cold comfort, but any comfort is better than none. O'Donahue's request for M'Shane to come inside was disregarded ; he was as tough as little Joey, at all events, and it would be a pity to interrupt the conversation. About four o'clock they had changed their horses at a small village, and were about three miles on their last stage, for that day's journey, when they passed through a pine forest.

"There's a nice place for an ambuscade, Joey, if there were any robbers about here," observed M'Shane. " Murder and Irish ! what's those chaps running among the trees so fast, and keeping pace with us ? I say, Dimitri," continued M'Shane, pointing to them, " what are those ? "

The courier looked in the direction pointed out, and as soon as he had done so, spoke to the driver, who, casting his eyes hastily in the direction, applied the lash to his horses, and set off with double speed.

"Wolves, sir," replied the courier, who then pulled out his pistols, and commenced loading them.

"Wolves !" said M'Shane, "and hungry enough, I'll warrant ; but they don't hope to make a meal of us, do they ? At all events, we will give them a little fight for it. Come, Joey, I see that Dimitri don't like it, so we must shake off the snow, and get our ammunition ready."

This was soon done ; the guns were unstrapped from the back of the coach-box, the pistols got from beneath their feet, and all were soon ready, loaded and primed.

"It's lucky there's such a mist on the windows of the carriage, that the lady can't see what we're after, or she'd be frightened, perhaps," said Joey.

The rapid pace at which the driver had put his horses had for a time left the wolves in the rear ; but now they were seen following the carriage at about a quarter of a mile distant, having quitted the forest and taken to the road.

THE POACHER

"Here they come, the devils! one, two, three—there are seven of them. I suppose this is what they call a covey in these parts. Were you ever wolf-hunting before, Joey?"

"I don't call this wolf-hunting," replied Joey; "I think the wolves are hunting us."

"It's all the same, my little poacher—it's a hunt, at all events. They are gaining on us fast; we shall soon come to an explanation."

The courier now climbed up to the coach-box to reconnoitre, and he shook his head, telling them in very plain English that he did not like it; that he had heard that the wolves were out in consequence of the extreme severity of the weather, and that he feared that these seven were only the advance of a whole pack; that they had many versts to go, for the stage was a long one, and it would be dark before they were at the end of it.

"Have you ever been chased by them before?" said Joey.

"Yes," replied the courier, "more than once; it's the horses that they are so anxious to get hold of. Three of our horses are very good, but the fourth is not very well, the driver says, and he is fearful that he will not hold out; however, we must keep them off as long as we can; we must not shoot at them till the last moment."

"Why not?" inquired M'Shane.

"Because the whole pack would scent the blood at miles, and redouble their efforts to come up with us. There is an empty bottle by you, sir; throw it on the road behind the carriage; that will stop them for a time."

"An empty bottle stop them! well, that's queer: it may stop a man drinking, because he can get no more out of it. However, as you please, gentlemen; here's to drink my health, bad manners to you," said M'Shane, throwing the bottle over the carriage.

The courier was right: at the sight of the bottle in the road, the wolves, who are of a most suspicious nature, and think that there is a trap laid for them in everything, stopped short, and gathered round it cautiously; the carriage proceeded, and in a few minutes the animals were nearly out of sight.

"Well, that bothers me entirely," said M'Shane; "an empty bottle is as good to them as a charged gun."

75

"But look, sir, they are coming on again," said Joey, "and faster than ever. I suppose they were satisfied that there was nothing in it."

The courier mounted again to the box where Joey and M'Shane were standing. "I think you had a ball of twine," said he to Joey, "when you were tying down the baskets; where is it?"

"It is here under the cushion," replied Joey, searching for and producing it.

"What shall we find to tie to it?" said the courier; "something not too heavy—a bottle won't do."

"What's it for?" inquired M'Shane.

"To trail, sir," replied the courier.

"To trail! I think they're fast enough upon our trail already; but if you want to help them, a red herring's the thing."

"No, sir, a piece of red cloth would do better," replied the courier.

"Red cloth! One would think you were fishing for mackerel," replied M'Shane.

"Will this piece of black cloth do, which was round the lock of the gun?" said Joey.

"Yes, I think it will," replied the courier.

The courier made fast the cloth to the end of the twine, and throwing it clear of the carriage, let the ball run out, until he had little more than the bare end in his hand, and the cloth was about forty yards behind the carriage, dragging over the snow.

"They will not pass the cloth, sir," said the courier; "they think that it's a trap."

Sure enough the wolves, who had been gaining fast on the carriage, now retreated again; and although they continued the pursuit, it was at a great distance.

"We have an hour and a half more to go before we arrive, and it will be dark, I'm afraid," said the courier; "all depends upon the horse holding out; I'm sure the pack is not far behind."

"And how many are there in a pack?" inquired M'Shane.

The courier shrugged up his shoulders. "Perhaps two or three hundred."

"Oh! the devil! Don't I wish I was at home with Mrs. M'Shane."

For half-an-hour they continued their rapid pace, when the horse referred to showed symptoms of weakness. Still the wolves had not advanced beyond the piece of black cloth which trailed behind the carriage.

"I think that, considering that they are so hungry, they are amazing shy of the bait," said M'Shane. "By all the powers, they've stopped again!"

"The string has broke, sir, and they are examining the cloth," cried Joey.

"Is there much line left?" inquired the courier, with some alarm.

"No, it has broken off by rubbing against the edge of the carriage behind."

The courier spoke to the driver, who now rose from his seat and lashed his horses furiously; but although three of the horses were still fresh, the fourth could not keep up with them, and there was every prospect of his being dragged down on his knees, as more than once he stumbled and nearly fell. In the meantime the wolves had left the piece of cloth behind them, and were coming up fast with the carriage.

"We must fire on them now, sir," said the courier, going back to his seat, "or they will tear the flanks of the horses."

M'Shane and Joey seized their guns, the headmost wolf was now nearly ahead of the carriage; Joey fired, and the animal rolled over in the snow.

"That's a good shot, Joey; load again; here's at another."

M'Shane fired, and missed the animal, which rushed forward; the courier's pistol, however, brought it down, just as he was springing on the hindmost horses.

O'Donahue, astonished at the firing, now lowered down the glass, and inquired the reason. M'Shane replied, that the wolves were on them, and that he'd better load his pistols in case they were required.

The wolves hung back a little upon the second one falling, but still continued the chase, although at a more respectable distance. The road was now on a descent, but the sick horse could hardly hold on his legs.

"A little half-hour more and we shall be in the town," said the courier, climbing up to the coach-seat, and looking up the road they had passed; "but St. Nicholas preserve us!"

he exclaimed; and he turned round and spoke in hurried accents to the driver in the Russian language.

Again the driver lashed furiously, but in vain; the poor horse was dead-beat.

"What is the matter now?" inquired M'Shane.

"Do you see that black mass coming down the hill? it's the main pack of wolves; I fear we are lost; the horse cannot go on."

"Then why not cut his traces, and go on with the three others?" cried Joey.

"The boy is right," replied the man, "and there is no time to lose." The courier went down on the sleigh, spoke to the driver in Russian, and the horses were pulled up. The courier jumped out with his knife, and commenced cutting the traces of the tired horse, while the other three, who knew that the wolves were upon them, plunged furiously in their harness, that they might proceed. It was a trying moment. The five wolves now came up; the first two were brought down by the guns of M'Shane and Joey, and O'Donahue killed a third from the carriage windows.

One of the others advanced furiously, and sprang upon the horse which the courier was cutting free. Joey leapt down, and put his pistol to the animal's head, and blew out his brains, while M'Shane, who had followed our hero, with the other pistol disabled the only wolf that remained.

But this danger which they had escaped from was nothing compared to that which threatened them; the whole pack now came sweeping like a torrent down the hill, with a simultaneous yell which might well strike terror into the bravest. The horse, which had fallen down when the wolf seized him, was still not clear of the sleigh, and the other three were quite unmanageable. M'Shane, Joey, and the courier, at last drew him clear from the track; they jumped into their places, and away they started again like the wind, for the horses were maddened with fear. The whole pack of wolves was not one hundred yards from them when they recommenced their speed, and even then M'Shane considered that there was no hope. But the horse that was left on the road proved their salvation; the starved animals darted upon it, piling themselves one on the other, snarling and tearing each other in their conflict for the feast. It was soon over;

in the course of three minutes the carcass had disappeared, and the major portion of the pack renewed their pursuit; but the carriage had proceeded too far ahead of them, and their speed being now uninterrupted, they gained the next village, and O'Donahue had the satisfaction of leading his terrified bride into the chamber of the post-house, where she fainted as soon as she was placed in a chair.

" I'll tell you what, Joey, I've had enough of wolves for all my life," said M'Shane; "and Joey, my boy, you're a good shot in the first place, and a brave little fellow in the next; here's a handful of roubles, as they call them, for you to buy lollipops with, but I don't think you'll find a shop that sells them hereabouts. Never mind, keep your sweet tooth till you get to old England again; and after I tell Mrs. M'Shane what you have done for us this day, she will allow you to walk into a leg of beef, or round a leg of mutton, or dive into a beefsteak pie, as long as you live, whether it be one hundred years more or less. I've said it, and don't you forget it; and now, as the wolves have not made their supper upon us, let us go and see what we can sup upon ourselves."

CHAPTER XVI

Return to England.

THE remainder of the journey was completed without any further adventure, and they at last found themselves out of the Russian dominions, when they were met by the uncle of the princess, who, as ? Pole, was not sorry that his niece had escaped from being wedded to a Russian. He warmly greeted O'Donahue as his connection, and immediately exerted all the interest which he had at the court to pacify the emperor. When the affair first became known, which it soon did, by the princess not returning to court, his Majesty was anything but pleased at being outwitted; but the persuasions of the empress, the pleading of the English ambassador, who exerted himself strenuously for O'Donahue, with the efforts made in other quarters, and more than all, the letter of O'Donahue, proving that the emperor had given his consent

79

(unwittingly, it is true), coupled with his wish to enter into his service, at last produced the desired effect, and after two months a notice of their pardon and permission to return was at last despatched by the empress. O'Donahue considered that it was best to take immediate advantage of this turn in his favour, and retrace his way to the capital. M'Shane, who had been quite long enough in the situation of a domestic, now announced his intention to return home; and O'Donahue, aware that he was separating him from his wife, did not, of course, throw any obstacle in the way of his departure. Our little hero, who has lately become such a cipher in our narrative, was now the subject of consideration. O'Donahue wished him to remain with him, but M'Shane opposed it.

"I tell you, O'Donahue, that it's no kindness to keep him here; the boy is too good to be a page at a lady's shoestring, or even a servant to so great a man as you are yourself now; besides, how will he like being buried here in a foreign country, and never go back to old England?"

"But what will he do better in England, M'Shane?"

"Depend upon it, major," said the princess, for she was now aware of M'Shane's rank, "I will treat him like a son."

"Still he will be a servant, my lady, and that's not the position—although, begging your pardon, an emperor might be proud to be your servant—yet that's not the position for little Joey."

"Prove that you will do better for him, M'Shane, and he is yours: but without you do, I am too partial to him to like to part with him. His conduct on the journey——"

"Yes, exactly, his conduct on the journey, when the wolves would have shared us out between them, is one great reason for my objection. He is too good for a menial, and that's the fact. You ask me what I intend to do with him; it is not so easy to answer that question, because you see, my lady, there's a certain Mrs. M'Shane in the way, who must be consulted; but I think that when I tell her, what I consider to be as near the truth as most things which are said in this world, that if it had not been for the courage and activity of little Joey, a certain Major M'Shane would have been by this time eaten and digested by a pack of wolves, why, I then think, as Mrs. M'Shane and I have no child, nor prospect of any, as I know of, that she may be well inclined to come into my way of

80

thinking, and of adopting him as her own son; but, of course, this cannot be said without my consulting with Mrs. M'Shane, seeing as how the money is her own, and she has a right to do as she pleases with it."

"That, indeed, alters the case," replied O'Donahue; "and I must not stand in the way of the boy's interest; still I should like to do something for him."

"You have done something for him, O'Donahue; you have prevented his starving; and if he has been of any use to you, it is but your reward—so you and he are quits. Well, then, it is agreed that I take him with me?"

"Yes," replied O'Donahue. "I cannot refuse my consent after what you have said."

Two days after this conversation the parties separated; O'Donahue, with his wife, accompanied by Dimitri, set off on their return to St. Petersburg; while M'Shane, who had provided himself with a proper passport, got into the diligence, accompanied by little Joey, on his way back to England.

CHAPTER XVII

The day after the murder.

W E must now return to the village of Grassford, and the cottage in which we left Rushbrook and his wife, who had been raised up from the floor by her husband, and, having now recovered from her swoon, was crying bitterly for the loss of her son, and the dread of her husband's crime being discovered. For some time Rushbrook remained in silence, looking at the embers in the grate; Mum sometimes would look piteously in his master's face, at other times he would slowly approach the weeping woman. The intelligence of the animal told him that something was wrong. Finding himself unnoticed, he would then go to the door by which Joey had quitted, snuff at the crevice, and return to his master's side.

"I'm glad that he's off," at last muttered Rushbrook; "he's a fine boy, that."

"Yes, he is," replied Jane; "but when shall I behold him again?"

"By-and-by, never fear, wife. We must not stay in this place, provided this affair blows over."

"If it does, indeed!"

"Come, come, Jane, we have every reason to hope it will; now, let's go to bed; it would not do, if any one should happen to have been near the spot, and to have found out what has taken place, for us to be discovered not to have been in bed all night, or even for a light to be seen at the cottage by any early riser. Come, Jane, let's to bed."

Rushbrook and his wife retired, the light was extinguished, and all was quiet, except conscience, which still tormented and kept Rushbrook turning to the right and left continually. Jane slept not: she listened to the wind; the slightest noise—the crowing of the cock—startled her, and soon footsteps were heard of those passing the windows. They could remain in bed no longer. Jane arose, dressed, and lighted the fire: Rushbrook remained sitting on the side of the bed in deep thought.

"I've been thinking, Jane," said he, at last, "it would be better to make away with Mum."

"With the dog? Why, it can't speak, poor thing. No—no—don't kill the poor dog."

"He can't speak, but the dog has sense; he may lead them to the spot."

"And if he were to do so, what then? it would prove nothing."

"No! only it would go harder against Joey."

"Against the boy! yes, it might convince them that Joey did the deed; but still, the very killing of the animal would look suspicious: tie him up, Rushbrook; that will do as well."

"Perhaps better," replied he; "tie him up in the back-kitchen, there's a good woman."

Jane did so, and then commenced preparing the breakfast; they had taken their seats, when the latch of the door was lifted up, and Furness, the schoolmaster, looked in. This he was often in the habit of doing, to call Joey out to accompany him to school.

"Good morning," said he; "now, where's my friend Joey?"

"Come in, come in, neighbour, and shut the door," said Rushbrook; "I wish to speak to you. Mayhap you'll take a cup of tea; if so, my missus will give you a good one."

THE POACHER

"Well, as Mrs. Rushbrook does make everything so good, I don't care if I do, although I have had breakfast. But where's my friend Joey? the lazy little dog; is he not up yet? Why, Mrs. Rushbrook, what's the matter? you look distressed."

"I am, indeed," replied Jane, putting her apron to her eyes.

"Why, Mrs. Rushbrook, what is it?" inquired the pedagogue.

"Just this; we are in great trouble about Joey. When we got up this morning we found that he was not in bed, and he has never been home since."

"Well, that is queer; why, where can the young scamp be gone to?"

"We don't know; but we find that he took my gun with him, and I'm afraid——" and here Rushbrook paused, shaking his head.

"Afraid of what?"

"That he has gone poaching, and has been taken by the keepers."

"But did he ever do so before?"

"Not by night, if he did by day. I can't tell; he always has had a hankering that way."

"Well, they do whisper the same of you, neighbour. Why do you keep a gun?"

"I've carried a gun all my life," replied Rushbrook, "and I don't choose to be without one: but that's not to the purpose; the question is, what would you advise us to do?"

"Why, you see, friend Rushbrook," replied the schoolmaster, "advice in this question becomes rather difficult. If Joey has been poaching, as you imagine, and has been taken up, as you suspect, why, then, you will soon hear of it: you, of course, have had no hand in it?"

"Hand in it—hand in what?" replied Rushbrook. "Do you think we trust a child like him with a gun?"

"I should think not; and therefore it is evident that he has acted without the concurrence of his parents. That will acquit you; but still, it will not help Joey; neither do I think you will be able to recover the gun, which I anticipate will become a deodand to the lord of the manor."

"But, the child—what will become of him?" exclaimed Jane.

"What will become of him?—why, as he is of tender years, they will not transport him—at least, I should think not; they may imprison him for a few months, and order him to be privately whipped. I do not see what you can do but remain quiet. I should recommend you not to say one syllable about it until you hear more."

"But suppose we do not hear?"

"That is to suppose that he did not go out with the gun to poach, but upon some other expedition."

"What else could the boy have gone out for?" said Rushbrook hastily.

"Very true; it is not very likely that he went out to commit murder," replied the pedagogue.

At the word "murder" Rushbrook started from his chair; but, recollecting himself, he sat down again.

"No, no, Joey commit murder?" cried he. "Ha, ha, ha!—no, no, Joey is no murderer."

"I should suspect not. Well, Master Rushbrook, I will dismiss my scholars this morning, and make every inquiry for you. Byres will be able to ascertain very soon, for he knows the new keeper at the manor-house."

"Byres help you, did you say? No, no, Byres never will," replied Rushbrook solemnly.

"And why not, my friend?"

"Why," replied Rushbrook, recollecting himself, "he has not been over cordial with me lately."

"Nevertheless, depend upon it, he will if he can," replied Furness; "if not for you, he will for me. Good morning, Mrs. Rushbrook, I will hasten away now; but will you not go with me?" continued Furness, appealing to Rushbrook.

"I will go another way; it's no use both going the same road."

"Very true," replied the pedagogue, who had his reasons for not wishing the company of Rushbrook, and Furness then left the house.

Mr. Furness found all his boys assembled in the schoolroom, very busily employed thumbing their books; he ordered silence, and informed them that in consequence of Joey being missing, he was going to assist his father to look after him; and therefore they would have a holiday for that day. He then ranged them all in a row, made them turn to the right face, clap their hands simultaneously, and disperse.

Although Mr. Furness had advised secrecy to the Rushbrooks, he did not follow the advice he had given; indeed, his reason for not having wished Rushbrook to be with him was, that he might have an opportunity of communicating his secret through the village, which he did by calling at every cottage, and informing the women who were left at home, that Joey Rushbrook had disappeared last night, with his father's gun, and that he was about to go in quest of him. Some nodded and smiled, others shook their heads, some were not at all surprised at it, others thought that things could not go on so for ever.

Mr. Furness having collected all their various opinions, then set off to the ale-house, to find Byres the pedlar. When he arrived, he found that Byres had not come home that night, and where he was nobody knew, which was more strange, as his box was up in his bed-chamber. Mr. Furness returned to the village intending to communicate this information to Rushbrook, but on calling, he found that Rushbrook had gone out in search of the boy. Furness then resolved to go up at once to the keeper's lodge, and solve the mystery. He took the highroad, and met Rushbrook returning.

"Well, have you gained any tidings?" inquired the pedagogue.

"None," replied Rushbrook.

"Then it's my opinion, my worthy friend, that we had better at once proceed to the keeper's cottage and make inquiry; for, strange to say, I have been to the ale-house, and my friend Byres is also missing."

"Indeed!" exclaimed Rushbrook, who had now completely recovered his self-possession. "Be it so, then; let us go to the keeper's."

They soon arrived there, and found the keeper at home, for he had returned to his dinner. Rushbrook, who had been cogitating how to proceed, was the first to speak.

"You haven't taken my poor Joey, have you, sir?" said he to the keeper.

"Not yet," replied the keeper surlily.

"You don't mean to say that you know nothing about him?" replied Rushbrook.

85

THE POACHER

"Yes, I know something about him and about you too, my chap," replied the keeper.

"But, Mr. Lucas," interrupted the pedagogue, "allow me to put you in possession of the facts. It appears that this boy —a boy of great natural parts, and who has been for some time under my tuition, did last night, but at what hour is unknown to his disconsolate parents, leave the cottage, taking with him his father's gun, and has not been heard of since."

"Well, I only hope he's shot himself, that's all," replied the keeper. "So you have a gun, then, have you, my honest chap?" continued he, turning to Rushbrook.

"Which," replied Furness, "as I have informed him already, will certainly be forfeited as a deodand to the lord of the manor; but, Mr. Lucas, this is not all; our mutual friend, Byres, the pedlar, is also missing, having left the Cat and Fiddle last night, and not having been heard of since."

"Indeed! that makes out a different case, and must be inquired into immediately. I think you were not the best of friends, were you?" said the keeper, looking at Rushbrook; and then he continued, "Come, Mary, give me my dinner, quick, and run up as fast as you can for Dick and Martin: tell them to come down with their retrievers only. Never fear, Mr. Furness, we will soon find it out. Never fear, my chap, we'll find your son also, and your gun to boot. You may hear more than you think for."

"All I want to know," replied Rushbrook fiercely, for his choler was raised by the sneers of the keeper, "is, where my boy may be." So saying, he quitted the cottage, leaving the schoolmaster with the keeper.

As Rushbrook returned home, he revolved in his mind what had passed, and decided that nothing could be more favourable for himself, however it might turn out for Joey. This conviction quieted his fears, and when the neighbours came in to talk with him, he was very cool and collected in his replies. In the meantime the keeper made a hasty meal, and, with his subordinates and the dogs, set off to the covers, which they beat till dark without success. The gun, however, which Joey had thrown down in the ditch, had been picked up by one of the labourers returning from his work, and taken by him to the ale-house. None could identify the gun, as Rushbrook had never permitted it to be seen. Lucas, the keeper, came in about an hour after dusk, and immediately took possession of it.

Such were the events of the first day after Joey's departure. Notwithstanding that the snow fell fast, the Cat and Fiddle was, as it may be supposed, unusually crowded on that night. Various were the surmises as to the disappearance of the pedlar and of little Joey. The keeper openly expressed his opinion that there was foul play somewhere, and it was not until near midnight that the ale-house was deserted, and the doors closed.

Rushbrook and his wife went to bed; tired with watching and excitement, they found oblivion for a few hours in a restless and unrefreshing sleep.

CHAPTER XVIII

A coroner's inquest.

DAY had scarcely dawned when the keeper and his satellites were again on the search. The snow had covered the ground for three or four inches, and, as the covers had been well examined on the preceding day, they now left them and went on in the direction towards where the gun had been picked up. This brought them direct to the furze bottom, where the dogs appeared to quicken their movements, and when the keepers came up with them again, they found them lying down by the frozen and stiffened corpse of the pedlar.

"Murder, as I expected," said Lucas, as they lifted up the body, and scraped off the snow which covered it; "right through his heart, poor fellow; who would have expected this from such a little varmint? Look about, my lads, and see if we can find anything else. What is Nap scratching at?—a bag—take it up, Martin. Dick, do you go for some people to take the body to the Cat and Fiddle, while we see if we can find anything more."

In a quarter of an hour the people arrived, the body was carried away, while the keeper went off in all haste to the authorities.

87

Furness, the schoolmaster, as soon as he had obtained the information, hastened to Rushbrook's cottage, that he might be the first to convey the intelligence. Rushbrook, however, from the back of the cottage, had perceived the people carrying in the body, and was prepared.

"My good people, I am much distressed, but it must be told; believe me, I feel for you—your son, my pupil, has murdered the pedlar."

"Impossible!" cried Rushbrook.

"It is but too true; I cannot imagine how a boy, brought up under my tuition—nay, Mrs. Rushbrook, don't cry— brought up, I may say, with such strict notions of morality, promising so fairly, blossoming so sweetly——"

"He never murdered the pedlar!" cried Jane, whose face was buried in her apron.

"Who then could have?" replied Furness.

"He never shot him intentionally, I'll swear," said Rushbrook; "if the pedlar has come to his death, it must have been by some accident. I suppose the gun went off somehow or other; yes, that must be it: and my poor boy, frightened at what had taken place, has run away."

"Well," replied the schoolmaster, "such may have been the case; and I do certainly feel as if it were impossible that a boy like Joey, brought up by me, grounded in every moral duty—I may add, religiously and piously instructed—could ever commit such a horrible crime."

"Indeed, he never did," replied Jane; "I am sure he never would do such a thing."

"Well, I must wish you good-bye now, my poor people; I will go down to the Cat and Fiddle, and hear what they say," cried the pedagogue, quitting the cottage.

"Jane, be careful," said Rushbrook; "our great point now is to say nothing. I wish that man would not come here."

"Oh, Rushbrook!" cried Jane, "what would I give if we could live these last three days over again."

"Then imagine, Jane, what I would give!" replied Rushbrook, striking his forehead; "and now say no more about it."

At twelve o'clock the next day the magistrates met, and the coroner's inquest was held upon the body of the pedlar.

THE POACHER

On examination of the body, it was ascertained that a charge of small shot had passed directly through the heart, so as to occasion immediate death; that the murder had not been committed with the view of robbing, it was evident, as the pedlar's purse, watch, and various other articles were found upon his person.

The first person examined was a man of the name of Green, who had found the gun in the ditch. The gun was produced, and he deposed to its being the one which he had picked up, and given into the possession of the keeper; but no one could say to whom the gun might belong.

The next party who gave his evidence was Lucas, the gamekeeper. He deposed that he knew the pedlar, Byres, and that being anxious to prevent poaching, he had offered him a good sum if he would assist him in convicting any poacher; that Byres had then confessed to him that he had often received game from Rushbrook, the father of the boy, and still continued to do so, but Rushbrook had treated him ill, and he was determined to be revenged upon him, and get him sent out of the country; that Byres had informed him on the Saturday night before the murder was committed, that Rushbrook was to be out on Monday night to procure game for him, and that if he looked out sharp he was certain to be taken. Byres had also informed him that he had never yet found out when Rushbrook left his cottage or returned, although he had been tracking the boy, Joey. As the boy was missing on Monday morning, and Byres did not return to the ale-house after he went out on Saturday night, he presumed that it was on the Sunday night that the pedlar was murdered.

The keeper then farther deposed as to the finding of the body, and also of a bag by the side of it; that the bag had evidently been used for putting game in, not only from the smell, but from the feathers of the birds which were still remaining inside of it.

The evidence as to the finding of the body and the bag was corroborated by that of Martin and Dick, the under-keepers.

Mr. Furness then made his appearance to give *voluntary* evidence, notwithstanding his great regard expressed for the Rushbrooks. He deposed that, calling at the cottage, on

Monday morning, for his pupil, he found the father and
mother in great distress at the disappearance of their son,
whom they stated to have left the cottage some time during
the night, and to have taken away his father's gun with him,
and that their son had not since returned; that he pointed
out to Rushbrook the impropriety of his having a gun, and
that Rushbrook had replied that he had carried one all his
life, and did not choose to be without one; that they told
him they supposed that he had gone out to poach, and was
taken by the keepers, and had requested him to go and
ascertain if such was the fact. Mr. Furness added that he
really imagined that to be the case now that he saw the bag,
which he recognised as having been once brought to him
by little Joey with some potatoes, which his parents had
made him a present of; that he could swear to the bag, and
so could several others as well as himself. Mr. Furness then
commenced a long flourish about his system of instruction,
in which he was stopped by the coroner, who said that it
had nothing to do with the business.

It was then suggested that Rushbrook and his wife should
be examined. There was a demur at the idea of the father
and mother giving evidence against their child, but it was
overruled, and in ten minutes they both made their appearance.

Mrs. Rushbrook, who had been counselled by her husband,
was the first examined; but she would not answer any question put to her. She did nothing but weep; and to every
question her only reply was, "If he did kill him, it was by
accident; my boy would never commit murder." Nothing
more was to be obtained from her; and the magistrates were
so moved by her distress, that she was dismissed.

Rushbrook trembled as he was brought in and saw the
body laid out on the table; but he soon recovered himself,
and became nerved and resolute, as people often will do in
extremity. He had made up his mind to answer some
questions, but not all.

"Do you know at what time your son left the cottage?"

"I do not."

"Does that gun belong to you?"

"Yes, it is mine."

"Do you know that bag?"

"Yes, it belongs to me."

"It has been used for putting game into—has it not ?"

"I shall not answer that question. I'm not on trial."

Many other questions were put to him, but he refused to answer them ; and as they would all more or less have criminated himself as a poacher, his refusals were admitted. Rushbrook had played his game well in admitting the gun and bag to be his property, as it was of service to him, and no harm to Joey. After summing up the whole evidence, the coroner addressed the jury, and they returned a unanimous verdict of wilful murder against Joseph Rushbrook the younger; and the magistrates directed the sum of £200 to be offered for our hero's apprehension.

CHAPTER XIX

A friend in need is a friend indeed.

RUSHBROOK and Jane returned to their cottage. Jane closed the door, and threw herself into her husband's arms. "You are saved at least," she cried : "thank Heaven for that ! You are spared. Alas! we do not know how much we love till danger comes upon us."

Rushbrook was much affected : he loved his wife, and had good reason to love her. Jane was a beautiful woman, not yet thirty ; tall in her person, her head was finely formed, yet apparently small for her height : her features were full of expression and sweetness. Had she been born to a high station, she would have been considered one of the greatest belles. As it was, she was loved by those around her; and there was a dignity and commanding air about her which won admiration and respect. No one could feel more deeply than she did the enormity of the offence committed by her husband ; and yet never in any moment since her marriage did she cling so earnestly and so closely by him as she did now. She was of that bold and daring temperament, that she could admire the courage that propelled to the crime, while the crime itself she abhorred. It was not, therefore, anything surprising that, at such a moment, with regard to a husband

91

to whom she was devoted, she thought more of the danger to which he was exposed than she did of the crime which had been committed.

To do Rushbrook himself justice, his person and mind were of no plebeian mould. He was a daring, venturous fellow, ready at any emergency, cool and collected in danger, had a pleasure in the excitement created by the difficulty and risk attending his nocturnal pursuits, caring little or nothing for the profits. He, as well as his wife, had not been neglected in point of education : he had been born in humble life, and had, by enlisting, chosen a path by which advancement became impossible ; but had Rushbrook been an officer instead of a common soldier, his talents would probably have been directed to more noble channels, and the poacher and pilferer for his captain might have exerted his dexterity so as to have gained honourable mention. His courage had always been remarkable, and he was looked upon by his officers—and so he was by his companions—as the most steady and collected man under fire to be found in the whole company.

We are the creatures of circumstances. Frederick **of** Prussia had no opinion of phrenology ; and one day he sent for the professor, and dressing up a highwayman and a pick-pocket in uniforms and orders, he desired the phrenologist to examine their heads, and give his opinion as to their qualifications. The *savant* did so, and turning to the king, said, " Sire, this person," pointing to the highwayman, " whatever he may be, would have been a great general, had he been employed. As for the other, he is quite in a different line. He may be, or, if he is not, he would make, an admirable financier." The king was satisfied that there was some truth in the science ; " for," as he very rightly observed, " what is a general but a highwayman, and what is a financier but a pickpocket ? "

" Calm yourself, dear Jane," said Rushbrook; " all is well now."

" All well !—yes ; but my poor child—£200 offered for his apprehension ! If they were to take him ! "

" I have no fear of that ; and if they did, they could not hurt him. It is true that they have given their verdict; but still they have no positive proof."

" But they have hanged people upon less proof before now, Rushbrook."

" Jane," replied Rushbrook, " our boy shall never be hanged
—I promise you that ; so make your mind easy."

"Then you must confess, to save him ; and I shall lose you."

A step at the door interrupted their colloquy. Rushbrook
opened it, and Mr. Furness, the schoolmaster, made his appearance.

" Well, my good friends, I am very sorry the verdict has
been such as it is, but it cannot be helped ; the evidence was
too strong, and it was a sad thing for me to be obliged to
give mine."

"You !" exclaimed Rushbrook; "why, did they call you up?"

" Yes, and put me on my oath. An oath, to a moral man,
is a very serious responsibility ; the nature of an oath is awful ;
and when you consider my position in this place, as the incul-
cator of morals and piety to the younger branches of the community, you must not be surprised at my telling the truth."

" And what had you to tell ?" inquired Rushbrook, with
surprise.

" Had to tell !—why, I had to tell what you told me
yesterday morning ; and I had to prove the bag as belonging
to you ; for you know you sent me some potatoes in it by
little Joey, poor fellow. Wilful Murder, and £200 upon
apprehension and conviction !"

Rushbrook looked at the pedagogue with surprise and
contempt.

" Pray, may I ask how they came to know that anything
had passed between us yesterday morning, for if I recollect
right, you desired me to be secret."

" Very true, and so I did ; but then they knew what good
friends we always were, I suppose, and so they sent for me,
and obliged me to speak upon my oath."

" I don't understand it," replied Rushbrook ; "they might
have asked you questions, but how could they have guessed
that I had told you anything ?"

" My dear friend, you don't understand it ; but in my situation, looking up to me, as every one does, as an example of
moral rectitude and correctness of conduct—as a pattern to
the juvenile branches of the community,—you see——"

" Yes, I do see that, under such circumstances, you should
not go to the ale-house and get tipsy two days, at least, out
of the week," replied Rushbrook, turning away.

"And why do I go to the ale-house, my dear friend, but to look after those who indulge too freely—yourself, for instance? How often have I seen you home?"

"Yes, when you were drunk and I was——" Jane put her hand upon her husband's mouth.

"And you were what, friend?" inquired Furness anxiously.

"Worse than you, perhaps. And now, friend Furness, as you must be tired with your long evidence, I wish you a good night."

"Shall I see you down at the Cat and Fiddle?"

"Not for some time, if ever, friend Furness, that you may depend upon."

"Never go to the Cat and Fiddle! A little wholesome drink drowns care, my friend; and, therefore, although I should be sorry that you indulged too much, yet, with me to look after you——"

"And drink half my ale, eh? No, no, friend Furness, those days are gone."

"Well, you are not in a humour for it now—but another time. Mrs. Rushbrook, have you a drop of small beer?"

"I have none to spare," replied Jane, turning away; "you should have applied to the magistrates for beer."

"Oh, just as you please," replied the pedagogue; "it certainly does ruffle people's temper when there is a verdict of wilful murder, and £200 for apprehension and conviction of the offender. Good night."

Furness banged the cottage door as he went out.

Rushbrook watched till he was out of hearing, and then said, "He's a scoundrel."

"I think so too," replied Jane; "but never mind, we will go to bed now, thank God for His mercies, and pray for His forgiveness. Come, dearest."

The next morning Mrs. Rushbrook was informed by the neighbours that the schoolmaster had volunteered his evidence. Rushbrook's indignation was excited, and he vowed revenge.

Whatever may have been the feelings of the community at the time of the discovery of the murder, certain it is that, after all was over, there was a strong sympathy expressed for Rushbrook and his wife, and the condolence was very general. The gamekeeper was avoided, and his friend Furness fell

94

into great disrepute, after his voluntarily coming forward and giving evidence against old and sworn friends. The consequence was, his school fell off, and the pedagogue, whenever he could raise the means, became more intemperate than ever.

One Saturday night, Rushbrook, who had resolved to pick a quarrel with Furness, went down to the ale-house. Furness was half drunk, and pot-valiant. Rushbrook taunted him so as to produce replies. One word brought on another, till Furness challenged Rushbrook to come outside and have it out. This was just what Rushbrook wished, and after half-an-hour Furness was carried home beaten to a mummy, and unable to leave his bed for many days. As soon as this revenge had been taken, Rushbrook, who had long made up his mind so to do, packed up and quitted the village, no one knowing whither he and Jane went; and Furness, who had lost all means of subsistence, did the same in a very few days afterwards, his place of retreat being equally unknown.

CHAPTER XX

In which we again follow up our hero's destiny.

AFTER the resolution that Major M'Shane came to, it is not to be surprised that he made, during the journey home, every inquiry of Joey relative to his former life. To these Joey gave him a very honest reply in everything except that portion of his history in which his father was so seriously implicated; he had the feeling that he was bound in honour not to reveal the circumstances connected with the murder of the pedlar. M'Shane was satisfied, and they arrived in London without further adventure. As soon as M'Shane had been embraced by his wife, he gave a narrative of his adventures, and did not forget to praise little Joey as he deserved. Mrs. M'Shane was all gratitude, and then it was that M'Shane expressed his intentions towards our hero, and, as he expected, he found his amiable wife wholly coincide with him in opinion. It was therefore decided that Joey should be put to a school, and be properly educated, as soon as an establishment that was eligible could be found.

95

THE POACHER

Their full intentions towards him, however, were not communicated to our hero; he was told that he was to go to school, and he willingly submitted. It was not, however, for three months that M'Shane would part with him; a difficulty was raised against every establishment that was named. During this time little Joey was very idle, for there was nothing for him to do. Books there were none, for Mrs. M'Shane had no time to read, and Major M'Shane no inclination. His only resort was to rummage over the newspapers which were taken in for the benefit of the customers, and this was his usual employment. One day, in turning over the file, he came to the account of the murder of the pedlar, with the report of the coroner's inquest. He read all the evidence, particularly that of Furness, the schoolmaster, and found that the verdict was wilful murder, with a reward of £200 for his apprehension. The term, wilful murder, he did not exactly comprehend; so, after laying down the paper, with a beating heart he went to Mrs. M'Shane, and asked her what was the meaning of it.

"Meaning, child?" replied Mrs. M'Shane, who was then very busy in her occupation, "it means, child, that a person is believed to be guilty of murder, and, if taken up, he will be hanged by the neck till he is dead."

"But," replied Joey, "suppose he has not committed the murder?"

"Well then, child, he must prove that he has not."

"And suppose, although he has not committed it, he cannot prove it?"

"Mercy on me, what a number of supposes! why, then he will be hanged all the same, to be sure."

A fortnight after these queries, Joey was sent to school; the master was a very decent man, the mistress a very decent woman, the tuition was decent, the fare was decent, the scholars were children of decent families; altogether, it was a decent establishment, and in this establishment little Joey made very decent progress, going home every half-year. How long Joey might have remained there it is impossible to say; but having been there for a year and a half, and arrived at the age of fourteen, he had just returned from the holidays with three guineas in his pocket, for M'Shane and his wife were very generous and very fond of their *protégé*, when a circumstance occurred which again ruffled the smooth current of our hero's existence.

He was walking out as all boys do walk out in decent schools, that is, in a long line, two by two, as the animals entered Noah's Ark, when a sort of shabby-genteel man passed their files. He happened to cast his eyes upon Joey, and stopped. "Master Joseph Rushbrook, I am most happy to see you once more," said he, extending his hand. Joey looked up into his face; there was no mistake; it was Furness, the schoolmaster. "Don't you recollect me, my dear boy? Don't you recollect him who taught the infant idea how to shoot? Don't you recollect your old preceptor?"

"Yes," replied Joey, colouring up, "I recollect you very well."

"I am delighted to see you; you know you were my fairest pupil, but we are all scattered now; your father and mother have gone no one knows where; you went away, and I also could no longer stay. What pleasure it is to meet you once more!"

Joey did not respond exactly to the pleasure. The stoppage of the line had caused some confusion, and the usher, who had followed it, now came up to ascertain the cause. "This is my old pupil, or rather I should say, my young pupil; but the best pupil I ever had. I am most delighted to see him, sir," said Furness, taking off his hat. "May I presume to ask who has the charge of this dear child at this present moment?"

The usher made no difficulty in stating the name and residence of the preceptor, and having gained this information, Furness shook Joey by the hand, bade him farewell, and, wishing him every happiness, walked away.

Joey's mind was confused during the remainder of his walk, and it was not until their return home that he could reflect on what had passed. That Furness had given evidence upon the inquest he knew, and he had penetration, when he read it, to feel that there was no necessity for Furness having given such evidence. He also knew that there was a reward of two hundred pounds for his apprehension; and when he thought of Furness's apparent kindness, and his not reverting to a subject so important as wilful murder having been found against him, he made up his mind that Furness had behaved so with the purpose of lulling him into security, and that the next day he would certainly take him up, for the sake of the reward.

Now, although we have not stopped our narrative to introduce the subject, we must here observe that Joey's love for his parents, particularly his father, was unbounded; he longed to see them again; they were constantly in his thoughts, and yet he dared not mention them, in consequence of the mystery connected with his quitting his home. He fully perceived his danger: he would be apprehended, and being so, he must either sacrifice his father or himself. Having weighed all this in his mind, he then reflected upon what should be his course to steer. Should he go home to acquaint Major M'Shane? He felt that he could trust him, and would have done so, but he had no right to entrust any one with a secret which involved his father's life. No, that would not do; yet, to leave him and Mrs. M'Shane after all their kindness, and without a word, this would be too ungrateful. After much cogitation he resolved that he would run away, so that all clue to him should be lost; that he would write a letter for M'Shane, and leave it. He wrote as follows:—

"DEAR SIR,—Do not think me ungrateful, for I love you and Mrs. M'Shane dearly, but I have been met by a person who knows me, and will certainly betray me. I left my father's home, not for poaching, but a murder that was committed; *I was not guilty.* This is the only secret I have held from you, and the secret is not MINE. I could not disprove it, and never will. I now leave because I have been discovered by a bad man, who will certainly take advantage of having fallen in with me. We may never meet again. I can say no more, except that I shall always pray for you and Mrs. M'Shane, and remember your kindness with gratitude.—Yours truly,   JOEY M'SHANE."

Since his return from St. Petersburg Joey had always, by their request, called himself Joey M'Shane, and he was not sorry when they gave him the permission, although he did not comprehend the advantages which were to accrue from taking the name.

THE POACHER

Joey, having finished his letter, sat down and cried bitterly —but in a school there is no retiring place for venting your feelings, and he was compelled to smother his tears. He performed his exercise, and repeated his lessons, as if nothing had happened, and nothing was about to happen, for Joey was in essence a little stoic. At night he went to his room with the other boys; he could only obtain a small portion of his clothes; these he put up in a handkerchief, went softly downstairs about one o'clock in the morning, put his letter addressed to M'Shane on the hall-table, opened the back door, climbed over the playground wall, and was again on the road to seek his fortune.

But Joey was much improved during the two years since he had quitted his father's house. Before that, he was a reflective boy; now, he was more capable of action and decision. His ideas had been much expanded from the knowledge of the world gained during his entry, as it were, into life; he had talked much, seen much, listened much, and thought more; and naturally quiet in his manner, he was now a gentlemanlike boy. At the eating-house he had met with every variety of character; and as there were some who frequented the house daily, with those Joey had become on intimate terms. He was no longer a child, but a lad of undaunted courage and presence of mind; he had only one fear, which was that his father's crime should be discovered.

And now he was again adrift, with a small bundle, three guineas in his pocket, and the world before him. At first he had but one idea—that of removing to a distance which should elude the vigilance of Furness, and he therefore walked on, and walked fast. Joey was capable of great fatigue; he had grown considerably, it is true, during the last two years, still he was small for his age; but every muscle in his body was a wire, and his strength, as had been proved by his schoolmates, was proportionate. He was elastic as india-rubber, and bold and determined as one who had been all his life in danger.

99

CHAPTER XXI

The scene is again shifted, and the plot advances.

IT will be necessary that for a short time we again follow up the fortunes of our hero's parents. When Rushbrook and Jane had quitted the village of Grassford, they had not come to any decision as to their future place of abode; all that Rushbrook felt was a desire to remove as far as possible from the spot where the crime had been committed. Such is the feeling that will ever possess the guilty, who, although they may increase their distance, attempt in vain to fly from their consciences, or that All-seeing Eye which follows them everywhere. Jane had a similar feeling, but it arose from her anxiety for her husband. They wandered away, for they had sold everything before their departure, until they found themselves in the West Riding of Yorkshire, and there they at length settled in a small village. Rushbrook easily obtained employment, for the population was scanty, and some months passed away without anything occurring of interest.

Rushbrook had never taken up his employment as a poacher since the night of the murder of the pedlar; he had abjured it from that hour. His knowledge of woodcraft was, however, discovered, and he was appointed first as under, and eventually as head keeper to a gentleman of landed property in the neighbourhood. In this situation they had remained about a year, Rushbrook giving full satisfaction to his employer, and comparatively contented (for no man could have such a crime upon his conscience, and not pass occasional hours of misery and remorse), and Jane was still mourning in secret for her only and darling child, when one day a paper was put into Rushbrook's hands by his master, desiring him to read an advertisement which it contained, and which was as follows:—"If Joseph Rushbrook, who formerly lived in the village of Grassford, in the county of Devon, should be still alive, and will make his residence known to Messrs. Pearce, James, and Simpson, of 14 Chancery Lane, he will hear of something greatly to his advantage. Should he be dead, and this advertisement meet the eye of his heirs, they are equally requested to make the communication to the above address."

"What does it mean, sir?" inquired Rushbrook.

"It means that, if you are that person, in all probability there is some legacy bequeathed to you by a relative," replied Mr. S——; "is it you?"

"Yes, sir," replied Rushbrook, changing colour; "I did once live at Grassford."

"Then you had better write to the parties and make yourself known. I will leave you the newspaper."

"What think you, Jane?" said Rushbrook, as soon as Mr. S—— had quitted.

"I think he is quite right," replied Jane.

"But, Jane, you forget—this may be a trap; they may have discovered something about—you know what I mean."

"Yes, I do, and I wish we could forget it; but in this instance I do not think you have anything to fear. There is no reward offered for your apprehension, but for my poor boy's, who is now wandering over the wide world; and no one would go to the expense to apprehend you, if there was nothing to be gained by it."

"True," replied Rushbrook, after a minute's reflection; "but, alas! I am a coward now: I will write."

Rushbrook wrote accordingly, and in reply received a letter enclosing a bank-bill for £20, and requesting that he would come to town immediately. He did so, and found, to his astonishment, that he was the heir-at-law to a property of £7000 per annum—with the only contingency, that he was, as nearest of kin, to take the name of Austin. Having entered into all the arrangements required by the legal gentlemen, he returned to Yorkshire, with £500 in his pocket, to communicate the intelligence to his wife; and when he did so, and embraced her, she burst into tears.

"Rushbrook, do not think I mean to reproach you by these tears; but I cannot help thinking that you would have been happier had this never happened. Your life will be doubly sweet to you now, and Joey's absence will be a source of more vexation than ever. Do you think that you will be happier?"

"Jane, dearest! I have been thinking of it as well as you,

and on reflection I think I shall be safer. Who would know the poacher Rushbrook in the gentleman of £7000 a year, of the name of Austin? Who would dare accuse him, even if there were suspicion? I feel that once in another county, under another name, and in another situation, I shall be safe."

"But our poor boy, should he ever come back——"

"Will also be forgotten. He will have grown up a man, and, having another name, will never be recognised: they will not even know what our former name was."

"I trust that it will be as you say. What do you now mean to do?"

"I shall say that I have a property of four or five hundred pounds left me, and that I intend to go up to London," replied Rushbrook.

"Yes, that will be wise; it will be an excuse for our leaving this place, and will be no clue to where we are going," replied Jane.

Rushbrook gave up his situation, sold his furniture, and quitted Yorkshire. In a few weeks afterwards he was installed into his new property, a splendid mansion, and situated in the west of Dorsetshire. Report had gone before them; some said that a common labourer had come into the property, others said it was a person in very moderate circumstances; as usual, both these reports were contradicted by a third, which represented him as a half-pay lieutenant in the army. Rushbrook had contrived to mystify even the solicitor as to his situation in life; he stated to him that he had retired from the army, and lived upon the government allowance; and it was in consequence of a reference to the solicitor, made by some of the best families in the neighbourhood, who wished to ascertain if the new-comers were people who could be visited, that this third report was spread, and universally believed. We have already observed that Rushbrook was a fine, tall man; and if there is any class of people who can be transplanted with success from low to high life, it will be those who have served in the army. The stoop is the evidence of a low-bred, vulgar man; the erect bearing equally so that of the gentleman. Now, the latter is gained in the army, by drilling and discipline, and being well dressed will provide for all else that is required, as far as mere personal appearance is con-

102

cerned. When, therefore, the neighbours called upon Mr. and Mrs. Austin, they were not surprised to find an erect, military-looking man, but they were very much surprised to find him matched with such a fine, and even elegant-looking woman as his wife. Timid at first, Jane had sufficient tact to watch others and copy; and before many months were passed in their new position, it would have been difficult to suppose that Mrs. Austin had not been born in the sphere in which she then moved. Austin was brusque and abrupt in his manners as before; but still there was always a reserve about him, which he naturally felt, and which assisted to remove the impression of vulgarity. People who are distant are seldom considered ungentlemanlike, although they may be considered unpleasant in their manners. It is those who are too familiar who obtain the character of vulgarity.

Austin, therefore, was respected, but not liked; Jane, on the contrary, whose beauty had now all the assistance of dress, and whose continued inward mourning for her lost son had improved that beauty by the pensive air which she wore, was a deserved and universal favourite. People of course said that Austin was a harsh husband, and pitied poor Mrs. Austin; but that people always do say if a woman is not inclined to mirth.

Austin found ample amusement in sporting over his extensive manor, and looking after his game. In one point the neighbouring gentlemen were surprised, that, although so keen a sportsman himself, he never could be prevailed upon to convict a poacher. He was appointed a magistrate, and being most liberal in all his subscriptions, was soon considered as a great acquisition to the county. His wife was much sought after, but it was invariably observed that, when children were mentioned, the tears stood in her eyes. Before they had been a year in their new position, they had acquired all the knowledge and tact necessary; their establishment was on a handsome scale; they were visited and paid visits to all the aristocracy and gentry, and were as popular as they could have desired to be. But were they happy? Alas! no. Little did those who envied Austin his property and establishment imagine what a load was on his mind—what a corroding care was wearing out his existence. Little did they imagine that he would gladly have resigned all, and been once more the poacher in the village of Grassford, to have removed from his conscience the deed of darkness which he had committed, and once more have his son by his side. And poor Jane, her thoughts were day and night upon one object—where was her child? It deprived her of rest at night; she remained meditating on his fate for hours during the day; it would rush into her mind in the gayest scenes and the happiest moments; it was one incessant incubus—one continual source of misery. Of her husband she thought less; for she knew how sincerely contrite he was for the deed he had done—how bitterly he had repented it ever since, and how it would, as long as he lived, be a source of misery—a worm that would never die, but gnaw till the last hour of his existence. But her boy—her noble, self-sacrificed little Joey!—he and his destiny were ever in her thoughts; and gladly would she have been a pauper applying for relief, if she had but that child to have led up in her hand. And yet all the county thought how happy and contented the Austins ought to be, to have suddenly come into possession of so much wealth. 'Tis God alone that knows the secrets of the heart of man.

CHAPTER XXII

A very long chapter, but in which our hero obtains employment in a very short time.

THE preparatory establishment for young gentlemen to which our hero had been sent was situated on Clapham Rise. Joey did not think it prudent to walk in the direction of London; he therefore made a cut across the country, so as to bring him, before seven o'clock in the morning, not very far from Gravesend. The night had been calm and beautiful, for it was in the month of August; and it had for some time been broad daylight when our hero, who had walked fifteen or sixteen miles, sat down to repose himself; and as he remained quietly seated on the green turf on the wayside, he thought of his father and mother, of the kindness of the M'Shanes, and his own hard fate, until he became melancholy and wept; and as the tears were rolling down his cheeks, a little girl of about ten years old, very neatly dressed, and evidently above the lower rank of life, came along the road, her footsteps so light as not to be perceived by Joey; she looked at him as she passed, and perceived that he was in tears, and her own bright, pretty face became clouded in a moment. Joey did not look up, and after hesitating awhile she passed on a few steps, and then she looked round, and observing that he was still weeping she paused, turned round, and came back to him. For a minute or two she stood before him; but Joey was unconscious of her presence, for he was now in the full tide of his grief, and not having forgotten the precepts which had been carefully instilled into him, he thought of the God of Refuge, and he arose, fell on his knees, and prayed. The little girl, whose tears had already been summoned by pity and sympathy, dropped her basket and knelt by his side—not that she prayed, for she knew not what the prayer was for, but from an instinctive feeling of respect towards the Deity which her new companion was addressing, and a feeling of kindness towards one who was evidently suffering. Joey lifted up his eyes and beheld the child on her knees, the tears rolling down her cheeks; he hastily wiped his eyes, for until that moment he imagined that he had been alone; he had been praying on account of his loneliness—he looked up, and he was not alone, but there was one by his side who pitied him, without knowing wherefore; he felt relieved by the sight. They both regained their feet at the same time, and Joey went up to the little girl, and taking her by the hand, said, "Thank you."

"Why do you cry?" said the little girl.

"Because I am unhappy; I have no home," replied Joey.

"No home!" said the little girl; "it is boys who are in rags and starving who have no home, not young gentlemen dressed as you are."

"But I have left my home," replied Joey.

"Then go back again—how glad they will be to see you!"

"Yes, indeed they would," replied Joey, "but I must not."

"You have not done anything wrong, have you? No, I'm sure you have not—you must have been a good boy, or you would not have prayed."

"No, I have done nothing wrong, but I must not tell you any more."

Indeed, Joey was much more communicative with the little girl than he would have been with anybody else ; but he had been surprised into it, and, moreover, he had no fear of being betrayed by such innocence. He now recollected himself, and changed the conversation.

"And where are you going to ?" inquired he.

"I am going to school at Gravesend. I go there every morning, and stay till the evening. This is my dinner in my basket. Are you hungry ?"

"No, not particularly."

"Are you going to Gravesend ?"

"Yes," replied Joey. "What is your name ?"

"Emma Phillips."

"Have you a father and mother ?"

"I have no father ; he was killed fighting, a little while after I was born."

"And your mother——"

"Lives with grandmother, at that house you see there through the large trees. And what are you going to do with yourself? Will you come home with me ? and I'll tell my mother all you have told me, and she is very kind, and will write to your friends."

"No, no ; you must not do that ; I am going to seek for employment."

"Why, what can you do ?"

"I hardly know," replied Joey ; "but I can work, and am willing to work, so I hope I shall not starve."

With such conversation they continued their way, until the little girl said, "There is my school, so now I must wish you good-bye."

"Good-bye ; I shall not forget you," replied Joey, "although we may never meet again." Tears stood in the eyes of our hero, as they reluctantly unclasped their hands and parted.

Joey, once more left alone, now meditated what was the best course for him to pursue. The little Emma's words, "Not young gentlemen dressed as you are," reminded him of the remarks and suspicions which must ensue if he did not alter his attire. This he resolved to do immediately ; the only idea which had presented itself to his mind was, if possible, to find some means of getting back to Captain O'Donahue, who, he was sure, would receive him, if he satisfied him that it was not safe for him to remain in England; but then, must he confess to him the truth or not? On this point our hero was not decided, so he put off the solution of it till another opportunity. A slop warehouse now attracted his attention; he looked into the door after having examined the articles outside, and seeing that a sailor boy was bargaining for some clothes, he went in as if waiting to be served, but, in fact, more to ascertain the value of the articles which he wished to purchase. The sailor had cheapened a red frock and pair of blue trousers, and at last obtained them from the Jew for 14s. Joey argued that, as he was much smaller than the lad, he ought to pay less; he asked for the same articles, but the Jew, who had scanned in his own mind the suit of clothes which Joey had on, argued that he ought to pay more. Joey was, however, firm, and about to leave the shop when the Jew called him back, and after much haggling Joey obtained the dress for 12s. Having paid for the clothes, Joey begged permission to be permitted to retire to the back shop and put them on, to ascertain if they fitted him, to which the Jew consented. A Jew asks no questions when a penny is to be turned; who Joey was, he cared little; his first object was to sell him the clothes, and having so done he hoped to make another penny by obtaining those of Joey at a moderate price. Perceiving that our hero was putting his own clothes, which he had taken off, into a bundle, the Jew asked him whether he would sell them, and Joey immediately agreed; but the price offered by the Jew was so small, that they were returned to the bundle, and once more was Joey leaving the shop, when the Jew at last offered to return to him the money he had paid for the sailor's dress, and take his own clothes in exchange, provided that Joey would also exchange his hat for one of tarpaulin, which would be more fitting to his present costume. To this our hero consented, and thus was the bargain concluded without Joey having parted with any of his small stock of ready money. No one who had only seen him dressed as when he quitted the school, would have easily recognised Joey in his new attire. Joey sallied forth from the shop with his bundle under his arm, intending to look out for a breakfast, for he was very hungry. Turning his head right and left to discover some notice of where provender might be obtained, he observed the sailor lad, who had been in the shop

when he went in, with his new purchase under his arm, looking very earnestly at some prints in a shop window. Joey
ranged up alongside of him, and inquired of him where he
could get something to eat; the lad turned round, stared,
and after a little while cried, " Well, now, you're the young
gentleman chap that came into the shop; I say, aren't you
after a rig, eh? Given them leg-bail, I'll swear. No consarn
of mine, old fellow. Come along, I'll show you."

Joey walked by his new acquaintance a few yards, when
the lad turned to him, " I say, did your master whop you
much?"

" No," replied Joey.

" Well, then, that's more than I can say of mine, for he
was at it all day. Hold out your right hand, now your left,"
continued he, mimicking; " my eyes! how it used to sting.
I don't think I should mind it much now," continued the lad,
turning up his hand; " it's a little harder than it was then.
Here's the shop, come in; if you haven't no money I'll give
you a breakfast."

The lad took his seat on one side of a narrow table, Joey on
the other, and his new acquaintance called for two pints of
tea, a twopenny loaf, and two penny bits of cheese. The loaf
was divided between them, and with their portion of cheese
and pint of tea each they made a good breakfast. As soon as
it was over the young sailor said to Joey, " Now, what are
you going arter; do you mean to ship?"

" I want employment," replied Joey; " and I don't much
care what it is."

" Well, then, look you; I ran away from my friends and
went to sea, and do you know, I've only repented of it once,
and that's ever since. Better do anything than go to sea—
winter coming on and all; besides, you don't look strong
enough; you don't know what it is to be coasting in winter-
time, thrashed up to furl the top-gallant sail when it is so
dark you can't see your way, and so cold that you can't feel
your fingers, holding on for your life, and feeling as if life,
after all, was not worth caring for; cold and misery aloft,
kicks and thumps below. Don't you go to sea; if you do,
after what I've told you, why, then, you're a greater fool than
you look to be."

" I don't want to be a sailor," replied Joey, " but I must do something to get my living. You are very kind : will you tell me what to do ? "

" Why, do you know, when I saw you come up to me when I was looking at the pictures, in your frock and trousers, you put me in mind, because you are so much like him, of a poor little boy who was drowned the other day alongside of an India ship ; that's why I stared, for I thought you were he at first."

" How was he drowned, poor fellow ? " responded Joey.

" Why, you see, his aunt is a good old soul, who keeps a bumboat, and goes off to the shipping."

" What's a bumboat ? "

" A boat full of soft tommy, soldiers, pipes and backey, rotten apples, stale pies, needles and threads, and a hundred other things ; besides a fat old woman sitting in the stern-sheets."

Joey stared ; he did not know that " soft tommy " meant loaves of bread, or that " soldiers " was the term for red herrings. He only thought that the boat must be very full.

" Now, you see that little Peter was her right-hand man, for she can't read and write. Can you ?—But of course you can."

" Yes, I can," replied Joey.

" Well little Peter was holding on by the painter against a hard sea, but his strength was not equal to it, and so when a swell took the boat he was pulled right overboard, and he was drowned."

" Was the painter drowned too ? " inquired Joey.

" Ha ! ha ! that's capital ; why, the painter is a rope. Now, the old woman has been dreadfully put out, and does nothing but cry about little Peter, and not being able to keep her accounts. Now, you look very like him, and I think it very likely the old woman would take you in his place, if I went and talked her over ; that's better than going to sea, for at all events you sleep dry and sound on shore every night, even if you do have a wet jacket sometimes. What d'ye think ? "

" I think you are very kind ; and I should be glad to take the place."

" Well, she's a good old soul, and has a warm heart, and trusts them who have no money ; too much, I'm afraid, for she loses a great deal. So now I'll go and speak to her, for she'll

109

be alongside of us when I go on board; and where shall I find you when I come on shore in the evening?"

"Wherever you say, I will be."

"Well then, meet me here at nine o'clock; that will make all certain. Come, I must be off now. I'll pay for the breakfast."

"I have money, I thank you," replied Joey.

"Then keep it, for it's more than I can do; and what's your name?"

"Joey."

"Well then, Joey, my hearty, if I get you this berth, when we come in, and I am short, you must let me go on tick till I can pay."

"What's tick?"

"You'll soon find out what tick is, after you have been a week in the bumboat," replied the lad, laughing. "Nine o'clock, my hearty; good-bye."

So saying, the young sailor caught up his new clothes, and hastened down to the beach.

The room was crowded with seamen and women, but they were too busy talking and laughing to pay any attention to Joey and his comrade. Our little hero sat some little time at the table after his new acquaintance had left, and then walked out into the streets, telling the people of the house that he was coming back again, and requesting them to take care of his bundle.

"You'll find it here, my little fellow, all right when you ask for it," said the woman at the bar, who took it inside and put it away under the counter.

Joey went out with his mind more at ease. The nature of his new employment, should he succeed in obtaining it, he could scarcely comprehend, but still it appeared to him one that he could accomplish. He amused himself walking down the streets, watching the movements of the passers-by, the watermen in their wherries, and the people on board of the vessels which were lying off in the stream. It was a busy and animating sight. As he was lolling at the landing-place a boat came on shore, which, from the description given by his young sailor friend, he was convinced was a bumboat; it had all the articles described by him, as well as many others, such as porter in bottles, a cask probably containing beer; leeks, onions, and many other heterogenous matters, and, moreover, there was a fat woman seated in the stern.

The waterman shoved in with his boat-hook, and the wherry grounded. The fat personage got out, and the waterman handed to her a basket, a long book, and several other articles, which she appeared to consider indispensable; among others, a bundle which looked like dirty linen for the wash.

"Dear me! how shall I get up all these things?" exclaimed the woman; "and, William, you can't leave the boat, and there's nobody here to help me."

"I'll help you," said Joey, coming down the steps; "what shall I carry for you?"

"Well, you are a good kind boy," replied she; "can you carry that bundle? I'll manage all the rest."

Joey tossed the bundle on his shoulder in a moment.

"Well, you are a strong little chap," said the waterman.

"He is a very nice little fellow, and a kind one. Now, come along, and I'll not forget you."

Joey followed with the bundle until they arrived at a narrow door, not eighty yards from the landing-place, and the woman asked him if he would carry it upstairs to the first floor, which he did.

"Do you want me any more?" said Joey, setting down the bundle.

"No, dear, no; but I must give you something for your trouble. What do you expect?"

"Nothing at all," replied Joey; "and I shall not take anything; you're very welcome; good-bye;" and so saying, Joey walked downstairs, although the woman halloed after him, and recommenced his peregrination in the streets of Gravesend; but he was soon tired of walking on the pavement, which was none of the best, and he then thought that he would go out into the country and enjoy the green fields; so off he set, the same way that he came into the town, passed by the school of little Emma, and trudged away on the road, stopping every now and then to examine what attracted his notice; watching a bird if it sang on the branch of a tree, and not moving lest he should frighten it away; at times sitting down by the road-side, and meditating on the past and the future. The day was closing in, and Joey was still amusing himself as every boy who has been confined to a schoolroom would do;

he sauntered on until he came to the very spot where he had been crying, and had met with little Emma Phillips; and as he sat down again, he thought of her sweet little face, and her kindness towards him—and there he remained some time till he was roused by some one singing as they went along the road. He looked up, and perceived it was the little girl, who was returning from school. Joey rose immediately, and walked towards her to meet her, but she did not appear to recognise him, and would have passed him if he had not said, "Don't you know me?"

"Yes, I do now," replied she, smiling, "but I did not at first—you have put on another dress; I have been thinking of you all day—and, do you know, I've got a black mark for not saying my lesson," added the little girl, with a sigh.

"And then it is my fault," replied Joey; "I'm very sorry."

"Oh, never mind; it is the first that I have had for a long while, and I shall tell mamma why. But you are dressed as a sailor boy—are you going to sea?"

"No, I believe not—I hope to have employment in the town here, and then I shall be able to see you sometimes, when you come from school. May I walk with you as far as your own house?"

"Yes, I suppose so, if you like it."

Joey walked with her until they came to the house, which was about two hundred yards farther.

"But," said Joey, hesitating, "you must make me a promise."

"What is that?"

"You must keep my secret. You must not tell your mother that you saw me first in what you call gentleman's clothes— it might do me harm—and indeed it's not for my own sake I ask it. Don't say a word about my other clothes, or they may ask me questions which I must not answer, for it's not my secret. I told you more this morning than I would have told any one else—I did, indeed."

"Well," replied the little girl, after thinking a little, "I suppose I have no right to tell a secret, if I am begged not to do it, so I will say nothing about your clothes. But I must tell mother that I met you."

"Oh yes; tell her you met me, and that I was looking for some work, and all that, and to-morrow or next day I will let you know if I get any."

112

"Will you come in now?" said Emma.

"No, not now; I must see if I can get this employment promised for me, and then I shall see you again; if I should not see you again, I shall not forget you, indeed I won't—Good-bye."

Emma bade him adieu, and they separated, and Joey remained and watched her till she disappeared under the porch of the entrance.

Our hero returned towards Gravesend in rather a melancholy mood; there was something so unusual in his meeting with the little girl—something so uncommon in the sympathy expressed by her—that he felt pain at parting. But it was getting late, and it was time that he kept his appointment with his friend the sailor boy.

Joey remained at the door of the eating-house for about a quarter of an hour, when he perceived the sailor lad coming up the street. He went forward to meet him.

"Oh, here we are. Well, young fellow, I've seen the old woman, and had a long talk with her, and she won't believe there can be another in the world like her Peter, but I persuaded her to have a look at you, and she has consented; so come along, for I must be on board again in half-an-hour."

Joey followed his new friend down the street, until they came to the very door to which he had carried the bundle. The sailor boy mounted the stairs, and turning into the room at the first landing, Joey beheld the woman whom he had assisted in the morning.

"Here he is, Mrs. Chopper, and if he won't suit you, I don't know who will," said the boy. "He's a regular scholar, and can sum up like winkin'."

This character, given so gratuitously by his new acquaintance, made Joey stare, and the woman looked hard into Joey's face.

"Well, now," said she, "where have I seen you before? Dear me! and he *is* like poor Peter, as you said, Jim; I vow he is."

"I saw you before to-day," replied Joey, "for I carried a bundle up for you."

"And so you did, and would have no money for your trouble. Well, Jim, he is like poor Peter."

"I told you so, old lady; ay, and he'll just do for you as

113   H

well as Peter did; but I'll leave you to settle matters, for I must be a-board."

So saying, the lad tipped a wink to Joey, the meaning of which our hero did not understand, and went downstairs.

"Well, now, it's very odd; but do you know you are like poor Peter, and the more I look at you the more you are like him: poor Peter! did you hear how I lost him?"

"Yes, the sailor lad told me this morning."

"Poor fellow! he held on too fast; most people drown by not holding on fast enough: he was a good boy, and very smart indeed. And so it was you who helped me this morning when I missed poor Peter so much? Well, it showed you had a good heart, and I love that; and where did you meet with Jim Paterson?"

"I met him first in a slop-shop, as he calls it, when I was buying my clothes."

"Well, Jim's a wild one, but he has a good heart, and pays when he can. I've been told by those who know his parents, that he will have property by-and-by. Well, and what can you do? I am afraid you can't do all Peter did."

"I can keep your accounts, and I can be honest and true to you."

"Well, Peter could not do more: are you sure you can keep accounts, and sum up totals?"

"Yes, to be sure I can; try me."

"Well, then, I will: here is pen, ink, and paper. Well, you are the very image of Peter, and that's a fact. Now write down beer, 8d.; tobacco, 4d.; is that down?"

"Yes."

"Let me see: duck for trousers, 3s. 6d.; beer again, 4d.; tobacco, 4d.; is that down? Well, then, say beer again, 8d. Now sum that all up."

Joey was perfect master of the task, and, as he handed over the paper, announced the whole sum to amount to 5s. 10d.

"Well," says Mrs. Chopper, "it looks all right; but just stay here a minute while I go and speak to somebody." Mrs. Chopper left the room, went downstairs, and took it to the bar-girl at the next public-house to ascertain if it was all correct.

"Yes, quite correct, Mrs. Chopper," replied the lass.

"And is it as good as Peter's was, poor fellow?"

114

"Much better," replied the girl.

"Dear me! Who would have thought it? and so like Peter too!"

Mrs. Chopper came upstairs again, and took her seat.— "Well," said she, "and now what is your name?"

"Joey."

"Joey what?"

"Joey—O'Donahue," replied our hero, for he was fearful of giving the name of M'Shane.

"And who are your parents?"

"They are poor people," replied Joey, "and live a long way off."

"And why did you leave them?"

Joey had already made up his mind to tell his former story: "I left there because I was accused of poaching, and they wished me to go away."

"Poaching; yes, I understand that—killing hares and birds. Well, but why did you poach?"

"Because father did."

"Oh, well, I see; then, if you only did what your father did we must not blame his child; and so you come down here to go to sea?"

"If I could not do better."

"But you shall do better, my good boy. I will try you instead of poor Peter, and if you are an honest and good, careful boy, it will be much better than going to sea. Dear me! how like he is—but now I *must* call you Peter; it will make me think I have him with me, poor fellow!"

"If you please," said Joey, who was not sorry to exchange his name.

"Well, then, where do you sleep to-night?"

"I did intend to ask for a bed at the house where I left my bundle."

"Then, don't do so; go for your bundle, and you shall sleep in Peter's bed (poor fellow, his last was a watery bed, as the papers say), and then to-morrow morning you can go off with me."

Joey accepted the offer, went back for his bundle, and returned to Mrs. Chopper in a quarter of an hour; she was then preparing her supper, which Joey was not sorry to partake of; after which she led him into a small room, in which

115

was a small bed without curtains; the room itself was hung round with strings of onions, papers of sweet herbs, and flitches of bacon; the floor was strewed with empty ginger-beer bottles, oakum in bags, and many other articles. Altogether, the smell was anything but agreeable.

" Here is poor Peter's bed," said Mrs. Chopper; " I changed his sheets the night before he was drowned, poor fellow ! Can I trust you to put the candle out ? "

" Oh yes; I'll be very careful."

" Then, good-night, boy. Do you ever say your prayers ? poor Peter always did."

" Yes, I do," replied Joey ; " good-night."

Mrs. Chopper left the room. Joey threw open the window —for he was almost suffocated—undressed himself, put out the light, and, when he had said his prayers, his thoughts naturally reverted to the little Emma who had knelt with him on the roadside.

CHAPTER XXIII

In which our hero goes on duty.

AT five o'clock the next morning Joey was called up by Mrs. Chopper; the waterman was in attendance, and, with the aid of Joey, carried down the various articles into the boat. When all was ready, Mrs. Chopper and Joey sat down to their break-fast, which consisted of tea, bread and butter, and red herrings ; and, as soon as it was finished, they embarked, and the boat shoved off.

" Well, Mrs. Chopper," said the waterman, " so I perceive you've got a new hand."

" Yes," replied Mrs. Chopper; " don't you think he's the moral of poor Peter ? "

" Well, I don't know; but there is a something about the cut of his jib which reminds me of him, now you mention it. Peter was a good boy."

" Ay, that he was, and as sharp as a needle. You see," said Mrs. Chopper, turning to Joey, " sharp's the word in a bumboat. There's many who pay, and many who don't; some I trust, and some I don't—that is, those who won't pay me old debts. We

lose a bit of money at times, but it all comes round in the end;
but I lose more by not booking the things taken than in any
other way, for sailors do pay when they have the money—that
is, if ever they come back again, poor fellows. Now, Peter."

"What! is his name Peter, too?"

"Yes, I must call him Peter, William; he is so like poor
Peter."

"Well, that will suit me; I hate learning new names."

"Well, but, Peter," continued Mrs. Chopper, "you must be
very careful; for, you see, I'm often called away here and
there after wash clothes and such things; and then you must
look out, and if they do take up anything, why, you must book
it, at all events. You'll learn by-and-by who to trust, and
who not to trust, for I know the most of my customers. You
must not trust a woman—I mean any of the sailors' wives—
unless I tell you; and you must be very sharp with them, for
they play all manner of tricks; you must look two ways at
once. Now, there's a girl on board the brig we are pulling to,
called Nancy; why, she used to weather poor Peter, sharp as
he was. She used to pretend to be very fond of him, and hug
him close to her with one arm, so as to blind him, while she
stole the tarts with the other; so, don't admit her famili-
arities; if you do, I shall pay for them."

"Then, who am I to trust?"

"Bless the child! you'll soon find out that; but mind one
thing; never trust a tall, lanky seaman, without his name's on
the books; those chaps never pay. There's the book kept by
poor Peter; and you see names upon the top of each score—
at least, I believe so; I have no learning myself, but I've a
good memory; I can't read nor write, and that's why Peter
was so useful."

That Peter could read his own writing it is to be presumed;
but certain it was that Joey could not make it out until after
many days' examination, when he discovered that certain
hieroglyphics were meant to represent certain articles; after
which it became more easy.

They had now reached the side of the vessel, and the sailors
came down into the boat, and took up several articles upon
credit; Joey booked them very regularly.

"Has Bill been down yet?" said a soft voice from the
gangway.

"No, Nancy, he has not."

"Then he wants two red herrings, a sixpenny loaf, and some 'baccy."

Joey looked up, and beheld a very handsome, fair, blue-eyed girl, with a most roguish look, who was hanging over the side.

"Then he must come himself, Nancy," replied Mrs. Chopper, "for, you know, the last time you took up the things he said that you were never told to do so, and he would not pay for them."

"That's because the fool was jealous; I lost the tobacco, Mrs. Chopper, and he said I had given it to Dick Snapper."

"I can't help that; he must come himself."

"But he's away in the boat, and he told me to get the things for him. Who have you there? Not Peter; no, it's not Peter; but what'a dear little boy."

"I told you so," said Mrs. Chopper to our hero; "now, if I wasn't in the boat, she would be down in it in a minute, and persuade you to let her have the things—and she never pays."

Joey looked up again, and, as he looked at Nancy, felt that it would be very unkind to refuse her.

"Now, what a hard-hearted old woman you are, Mrs. Chopper. Bill will come on board; and, as sure as I stand here, he'll whack me. He will pay you, you may take my word for it."

"Your word, Nancy!" replied Mrs. Chopper, shaking her head.

"Stop a moment," said Nancy, coming down the side with very little regard as to showing her well-formed legs; "stop, Mrs. Chopper, and I'll explain to you."

"It's no use coming down, Nancy, I tell you," replied Mrs. Chopper.

"Well, we shall see," replied Nancy, taking her seat in the boat, and looking archly in Mrs. Chopper's face; "the fact is, Mrs. Chopper, you don't know what a good-tempered woman you are."

"I know, Nancy, what you are," replied Mrs. Chopper.

"Oh, so does everybody: I'm nobody's enemy but my own, they say."

"Ah! that's very true, child; more's the pity."

"Now, I didn't come down to wheedle you out of anything,

Mrs. Chopper, but merely to talk to you, and look at this pretty boy."

" There you go, Nancy ; but ain't he like Peter ? "

" Well, and so he is ! very like Peter ; he has Peter's eyes and his nose, and his mouth is exactly Peter's—how very strange ! "

" I never see'd such a likeness ! " exclaimed Mrs. Chopper.

" No, indeed," replied Nancy, who, by agreeing with Mrs. Chopper in all she said, and praising Joey, and his likeness to Peter, at last quite came over the old bumboat-woman ; and Nancy quitted her boat with the two herrings, the loaf, and the paper of tobacco.

" Shall I put them down, Mrs. Chopper ? " said Joey.

" Oh, dear," replied Mrs. Chopper, coming to her recollection, " I'm afraid that it's no use ; but put them down, anyhow ; they will do for bad debts. Shove off, William, we must go to the large ship now."

" I do wish that that Nancy was at any other port," exclaimed Mrs. Chopper, as they quitted the vessel's side ; " I do lose so much money by her."

" Well," said the waterman, laughing, " you're not the only one ; she can wheedle man or woman, or, as they say, the devil to boot, if she would try."

During the whole of the day the wherry proceeded from ship to ship, supplying necessaries ; in many instances they were paid for in ready money, in others Joey's capabilities were required, and they were booked down against the customers. At last, about five o'clock in the evening, the beer-barrel being empty, most of the contents of the baskets nearly exhausted, and the wherry loaded with the linen for the wash, biscuits, empty bottles, and various other articles of traffic or exchange, Mrs. Chopper ordered William, the waterman, to pull on shore to the landing-place.

As soon as the baskets and other articles had been carried up to the house, Mrs. Chopper sent out for the dinner, which was regularly obtained from a cook's-shop. Joey sat down with her, and when his meal was finished, Mrs. Chopper told him he might take a run and stretch his legs a little if he pleased, while she attended to the linen which was to go to the wash. Joey was not sorry to take advantage of this considerate permission, for his legs were quite cramped from sitting so

119

long jammed up between baskets of eggs, red herrings, and the other commodities which had encompassed him.

We must now introduce Mrs. Chopper to the reader a little more ceremoniously. She was the widow of a boatswain, who had set her up in the bumboat business with some money he had acquired a short time before his death, and she had continued it ever since on her own account. People said that she was rich, but riches are comparative, and if a person in a seaport town, and in her situation, could show £200 or £300 at her bankers, she was considered rich. If she was rich in nothing else, she certainly was in bad and doubtful debts, having seven or eight books like that which Joey was filling up for her during the whole day, all containing accounts of long standing, and most of which probably would stand for ever. But if the bad debts were many, the profits were in proportion; and what with the long-standing debts being occasionally paid, the ready-money she continually received, and the profitable traffic which she made in the way of exchange, &c., she appeared to do a thriving business, although it is certain the one-half of her goods were as much given away as were the articles obtained from her in the morning by Nancy.

It is a question whether these books of bad debts were not a source of enjoyment to her, for every night she would take one of the books down, and although she could not read, yet, by having them continually read to her, and knowing the pages so exactly, she could almost repeat every line by heart which the various bills contained; and then there was always a story which she had to tell about each—something relative to the party of whom the transaction reminded her; and subsequently, when Joey was fairly domiciled with her, she would make him hand down one of the books, and talk away from it for hours; they were the ledgers of her reminiscences; the events of a considerable portion of her life were all entered down along with the 'baccy, porter, pipes, and red herrings; a bill for these articles was to her time, place, and circumstance; and what with a good memory, and bad debts to assist it, many were the hours which were passed away (and pleasantly enough, too, for one liked to talk, and the other to listen) between Mrs. Chopper and our little hero. But we must not anticipate.

THE POACHER

The permission given to Joey to stretch his legs induced him to set off as fast as he could to gain the highroad before his little friend, Emma Phillips, had left her school. He sat down in the same place, waiting for her coming. The spot had become hallowed to the poor fellow, for he had there met with a friend—with one who sympathised with him when he most required consolation. He now felt happy, for he was no longer in doubt about obtaining his livelihood, and his first wish was to impart the pleasing intelligence to his little friend. She was not long before she made her appearance in her little straw bonnet with blue ribbons. Joey started up, and informed her that he had got a very nice place, explained to her what it was, and how he had been employed during the day.

" And I can very often come out about this time, I think," added Joey, " and then I can walk home with you, and see that you come to no harm."

" But," replied the little girl, " my mother says that she would like to see you, as she will not allow me to make acquaintance with people I meet by accident. Don't you think that mother is right ? "

" Yes, I do ; she's very right," replied Joey ; " I didn't think of that."

" Will you come and see her, then ? "

" Not now, because I am not very clean. I'll come on Sunday, if I can get leave."

They separated, and Joey returned back to the town. As he walked on, he thought he would spend the money he had got in a suit of Sunday clothes, of a better quality than those he had on, the materials of which were very coarse. On second thoughts, he resolved to apply to Mrs. Chopper, as he did not exactly know where to go for them, and was afraid that he would be imposed upon.

" Well, Peter," said his new mistress, " do you feel better for your walk ? "

" Yes, thank you, ma'am."

" Peter," continued Mrs. Chopper, " you appear to be a very handy, good boy, and I hope we shall live together a long while. How long have you been at sea ? "

" I was going to sea ; I have never been to sea yet, and I don't want to go ; I would rather stay with you."

121

"And so you shall, that's a settled thing. What clothes have you got, Peter?"

"I have none but what I stand in, and a few shirts in a bundle, and they are Sunday ones; but when I left home I had some money given me, and I wish to buy a suit of clothes for Sunday, to go to church in."

"That's a good boy, and so you shall; but how much money have you got?"

"Quite enough to buy a suit of clothes," replied Joey, handing out two sovereigns, and seventeen shillings in silver.

"Oh, I suppose they gave you all that to fit you out with when you left home; poor people, I dare say they worked hard for it. Well, I don't think the money will be of any use to you; so you had better buy a Sunday suit, and I will take care you want for nothing afterwards. Don't you think I'm right?"

"Yes, I wish to do so. To-day is Tuesday; I may have them made by next Sunday?"

"So you can; and as soon as William comes in, which he will soon, from the washerwoman's, we will go out and order them. Here he comes up the stairs—no, that foot's too light for his. Well, it's Nancy, I declare! Why, Nancy, now," continued Mrs. Chopper, in a deprecating tone, "what do you want here?"

"Well, I leave you to guess," replied Nancy, looking very demure, and taking a seat upon a hamper.

"Guess, I fear there's no guess in it, Nancy; but I will not —now it's no use—I will not trust another shilling."

"But I know you will, Mrs. Chopper. Lord love you, you're such a good-natured creature, you can't refuse any one, and certainly not me. Why don't you take me in your boat with you as your assistant? then there would be something in it worth looking at. I should bring you plenty of custom."

"You're too wild, Nancy; too wild, girl. But, now, what do you want? recollect you've already had some things to-day."

"I know I have, and you are a good-natured old trump, that you are. Now I'll tell you—gold must pass between us this time."

"Mercy on me, Nancy, why, you're mad. I've no gold— nothing but bad debts."

"Look you, Mrs. Chopper, look at this shabby old bonnet of mine. Don't I want a new one?"

"Then you must get somebody else to give you money, Nancy," replied Mrs. Chopper, coolly and decidedly.

"Don't talk so fast, Mrs. Chopper: now, I'll let you know how it is. When Bill came on board he asked the captain for an advance; the captain refused him before, but this time he was in a good humour, and he consented. So then I coaxed Bill out of a sovereign to buy a new bonnet, and he gave it me; and then I thought what a kind soul you were, and I resolved that I would bring you the sovereign, and go without the new bonnet; so here it is, take it quick, or I shall repent."

"Well, Nancy," said Mrs. Chopper, "you said right; gold has passed between us, and I am surprised. Now I shall trust you again."

"And so you ought; it's not every pretty girl, like me, who will give up a new bonnet. Only look what a rubbishy affair this is," continued Nancy, giving her own a kick up in the air.

"I wish I had a sovereign to give away," said Joey to Mrs. Chopper; "I wish I had not said a word about the clothes."

"Do as you like with your own money, my dear," said the bumboat-woman.

"Then, Nancy, I'll give you a sovereign to buy yourself a new bonnet with," said Joey, taking one out of his pocket and putting it into her hand.

Nancy looked at the sovereign, and then at Joey. "Bless the boy!" said she at last, kissing him on the forehead; "he has a kind heart; may the world use him better than it has me! Here, take your sovereign, child; any bonnet's good enough for one like me." So saying, Nancy turned hastily away, and ran downstairs.

CHAPTER XXIV

In which Mrs. Chopper reads her ledger.

Ah, poor girl," said Mrs. Chopper, with a sigh, as Nancy disappeared. "You are a good boy, Peter; I like to see boys not too fond of money, and if she had taken it (and I wish she had, poor thing) I would have made it up to you."

"Is the man she calls Bill her husband?" inquired Joey.

"Oh, I know nothing about other people's husbands,"

replied Mrs. Chopper hastily. "Now then, let us go and order the clothes, and then you'll be able to go to church on Sunday; I will do without you."

"What, won't you go to church?"

"Bless you, child! who is to give the poor men their break-fast and their beer? A bumboat-woman can't go to church any more than a baker's man, for people must eat on a Sunday. Church, like everything else in this world, appears to me only to be made for the rich; I always take my Bible in the boat with me on Sunday, but then I can't read it, so it's of no great use. No, dear, I can't go to church, but I can contrive, if it don't rain in the evening, to go to meeting and hear a little of the Word; but you can go to church, dear."

A suit of blue cloth, made in sailor's fashion, having been ordered by Mrs. Chopper, she and Joey returned home; and, after their tea, Mrs. Chopper desired Joey to hand her one of the account-books, which she put upon her knees and opened.

"There," said she, looking at the page, "I know that account well; it was Tom Alsop's—a fine fellow he was, only he made such a bad marriage: his wife was a very fiend, and the poor fellow loved her, which was worse. One day he missed her, and found she was on board another vessel; and he came on shore, distracted like, and got very tipsy, as sailors always do when they're in trouble, and he went down to the wharf, and his body was picked up next day."

"Did he drown himself?"

"Yes, so people think, Peter; and he owed me £1, 3s. 4d., if I recollect right. Aren't that the figure, Peter?"

"Yes, ma'am," replied Joey; "that's the sum total of the account, exactly."

"Poor fellow!" continued Mrs. Chopper, with a sigh, "he went to his long account without paying me my short one. Never mind; I wish he was alive, and twice as much in my debt. There's another—I recollect that well, Peter, for it's a proof that sailors are honest; and I do believe that, if they don't pay, it's more from thoughtlessness than anything else; and then the women coax all their money from them, for sailors don't care for money when they do get it—and then those Jews are such shocking fellows; but look you, Peter, this is almost the first bill run up after I took up the business. He was a nice fair-haired lad from Shields; and the boy was cast away, and he was picked up by another vessel, and brought here; and I let him have things and lent him money to the amount of a matter of £20, and he said he would save all and pay me, and he sailed away again, and I never heard of him for nine years. I thought that he was drowned, or that he was not an honest lad; I didn't know which, and it was a deal of money to lose; but I gave it up; when one day a tall, stout fellow, with great red whiskers, called upon me, and said, 'Do you know me?' 'No,' said I, half-frightened; 'how should I know you? I never see'd you before.'—'Yes, you did,' says he, 'and here's a proof of it;' and he put down on the table a lot of money, and said, 'Now, missus, help yourself: better late than never. I'm Jim Sparling, who was cast away, and who you were as good as a mother to; but I've never been able to get leave to come to you since. I'm boatswain's mate of a man-of-war, and have just received my pay, and now I've come to pay my debts.' He would make me take £5 more than his bill, to buy a new silk gown for his sake. Poor fellow! he's dead now. Here's another, that was run up by one of your tall, lanky sailors, who wear their knives in a sheath, and not with a lanyard round their waists; those fellows never pay, but they swear dreadfully. Let me see, what can this one be? Read it, Peter; how much is it?"

"£4, 2s. 4d.," replied our hero.

"Yes, yes, I recollect now—it was the Dutch skipper. There's murder in that bill, Peter: it was things I supplied to him just before he sailed; and an old man was passenger in the cabin: he was a very rich man, although he pretended to be poor. He was a diamond merchant, they say; and as soon as they were at sea, the Dutch captain murdered him in the night, and threw him overboard out of the cabin-window; but one of the sailors saw the deed done, and the captain was taken up at Amsterdam, and had his head cut off. The crew told us when the galliot came back with a new captain. So the Dutch skipper paid the forfeit of his crime; he paid my bill, too, that's certain. Oh, deary me!" continued the old lady, turning to another page. "I shan't forget this in a hurry. I never see poor Nancy now without recollecting it. Look, Peter; I know the sum—£8, 4s. 6d. exactly: it was the things taken up when Tom Freelove married Nancy—it was the wedding dinner and supper."

125

"What, Nancy who was here just now?"

"Yes, that Nancy; and a sweet, modest young creature she was then, and had been well brought up too; she could read and write beautifully, and subscribed to a circulating library, they say. She was the daughter of a baker in this town. I recollect it well: such a fine day it was when they went to church, she looking so handsome in her new ribbons and smart dress, and he such a fine-looking young man. I never seed such a handsome young couple; but he was a bad one, and so it all ended in misery."

"Tell me how," said Joey.

"I'll tell all you ought to know, boy; you are too young to be told all the wickedness of this world. Her husband treated her very ill; before he had been married a month he left her, and went about with other people, and was always drunk, and she became jealous and distracted, and he beat her cruelly, and deserted her; and then, to comfort her, people would persuade her to keep her spirits up, and gave her something to drink, and by degrees she became fond of it. Her husband was killed by a fall from the mast-head; and she loved him still and took more to liquor, and that was her ruin. She don't drink now, because she don't feel as she used to do; she cares about nothing; she is much to be pitied, poor thing, for she is still young, and very pretty. It's only four years ago when I saw her come out of church, and thought what a happy couple they would be."

"Where are her father and mother?"

"Both dead. Don't let's talk about it any more. It's bad enough when a man drinks; but if a woman takes to it, it is all over with her; but some people's feelings are so strong, that they fly to it directly to drown care and misery. Put up the book, Peter; I can't look at it any more to-night; we'll go to bed."

Joey every day gave more satisfaction to his employer, and upon his own responsibility, allowed his friend the sailor lad to open an account as soon as his money was all gone. Finding that the vessel was going up the river to load, Joey determined to write a few lines to the M'Shanes, to allay the uneasiness which he knew his absence must have occasioned, Jim Paterson promising to put the letter in the post as soon as he arrived at London.

Our hero simply said, "My dear Sir,—I am quite well, and have found employment, so pray do not grieve about me, as I never shall forget your kindness.—JOEY M'SHANE."

On the following Sunday Joey was dressed in his sailor's suit, and looked very well in it. He was not only a very good-looking, but a gentlemanlike boy in his manners. He went to church, and after church he walked out to the abode of his little friend, Emma Phillips. She ran out to meet him, was delighted with his new clothes, and took him by the hand to present him to her mother. Mrs. Phillips was a quiet-looking, pleasing woman, and the old lady was of a very venerable appearance. They made many inquiries about his friends, and Joey continued in the same story, that he and his father had been poachers, that he had been discovered and obliged to go away, and that he went with the consent of his parents. They were satisfied with his replies, and prepossessed in his favour; and as Joey was so patronised by her little daughter, he was desired to renew his visits, which he occasionally did on Sundays, but preferred meeting Emma on the road from school; and the two children (if Joey could be called a child) became very intimate, and felt annoyed if they did not every day exchange a few words. Thus passed the first six months of Joey's new life. The winter was cold, and the water rough, and he blew his fingers, while Mrs. Chopper folded her arms up in her apron; but he had always a good dinner and a warm bed after the day's work was over. He became a great favourite with Mrs. Chopper, who at last admitted that he was much more useful than even Peter; and William, the waterman, declared that such was really the case, and that he was, in his opinion, worth two of the former Peter, who had come to such an untimely end.

CHAPTER XXV

In which the biter is bit.

THE disappearance of Joey from the school was immediately communicated to M'Shane by the master, who could not imagine how such an incident could have occurred in such a decent establishment as his preparatory seminary; it was an epoch in his existence, and ever afterwards his chronology was founded upon it, and everything that occurred was so many months or weeks before or after the absconding of young Master M'Shane. The letter had, of course, been produced, and as soon as the schoolmaster had taken his departure, M'Shane and his wife were in deep council. " I recollect," said Mrs. M'Shane, who was crying in an easy-chair—" I recollect now, that one day the boy came up and asked me the meaning of wilful murder, and I told him. And now I think of it, I do also remember the people at No. 1 table, close to the counter, some time ago, talking about a murder having been committed by a mere child, and a long report of it in the newspapers. I am sure, however (as Joey says in his letter), that he is not guilty."

" And so am I," replied M'Shane. " However, bring up the file of newspapers, dear, and let me look over them. How long back do you think it was ? "

" Why, let me see ; it was about the time you went away with Captain O'Donahue, I think, or a little before—that was in October."

M'Shane turned over the file of newspapers, and after a quarter of an hour's search found the report of the coroner's inquest.

" Here it is, my dear, sure enough," said M'Shane.

As soon as he had read it over, and came to the end, he said, " Yes ; wilful murder against Joseph Rushbrook the younger, and £200 for his apprehension. This it was that drove the boy away from home, and not poaching, although I have no doubt that poaching was the cause of the murder. Now, my dear," continued M'Shane, " I think I can unravel all this ; the murder has been committed, that's evident, by somebody, but not by Joey, I'll be sworn ; he says that he is not guilty, and I believe him. Nevertheless, Joey runs away, and a verdict is found against him. My dear wife, I happen to know the father of Joey well ; he was a fine, bold soldier, but one who would stick at nothing ; and if I could venture an opinion, it is, that the murder was committed by Rushbrook, and not by the boy, and that the boy has absconded to save his father."

The reader will acknowledge that M'Shane was very clear-sighted.

128

"That's my opinion," continued M'Shane. "How it has been managed to make the boy appear as the party, I cannot tell ; but knowing the father, and knowing the son, I'd stake my commission that I've guessed at the truth."

"Poor boy !" exclaimed Mrs. M'Shane ; "well, the Commandments say that the sins of the father shall be visited upon the children. What can be done, M'Shane ? "

"Nothing at present ; it would injure Joey to raise a hue and cry after him ; for, you see, if he is apprehended, he must either be tried for his life, and convicted himself, or prove that he did not do it, which probably he could not do without convicting his father ; I will, however, make some inquiries about Rushbrook himself, and if I can I will see him."

The same evening the schoolmaster again called upon M'Shane, to say that two persons had come to the school in the afternoon and asked to see him ; that one of them, shabbily dressed, but evidently a person who was not of so low a class in life as the other, had accosted him when he came into the parlour, with, "I believe I have the pleasure of speaking to Mr. Slappum ; if so, may I request the favour to see my little friend Joey, whom I met yesterday walking out with the other young gentlemen under your care, as I have a message to him from his father and mother ? The dear boy was once under my tuition, and did me much credit, as I have no doubt that he has done you."

Now, the usher had told Mr. Slappum that Joey had been addressed by this person the day before, and the schoolmaster presuming, of course, that it was Joey M'Shane, replied, "I am sorry to say that he left this house last night, and has absconded we know not where. He left a letter for Major M'Shane, which I have this day delivered to him, acquainting him with the unpleasant circumstance."

"Bolted, by all that's clever !" said the second personage to the first, who looked very much surprised and confounded.

"You really have astonished me, my dear sir," replied the first person, whom the reader will of course recognise to be Furness ; "that a lad brought up by me in such strict moral principles, such correct notions of right and wrong, and, I may add, such pious feelings, should have taken such a step, is to me incomprehensible. Major M'Shane, I think you said, lives at—— ? "

"Major M'Shane lives at No. — in Holborn," replied the schoolmaster.

"And the lad has not gone home to him?"

"No, he has not; he left a letter, which I took to Major M'Shane; but I did not break the seal, and am ignorant of its contents."

"I really am stupefied with grief and vexation," replied Furness, "and will not intrude any longer. Bless the poor boy! what can have come of him?"

So saying, Furness took his departure with the peace-officer, whom he had entrusted with the warrant which he had taken out to secure the person of our hero.

M'Shane heard the schoolmaster's account of this visit without interruption, and then said, "I have no doubt but that this person who has called upon you will pay me a visit; oblige me, therefore, by describing his person particularly, so that I may know him at first sight."

The schoolmaster gave a most accurate description of Furness, and then took his leave.

As the eating-house kept by Mrs. M'Shane had a private door, Furness (who, as M'Shane had prophesied, came the next afternoon), after having read the name on the private door, which was not on the eating-house, which went by the name of the Chequers, imagined that it was an establishment apart, and thought it advisable to enter into it, and ascertain a little about Major M'Shane before he called upon him. Although M'Shane seldom made his appearance in the room appropriated for the dinners, it so happened that he was standing at the door when Furness entered and sat down in a box, calling for the bill of fare, and ordering a plate of beef and cabbage. M'Shane recognised him by the description given of him immediately, and resolved to make his acquaintance incog., and ascertain what his intentions were; he therefore took his seat in the same box, and winking to one of the girls who attended, also called for a plate of beef and cabbage. Furness, who was anxious to pump any one he might fall in with, immediately entered into conversation with the major.

"A good house this, sir, and well attended apparently?"

"Yes, sir," replied M'Shane; "it is considered a very good house."

"Do you frequent it much yourself?"

130

"Always, sir; I feel much interested in its success," replied M'Shane; "for I know the lady who keeps it well, and have a high respect for her."

"I saw her as I passed by—a fine woman, sir! Pray may I ask who is Major M'Shane, who I observe lives in the rooms above?"

"He is a major in the army, sir—now on half-pay."

"Do you know him?"

"Remarkably well," replied M'Shane; "he's a countryman of mine."

"He's married, sir, I think? I'll trouble you for the pepper."

"He is married, sir, to a very amiable woman."

"Any family, sir?"

"Not that I know of; they have a young *protégé*, I believe, now at school—a boy they call Joey."

"Indeed! how very kind of them; really, now, it's quite refreshing for me to see so much goodness of heart still remaining in this bad world. Adopted him, I presume?"

"I really cannot exactly say that; I know that they treat him as their own child."

"Have you seen Major M'Shane lately, sir?"

"Saw him this morning, sir, just after he got up."

"Indeed! This is remarkably good ale, sir—will you honour me by tasting it?"

"Sir, you are very kind; but the fact is I never drink malt liquor. Here, girl, bring a half-pint of brandy. I trust, sir, you will not refuse to join me in a glass, although I cannot venture to accept your polite offer."

Furness drank off his pot of ale, and made ready for the brandy which had been offered him; M'Shane filled his own glass, and then handed the decanter over to Furness.

"I have the pleasure of drinking your good health, sir," said M'Shane. "You are from the country, I presume; may I inquire from what part?"

"I am from Devonshire; I was formerly head of the grammar-school at ——; but, sir, my principles would not allow me to retain my situation; rectitude of conduct, sir, is absolutely necessary to the profession which inculcates morality and virtue, as well as instruction to youth, sir. Here's to our better acquaintance, sir."

131

"Sir, to yours; I honour your sentiments. By the powers! but you're right, Mr.——, I beg your pardon—but I don't catch your name exactly."

"Furness, sir, at your service. Yes, sir, the directors of the foundation which I presided over, I may say, with such credit to myself, and such advantage to the pupils under my care, wished to make a job—yes, sir—of a charity; I could not consent to such deeds, and I resigned."

"And you have been in London ever since?"

"No, sir; I repaired to the small village of Grassford, where I set up a school, but circumstances compelled me to resign, and I am now about to seek for employment in another hemisphere; in short, I have an idea of going out to New South Wales as a preceptor. I understand they are in great want of tuition in that quarter."

"I should think so," replied M'Shane; "and they have a great deal to unlearn as well as to learn."

"I speak of the junior branches—the scions or offsets, I may say—born in the colony, and who, I trust, will prove that crime is not hereditary."

"Well, I wish you luck, sir," replied M'Shane; "you must oblige me by taking another glass, for I never shall be able to finish this decanter myself."

"I gladly avail myself of the pleasure of your company, sir."

As the reader is well aware that Furness was an intemperate man, it is not surprising that he accepted the offer; and before the second glass was finished, the ale and brandy had begun to have the effect, and he had become very communicative.

"What was the name of the village which you stated you had resided in lately, sir?" inquired M'Shane.

"The village of Grassford."

"There is something I recollect about that village; let me see—something that I read in the newspapers. I remember now—it was the murder of a pedlar."

"Very true, sir, such a circumstance did take place; it was a dreadful affair—and, what is more strange, committed by a mere child, who absconded."

"Indeed! What was his name?"

"Rushbrook, sir; his father was a well-known poacher—a man who had been in the army, and had a pension for wounds. There is an old saying, sir, of high authority—'Bring up a

132

child in the way he should go, and he will not depart from it.' I instructed that boy, sir; but alas! what avails the instruction of a preceptor when a father leads a child into evil ways?"

"That's the truth, and no mistake," replied M'Shane. "So the boy ran away? Yes; I recollect now. And what became of the father?"

"The father, sir, and mother have since left the village, and gone nobody knows where."

"Indeed! are you sure of that?"

"Quite sure, sir; for I was most anxious to discover them, and took great pains, but without success."

"What did the people say thereabouts? Was there no suspicion of the father being implicated?"

"I do not think there was. He gave evidence at the inquest, and so did I, sir, as you may suppose, most unwillingly; for the boy was a favourite of mine. I beg your pardon, sir—you say you are acquainted with Major M'Shane, and saw him this morning; is the interesting little boy you speak of as under his protection now at home, or still at school?"

"I really cannot positively say," replied M'Shane; "but this is not holiday-time. Come, sir, we must not part yet; your conversation is too interesting. You must allow me to call for some more brandy; poor as I am, I must treat myself and you too. I wish I knew where I could pick up a little money; for, to tell you the truth, cash begins to run low."

Furness was now more than half drunk. "Well, sir," said he, "I have known money picked up without any difficulty; for instance, now, suppose we should fall in with this young rascal who committed the murder; there is £200 offered for his apprehension and conviction."

"I thought as much," muttered M'Shane; "the infernal scoundrel!—I suspect that you will find him where you are going to, Mr. Furbish, he's got that far by this time."

"Between you and I, I think not, sir. My name is Furness, sir—I beg your pardon—not Furbish."

"Why, you do not think he would be such a fool as to remain in the country after such an act?"

"The wicked are foolish, sir, as well as others," replied

Furness, putting his finger to his nose, and looking very knowingly.

"That's truth, sir. Help yourself; you drink nothing. Excuse me one minute; I'll be back directly."

M'Shane left the box for a few minutes to explain to his wife what he was about, and to give time for the liquor to operate upon Furness. As he expected, he found on his return that Furness had finished his glass, and was more tipsy than when he left him.

The conversation was renewed, and M'Shane again pleading his poverty, and his wish to obtain money, brought out the proposal of Furness, who informed him that he had recognised the *protégé* of Major M'Shane to be the identical Joseph Rushbrook; that the boy had absconded from the school, and was concealed in the house. He concluded by observing to M'Shane, that, as he was so intimate with the major, it would be very easy for him to ascertain the fact, and offered him £50 as his share of the reward, if he would assist him in the boy's capture. It was lucky for Furness that M'Shane was surrounded by others, or in all probability there would have been another murder committed. The major, however, said he would think of it, and fell back in deep thought; what he was thinking of was, what he should do to punish Furness. At last an idea came into his head; the rascal was drunk, and he proposed that he should go to another house, where they might find the major, and he would present him. Furness consented, and reeled out of the box; M'Shane, although he would as soon have touched a viper, controlled himself sufficiently to give Furness his arm, and leading him down by two or three back courts, he took him into an ale-house where there was a rendezvous for enlisting marines for the navy. As soon as they were seated, and had liquor before them, M'Shane spoke to the sergeant, tipped him a guinea, and said he had a good recruit for him, if he could be persuaded to enlist. He then introduced the sergeant as the major, and advised Furness to pretend to agree with him in everything. The sergeant told long stories, clapped Furness, who was now quite intoxicated, on the back, called him a jolly fellow, and asked him to enlist. "Say 'yes,' to please him," said M'Shane in his ear. Furness did so, received the shilling, and when he came to his senses next day, found his friend had disappeared, and that he was under an escort for Portsmouth. All remonstrances were unavailing; M'Shane had fee'd the sergeant, and had promised him a higher fee not to let Furness off; and the latter, having but a few shillings in his pocket, was compelled to submit to his fate.

CHAPTER XXVI

In which our hero again falls in with an old acquaintance.

FOR nearly two years Joey had filled his situation as chancellor of the exchequer to Mrs. Chopper. He certainly did not feel himself always in the humour or the disposition for business, especially during the hard winter months, when, seated almost immovably in the boat during the best portion of the day, he would find his fingers so completely dead, that he could not hold his pen. But there is no situation, under any of the powers that be, that has not some drawback. People may say that a sinecure is one that has not its disadvantages; but such is not the case—there is the disgrace of holding it. At all events, Joey's place was no sinecure, for he was up early, and was employed the whole of the day.

Nancy, the young woman we have introduced to our readers, had contracted a great regard for our hero, ever since his offering her his money; and Joey was equally partial to her, for she possessed a warm heart and much good feeling; she would very often run upstairs into Mrs. Chopper's room, to talk with the old lady and to see Joey, and would then take out her thimble and needle, examine his clothes, and make the necessary repairs.

"I saw you walking with little Emma Phillips, Peter," said Nancy; "where did you come to know her?"

"I met her in the road the day that I came down to Gravesend."

"Well, I'm sure! and do you speak to every young lady you chance to meet?"

"No; but I was unhappy, and she was very kind to me."

"She's a very sweet child, or rather, I can only say that she was when I knew her."

135

" When did you know her ? "

" Four or five years ago. I lived for a short time with Mrs. Phillips; that was when I was a good girl."

" Yes, indeed, Nancy," said Mrs. Chopper, shaking her head.

" Why ain't you good now, Nancy ? " replied Joey.

" Because——" said Nancy.

" Because why ? "

" Because I am not good," replied the girl; " and now, Peter, don't ask any more questions, or you'll make me cry. Heigho ! I think crying very pleasant now and then ; one's heart feels fresher, like flowers after the rain. Peter, where are your father and mother ? "

" I don't know ; I left them at home."

" You left them at home ! but do you never hear from them ? do you never write ? "

" No."

" But why not ? I am sure they have brought you up well. They must be very good people—are they not ? "

Joey could not answer; how could he say that his father was a good man after what had passed ?

" You don't answer me, Peter ; don't you love your father and mother dearly ? "

" Yes, indeed I do ; but I must not write to them."

" Well, I must say there is something about Peter and his parents which I cannot understand, and which I have often tried to make him tell, and he will not," said Mrs. Chopper. " Poaching ain't such a great crime, especially in a boy. I can't see why he should not write to his father and mother, at all events. I hope, Peter, you have told me the truth ? "

" I have told you what is true ; but my father was a poacher, and they know it ; and if they did not punish me, they would him, and transport him, too, if I gave evidence against him, which I must do, if put to my oath. I've told you all I can tell ; I must not tell of father, must I ? "

" No, no, child; I dare say you are right," replied Mrs. Chopper.

" Now, I don't ask you to tell me, Peter," said Nancy, " for I can guess what has taken place : you and your father have been out poaching, there has been a scuffle with the keepers, and there has been blood shed ; and that's the reason why you keep out of the way. Ain't I right ? "

"You are not far wrong," replied Joey; "but I will not say a word more upon it."

"And I won't ask you, my little Peter; there—that's done —and now I shall have a peep out of the window, for it's very close here, Mrs. Chopper."

Nancy threw the window open and leaned out of it, watching the passers-by. "Mercy on us! here's three soldiers coming up the street with a deserter handcuffed," cried she. "Who can it be? he's a sailor. Why, I do believe it's Sam Oxenham, that belongs to the *Thomas and Mary* of Sunderland. Poor fellow! Yes, it is him."

Joey went to the window, and took his stand by the side of Nancy. "What soldiers are those?" inquired he.

"They're not soldiers, after all," replied Nancy; "they are jollies—a sergeant and two privates."

"Jollies! what are they?"

"Why, marines, to be sure."

Joey continued looking at them until they passed under the window, when Nancy, who had a great disgust at anything like arbitrary power, could not refrain from speaking.

"I say, master sergeant, you're a nice brave fellow, with your two jollies. D'ye think the young man will kill you all three, that you must put the darbies on so tight?"

At this appeal the sergeant and privates looked up at the window, and laughed when they saw such a pretty girl as Nancy. The eyes of one of the privates were, however, soon fixed on our hero's face, and deeply scrutinising it, when Joey looked at him. As soon as Joey recognised him he drew back from the window, pale as death, the private still remaining staring at the window.

"Why, what's the matter, Peter?" said Nancy; "what makes you look so pale? do you know that man?"

"Yes," replied Joey, drawing his breath, "and he knows me, I'm afraid."

"Why do you fear?" replied Nancy.

"See if he's gone," said Joey.

"Yes, he has; he has gone up the street with the sergeant, but every now and then he looks back at this window; but perhaps that's to see me."

"Why, Peter, what harm can that marine do you?" inquired Mrs. Chopper.

"A great deal; he will never be quiet until he has me taken up, and then what will become of my poor father?" continued Joey, with the tears running down his cheeks.

"Give me my bonnet, Peter. I'll soon find out what he is after," said Nancy, leaving the window. She threw her bonnet on her head, and ran downstairs.

Mrs. Chopper in vain endeavoured to console our hero, or make him explain—he did nothing but sit mournfully by her side, thinking what he had best do, and expecting every minute to hear the tramp of Furness (for it was he who had recognised Joey) coming up the stairs.

"Mrs. Chopper," at last said Joey, "I must leave you, I'm afraid; I was obliged to leave my former friends on this man's account."

"Leave me, boy! no, no, you must not leave me—how could I get on without you?"

"If I don't leave you myself, I shall be taken up, that is certain; but indeed I have not done wrong—don't think that I have."

"I'm sure of it, child; you've only to say so, and I'll believe you; but why should he care about you?"

"He lived in our village, and knows all about it; he gave evidence at——"

"At what, boy?"

"At the time that I ran away from home; he proved that I had the gun and bag which were found."

"Well, and suppose you had; what then?"

"Mrs. Chopper, there was a reward offered, and he wants to get the money."

"Oh, I see now—a reward offered; then it must be as Nancy said, there was blood shed," and Mrs. Chopper put her apron up to her eyes.

Joey made no answer. After a few minutes' silence he rose, and went to the room where he slept, and put his clothes up in a bundle. Having so done, he sat down on the side of his bed, and reflected what was the course he ought to pursue.

Our hero was now sixteen, and much increased in stature; he was no longer a child, although, in heart, almost as innocent. His thoughts wandered—he yearned to see his father and mother, and reflected whether he might not venture back to the village, and meet them by stealth; he thought of the M'Shanes, and imagined that he might in the same way return to them; then little Emma Phillips rose in his imagination, and his fear that he should never see her again; Captain O'Donahue was at last brought to his recollection, and he longed to be once more with him in Russia; and, lastly, he reviewed the happy and contented life he had lately led with his good friend Mrs. Chopper, and how sorry he should be to part with her. After a time he threw himself on his bed and hid his face in the pillow; and, overcome with the excess of his feelings, he at last fell asleep.

In the meantime Nancy had followed the marines up the street, and saw them enter, with their prisoner, into a small public-house where she was well known; she followed them, spoke a few kind words to the seaman who had been apprehended, and with whom she was acquainted, and then sat down by Furness to attract his attention.

Furness had certainly much improved in his appearance since he had (much against his will) been serving his Majesty. Being a tall man, he had, by drilling, become perfectly erect, and the punishment awarded to drunkenness, as well as the difficulty of procuring liquor, had kept him from his former intemperance, and his health had in consequence improved. He had been more than once brought up to the gangway upon his first embarkation, but latterly had conducted himself properly, and was in expectation of being made a corporal, for which situation his education certainly qualified him. On the whole, he was now a fine-looking marine, although just as unprincipled a scoundrel as ever.

"Well, my pretty lass, didn't I see you looking out of window just now?"

"To be sure you did, and you might have heard me too," replied Nancy; "and when I saw such a handsome fellow as you, didn't I put on my bonnet in a hurry, and come after you? What ship do you belong to?"

"The *Mars*, at the Nore."

"Well, I should like to go on board of a man-of-war. Will you take me?"

"To be sure I will; come, have a drink of beer."

"Here's to the jollies," said Nancy, putting the pewter pot to her lips. "When do you go on board again?"

139

"Not till to-morrow; we've caught our bird, and now we'll amuse ourselves a little. Do you belong to this place?"

"Yes, bred and born here; but we hardly ever see a man-of-war; they stay at the Nore, or go higher up."

Nancy did all she could to make Furness believe she had taken a fancy to him, and knew too well how to succeed. Before an hour had passed, Furness had, as he thought, made every arrangement with her, and congratulated himself on his good fortune. In the meantime the beer and brandy went round; even the unfortunate captive was persuaded to drink with them, and drown reflection. At last Furness said to Nancy, "Who was that lad that was looking out of the window with you? Was it your brother?"

"My brother! bless you, no. You mean that scamp, Peter, who goes in the bumboat with old Mother Chopper."

"Does he?—well, I have either seen him before, or some one like him."

"He's not of our town," replied Nancy; "he came here about two years ago, nobody knows where from, and has been with Mrs. Chopper ever since."

"Two years ago," muttered Furness, "that's just the time. Come, girl, take some more beer."

Nancy drank a little, and put down the pot.

"Where does Mrs. Chopper live?" inquired Furness.

"Where you saw me looking out of the window," replied Nancy.

"And the boy lives with her? I will call upon Mrs. Chopper by-and-by."

"Yes, to be sure he does; but why are you talking so about the boy? Why don't you talk to me, and tell me what a pretty girl I am, for I like to be told that."

Furness and his comrades continued the carouse, and were getting fast into a state of intoxication; the sergeant only was prudent; but Furness could not let pass this opportunity of indulging without fear of punishment. He became more loving towards Nancy as he became more tipsy, when Nancy, who cajoled him to the utmost of her power, again mentioned our hero; and then it was that Furness, who, when inebriated, could never hold a secret, first told her there was a reward offered for his apprehension, and that if she would remain with him they would spend the money together. To this

Nancy immediately consented, and offered to assist him as much as she could, as she had the entrance into Mrs. Chopper's house, and knew where the lad slept. But Nancy was determined to gain more from Furness, and as he was now pretty far gone, she proposed that they should take a walk out, for it was a beautiful evening. Furness gladly consented. Nancy again explained to him how she should manage to get Joey into her power, and appeared quite delighted at the idea of there being a reward, which they were to obtain; and finding that Furness was completely deceived, and that the fresh air had increased his inebriety, she then persuaded him to confide to her all the circumstances connected with the reward offered for our hero's apprehension. She then learned what had occurred at the inquest—Joey's escape—his being again discovered by Furness—and his second escape from the school, to which he had been put by the M'Shanes.

"And his father and mother, where are they? When I think of them I must say that I do not much like to assist in taking up the boy. Poor people, how they will suffer when they hear of it! Really I don't know what to say," continued Nancy, biting the tip of her finger, as if hesitating.

"Don't let them stop you," said Furness; "they will not be likely even to hear of it; they left the village before me, and no one knows where they are gone. I tried to find out myself, but could not. It's very clear that they are gone to America."

"Indeed!" said Nancy, who had put the question because she wished to give Joey some information relative to his parents; "gone to America, do you say?"

"Yes, I am inclined to think so, for I lost all trace of them."

"Well then," replied Nancy, "that scruple of mine is got over."

She then pointed out to Furness the propriety of waiting an hour or two, till people were in bed, that there might be no chance of a rescue; and they returned to the public-house. Furness took another glass of ale, and then fell fast asleep on the bench, with his head over the table.

"So," thought Nancy, as she left the public-house, "the drunken fool makes sure of his £200; but there is no time to be lost."

Nancy hastened back to Mrs. Chopper, whom she found

141

sitting with a candle turning over the leaves of one of the old account-books.

"O Nancy, is that you? I was just sighing over you; here's the things that were ordered for your wedding. Poor girl! I fear you have not often been to church since."

Nancy was silent for a short time. "I'm sick of my life, and sick of myself, Mrs. Chopper; but what can I do?—a wretch like me! I wish I could run away, as poor Peter must directly, and go to where I never was known; I should be so happy."

"Peter must go, do you say, Nancy? Is that certain?"

"Most certain, Mrs. Chopper, and he must be off directly. I have been with the marines, and the fellow has told me everything; he is only waiting now for me to go back, to come and take him."

"But tell me, Nancy, has Peter been guilty?"

"I believe from my heart that he has done nothing; but still murder was committed, and Peter will be apprehended, unless you give him the means of running away. Where is he now?"

"Asleep, fast asleep: I didn't like to wake him, poor fellow!"

"Then he must be innocent, Mrs. Chopper: they say the guilty never sleep. But what will he do—he has no money?"

"He has saved me a mint of money, and he shall not want it," replied Mrs. Chopper. "What shall I do without him? I can't bear to part with him."

"But you must, Mrs. Chopper; and, if you love him, you will give him the means, and let him be off directly. I wish I was going too," continued Nancy, bursting into tears.

"Go with him, Nancy, and look after him, and take care of my poor Peter," said Mrs. Chopper, whimpering; "go, my child, go, and lead a good life. I should better part with him if I thought you were with him, and away from this horrid place."

"Will you let me go with him, Mrs. Chopper—will you, indeed?" cried Nancy, falling on her knees. "Oh! I will watch him as a mother would her son, as a sister would her brother! Give us but the means to quit this place, and the good and the wicked both will bless you."

142

"That you shall have, my poor girl; it has often pained my heart to look at you, for I felt that you are too good for what you are, and you will be again a good honest girl. You both shall go. Poor Peter! I wish I were young enough, I would go with you; but I can't. How I shall be cheated again when he is gone! but go he must. Here, Nancy, take the money; take all I have in the house:" and Mrs. Chopper put upwards of £20 into Nancy's hand as she was kneeling before her. Nancy fell forward with her face in the lap of the good old woman, suffocated with emotion and tears. "Come, come, Nancy," said Mrs. Chopper, after a pause, and wiping her eyes with her apron, "you mustn't take on so, my poor girl. Recollect poor Peter; there's no time to lose."

"That is true," replied Nancy, rising up. "Mrs. Chopper, you have done a deed this night for which you will have your reward in heaven. May the God of mercy bless you! and, as soon as I dare, night and morning will I pray for you."

Mrs. Chopper went into Joey's room with the candle in her hand, followed by Nancy. "See, how sound he sleeps!" said the old woman; "he is not guilty. Peter! Peter! come, get up, child."

Joey rose from his bed, confused at first with the light in his eyes, but soon recovered himself.

"Peter, you must go, my poor boy, and go quickly, Nancy says."

"I was sure of it," replied Joey: "I am very, very sorry to leave you, Mrs. Chopper. Pray think well of me, for, indeed, I have done nothing wrong."

"I am sure of it; but Nancy knows it all, and away you must go. I wish you were off; I'm getting fidgety about it, although I cannot bear to lose you; so good-bye at once, Peter, and God bless you! I hope we shall meet again yet."

"I hope so, indeed, Mrs. Chopper; for you have been very kind to me, as kind as a mother could be."

Mrs. Chopper hugged him to her breast, and then said, in a hurried tone, as she dropped on the bed, "There; go, go."

Nancy took up Joey's bundle in one hand and Joey by the other, and they went downstairs. As soon as they were in the street, Nancy turned short round, and went to the house where she usually slept, desiring Joey to wait a moment at

143

the door. She soon returned with her own bundle, and then, with a quick pace, walked on, desiring Joey to follow her. They proceeded in this manner until they were clear of the town, when Joey came up to Nancy, and said, " Thank you, Nancy ; I suppose we'd better part now."

" No, we don't part yet, Peter," replied Nancy.

" But where are you going, and why have you that bundle?"

" I am going with you, Peter," replied Nancy.

" But, Nancy——" replied Joey ; and then, after a pause : " I will do all I can for you—I will work for you—but I have no money, and I hope we shall not starve."

" Bless you, boy ! bless you for that kind feeling ! But we shall not starve ; I have Mrs. Chopper's leave to go with you ; indeed, she wished me so to do, and she has given me money for you—it is for you, although she said for both."

" She is very kind ; but why should you go with me, Nancy ? You have nothing to fear."

" We must not talk now, Peter ; let us walk on ; I have more to fear than you."

" How is that ?   I fear being taken up for that of which I am not guilty, but you have nothing to fear."

" Peter, dear," replied Nancy solemnly, " I do not fear for anything the world can do to me—but don't talk now ; let us go on."

CHAPTER XXVII

In which the wheel of fortune brings our hero's nose to the grindstone.

WHEN Nancy and our hero had proceeded about three miles on their way, Nancy slackened her pace, and they entered into conversation.

" Which way are you going?" demanded Joey.

" I'm cutting right across the country, Peter, or rather Joey, as I shall in future call you, for that is your real name—the marine told me it was Joseph Rushbrook ; is it not?"

" Yes, it is," replied Joey.

" Then in future I shall call you so, for I do not want to hear even a name which would remind me of the scene of my

144

misery; and, Joey, do you never call me Nancy again, the name is odious to me; call me Mary."

"I will if you wish it; but I cannot imagine why you should run away from Gravesend, Mary. What do you mean to do? I ran away from fear of being taken up."

"And I, Joey, do more; I fly from the wrath to come. You ask me what I intend to do; I will answer you in the words of the catechism which I used once to repeat, 'to lead a new life, have a thankful remembrance of Christ's death, and be in charity with all men.' I shall seek for service; I care not how humble—it will be good enough. I will sift cinders for brick-making, make bricks, do anything, as long as what I do is honest."

"I am very glad to hear you say that, Mary," replied Joey, "for I was always very fond of you."

"Yes, Joey, and you were the first who offered to do a kind thing for me for a long while; I have never forgotten it, and this night I have done something to repay it."

Nancy then entered into a detail of all that had passed between her and Furness, of which Joey had been ignorant, and which proved to him what a narrow escape he had had.

"I little thought you had done all this while I slept," replied Joey; "but I am very grateful, Mary."

"I know you are, so say no more about it. You see, Joey, he gave me all your history, and appears to believe that you committed the murder. I do not believe it; I do not believe you would do such a thing, although your gun might have gone off by accident."

"No, Mary, I did not do it, either on purpose or by accident; but you must ask me no more questions, for if I were put on my trial I should not reveal the secret."

"Then I will never speak to you any more about it, if I can help it. I have my own thoughts on the business, but now I drop it. It is nearly daylight, and we have walked a good many miles; I shall not be sorry to sit down and rest myself."

"Do you know how far we have to go before we come to any town, Mary?"

"We are not far from Maidstone; it is on our right, but it will be as well not to go through so large a town so near to Gravesend. Besides, some of the soldiers may know me. As

145   K

soon as we come to a good place, where we can find a drink of water, we will sit down and rest ourselves."

About a mile farther on they came to a small rivulet which crossed the road.

"This will do, Joey," said Nancy; "now we'll sit down."

It was then daylight; they took their seats on their bundles as soon as they had drunk from the stream.

"Now, Joey," said Mary (as we shall call her for the future), "let us see what money we have. Mrs. Chopper put all she had in my hands; poor, good old woman, bless her! Count it, Joey; it is yours."

"No, Mary; she gave it for both of us."

"Never mind; do you keep it: for you see, Joey, it might happen that you might have to run off at a moment's warning, and it would not do for you to be without money."

"If I was to run off at a minute's warning, I should then take it all with me, and it would not do for you to be left without any money, Mary; so we must halve it between us, although we will always make one purse."

"Well, be it so; for if you were robbed, or I were robbed, on the way, the other might escape."

They then divided the money, Joey putting his share into his pocket, and tying it in with a string. Mary dropped hers down into the usual deposit of women for bank-notes and billets-doux. As soon as this matter had been arranged, Mary opened her bundle, and took out a handkerchief, which she put on her shoulders; combed out the ringlets which she had worn, and dressed her hair flat on her temples; removed the gay ribbons from her bonnet, and substituted some plain brown in their stead.

"There," says she; "now, Joey, don't I look more respectable?"

"You do look more neat and more——"

"More modest, you would say, Joey. Well, and I hope in future to become what I look. But I look more fit to be your sister, Joey, for I have been thinking we had better pass off as brother and sister to avoid questioning. We must make out some story to agree in. Who shall we say that we are (as we dare not say who we really are)? I am looking out for service, and so are you, that's very clear; father and mother are both dead; father was a baker. That's all true, as far as relates to me ; and as you are my brother, why you must take my father and mother. It's no very great story, after all."

" But it won't do to say we came from Gravesend."

" No ; we need not say that, and yet tell no story ; the village we passed through last night was Wrotham, so we came from thence."

" But where do you think of going, Mary ? "

" A good way farther off yet ; at all events, before we look out for service, we will get into another county. Now, if you are ready, we will go on, Joey, and look out for some breakfast, and then I shall be able to change my gown for a quieter one."

In half-an-hour they arrived at a village, and went into a public-house. Mary went upstairs and changed her dress ; and now that she had completed her arrangements, she looked a very pretty, modest young woman, and none could have supposed that the day before she had been flaunting in the street of a seafaring town. Inquiries were made, as might be supposed, and Mary replied that she was going to service, and that her brother was escorting her. They had their breakfast, and after resting two hours, they proceeded on their journey.

For some days they travelled more deliberately, until they found themselves in the village of Manstone, in Dorsetshire, where they, as usual, put up at an humble public-house. Here Mary told a different story ; she had been disappointed in a situation, and they intended to go back to their native town.

The landlady of the hotel was prepossessed in favour of such a very pretty girl as Mary, as well as with the appearance of Joey, who, although in his sailor's dress, was very superior in carriage and manners to a boy in his supposed station in life, and she said that if they would remain there a few days she would try to procure them some situation. The third day after their arrival she informed Mary that she had heard of a situation as under-housemaid at the squire's, about a mile off, if she would like to take it, and Mary gladly consented. Mrs. Derborough sent up word, and received orders for Mary to make her appearance, and Mary accordingly went up to the hall, accompanied by Joey. When she arrived there, and made known her business, she was desired to wait in the servants' hall until she was sent for. In about a quarter of an hour she was summoned, and, leaving Joey in the hall, she went up to see the lady of the house, who inquired whether she had ever been out at service before, and if she had a good character.

Mary replied that she had never been out at service, and that she had no character at all (which, by-the-bye, was very true). The lady of the house smiled at this apparently *naïve* answer from so very modest-looking and pretty a girl, and asked who her parents were.

To this question Mary's answer was ready, and she further added that she had left home in search of a place, and had been disappointed; that her father and mother were dead, but her brother was down below, and had escorted her; and that Mrs. Chopper was an old friend of her mother's, and could answer to her character.

The lady was prepossessed by Mary's appearance, by the report of Mrs. Derborough, and by the respectability of her brother travelling with her, and agreed to try her; but at the same time said she must have Mrs. Chopper's address, that she might write to her; but, the place being vacant, she might come to-morrow morning: her wages were named, and immediately accepted; and thus did Mary obtain her situation.

People say you cannot be too particular when you choose servants; and, to a certain degree, this is true; but this extreme caution, however selfishness and prudence may dictate it, is but too often the cause of servants who have committed an error, and have in consequence been refused a character, being driven to destitution and misery, when they had a full intention, and would have, had they been permitted, redeemed their transgression.

Mary was resolved to be a good and honest girl. Had the lady of the house been very particular, and had others to whom she might afterwards have applied been the same, all her good intentions might have been frustrated, and she might have been driven to despair, if not to her former evil courses. It is perhaps fortunate that everybody in the world is not so particular as your very good people, and that there is an occasional loophole by which those who have erred are permitted to return to virtue. Mary left the room delighted with her success, and went down to Joey in the servants' hall. The servants soon found out from Mary that she was coming to the house, and one of the men chucked her under the chin, and told her she was a very pretty girl. Mary drew back, and Joey immediately resented the liberty, stating that he would not allow any man to insult his sister, for Joey was wise enough to see that he could not do a better thing to serve Mary. The servant was insolent in return, and threatened to chastise Joey, and ordered him to leave the house. The women took our hero's part. The housekeeper came down at the time, and hearing the cause of the dispute, was angry with the footman; the butler took the side of the footman; and the end of it was that the voices were at the highest pitch when the bell rang, and the men being obliged to answer it, the women were for the time left in possession of the field.

"What is that noise below?" inquired the master of the house.

"It is a boy, sir—the brother, I believe, of the girl who has come as under-housemaid, who has been making a disturbance."

"Desire him to leave the house instantly."

"Yes, sir," replied the butler, who went down to enforce the order.

Little did the master of the house imagine that in giving that order he was turning out of the house his own son; for the squire was no other than Mr. Austin. Little did the inconsolable Mrs. Austin fancy that her dear, lamented boy was at that moment under the same roof with her, and been driven out of it by her menials; but such was the case. So Joey and Mary quitted the hall, and bent their way back to the village inn.

"Well, Mary," said Joey, "I am very glad that you have found a situation."

"And so I am very thankful, indeed, Joey," replied she; "and only hope that you will be able to get one somewhere about here also, and then we may occasionally see something of one another."

"No, Mary," replied Joey, "I shall not look for a situation about here; the only reason I had for wishing it was that I might see you; but that will be impossible now."

"Why so?"

"Do you think that I will ever put my foot into that house again, after the manner I was treated to-day? Never."

"I was afraid so," replied Mary mournfully.

"No, Mary, I am happy that you are provided for; for I can seek my own fortune, and I will write to you, and let you know what I do; and you will write to me, Mary, won't you?"

"It will be the greatest pleasure that will be left to me, Joey; for I love you as dearly as if you were my own brother."

The next day our hero and Mary parted, with many tears on her side, and much sorrow on his. Joey refused to take more of the money than what he had in his possession, but promised, in case of need, to apply to Mary, who said that she would hoard up everything for him; and she kept her word. Joey, having escorted Mary to the hall lodge, remained at the inn till the next morning, and then set off once more on his travels.

Our hero started at break of day, and had walked, by a western road, from Manstone, about six miles, when he met two men coming towards him. They were most miserably clad —neither of them had shoes or stockings; one had only a waistcoat and a pair of trousers, with a sack on his back; the other had a pair of blue trousers torn to ribbons, a Guernsey frock, and a tarpaulin hat. They appeared what they represented themselves to be, when they demanded charity, two wrecked seamen, who were travelling to a northern port to obtain employment; but had these fellows been questioned by a sailor, he would soon have discovered, by their total ignorance of anything nautical, that they were impostors. Perhaps there is no plan more successful than this, which is now carried on to an enormous extent by a set of rogues and depredators, who occasionally request charity, but too often extort it, and add to their spoils by robbing and plundering everything in their way. It is impossible for people in this country to ascertain the truth of the assertions of these vagabonds, and it appears unfeeling to refuse assistance to a poor seaman who has lost his all: even the cottager offers his mite, and thus do they levy upon the public to an extent which is scarcely credible; but it should be known that, in all cases of shipwreck, sailors are now invariably relieved and decently clothed, and supplied with the means of travelling to obtain employment; and whenever a man appeals for charity in a half-naked state, he is invariably an impostor or a worthless scoundrel.

The two men were talking loud and laughing when they approached our hero. As soon as they came near, they looked

"Joey, aiming the stone with great precision, hit him on the
forehead, and the fellow fell down senseless."

hard at him, and stopped right before him, so as to block up
the footpath.

"Hilloa, my little sailor! where are you bound to?" said
one to Joey, who had his common sailor's dress on.

"And, I say, what have you got in that bundle?" said the
other; "and how are you off for brads?—haven't you something to spare for brother-seamen? Come, feel in your
pockets; or shall I feel for you?"

Joey did not much like this exordium; he replied, stepping
into the road at the same time, "I've no money, and the
bundle contains my clothes."

"Come, come," said the first, "you're not going to get off
that way. If you don't wish your brains beaten out, you'll
just hand over that bundle for me to examine;" and so saying,
the man stepped into the road towards Joey, who continued
to retreat to the opposite side.

There was no footpath at the side of the road to which
Joey retreated, but a very thick quick-set hedge, much too
strong for any man to force his way through. Joey perceived
this; and as the man came at him to seize his bundle, he
contrived by a great effort to swing it over the hedge into
the field on the other side. The man, exasperated at this
measure on the part of our hero, ran to seize him; but Joey
dodged under him, and ran away down the road for a few
yards, where he picked up a heavy stone for his defence, and
there remained, prepared to defend himself, and not lose his
bundle if he could help it.

"You get hold of him, Bill, while I go round for the
bundle," said the man who had followed across the road, and
he immediately set off to find the gate, or some entrance into
the field, while the other man made after Joey. Our hero
retreated at full speed; the man followed, but could not keep
pace with our hero, as the road was newly gravelled, and he
had no shoes. Joey, perceiving this, slackened his pace, and
when the man was close to him, turned short round, and
aiming the stone with great precision, hit him on the forehead,
and the fellow fell down senseless. In the meantime the
other miscreant had taken the road in the opposite direction
to look for the gate; and Joey, now rid of his assailant, perceived that in the hedge, opposite to the part of the road
where he now stood, there was a gap which he could get

through. He scrambled into the field, and ran for his bundle. The other man, who had been delayed, the gate being locked, and fenced with thorns, had but just gained the field when Joey had his bundle in his possession. Our hero caught it up, and ran like lightning to the gap, tossed over his bundle, and followed it, while the man was still a hundred yards from him. Once more in the highroad, Joey took to his heels, and having run about two hundred yards, he looked back to ascertain if he was pursued, and perceived the man standing over his comrade, who was lying where he had fallen. Satisfied that he was now safe, Joey pursued his journey at a less rapid rate, although he continued to look back every minute, just by way of precaution; but the fellows, although they would not lose an opportunity of what appeared such an easy robbery, had their own reasons for continuing their journey, and getting away from that part of the country.

Our hero pursued his way for two miles, looking out for some water by the wayside to quench his thirst, when he observed in the distance that there was something lying on the roadside. As he came nearer he made it out to be a man prostrate on the grass, apparently asleep, and a few yards from where the man lay was a knife-grinder's wheel, and a few other articles in the use of a travelling tinker; a fire, nearly extinct, was throwing up a tiny column of smoke, and a saucepan, which appeared to have been upset, was lying beside it. There was something in the scene before him which created a suspicion in the mind of our hero that all was not right; so, instead of passing on, he walked right up to where the man lay, and soon discovered that his face and dress were bloody. Joey knelt down by the side of him, and found that he was senseless but breathing heavily. Joey untied the handkerchief which was round his neck, and which was apparently very tight, and almost immediately afterwards the man appeared relieved, and opened his eyes. After a little time he contrived to utter one word—"Water!" and Joey, taking up the empty saucepan, proceeded in search of it. He soon found some, and brought it back. The tinker had greatly recovered during his absence, and as soon as he had drunk the water sat upright.

"Don't leave me, boy," said the tinker; "I feel very faint."

"I will stay by you as long as I can be of any use to you," replied Joey; "what has happened?"

"Robbed and almost murdered!" replied the man, with a groan.

"Was it by those two rascals without shoes and stockings who attempted to rob me?" inquired Joey.

"Yes, the same, I've no doubt. I must lie down for a time, my head is so bad," replied the man, dropping back upon the grass.

In a few minutes the exhausted man fell asleep, and Joey remained sitting by his side for nearly two hours. At last, his new companion awoke, raised himself up, and, dipping his handkerchief into the saucepan of water, washed the blood from his head and face.

"This might have been worse, my little fellow," said he to Joey, after he had wiped his face; "one of those rascals nearly throttled me, he pulled my handkerchief so tight. Well, this is a wicked world, this, to take away a fellow-creature's life for thirteenpence-halfpenny, for that was all the money they found in my pocket. I thought an itinerant tinker was safe from highway robbery, at all events. Did you not say that they attacked you, or did I dream it?"

"I did say so; it was no dream."

"And how did a little midge like you escape?"

Joey gave the tinker a detail of what had occurred.

"Cleverly done, boy, and kindly done now to come to my help, and to remain by me. I was going down the road, and as you have come down, I presume we are going the same way," replied the tinker.

"Do you feel strong enough to walk now?"

"Yes, I think I can; but there's the grindstone."

"Oh, I'll wheel that for you."

"Do, that's a good boy, for I tremble very much, and it would be too heavy for me now."

Joey fixed his bundle, with the saucepan, &c., upon the knife-grinder's wheel, and rolled it along the road, followed by the tinker, until they came to a small hamlet, about two miles from the spot from which they had started; they halted when they were fifty yards from the first cottage, and the tinker, having selected a dry place under the hedge, said, "I must stop here a little while."

Joey, who had heard the tinker say that the men had robbed him of thirteenpence-halfpenny, imagined that he was destitute, and as he wished to proceed on his way, he took out two shillings, and held them out to the man, saying, "This will keep you till you can earn some more. Good-bye now ; I must go on."

The tinker looked at Joey. "You're a kind-hearted lad, at all events, and a clever, bold one, if I mistake not," said he ; "put up your money, nevertheless, for I do not want any. I have plenty, if they had only known where to look for it."

Joey was examining his new companion during the time that he was speaking to him. There was a free and independent bearing about the man, and a refinement of manner and speech very different from what might be expected from one in so humble a situation. The tinker perceived this scrutiny, and, after meeting our hero's glance, said, "Well, what are you thinking of now ? "

"I was thinking that you have not always been a tinker."

"And I fancy that you have not always been a sailor, my young master ; but, however, oblige me by going into the village and getting some breakfast for us. I will pay you the money when you return, and then we can talk a little."

Joey went into the village, and finding a small chandler's shop, bought some bread and cheese, and a large mug which held a quart of beer, both of which he also purchased, and then went back to the tinker. As soon as they had made their breakfast, Joey rose up and said—"I must go on now ; I hope you'll find yourself better to-morrow."

"Are you in a very great hurry, my lad ?" inquired the tinker.

"I want to find some employment," replied Joey ; "and, therefore, I must look for it."

"Tell me what employment you want. What can you do ? "

"I don't exactly know ; I have been keeping accounts for a person."

"Then you are a scholar, and not a seafaring person ? "

"I am not a sailor, if you mean that ; but I have been on the river."

"Well, if you wish to get employment, as I know this country well and a great many people, I think I may help you. At all events, a few days can make no difference ; for you see, my boy, to-morrow I shall be able to work, and then, I'll answer for it, I'll find meat and drink for both of us ; so, what do you say? Suppose you stay with me, and we'll travel together for a few days, and when I have found work that will suit you, then we can part?"

" I will, if you wish it," replied Joey.

" Then that's agreed," said the tinker; " I should like to do you a good turn before we part, and I hope I shall be able; at all events, if you stay with me a little while, I will teach you a trade which will serve you when all others fail."

"What, to mend kettles and to grind knives?"

" Exactly; and, depend upon it, if you would be sure of gaining your livelihood, you will choose a profession which will not depend upon the caprice of others, or upon patronage. Kettles, my boy, will wear out, knives will get blunt, and, therefore, for a good trade give me ' kettles to mend, knives to grind.' I've tried many trades, and there is none that suits me so well. And now that we've had our breakfast, we may just as well look out for lodgings for the night, for I suppose you would not like the heavens for your canopy, which I very often prefer. Now, put yourself to the wheel, and I'll try my old quarters."

The knife-grinder walked into the village, followed by Joey, who rolled the wheel, until they stopped at a cottage, where he was immediately recognised and welcomed. Joey was ordered to put the wheel under a shed, and then followed the tinker into the cottage. The latter told his story, which created a good deal of surprise and indignation, and then complained of his head and retired to lie down, while Joey amused himself with the children. They ate and slept there that night, the people refusing to take anything for their reception. The next day the tinker was quite recovered, and having mended a kettle and ground three or four knives for his hostess, he set off again, followed by Joey, who rolled the wheel

CHAPTER XXVIII

On the science of tinkering and the art of writing despatches.

THEY had proceeded about two miles when the tinker said, " Come, my lad, let us sit down now, and rest ourselves a bit, for it is past noon, and you must be tired with shoving that wheel along. I would have taken it from you before this, but the fact is, I'm rather stiff yet about the head and shoulders; I feel it more than I thought I should. Here's a nice spot; I like to sit down under a tree, not too well covered with leaves, like this ash; I like to see the sunshine playing here and there upon the green grass, shifting its spots as the leaves are rustled by the wind. Now, let us lie down here, and not care a fig for the world. I am a philosopher; do you know that?"

"I don't exactly know what it means; a very clever, good man—is it not?"

"Well, not exactly; a man may be a philosopher without being very good, or without being very clever. A philosopher is a man who never frets about anything, cares about nothing, is contented with a little, and doesn't envy any one who appears better off than himself, at least that is my school of philosophy. You stare, boy, to hear a tinker talk in this way—I perceive that; but you must know that I am a tinker by choice; and I have tried many other professions before, all of which have disgusted me."

"What other professions have you been?"

"I have been—let me see—I almost forget; but I'll begin at the beginning. My father was a gentleman, and until I was fourteen years old I was a gentleman, or the son of one; then he died, and that profession was over, for he left nothing. My mother married again, and left me; she left me at school, and the master kept me there for a year, in hopes of being paid; but, hearing nothing of my mother, and not knowing what to do with me, he at last (for he was a kind man) installed me as under-usher of the school; for, you see, my education had been good, and I was well qualified for the situation, as far as capability went: it was rather a bathos, though, to sink from a gentleman's son to an under-usher; but I was not a philosopher at that time. I handed the toast to the master and mistress, the head-ushers and parlour-boarders, but was not allowed any myself; I taught Latin and Greek, and English grammar, to the little boys, who made faces at me, and put crooked pins on the bottom of my chair; I walked at the head of the string when they went out for an airing, and walked upstairs the last when it was time to go to bed. I had all the drudgery, and none of the comforts; I was up first, and held answerable for all deficiencies; I had to examine all their nasty little trousers, and hold weekly conversation with the botcher, as to the possibility of repairs ; to run out if a hen cackled, that the boys should not get the egg; to wipe the noses of my mistress's children, and carry them if they roared ; to pay for all broken glass, if I could not discover the culprit ; to account for all bad smells, for all noise, and for all ink spilled; to make all the pens, and to keep one hundred boys silent and attentive at church ; for all which, with deductions, I received £40 a year and found my own washing. I stayed two years, during which time I contrived to save about £6; and with that, one fine morning, I set off on my travels, fully satisfied that, come what would, I could not change for the worse."

"Then you were about in the position that I'm in now," said Joey, laughing.

"Yes, thereabouts ; only a little older, I should imagine. I set off with good hopes, but soon found that nobody wanted educated people—they were a complete drug. At last I obtained a situation as waiter at a posting-house on the road, where I ran along all day long to the tinkling of bells, with hot brandy-and-water ever under my nose; I answered all the bells, but the head waiter took all the money. However, I made acquaintances there, and at last obtained a situation as clerk to a corn-chandler, where I kept the books; but he failed, and then I was handed over to the miller, and covered with flour for the whole time I was in his service. I stayed there till I had an offer from a coal-merchant (that was going from white to black); but, however, it was a better place. Then, by mere chance, I obtained the situation of clerk on board of a fourteen-gun brig, and cruised in the Channel for six months ; but, as I found that there was no chance of being a purser, and as I hated the confinement and discipline of a man-of-war, I cut and run as soon as I obtained my pay. Then I was shopman at a draper's, which was abominable, for if the customers would not buy the goods I got all the blame ; besides, I had to clean my master's boots and my mistress's shoes, and dine in the kitchen on scraps, with a slipshod, squinting girl, who made love to me. Then I was a warehouseman ; but they soon tacked on to it the office of light porter, and I had to carry weights enough to break my back. At last I obtained a situation as foreman in a tinman and cutler's shop, and by being constantly sent into the workshop I learnt something of the trade; I had made up my mind not to remain much longer, and I paid attention, receiving now and then a lesson from the workmen, till I found that I could do very well; for, you see, it's a very simple sort of business, after all."

"But still a travelling tinker is not so respectable as being in any of the situations you were in before," replied Joey.

"There I must beg your pardon, my good lad; I had often serious thoughts upon the subject, and I argued as follows :— What is the best profession in this world of ours ?—that of a gentleman; for a gentleman does not work, he has liberty to go where he pleases, he is not controlled, and is his own master. Many a man considers himself a gentleman who has not the indispensables that must complete the profession. A clerk in the Treasury, or public offices, considers himself a gentleman; and so he is by birth, but not by *profession;* for he is not his own master, but is as much tied down to his desk as the clerk in a banker's counting-house, or in a shop. A gentleman by profession must be his own master, and independent; and how few there are in this world who can say so ! Soldiers and sailors are obliged to obey orders, and therefore I do not put them down as perfect gentlemen according to my ideas of what a gentleman should be. I doubt whether the prime minister can be considered a gentleman until after he is turned out of office. Do you understand me, boy ?"

"Oh yes, I understand what you mean by a gentleman; I recollect reading a story of a negro who came to this country, and who said that the pig was the only gentleman in the country, for he was the only living being who did not work."

"The negro was not far wrong," resumed the tinker. "Well, after thinking a long while, I came to the decision that, as I could not be a perfect gentleman, I would be the nearest thing to it that was possible; and I considered that the most enviable situation was that of a travelling tinker. I learned enough of the trade, saved money to purchase a knife-grinder's wheel, and here I have been in this capacity for nearly ten years."

"And do you hold to the opinion that you formed ?"

"I do; for, look you, work I must; therefore, the only question was, to take up the work that was lightest and paid best. I know no trade where you can gain so much with so little capital and so little labour. Then, I am not controlled by any living being; I have my liberty and independence : I go where I please, stop where I please, work when I please, and idle when I please; and never know what it is to want a night's lodging. Show me any other profession which can say the same! I might be better clothed—I might be considered more respectable; but I am a philosopher, and despise all that; I earn as much as I want, and do very little work for it. I can grind knives and scissors and mend kettles enough in one day to provide for a whole week; for instance, I can grind a knife in two minutes, for which I receive twopence. Now, allowing that I work twelve hours in the day, at the rate of one penny per minute, I should earn £3 per day, which, deducting Sundays, is £939 a year. Put that against £40 a year as a drudge to a school, or confined to a desk in a shop, or any other profession, and you see how lucrative mine is in proportion. Then I am under no control; not ordered here or there, like a general or admiral; not attacked in the House of Commons or Lords, like a prime minister; on the contrary, half a day's work out of the seven is all I require; and I therefore assert that my profession is nearer to that of a gentleman than any other that I know of."

"It may be as you style it, but you don't look much like one," replied Joey, laughing.

"That's prejudice; my clothes keep me as warm as if they were of the best materials, and quite new. I enjoy my victuals quite as much as a well-dressed gentleman does—perhaps more; I can indulge in my own thoughts; I have leisure to read all my favourite authors, and can afford to purchase new books. Besides, as I must work a little, it is pleasant to feel that I am always in request, and respected by those who employ me."

"Respected! on what account?"

"Because I am always wanted, and therefore always welcome. It is the little things of this life which annoy, not the great; and a kettle that won't hold water, or a knife that won't cut, are always objects of execration; and as people heap their anathemas upon the kettle and the knife, so do they long for my return; and when I come they are glad to see me, glad to pay me, and glad to find that their knives are sharp, and their kettles, thrown on one side, are useful again,

159

at a trifling charge. I add to people's comforts; I become necessary to every poor person in the cottages; and there-fore, they like me and respect me. And, indeed, if it is only considered how many oaths and execrations are used when a person is hacking and sawing away with a knife which will not cut, and how by my wheel I do away with the cause of crime, I think that a travelling tinker may be considered, as to his moral influence upon society, more important than any parson in his pulpit. You observe that I have not rendered the profession degrading by marriage, as many do."

" How do you mean?"

" I hold that, whatever may be the means of a gentleman, he must be considered to lose the most precious advantages appertaining to his profession when he marries; for he loses his liberty, and can no longer be said to be under no control. It is very well for other professions to marry, as the world must be peopled; but a gentleman never should. It is true, he may contrive to leave his clog at home, but then he pays dear for a useless and galling appendage; but, in my situa-tion as a travelling tinker, I could not have done so; I must have dragged my clog after me through the mud and mire, and have had a very different reception than what I have at present."

" Why so?"

" Why, a man may stroll about the country by himself— find lodging and entertainment for himself; but not so if he had a wife in rags, and two or three dirty children at his heels. A single man, in every stage of society, if he pays his own way, more easily finds admission than a married one —that is, because the women regulate it; and, although they will receive him as a tinker, they invariably object to his wife, who is considered and stigmatised as the tinker's trull. No, that would not do—a wife would detract from my re-spectability, and add very much to my cares."

" But have you no home, then, anywhere?"

" Why, yes, I have, like all single men on the *pavé*, as the French say—just a sort of 'chambers' to keep my property in, which will accumulate in spite of me."

" Where are they?"

" In Dudstone, to which place I am now going. I have a room for six pounds a year; and the woman in the house takes charge of everything during my absence. And now, my boy, what is your name?"

"Joey Atherton," replied our hero, who had made up his mind to take the surname of his adopted sister, Nancy.

"Well, Joey, do you agree with me that my profession is a good one, and are you willing to learn it? If so, I will teach you."

"I shall be very glad to learn it, because it may one day be useful; but I am not sure that I should like to follow it."

"You will probably change your opinion; at all events, give it a fair trial. In a month or so you will have the theory of it by heart, and then we will come to the practice."

"How do you mean?"

"It's of no use your attempting anything till you're well grounded in the theory of the art, which you will gain by using your eyes. All you have to do at first is to look on; watch me when I grind a knife or a pair of scissors; be attentive when you see me soldering a pot, or putting a patch upon a kettle; see how I turn my hand when I'm grinding, how I beat out the iron when I mend; and learn how to heat the tools when I solder. In a month you will know how things are to be done in theory, and after that we shall come to the practice. One only thing, in the way of practice, must you enter upon at once, and that is turning the wheel with your foot; for you must learn to do it so mechanically, that you are not aware that you are doing it, otherwise you cannot devote your whole attention to the scissors or knife in your hand."

"And do you really like your present life, then, wandering about from place to place?"

"To be sure I do. I am my own master; go where I like; stop where I like; pay no taxes or rates. I still retain all the gentleman except the dress, which I can resume when I please. Besides, mine is a philanthropic profession; I go about doing good, and I've the means of resenting an affront like a despot."

"As how?"

"Why, you see, we travellers never interfere in each other's beats; mine is a circuit of many miles of country, and at the rate I travel it is somewhat about three months until I am at the same place again; they must wait for me if they want their jobs done, for they cannot get any one else. In one village they played me a trick one Saturday night, when all the men were at the ale-house, and the consequence was, I cut the village for a year; and there never was such a village full of old kettles and blunt knives in consequence. However, they sent me a deputation, hoping I would forget what had passed, and I pardoned them."

"What is your name?" inquired Joey.

"Augustus Spikeman. My father was Augustus Spikeman, Esq.; I was Master Augustus Spikeman, and now I'm Spikeman the tinker; so now we'll go on again. I have nearly come to the end of my beat; in two days we shall be at Dudstone, where I have my room, and where we shall probably remain for some days before we start again."

In the afternoon they arrived at a small hamlet, where they supped and slept. Spikeman was very busy till noon grinding and repairing; they then continued their journey, and on the second day, having waited outside the town till it was dusk, Spikeman left his wheel in the charge of the landlord of a small ale-house, to whom he appeared well known, then walked with Joey to the house in which he had a room, and led him upstairs to his apartment.

When our hero entered the chamber of Spikeman, he was very much surprised to find it was spacious, light, and airy, and very clean. A large bed was in one corner; a sofa, mahogany table, chest of drawers, and chairs, composed the furniture; there was a good-sized looking-glass over the chimney-piece, and several shelves of books round the room. Desiring Joey to sit down and take a book, Spikeman rang for water, shaved off his beard, which had grown nearly half an inch long, washed himself, and then put on clean linen, and a very neat suit of clothes. When he was completely dressed, Joey could hardly believe that it was the same person. Upon Joey expressing his astonishment, Spikeman replied, "You see, my lad, there is no one in this town who knows what my real profession is. I always go out and return at dusk, and the travelling tinker is not recognised; not that I care for it so much, only other people do, and I respect their prejudices. They know that I am in the ironmongery line, and that is all; so I always make it a rule to enjoy myself after my circuit, and live like a gentleman till part of my money is gone, and

then I set out again. I am acquainted with a good many
highly respectable people in this town, and that is the reason
why I said I could be of service to you. Have you any better
clothes ? "

" Yes ; much better."

" Then dress yourself in them, and keep those you wear
for our travels."

Joey did as he was requested, and Spikeman then proposed
that they should make a call at a friend's, where he would
introduce our hero as his nephew. They set off, and soon
came to the front of a neat-looking house, at the door of
which Spikeman rapped. The door was opened by one of
the daughters of the house, who, on seeing him, cried out,
" Dear me, Mr. Spikeman, is this you ? Why, where have
you been all this while ? "

" About the country for orders, Miss Amelia," replied
Spikeman ; " business must be attended to."

" Well, come in ; mother will be glad to see you," replied
the girl, at the same time opening the door of the sitting-
room for them to enter.

" Mr. Spikeman, as I live ! " exclaimed another girl, jumping up, and seizing his hand.

" Well, Mr. Spikeman, it's an age since we have seen you,"
said the mother, " so now sit down and tell us all the news ;
and Ophelia, my love, get tea ready ; and who is it you have
with you, Mr. Spikeman ? "

" My little nephew, madam ; he is about to enter into the
mysteries of the cutlery trade."

" Indeed ! well, I suppose, as you are looking out for a
successor, you soon intend to retire from business and take a
wife, Mr. Spikeman ? "

" Why, I suppose it will be my fate one of these days,"
replied Spikeman ; " but that's an affair that requires some
consideration."

" Very true, Mr. Spikeman, it is a serious affair," replied
the old lady ; " and I can assure you that neither my Ophelia
nor Amelia should marry a man, with my consent, without I
was convinced the gentleman considered it a very serious
affair. It makes or mars a man, as the saying is."

" Well, Miss Ophelia, have you read all the books I lent
you the last time I was here ? "

163

"Yes, that they have, both of them," replied the old lady; "they are so fond of poetry."

"But we've often wished that you were here to read to us," replied Miss Amelia, "you do read so beautifully; will you read to us after tea?"

"Certainly, with much pleasure."

Miss Ophelia now entered with the tea-tray; she and her sister then went into the kitchen to make some toast, and to see to the kettle boiling, while Mr. Spikeman continued in conversation with the mother. Mrs. James was the widow of a draper in the town, who had, at his death, left her sufficient to live quietly and respectably with her daughters, who were both very good, amiable girls; and it must be acknowledged, neither of them unwilling to listen to the addresses of Mr. Spikeman had he been so inclined; but they began to think that Mr. Spikeman was not a marrying man, which, as the reader must know by this time, was the fact.

The evening passed very pleasantly. Mr. Spikeman took a volume of poetry, and, as Miss Ophelia had said, he did read very beautifully: so much so, that Joey was in admiration, for he had never yet known the power produced by good reading. At ten o'clock they took their leave, and returned to Spikeman's domicile.

As soon as they were upstairs, and candles lighted, Spikeman sat down on the sofa. "You see, Joey," said he, "that it is necessary not to mention the knife-grinder's wheel, as it would make a difference in my reception. All gentlemen do not gain their livelihood as honestly as I do; but still, prejudices are not to be overcome. You did me a kind act, and I wished to return it; I could not do so without letting you into this little secret, but I have seen enough of you to think you can be trusted."

"I should hope so," replied Joey: "I have learnt caution, young as I am."

"That I have perceived already, and therefore I have said enough on the subject. I have but one bed, and you must sleep with me, as you did on our travels."

The next morning the old woman of the house brought up their breakfast. Spikeman lived in a very comfortable way, very different to what he did as a travelling tinker; and he really appeared to Joey to be, with the exception of his conversation, which was always superior, a very different person from what he was when Joey first fell in with him. For many days they remained at Dudstone, visiting the different houses, and were always well received.

"You appear so well known, and so well liked in this town," observed Joey, "I wonder you do not set up a business, particularly as you say you have money in the bank."

"If I did, Joey, I should no longer be happy, no longer be my own master, and do as I please; in fact, I should no longer be the gentleman, that is, the gentleman by profession, as near as I can be one—the man who has his liberty, and enjoys it. No, no, boy; I have tried almost everything, and have come to my own conclusions. Have you been reading the book I gave you?"

"Yes; I have nearly finished it?"

"I am glad to see that you like reading. Nothing so much improves or enlarges the mind. You must never let a day pass without reading two or three hours, and when we travel again, and are alone by the wayside, we will read together: I will choose some books on purpose."

"I should like very much to write to my sister Mary," said Joey.

"Do so, and tell her that you have employment; but do not say exactly how. There are pens and paper in the drawer. Stop, I will find them for you." Spikeman went to the drawer, and when taking out the pens and paper, laid hold of some manuscript writing. "By-the-bye," said he, laughing, "I told you, Joey, that I had been a captain's clerk on board the *Weasel*, a fourteen-gun brig; I wrote the captain's despatches for him; and here are two of them of which I kept copies, that I might laugh over them occasionally. I wrote all his letters; for he was no great penman in the first place, and had a very great confusion of ideas in the second. He certainly was indebted to me, as you will acknowledge, when you hear what I read and tell you. I served under him, cruising in the Channel; and I flatter myself that it was entirely through my writings that he got his promotion. He is now Captain Alcibiades Ajax Boggs, and all through me. We were cruising off the coast of France, close in to Ushant, where we perceived a fleet of small vessels, called chasse-marées (coasting luggers), laden with wine, coming round; and as we did not know of

165

any batteries thereabouts, we ran in to attempt a capture.
We cut off three of them, but just as we had compelled them,
by firing broadsides into them, to lower their sails, a battery,
which our commander did not know anything of, opened fire
upon us, and before we could get out of range, which we did
as soon as we could, one shot came in on deck, and cut the
topsail halyard's fall, at the very time that the men were
hoisting the sail (for we had been shaking another reef out),
and the rope being divided, as the men were hauling upon it,
of course they all tumbled on the deck, one over another.
The other shot struck our foremast, and chipped off a large
slice, besides cutting away one of the shrouds, and the signal
halyards. Now, you do not know enough about ships to
understand that there was very little harm done, or that the
coasting vessels were very small, with only three or four men
on board of each of them; it therefore required some little
management to make a flaming despatch. But I did it—
only listen, now—I have begun in the true Nelson style :—

"'TO THE SECRETARY OF THE ADMIRALTY.

"'SIR,—It has pleased the Great Disposer to grant a
decided victory to his Majesty's arms, through the efforts of
the vessel which I have the honour to command. On the
23rd day of August last, Ushant then bearing S.W. ¾ West,
wind W., distant from three to four leagues, perceived an
enemy's fleet, of three-masted vessels, rounding the point,
with the hopes, I presume, of gaining the port of Cherbourg.
Convinced that I should have every support from the gallant
officers and true British tars under my command, I immediately
bore down to the attack; the movements of the enemy fully
proved that they were astounded at the boldness of the
manœuvre, and instead of keeping their line, they soon
separated, and sheered off in different directions, so as to
receive the support of their batteries.'

"You see, Joey, I have said three-masted vessels, which
implies ships, although in this case, they were only small
coasting luggers.

"'In half-an-hour we were sufficiently close to the main
body to open our fire, and broadside after broadside were

poured in, answered by the batteries on the coast, with un-
erring aim. Notwithstanding the unequal contest, I have
the pleasure of informing you, that in less than half-an-hour
we succeeded in capturing three of the vessels (named as per
margin), and finding nothing more could be done for the
honour of his Majesty's arms, as soon as we could take possession, I considered it my duty to haul off from the incessant
and galling fire of the batteries.

" ' In this well-fought and successful contest, I trust that
the British flag has not been tarnished. What the enemy's
loss may have been it is impossible to say ; they acknowledge
themselves, however, that it has been severe.' "

" But did the enemy lose any men ? " demanded Joey.

" Not one; but you observe I do not say loss of life, although the Admiralty may think I refer to it—that's not my
fault. But I was perfectly correct in saying the enemy's
loss was great ; for the poor devils who were in the chasse-
marées, when they were brought on board, wrung their
hands, and said, that they had *lost their all*. Now, what loss
can be greater than *all* ?

" ' His Majesty's vessel is much injured in her spars and
rigging from the precision of the enemy's fire; her lower
rigging — running rigging being cut away, her foremast
severely wounded, and, I regret to add, severely injured in
the hull ; but such was the activity of the officers and men,
that with the exception of the foremast, which will require
the services of the dockyard, in twenty-four hours we were
ready to resume the contest. I am happy to say, that although
we have many men hurt, we have none killed; and I trust
that, under the care of the surgeon, they will, most of them,
be soon able to resume their duty.' "

" But you had no men wounded ? " interrupted Joey.

" None wounded ! I don't say wounded, I only say hurt.
Didn't a dozen of the men, who were hoisting the main-
topsail when the fall was cut away, all tumble backwards on
the deck ? And do you think they were not hurt by the
fall ?—of course they were ; besides, one man nearly had
his finger jammed off, and another burnt his hand by

167

putting too much powder to the touch-hole of his car-ronade. So I continue :—

"' It now becomes my duty to point out to their Lordships the very meritorious conduct of Mr. John Smith, an old and deserving officer, Mr. James Hammond, Mr. Cross, and Mr. Byfleet ; indeed, I may say that all the officers under my command vied in their exertions for the honour of the British flag.'

"You see the commander had quarrelled with some of his officers at that time, and would not mention them. I tried all I could to persuade him, but he was obstinate.

"' I have the honour to return a list of casualties, and the names of the vessels taken, and have the honour to be, Sir, your obedient servant, ALCIBIADES AJAX BOGGS.

"' Report of killed and wounded on board of his Majesty's brig *Weasel*, in the action of the 23rd of August :—Killed, none ; wounds and contusions, John Potts, William Smith, Thomas Snaggs, William Walker, and Peter Potter, able seamen ; John Hobbs, Timothy Stout, and Walter Pye, marines.

"' Return of vessels captured in the action of the 23rd of August, by his Majesty's brig *Weasel :—Notre Dame de Miséricorde*, de Rochelle ; *La Vengeur*, de Bourdeaux ; *L'Etoile du Matin*, de Charent.

(Signed)   "' ALCIBIADES AJAX BOGGS,
"' Commander.' "

"Well, I'm sure, if you had not told me otherwise, I should have thought it had been a very hard fight."

" That's what they did at the Admiralty, and just what we wanted ; but now I come to my other despatch, which obtained the rank for my captain ; and upon which I plume myself not a little. You must know, that when cruising in the Channel, in a thick fog, and not keeping a very sharp look-out, we ran foul of a French privateer. It was about nine o'clock in the evening, and we had very few hands on deck, and those on deck were most of them, if not all, asleep. We came bang against one another, and carried away both spars and yards ; and the privateer, who was by far the most alert after the accident happened, cut away a good deal of our rigging, and got clear of us before our men could be got up from below. Had they been on the look-out, they might have boarded us to a certainty, for all was confusion and amazement; but they cleared themselves and got off before our men could get up and run to their guns. She was out of sight immediately, from the thickness of the fog; however, we fired several broadsides in the direction we supposed she might be; and there was an end to the matter. Altogether, as you perceive, it was not a very creditable affair."

"Why, no," replied Joey; "I don't see how you could make much out of that."

"Well, if you can't see, now you shall hear:—

"'TO THE SECRETARY OF THE ADMIRALTY.

"'SIR,—I have the honour to acquaint you that, on the night of the 10th of November, cruising in the Channel, with the wind from S.E., and foggy, a large vessel hove in sight, on our weather bow.'

"You see, I didn't say we perceived a vessel, for that would not have been correct.

"'As she evidently did not perceive us, we continued our course towards her; the men were summoned to their quarters, and, in a very short time, were ready to uphold the honour of the English flag. The first collision between the two vessels was dreadful; but she contrived to disengage herself, and we were therefore prevented carrying her by boarding. After repeated broadsides, to which, in her disabled and confused state, she could make no return, she gradually increased her distance; still, she had remained in our hands, a proud trophy—I say, still she had been a proud trophy—had not the unequal collision '—[it was a very unequal collision, for she was a much smaller vessel than we were]—' carried away our fore-yard, cat-head, foretop-gallant mast, jibboom, and dolphin-striker, and rendered us, from the state of our rigging, a mere wreck. Favoured by the thick fog and darkness of the night, I regret that, after all our efforts, she contrived to escape, and the spoils of victory were wrested from us after all our strenuous exertions in our country's cause.

169

"'When all performed their duty in so exemplary a manner, it would be unfair, and, indeed, invidious, to particularise: still, I cannot refrain from mentioning the good conduct of Mr. Smith, my first lieutenant; Mr. Bowles, my second lieutenant; Mr. Chabb, my worthy master; Mr. Jones and Mr. James, master's mates; Messrs. Hall, Small, Ball, and Pall, midshipmen; and Messrs. Sweet and Sharp, volunteers. I also received every assistance from Mr. Grulf, the purser, who offered his services, and I cannot omit the conduct of Mr. Spikeman, clerk. I am also highly indebted to the attention and care shown by Mr. Thorn, surgeon, who is so well supported in his duties by Mr. Green, assistant-surgeon, of this ship. The activity of Mr. Bruce, the boatswain, was deserving of the highest encomiums; and it would be an act of injustice not to notice the zeal of Mr. Bile, the carpenter, and Mr. Sponge, gunner of the ship. James Anderson, quartermaster, received a severe contusion, but is now doing well; I trust I shall not be considered presumptuous in recommending him to a boatswain's warrant.

"'I am happy to say that our casualties, owing to the extreme panic of the enemy, are very few.—I have the honour to be, Sir, your very obedient and humble servant,

"'ALCIBIADES AJAX BOGGS.

"'Wounded—Very severely, James Anderson, quartermaster. Contusions—John Peters, able seaman; James Morrison, marine; Thomas Snowball, captain's cook.'

"There, now; that I consider a very capital letter; no Frenchman, not even an American, could have made out a better case. The Admiralty were satisfied that something very gallant had been done, although the fog made it appear not quite so clear as it might have been; and the consequence was, that my commander received his promotion. There, now, write your letter, and tell your sister that she must answer it as soon as possible, as you are going out with me for orders in three or four days, and shall be absent for three months."

Joey wrote a long letter to Mary; he stated the adventure with the two scoundrels who would have robbed him, his afterwards falling in with a gentleman who dealt in cutlery, and his being taken into his service; and, as Spikeman had told him, requested her to answer directly, as he was about to set off on a circuit with his master, which would occasion his absence for three months.

Mary's reply came before Joey's departure. She stated that she was comfortable and happy, that her mistress was very kind to her, but that she felt that the work was rather too much; however, she would do her duty to her employers. There was much good advice to Joey, much affectionate feeling, occasional recurrence to past scenes, and thankfulness that she was no longer a disgrace to her parents and her sex; it was a humble, grateful, contrite, and affectionate effusion, which did honour to poor Mary, and proved that she was sincere in her assertions of continuing in the right path, and dotingly attached to our hero. Joey read it over and over again, and shed tears of pleasure as he recalled the scenes which had passed. Poor Joey had lost his father and mother, as he supposed, for ever; and it was soothing to the boy's feelings to know that there were some people in the world who loved him; and he remained for hours thinking of Mary, Mrs. Chopper, and his good and kind friends, the M'Shanes.

Two days after the receipt of Mary's letter, Spikeman and Joey went to the houses of their various acquaintances, and bade them adieu, announcing their intention to set off on the circuit. Spikeman paid up everything, and put away many articles in his room which had been taken out for use. Joey and he then put on their travelling garments, and, waiting till it was dusk, locked the chambers and set off to the little public-house, where the knife-grinder's wheel had been deposited. Spikeman had taken the precaution to smudge and dirty his face, and Joey, at his request, had done the same. When they entered the public-house, the landlord greeted Spikeman warmly, and asked him what he had been about. Spikeman replied that, as usual, he had been to see his old mother, and now he must roll his grindstone a bit. After drinking a pot of beer at the kitchen fire, they retired to bed; and the next morning, at daylight, they once more proceeded on their travels.

CHAPTER XXIX

In which the tinker falls in love with a lady of high degree.

FOR many months Spikeman and our hero travelled together, during which time Joey had learnt to grind a knife or a pair of scissors as well as Spikeman himself, and took most of the work off his hands; they suited each other, and passed their time most pleasantly, indulging themselves every day with a few hours' repose and reading on the wayside.

One afternoon, when it was very sultry, they had stopped and ensconced themselves in a shady copse by the side of the road, not far from an old mansion, which stood on an eminence, when Spikeman said, "Joey, I think we are intruding here; and, if so, may be forcibly expelled, which will not be pleasant; so roll the wheel in, out of sight, and then we may indulge in a siesta, which, during this heat, will be very agreeable."

"What's a siesta?" said Joey.

"A siesta is a nap in the middle of the day, universally resorted to by the Spaniards, Italians, and, indeed, by all the inhabitants of hot climates; with respectable people it is called a siesta, but with a travelling tinker it must be, I suppose, called a snooze."

"Well then, a snooze let it be," said Joey, taking his seat on the turf by Spikeman in a reclining position.

They had not yet composed themselves to sleep, when they heard a female voice singing at a little distance. The voice evidently proceeded from the pleasure-grounds which were between them and the mansion.

"Hush!" said Spikeman, putting up his finger, as he raised himself on his elbow.

The party evidently advanced nearer to them, and carolled in very beautiful tones the song of Ariel :—

> "Where the bee sucks, there lurk I,
> In the cowslip's bell I lie," &c.

"Heigho!" exclaimed a soft voice, after the song had been finished; "I wish I could creep into a cowslip-bell. Miss

172

Araminta, you are not coming down the walk yet; it appears you are in no hurry, so I'll begin my new book."

After this soliloquy there was silence. Spikeman made a sign to Joey to remain still, and then, creeping on his hands and knees, by degrees arrived as far as he could venture to the other side of the copse.

In a minute or two another footstep was heard coming down the gravel-walk, and soon afterwards another voice.

"Well, Melissa, did you think I never would come? I could not help it. Uncle would have me rub his foot a little."

"Ay, there's the rub," replied the first young lady. "Well, it was a sacrifice of friendship at the altar of humanity. Poor papa! I wish I could rub his foot for him; but I always do it to a quadrille tune, and he always says I rub it too hard. I only follow the music."

"Yes, and so does he; for you sometimes set him a dancing, you giddy girl."

"I am not fit for a nurse, and that's the fact, Araminta. I can feel for him, but I cannot sit still a minute; that you know. Poor mamma was a great loss; and, when she died, I don't know what I should have done, if it hadn't been for my dear cousin Araminta."

"Nay, you are very useful in your way, for you play and sing to him, and that soothes him."

"Yes, I do it with pleasure, for I can do but little else; but, Araminta, my singing is that of the caged bird. I must sing where they hang my cage. Oh, how I wish I had been a man!"

"I believe that there never was a woman yet who has not, at one time of her life, said the same thing, however mild and quiet she may have been in disposition. But, as we cannot, why——"

"Why, the next thing is to wish to be a man's wife, Araminta—is it not?"

"It is natural, I suppose, to wish so," replied Araminta; "but I seldom think about it. I must first see the man I can love before I think about marrying."

"And now tell me, Araminta, what kind of a man do you think you could fancy?"

"I should like him to be steady, generous, brave, and handsome; of unexceptionable family, with plenty of money; that's all."

"Oh, that's all! I admire your 'that's all.' You are not very likely to meet with your match, I'm afraid. If he's steady, he is not very likely to be very generous; and if to those two qualifications you tack on birth, wealth, beauty, and bravery, I think your 'that's all' is very misplaced. Now, I have other ideas."

"Pray let me have them, Melissa."

"I do not want my husband to be very handsome; but I wish him to be full of fire and energy, a man that—in fact, a man that could keep me in tolerable order. I do not care about his having money, as I have plenty in my own possession to bestow on any man I love; but he must be of good education—very fond of reading—romantic, not a little; and his extraction must be, however poor, respectable,—that is, his parents must not have been tradespeople. You know I prefer riding a spirited horse to a quiet one; and, if I were to marry, I should like a husband who would give me some trouble to manage. I think I would master him."

"So have many thought before you, Melissa; but they have been mistaken."

"Yes, because they have attempted it by meekness and submission, thinking to disarm by that method. It never will do, any more than getting into a passion. When a man gives up his liberty, he does make a great sacrifice—that I'm sure of; and a woman should prevent him feeling that he is chained to her."

"And how would you manage that?" said Araminta.

"By being infinite in my variety, always cheerful, and instead of permitting him to stay at home, pinned to my apron-string, order him out away from me, join his amusements, and always have people in the house that he liked, so as to avoid being too much *tête-à-tête*. The caged bird ever wants to escape; open the doors, and let him take a flight, and he will come back of his own accord. Of course, I am supposing my gentleman to be naturally good-hearted and good-tempered. Sooner than marry what you call a steady, sober man, I'd run away with a captain of a privateer. And, one thing more, Araminta, I never would, passionately, distractedly fond as I might be, acknowledge to my husband the extent of my devotion and affection for him. I would always have him to suppose that I could still love him better than what I yet did—in short, that there was more to be gained; for, depend upon it, when a man is assured that he has nothing more to gain, his attentions are over. You can't expect a man to chase nothing, you know."

"You are a wild girl, Melissa. I only hope you will marry well."

"I hope I shall; but I can tell you this, that if I do make a mistake, at all events my husband will find that he has made a mistake also. There's a little lurking devil in me, which, if roused up by bad treatment, would, I expect, make me more than a match for him. I'm almost sorry that I've so much money of my own, for I suspect every man who says anything pretty to me; and there are but few in this world who would scorn to marry for money."

"I believe so, Melissa; but your person would be quite sufficient without fortune."

"Thanks, coz; for a woman that's very handsome of you. And so now we will begin our new book."

Miss Melissa now commenced reading; and Spikeman, who had not yet seen the faces of the two young ladies, crept softly nearer to the side of the copse, so as to enable him to satisfy his curiosity. In this position he remained nearly an hour; when the book was closed, and the young ladies returned to the house, Melissa again singing as she went.

"Joey," said Spikeman, "I did not think that there was such a woman in existence as that girl; she is just the idea that I have formed of what a woman ought to be; I must find out who she is; I am in love with her, and——"

"Mean to make her a tinker's bride," replied Joey, laughing.

"Joey, I shall certainly knock you down, if you apply that term to her. Come, let us go to the village,—it is close at hand."

As soon as they arrived at the village, Spikeman went into the ale-house. During the remainder of the day he was in a brown study, and Joey amused himself with a book. At nine o'clock the company had all quitted the tap-room, and then Spikeman entered into conversation with the hostess. In the course of conversation, she informed him that the mansion belonged to Squire Mathews, who had formerly been a great manufacturer, and who had purchased the place ; that the old gentleman had long suffered from the gout, and saw no company, which was very bad for the village; that Miss Melissa was his daughter, and he had a son, who was with his regiment in India, and, it was said, not on very good terms with his father; that the old gentleman was violent and choleric because he was always in pain ; but that every one spoke well of Miss Melissa and Miss Araminta, her cousin, who were both very kind to the poor people. Having obtained these particulars, Spikeman went to bed : he slept little that night, as Joey, who was his bedfellow, could vouch for ; for he allowed Joey no sleep either, turning and twisting round in the bed every two minutes. The next morning they arose early, and proceeded on their way.

"Joey," said Spikeman, after an hour's silence, "I was thinking a great deal last night."

"So I suppose, for you certainly were not sleeping."

"No, I could not sleep ; the fact is, Joey, I am determined to have that girl, Miss Mathews, if I can ; a bold attempt for a tinker, you will say, but not for a gentleman born as I was. I thought I never should care for a woman; but there is a current in the affairs of men. I shall now drift with the current, and if it leads to fortune, so much the better; if not, he who dares greatly does greatly. I feel convinced that I should make her a good husband, and it shall not be my fault if I do not gain her."

"Do you mean to propose in form with your foot on your wheel ?"

"No, saucebox, I don't ; but I mean to turn my knife-grinder's wheel into a wheel of fortune ; and with your help I will do so."

"You are sure of my help if you are serious," replied Joey ; "but how you are to manage I cannot comprehend."

"I have already made out a programme, although the interweaving of the plot is not yet decided upon ; but I must get to the next town as fast as I can, as I must make preparations."

On arrival, they took up humble quarters, as usual ; and then Spikeman went to a stationer's, and told them that he had got a commission to execute for a lady. He bought sealing-wax, a glass seal, with " Espérance " as a motto, gilt-edged notepaper, and several other requisites in the stationery line, and ordered them to be packed up carefully, that he might not soil them; he then purchased scented soap, a hair-brush, and other articles for the toilet; and having obtained all these requisites, he added to them one or two pair of common beaver gloves, and then went to the barber's to get his hair cut.

"I am all ready now, Joey," said he, when he returned to the ale-house; "and to-morrow we retrace our steps."

"What! back to the village?"

"Yes; and where we shall remain some time, perhaps."

On reaching the village next morning Spikeman hired a bedroom, and leaving Joey to work the grindstone, remained in his apartments. When Joey returned in the evening, he found Spikeman had been very busy with the soap, and had restored his hands to something like their proper colour; he had also shaved himself, and washed his hair clean, and brushed it well.

"You see, Joey, I have commenced operations already; I shall soon be prepared to act the part of the gentleman who has turned tinker to gain the love of a fair lady of high degree."

"I wish you success; but what are your plans?"

"That you will find out to-morrow morning; now we must go to bed."

CHAPTER XXX

Plotting, reading, and writing.

SPIKEMAN was up early the next morning. When they had breakfasted, he desired Joey to go for the knife-grinder's wheel, and follow him. As soon as they were clear of the village, Spikeman said, "It will not do to remain at the village; there's a cottage half a mile down the road where they once gave me a lodging; we must try if we can get it now."

When they arrived at the cottage, Spikeman made a very satisfactory bargain for board and lodging for a few days, stating that they charged so much at the village ale-house that he could not afford to stay there, and that he expected to have a good job at Squire Mathews', up at the mansion-house. As

soon as this arrangement was completed, they returned back
to the copse near to the mansion-house, Joey rolling the knife-
grinder's wheel.

"You see, Joey," said Spikeman, "the first thing necessary
will be to stimulate curiosity; we may have to wait a day or
two before the opportunity may occur; but, if necessary, I will
wait a month. That Miss Mathews will very often be found
on the seat by the copse, either alone or with her cousin, I
take to be certain, as all ladies have their favourite retreats.
I do not intend that they should see me yet; I must make an
impression first. Now, leave the wheel on the outside, and
come with me: do not speak."

As soon as they were in the copse, Spikeman reconnoitred
very carefully, to ascertain if either of the young ladies
were on the bench, and finding no one there, he returned
to Joey.

"They cannot come without our hearing their footsteps,"
said Spikeman; "so now we must wait here patiently."

Spikeman threw himself down on the turf in front of the
copse, and Joey followed his example.

"Come, Joey, we may as well read a little to pass away the
time; I have brought two volumes of Byron with me."

For half-an-hour they were thus occupied, when they heard
the voice of Miss Mathews singing as before as she came down
the walk. Spikeman rose and peeped through the foliage.
"She is alone," said he, "which is just what I wished. Now,
Joey, I am going to read to you aloud." Spikeman then
began to read in the masterly style which we have before
referred to:—

       " 'I loved, and was beloved again;
       They tell me, Sir, you never knew
       Those gentle frailties; if 'tis true
       I shorten all my joys and pain,
       To you 'twould seem absurd as vain;
       But all now are not born to reign,
       Or o'er their passions, or as you
       There, o'er themselves and nations too.
       I am, or rather was, a Prince,
       A chief of thousands, and could lead
       Them on when each would foremost bleed,
       But would not o'er myself

The like control. But to resume :
I loved, and was beloved again ;
In sooth it is a happy doom—
But yet where happiness ends in pain.'

"I am afraid that is but too true, my dear boy," said Spike-man, laying down the book ; "Shakspeare has most truly said, 'The course of true love never did run smooth.' Nay, he cannot be said to be original in that idea, for Horace and most of the Greek and Latin poets have said much the same thing before him ; however, let us go on again—

"'We met in secret, and the hour
Which led me to my lady's bower
Was fiery expectation's dower ;
The days and nights were nothing—all
Except the hour which doth recall,
In the long lapse from youth to age,
No other like itself.'

"Do you observe the extreme beauty of that passage ?" said Spikeman.

"Yes," said Joey, "it is very beautiful."

"You would more feel the power of it, my dear boy, if you were in love, but your time is not yet come ; but I am afraid we must leave off now, for I expect letters of consequence by the post, and it is useless, I fear, waiting here. Come, put the book by, and let us take up the wheel of my sad fortunes."

Spikeman and Joey rose on their feet. Joey went to the knife-grinder's wheel, and Spikeman followed him without looking back ; he heard a rustling, nevertheless, among the bushes, which announced to him that his manœuvres had succeeded ; and as soon as he was about fifty yards from the road, he took the wheel from Joey, desiring him to look back, as if accidentally. Joey did so, and saw Miss Mathews following them with her eyes.

"That will do," observed Spikeman ; "her curiosity is excited, and that is all I wish."

What Spikeman said was correct. Araminta joined Miss Mathews shortly after Spikeman and Joey had gone away.

"My dear Araminta," said Melissa, "such an adventure ! I can hardly credit my senses."

179

"Why, what is the matter, dear cousin?"

"Do you see that man and boy, with a knife-grinder's wheel, just in sight now?"

"Yes, to be sure I do; but what of them? Have they been insolent?"

"Insolent! they never saw me; they had no idea that I was here. I heard voices as I came down the walk, so I moved softly, and when I gained the seat, there was somebody reading poetry so beautifully; I never heard any one read with such correct emphasis and clear pronunciation. And then he stopped, and talked to the boy about the Greek and Latin poets, and quoted Shakspeare. There must be some mystery."

"Well, but if there is, what has that to do with the travelling tinkers?"

"What! why, it was the travelling tinker himself, dearest; but he cannot be a tinker, for I heard him say that he expected letters of consequence, and no travelling tinker could do that."

"Why, no; I doubt if most of them can read at all."

"Now, I would give my little finger to know who that person is."

"Did you see his face?"

"No; he never turned this way; the boy did when they were some distance off. It's very strange."

"What was he reading?"

"I don't know; it was very beautiful. I wonder if he will ever come this way again? If he does——"

"Well, Melissa, and if he does?"

"My scissors want grinding very badly; they won't cut a bit."

"Why, Melissa, you don't mean to fall in love with a tinker?" said Araminta, laughing.

"He is no tinker, I'm sure; but why is he disguised? I should like to know."

"Well, but I came out to tell you that your father wants you. Come along."

The two young ladies then returned to the house, but the mystery of the morning was broached more than once, and canvassed in every possible way.

Spikeman, as soon as he had returned to the cottage, took out his writing materials to concoct an epistle. After some

time in correcting, he made out a fair copy, which he read
to Joey.

"I tremble lest at the first moment you cast your eyes
over the page, you throw it away without deigning to peruse
it; and yet there is nothing in it which could raise a blush
on the cheek of a modest maiden. If it be a crime to have
seen you by chance, to have watched you by stealth, to consider hallowed every spot you visit—nay, more, if it be a
crime to worship at the shrine of beauty and of innocence, or,
to speak more boldly, to adore you—then am I guilty. You
will ask why I resort to a clandestine step. Simply, because,
when I discovered your name and birth, I felt assured that
an ancient feud between the two families, to which nor you
nor I were parties, would bar an introduction to your father's
house. You would ask me who I am. A gentleman, I trust,
by birth and education; a poor one, I grant; and you have
made me poorer, for you have robbed me of more than wealth
—my peace of mind and my happiness. I feel that I am
presumptuous and bold; but forgive me. Your eyes tell me
you are too kind, too good to give unnecessary pain; and if
you knew how much I have already suffered, you would
not oppress further a man who was happy until he saw
you. Pardon me, therefore, my boldness, and excuse the
means I have taken of placing this communication before
you."

"That will do, I think," said Spikeman; "and now, Joey,
we will go out and take a walk, and I will give you your
directions."

CHAPTER XXXI

In which the plot thickens.

THE next day our hero, having received the letter with his
instructions, went with the wheel down to the copse near to
the mansion-house. Here he remained quietly until he heard
Miss Melissa coming down the gravel-walk; he waited till
she had time to gain her seat, and then, leaving his wheel
outside, he walked round the copse until he came to her.
She raised her eyes from her book when she saw him.

181

"If you please, miss, have you any scissors or knives for me to grind?" said Joey, bowing with his hat in his hand.

Miss Mathews looked earnestly at Joey.

"Who are you?" said she at last; "are you the boy who was on this road with a knife-grinder and his wheel yesterday afternoon?"

"Yes, madam, we came this way," replied Joey, bowing again very politely.

"Is he your father?"

"No, madam, he is my uncle; he is not married."

"Your uncle. Well, I have a pair of scissors to grind, and I will go for them; you may bring your wheel in here, as I wish to see how you grind."

"Certainly, miss, with the greatest pleasure."

Joey brought in his wheel, and observing that Miss Mathews had left her book on the seat, he opened it at the marked page and slipped the letter in; and scarcely had done so, when he perceived Miss Mathews and her cousin coming towards him.

"Here are the scissors; mind you make them cut well."

"I will do my best, miss," replied Joey, who immediately set to work.

"Have you been long at this trade?" said Miss Mathews.

"No, miss, not very long."

"And your uncle, has he been long at it?"

Joey hesitated on purpose. "Why, I really don't know exactly how long."

"Why is your uncle not with you?"

"He was obliged to go to town, miss—that is, to a town at some distance from here—on business."

"Why, what business can a tinker have?" inquired Araminta.

"I suppose he wanted some soft solder, miss; he requires a great deal."

"Can you read and write, boy?" inquired Melissa.

"Me, miss! how should I know how to write and read?" replied Joey, looking up.

"Have you been much about here?"

"Yes, miss, a good deal; uncle seems to like this part; we never were so long before. The scissors are done now,

miss, and they will cut very well. Uncle was in hopes of
getting some work at the mansion-house when he came
back."

"Can your uncle write and read?"

"I believe he can a little, miss."

"What do I owe you for the scissors?"

"Nothing, miss, if you please; I had rather not take anything from you."

"And why not from me?"

"Because I never worked for so pretty a lady before.
Wish you good morning, ladies," said Joey, taking up his
wheel and rolling it away.

"Well, Araminta, what do you think now? That's no
knife-grinder's boy; he is as well-bred and polite as any lad
I ever saw."

"I suspect that he is a little story-teller, saying that he
could not write and read," Araminta replied.

"And so do I; what made him in such a hurry to go
away?"

"I suppose he did not like our questions. I wonder
whether the uncle will come. Well, Melissa, I must not
quit your father just now, so I must leave you with your
book," and so saying, Araminta took her way to the
house.

Miss Mathews was in a reverie for some minutes; Joey's
behaviour had puzzled her almost as much as what she
had overheard the day before. At last she opened the
book, and, to her great astonishment, beheld the letter.
She started—looked at it—it was addressed to her. She
demurred at first whether she should open it. It must
have been put there by the tinker's boy—it was evidently
no tinker's letter; it must be a love-letter, and she ought
not to read it. There was something, however, so very
charming in the whole romance of the affair, if it should
turn out, as she suspected, that the tinker should prove
a gentleman who had fallen in love with her, and had
assumed the disguise. Melissa wanted an excuse to herself
for opening the letter. At last she said to herself, "Who
knows but what it may be a petition from some poor
person or other who is in distress? I ought to read it, at
all events."

Had it proved to be a petition, Miss Melissa would have been terribly disappointed. "It certainly is very respectful," thought Melissa, after she had read it, "but I cannot reply to it; that would never do. There certainly is nothing I can take offence at. It must be the tinker himself, I am sure of that; but still he does not say so. Well, I don't know, but I feel very anxious as to what this will come to. Oh, it can come to nothing, for I cannot love a man I have never seen, and I would not admit a stranger to an interview; that's quite decided. I must show the letter to Araminta. Shall I? I don't know, she's so particular, so steady, and would be talking of propriety and prudence; it would vex her so, and put her quite in a fever, she would be so unhappy; no, it would be cruel to say anything to her, she would fret so about it; I won't tell her until I think it absolutely necessary. It is a very gentlemanlike hand, and elegant language too; but still I'm not going to carry on a secret correspondence with a tinker. It must be the tinker. What an odd thing altogether! What can his name be? An old family quarrel, too. Why, it's a Romeo and Juliet affair, only Romeo's a tinker. Well, one mask is as good as another. He acknowledges himself poor, I like that of him, there's something so honest in it. Well, after all, it will be a little amusement to a poor girl like me, shut up from year's end to year's end, with opodeldocs always in my nose; so I will see what the end of it may be," thought Melissa, rising from her seat to go into the house, and putting the letter into her pocket.

Joey went back to Spikeman and reported progress.

"That's all I wish, Joey," said Spikeman; "now you must not go there to-morrow; we must let it work a little; if she is at all interested in the letter, she will be impatient to know more."

Spikeman was right. Melissa looked up and down the road very often during the next day, and was rather silent during the evening. The second day after, Joey, having received his instructions, set off, with his knife-grinder's wheel, for the mansion-house. When he went round the copse where the bench was, he found Miss Mathews there.

"I beg your pardon, miss, but do you think there is any work at the house?"

"Come here, sir," said Melissa, assuming a very digni-
fied air.

"Yes, miss," said Joey, walking slowly to her.

"Now tell me the truth, and I will reward you with half-
a-crown."

"Yes, miss."

"Did you not put this letter in my book the day before
yesterday?"

"Letter, miss! what letter?"

"Don't you deny it, for you know you did; and if you
don't tell me the truth, my father is a magistrate, and I'll
have you punished."

"I was told not to tell," replied Joey, pretending to be
frightened.

"But you must tell; yes, and tell me immediately."

"I hope you are not angry, miss."

"No, not if you tell the truth."

"I don't exactly know, miss, but a gentleman——"

"What gentleman?"

"A gentleman that came to uncle, miss."

"A gentleman that came to your uncle; well, go on."

"I suppose he wrote the letter, but I'm not sure; and
uncle gave me the letter to put it where you might
see it."

"Oh, then, a gentleman, you say, gave your uncle this
letter, and your uncle gave it to you to bring to me. Is
that it?"

"Uncle gave me the letter, but I dare say uncle will tell
you all about it, and who the gentleman was."

"Is your uncle come back?"

"He comes back to-night, madam."

"You're sure your uncle did not write the letter?"

"La, miss! uncle write such a letter as that—and to a
lady like you—that would be odd."

"Very odd, indeed!" replied Miss Melissa, who remained
a minute or two in thought. "Well, my lad," said she at
last, "I must and will know who has had the boldness to
write this letter to me; and as your uncle knows, you will
bring him here to-morrow, that I may inquire about it; and
let him take care that he tells the truth."

"Yes, miss; I will tell him as soon as he comes home. I
185

hope you are not angry with me, miss ; I did not think there was any harm in putting into the book such a nice clean letter as that."

"No, I am not angry with you; your uncle is more to blame ; I shall expect him to-morrow about this time. You may go now."

CHAPTER XXXII

In which the tinker makes love.

JOEY made his obeisance, and departed as if he was frightened. Miss Melissa watched him ; at last she thought, "Tinker or no tinker? that is the question. No tinker, for a cool hundred, as my father would say ; for, no tinker's boy, no tinker ; and that is no tinker's boy. How clever of him to say that the letter was given him by a gentleman ! Now I can send to him to interrogate him, and have an interview without any offence to my feelings ; and if he is disguised, as I feel confident that he is, I shall soon discover it."

Miss Melissa Mathews did not sleep that night ; and at the time appointed she was sitting on the bench, with all the assumed dignity of a newly made magistrate. Spikeman and Joey were not long before they made their appearance. Spikeman was particularly clean and neat, although he took care to wear the outward appearance of a tinker ; his hands were, by continual washing in hot water, very white, and he had paid every attention to his person, except in wearing his rough and sullied clothes.

"My boy tells me, miss, that you wish to speak to me," said Spikeman, assuming the air of a vulgar man.

"I did, friend," said Melissa, after looking at Spikeman for a few minutes ; "a letter has been brought here clandestinely, and your boy confesses that he received it from you ; now, I wish to know how you came by it."

"Boy, go away to a distance," said Spikeman, very angrily ; "if you can't keep one secret, at all events you shall not hear any more."

Joey retreated, as had been arranged between them.

"Well, madam, or miss (I suppose miss)," said Spikeman,

186

"that letter was written by a gentleman that loves the very ground you tread upon."

"And he requested it to be delivered to me?"

"He did, miss; and if you knew, as I do, how he loves you, you would not be surprised at his taking so bold a step."

"I am surprised at your taking so bold a step, tinker, as to send it by your boy."

"It was a long while before I would venture, miss; but when he had told me what he did, I really could not help doing so; for I pitied him, and so would you, if you knew all."

"And pray what did he tell you?"

"He told me, miss," said Spikeman, who had gradually assumed his own manner of speaking, "that he had ever rejected the thoughts of matrimony—that he rose up every morning thanking Heaven that he was free and independent—that he had scorned the idea of ever being captivated with the charms of a woman; but that one day he had by chance passed down this road, and had heard you singing as you were coming down to repose on this bench. Captivated by your voice, curiosity induced him to conceal himself in the copse behind us, and from thence he had a view of your person: nay, miss, he told me more, that he had played the eaves-dropper, and heard all your conversation, free and uncon-strained as it was from the supposition that you were alone; he heard you express your sentiments and opinions, and find-ing that there was on this earth, what, in his scepticism, he thought never to exist—youth, beauty, talent, principle, and family, all united in one person—he had bowed at the shrine, and had become a silent and unseen worshipper."

Spikeman stopped speaking.

"Then it appears that this gentleman, as you style him, has been guilty of the ungentlemanly practice of listening to private conversation—no very great recommendation."

"Such was not his intention at first; he was seduced to it by you. Do not blame him for that—now that I have seen you, I cannot; but, miss, he told me more. He said that he felt that he was unworthy of you, and had not a competence to offer you, even if he could obtain your favour; that he discovered that there was a cause which prevented his gaining an introduction to your family; in fact, that he was hopeless and despairing, He had hovered near you for a long time, for he could not leave the air you breathed; and, at last, that he had resolved to set his life upon the die and stake the hazard. Could I refuse him, miss? He is of an old family, but not wealthy; he is a gentleman by birth and education, and therefore I did not think I was doing so very wrong in giving him the chance, trifling as it might be. I beg your pardon, madam, if I have offended; and any message you may have to deliver to him, harsh as it may be—nay, even if it should be his death—it shall be faithfully and truly delivered."

"When shall you see him, Master Tinker?" said Melissa, very gravely.

"In a week he will be here, he said, not before."

"Considering he is so much in love, he takes his time," replied Melissa. "Well, Master Tinker, you may tell him from me, that I've no answer to give him. It is quite ridiculous, as well as highly improper, that I should receive a letter or answer one from a person whom I never saw. I admit his letter to be respectful, or I should have sent a much harsher message."

"Your commands shall be obeyed, miss; that is, if you cannot be persuaded to see him for one minute."

"Most certainly not; I see no gentleman who is not received at my father's house, and properly presented to me. It may be the custom among people in your station of life, Master Tinker, but not in mine; and as for yourself, I recommend you not to attempt to bring another letter."

"I must request your pardon for my fault, miss; may I ask, after I have seen the poor young gentleman, am I to report to you what takes place?"

"Yes, if it is to assure me that I shall be no more troubled with his addresses."

"You shall be obeyed, miss," continued Spikeman; then, changing his tone and air, he said, "I beg your pardon, have you any knives or scissors to grind?"

"No," replied Melissa, jumping up from her seat, and walking towards the house to conceal her mirth. Shortly afterwards she turned round to look if Spikeman was gone; he had remained near the seat, with his eyes following her footsteps. "I could love that man," thought Melissa, as she walked on. "What an eye he has, and what eloquence; I shall run away with a tinker I do believe; but it is my destiny. Why does he say a week—a whole week? But how easy to see through his disguise! He had the stamp of a gentleman upon him. Dear me, I wonder how this is to end! I must not tell Araminta yet; she would be fidgeted out of her wits! How foolish of me! I quite forgot to ask the name of this *gentleman*. I'll not forget it next time."

CHAPTER XXXIII

Well done, tinker.

IT is beyond my hopes, Joey," said Spikeman, as they went back to the cottage; "she knows well enough that I was pleading for myself, and not for another, and she has said quite as much as my most sanguine wishes could desire; in fact, she has given me permission to come again, and report the result of her message to the non-existent gentleman, which is equal to an assignation. I have no doubt now I shall ultimately succeed, and I must make my preparations; I told her that I should not be able to deliver her message for a week, and she did not like the delay, that was clear; it will all work in my favour; a week's expectation will ripen the fruit more than daily meetings. I must leave this to-night; but you may as well stay here, for you can be of no use to me."

"Where are you going, then?"

"First to Dudstone, to take my money out of the bank; I have a good sum, sufficient to carry me on for many months after her marriage, if I do marry her. I shall change my dress at Dudstone, of course, and then start for London, by mail, and fit myself out with a most fashionable wardrobe and et-ceteras, come down again to Cobhurst, the town we were in the other day, with my portmanteau, and from thence return here in my tinker's clothes to resume operations. You must not go near her during my absence."

"Certainly not; shall I go out at all?"

"No, not with the wheel; you might meet her on the road, and she would be putting questions to you."

That evening Spikeman set off, and was absent for five days, when he again made his appearance early in the morning. Joey had remained almost altogether indoors, and had taken that opportunity of writing to Mary. He wrote on the day after Spikeman's departure, as it would give ample time for an answer before his return; but Joey received no reply to his letter.

"I am all prepared now, my boy," said Spikeman, whose appearance was considerably improved by the various little personal arrangements which he had gone through during the time he was in London. "I have my money in my pocket, my portmanteau at Cobhurst, and now it depends upon the rapidity of my success when the day is to come that I make the knife-grinder's wheel over to you. I will go down now, but without you this time."

Spikeman set off with his wheel, and soon arrived at the usual place of meeting; Miss Mathews, from the window, had perceived him coming down the road; she waited a quarter of an hour before she made her appearance; had not she had her eyes on the hands of the timepiece, and knew that it was only a quarter of an hour, she could have sworn that it had been two hours at least. Poor girl! she had, during this week, run over every circumstance connected with the meeting at least a thousand times; every word that had been exchanged had been engraven on her memory, and, without her knowledge almost, her heart had imperceptibly received the impression. She walked down, reading her book very attentively, until she arrived at the bench.

"Any knives or scissors to grind, ma'am?" asked Spikeman, respectfully coming forward.

"You here again, Master Tinker! Why, I had quite forgot all about you."

(Heaven preserve us! how innocent girls will sometimes tell fibs out of modesty.)

"It were well for others, Miss Mathews, if their memory were equally treacherous," rejoined Spikeman.

"And why so, pray?"

"I speak of the gentleman to whom you sent the message."

"And what was his reply to you?"

"He acknowledged, Miss Mathews, the madness of his communication to you, of the impossibility of your giving him an answer, and of your admitting him to your presence. He admired the prudence of your conduct, but, unfortunately, his admiration only increased his love. He requested me to say that he will write no more."

"He has done wisely, and I am satisfied."

"I would I could say as much for him, Miss Mathews; for it is my opinion, that his very existence is now so bound up with the possession of you, that if he does not succeed he cannot exist."

"That's not my fault," replied Melissa, with her eyes cast down.

"No, it is not. Still, Miss Mathews, when it is considered that this man had abjured, I may say, had almost despised women, it is no small triumph to you, or homage from him, that you have made him feel the power of your sex."

"It is his just punishment for having despised us."

"Perhaps so; yet if we were all punished for our misdeeds, as Shakspeare says, who should escape whipping?"

"Pray, Master Tinker, where did you learn to quote Shakspeare?"

"Where I learnt much more. I was not always a travelling tinker."

"So I presumed before this. And pray how came you to be one?"

"Miss Mathews, if the truth must be told, it arose from an unfortunate attachment."

"I have read in the olden poets that love would turn a god into a man; but I never heard of its making him a tinker," replied Melissa, smiling.

"The immortal Jove did not hesitate to conceal his thunder-bolts when he deigned to love; and Cupid but too often has recourse to the aid of Proteus to secure success. We have, therefore, no mean warranty."

"And who was the lady of thy love, good Master Tinker?"

"She was, Miss Mathews, like you in everything. She was as beautiful, as intelligent, as honest, as proud, and, unfortunately, she was, like you, as obdurate, which reminds me of the unfortunate gentleman whose emissary I now am. In his madness he requested me—yes, Miss Mathews, me a poor —tinker—to woo you for him—to say to you all that he would have said had he been admitted to your presence—to plead for him—to kneel for him at your feet, and entreat you to have some compassion for one whose only misfortune was to love—whose only fault was to be poor. What could I say, Miss Mathews—what could I reply to a person in his state of desperation? To reason with him, to argue with him, had been useless; I could only soothe him by making such a promise, provided that I was permitted to do it. Tell me, Miss Mathews, have I your permission to make the attempt?"

"First, Mr. Tinker, I should wish to know the name of this gentleman."

"I promised not to mention it, Miss Mathews; but I can evade the promise. I have a book which belongs to him in my pocket, on the inside of which are the arms of his family, with his father's name underneath them."

Spikeman presented the book. Melissa read the name, and then laid it on the bench without saying a word.

"And now, Miss Mathews, as I have shown you that the gentleman has no wish to conceal who he is, may I venture to hope that you will permit me to plead occasionally, when I may see you, in his behalf."

"I know not what to say, Master Tinker. I consider it a measure fraught with some danger, both to the gentleman and to myself. You have quoted Shakspeare—allow me now to do the same :—

  "'Friendship is constant in all other things
  Save in the office and affairs of love,
  Therefore all hearts in love use their own tongues.'

You observe, Master Tinker, that there is the danger of your pleading for yourself, and not for your client; and there is also the danger of my being insensibly moved to listen to the addresses of a tinker. Now, only reflect upon the awful consequences," continued Melissa, smiling.

"I pledge you my honour, Miss Mathews, that I will only plead for the person whose name you have read in the book, and that you shall never be humiliated by the importunities of a mender of pots and pans."

"You pledge the honour of a tinker; what may that be worth?"

"A tinker that has the honour of conversing with Miss Mathews, has an honour that cannot be too highly appreciated."

192

"Well, that is very polite for a mender of old kettles; but the schoolmaster is abroad, which, I presume, accounts for such strange anomalies as our present conversation. I must now wish you good morning."

"When may I have the honour of again presenting myself in behalf of the poor gentleman?"

"I can really make no appointments with tinkers," replied Melissa; "if you personate that young man, you must be content to wait for days or months to catch a glimpse of the hem of my garment; to bay the moon and bless the stars, and I do not know what else. It is, in short, catch me when you can; and now farewell, good Master Tinker," replied Melissa, leaving her own book and taking the one Spikeman had put into her hand, which she carried with her to the house. It was all up with Miss Melissa Mathews, that was clear.

We shall pass over a fortnight, during which Spikeman, at first every other day, and subsequently every day or evening, had a meeting with Melissa, in every one of which he pleaded his cause in the third person. Joey began to be very tired of this affair, as he remained idle during the whole time, when one morning Spikeman told him that he must go down to the meeting-place without the wheel, and tell Miss Mathews his uncle the tinker was ill, and not able to come that evening.

Joey received his instructions, and went down immediately. Miss Mathews was not to be seen, and Joey, to avoid observation, hid himself in the copse, awaiting her arrival. At last she came, accompanied by Araminta, her cousin. As soon as they had taken their seats on the bench, Araminta commenced: "My dear Melissa, I could not speak to you in the house, on account of your father; but Simpson has told me this morning that she thought it her duty to state to me that you have been seen, not only in the daytime, but late in the evening, walking and talking with a strange-looking man. I have thought it very odd that you should not have mentioned this mysterious person to me lately; but I do think it most strange that you should have been so imprudent. Now tell me everything that has happened, or I must really make it known to your father."

"And have me locked up for months—that's very kind of you, Araminta," replied Melissa.

"But consider what you have been doing, Melissa. Who is this man?"

"A travelling tinker, who brought me a letter from a gentleman, who has been so silly as to fall in love with me."

"And what steps have you taken, cousin?"

"Positively refused to receive a letter, or to see the gentleman."

"Then why does the man come again?"

"To know if we have any knives or scissors to grind."

"Come, come, Melissa, this is ridiculous. All the servants are talking about it; and you know how servants talk. Why do you continue to see this fellow?"

"Because he amuses me, and it is so stupid of him."

"If that is your only reason, you can have no objection to see him no more, now that scandal is abroad. Will you promise me that you will not? Recollect, dear Melissa, how imprudent and how unmaidenly it is."

"Why, you don't think that I am going to elope with a tinker, do you, cousin?"

"I should think not; nevertheless, a tinker is no companion for Miss Mathews, dear cousin. Melissa, you have been most imprudent. How far you have told me the truth I know not; but this I must tell you, if you do not promise me to give up this disgraceful acquaintance, I will immediately acquaint my uncle."

"I will not be forced into any promise, Araminta," replied Melissa indignantly.

"Well then, I will not hurry you into it. I will give you forty-eight hours to reply, and if by that time your own good sense does not point out your indiscretion, I certainly will make it known to your father; that is decided." So saying, Araminta rose from the bench and walked towards the house.

"Eight-and-forty hours," said Melissa thoughtfully; "it must be decided by that time."

Joey, who had wit enough to perceive how matters stood, made up his mind not to deliver his message. He knew that Spikeman was well, and presumed that his staying away was to make Miss Mathews more impatient to see him. Melissa remained on the bench in deep thought; at last Joey went up to her.

"You here, my boy! what have you come for?" said Melissa.

"I was strolling this way, madam."

"Come here; I want you to tell me the truth; indeed, it is useless to attempt to deceive me. Is that person your uncle?"

"No, miss, he is not."

"I knew that. Is he not the person who wrote the letter, and a gentleman in disguise? Answer me that question, and then I have a message to him which will make him happy."

"He is a gentleman, miss."

"And his name is Spikeman, is it not?"

"Yes, miss, it is."

"Will he be here this evening? This is no time for trifling."

"If you want him, miss, I am sure he will."

"Tell him to be sure and come, and not in disguise," said Melissa, bursting into tears. "That's no use, my die is cast," continued she, talking to herself. Joey remained by her side until she removed her hands from her face. "Why do you wait?"

"At what hour, miss, shall he come?" said Joey.

"As soon as it is dusk. Leave me, boy, and do not forget."

Joey hastened to Spikeman, and narrated what he had seen and heard, with the message of Melissa.

"My dear boy, you have helped me to happiness," said Spikeman. "She shed tears, did she? Poor thing! I trust they will be the last she shall shed. I must be off to Cobhurst at once. Meet me at dark at the copse, for I shall want to speak to you."

Spikeman set off for the town as fast as he could, with his bundle on his head. When half way he went into a field and changed his clothes, discarding his tinker's dress for ever, throwing it into a ditch for the benefit of the finder. He then went into the town to his rooms, dressed himself in a fashionable suit, arranged his portmanteau, and ordered a chaise to

195

be ready at the door at a certain time, so as to arrive at the village before dusk. After he had passed through the village he ordered the postboy to stop about fifty yards on the other side of the copse, and getting out desired him to remain till he returned. Joey was already there, and soon afterwards Miss M. made her appearance, coming down the walk in a hurried manner, in her shawl and bonnet. As soon as she gained the bench Spikeman was at her feet; he told her he knew what had passed between her and her cousin; that he could not, would not part with her; he now came without disguise to repeat what he had so often said to her, that he loved and adored her, and that his life should be devoted to make her happy.

Melissa wept, entreated, refused, and half consented; Spikeman led her away from the bench towards the road, she still refusing, yet still advancing, until they came to the door of the chaise. Joey let down the steps; Melissa, half fainting and half resisting, was put in; Spikeman followed, and the door was closed by Joey.

"Stop a moment, boy," said Spikeman. "Here, Joey, take this."

As Spikeman put a packet into our hero's hand, Melissa clasped her hands and cried, "Yes—yes! stop, do stop, and let me out; I cannot go, indeed I cannot."

"There's lights coming down the gravel walk," said Joey; "they are running fast."

"Drive on, boy, as fast as you can," said Spikeman.

"Oh yes! drive on," cried Melissa, sinking into her lover's arms.

Off went the chaise, leaving Joey on the road with the packet in his hand; our hero turned round and perceived the lights close to him, and not exactly wishing to be interrogated, he set off as fast as he could, and never checked his speed until he arrived at the cottage where he and Spikeman had taken up their quarters.

CHAPTER XXXIV

A very long chapter, necessary to fetch up the remainder of the convoy.

As it was late that night, Joey did not open the packet delivered to him by Spikeman until he arose the next morning, which he did very early, as he thought it very likely that he might be apprehended, if he was not off in good time. The packet contained a key, £20 in money, and a paper, with the following letter :—

" My dear Boy,—As we must now part, at least for some time, I have left you money sufficient to set you up for the present ; I have enclosed a memorandum, by which I make over to you the knife-grinder's wheel, and all the furniture, books, &c., that are in my rooms at Dudstone, the key of which is also enclosed. I should recommend you going there and taking immediate possession, and as soon as I have time, I shall write to the woman of the house, to inform her of the contents of the memorandum ; and I will also write to you, and let you know how I get on. Of course you will now do as you please ; at all events, I have taught you a profession, and have given you the means of following it. I only hope, if you do, that some day you may be able to retire from business as successfully as I have done. You will, of course, write to me occasionally, after you know where I am. Depend upon it, there is no profession so near to that of a gentleman as that of a travelling tinker.—Yours ever truly,
" Augustus Spikeman.

" N.B.—There is some money in the old place to pay the bill at the cottage."

Our hero considered that he could not do better than follow the advice of Spikeman. He first wrote a few lines to Mary, requesting that she would send her answer to Dudstone ; and then, having settled with the hostess, he set off with his knife-grinder's wheel on his return home to what were now his apartments. As he was not anxious to make money, he did not delay on his road, and on the fifth day he found himself at the door of the ale-house near to Dudstone, where he had before left the wheel. Joey thought it advisable to do so now, telling the landlord that Spikeman had requested him so to do; and as soon as it was dusk our hero proceeded to the town, and knocked at the door of the house in which were Spikeman's apartments. He informed the landlady that Spikeman would not in all probability return, and had sent him to take possession, showing her the key. The dame was satisfied, and Joey went upstairs. As soon as he had lighted the candle, and fairly installed himself, our hero threw himself down on the sofa and began to reflect. It is pleasant to have property of our own, and Joey never had had any before; it was satisfactory to look at the furniture, bed, and books, and say, "All this is *mine*." Joey felt this, as it is to be presumed everybody would in the same position, and for some time he continued looking round and round at his property. Having satisfied himself with a review of it externally, he next proceeded to open all the drawers, the chests, &c. There were many articles in them which Joey did not expect to find, such as a store of sheets, table-linen, and all Spikeman's clothes, which he had discarded when he went up to London, some silver spoons, and a variety of little odds and ends; in short, Spikeman had left our hero everything as it stood. Joey put his money away, and then went to bed, and slept as serenely as the largest landed proprietor in the kingdom. When he awoke next morning, our hero began to reflect upon what he should do. He was not of Spikeman's opinion that a travelling tinker was the next thing to a gentleman, nor did he much like the idea of rolling the wheel about all his life; nevertheless, he agreed with Spikeman that it was a trade by which he could earn his livelihood, and if he could do no better, it would always be a resource. As soon as he had taken his breakfast he sat down and wrote to Mary, acquainting her with all that had taken place, and stating what his own feelings were upon his future prospects. Having finished his letter, he dressed himself neatly, and went out to call upon the widow James. Miss Ophelia and Miss Amelia were both at home.

"Well, Master Atherton, how do you do? and pray where is Mr. Spikeman?" said both the girls in a breath.

"He is a long way from this!" replied Joey.

"A long way from this! Why, has he not come back with you?"

"No! and I believe he will not come back any more. I am come, as his agent, to take possession of his property."

"Why, what has happened?"

"A very sad accident," replied our hero, shaking his head; "he fell——"

"Fell!" exclaimed the two girls in a breath.

"Yes, fell in love, and is married."

"Well now!" exclaimed Miss Ophelia, "only to think!"
Miss Amelia said nothing.

"And so he is really married?"

"Yes; and he has given up business."

"He did seem in a great hurry when he last came here," observed Amelia. "And what are you going to do?"

"I am not going to follow his example just yet," replied Joey.

"I suppose not; but what are you going to do?" replied Ophelia.

"I shall wait here for his orders; I expect to hear from him. Whether I am to remain in this part of the country, or sell off and join him, or look out for some other business, I hardly know; I think myself I shall look out for something else; I don't like the cutlery line and travelling for orders. How is your mamma, Miss Ophelia?"

"She is very well, and has gone to market. Well, I never did expect to hear of Mr. Spikeman being married! Who is he married to, Joseph?"

"To a very beautiful young lady, daughter of Squire Mathews, with a large fortune."

"Yes; men always look for money nowadays," said Amelia.

"I must go now," said Joey, getting up; "I have some calls and some inquiries to make. Good morning, young ladies."

It must be acknowledged that the two Misses James were not quite so cordial towards Joey as they were formerly; but unmarried girls do not like to hear of their old acquaintances marrying anybody save themselves. There is not only a flirt the less, but a chance the less in consequence; and it should be remarked, that there were very few *beaux* at Dudstone.

THE POACHER

Our hero was some days at Dudstone before he received a letter from Spikeman, who informed him that he had arrived safely at Gretna (indeed, there was no male relation of the family to pursue him), and the silken bonds of Hymen had been made more secure by the iron rivets of the blacksmith; that three days after he had written a letter to his wife's father, informing him that he had *done him the honour* of marrying his daughter; that he could not exactly say when he could find time to come to the mansion and pay him a visit, but that he would as soon as he conveniently could; that he begged that the room prepared for them upon their arrival might have a *large* dressing-room attached to it, as he could not dispense with that convenience; that he was not aware whether Mr. Mathews was inclined to part with the mansion and property, but as his wife had declared that she would prefer living there to anywhere else, he had not any objection to purchase it of Mr. Mathews, if they could come to terms; hoped his gout was better, and was his "very faithfully, AUGUSTUS SPIKEMAN." Melissa wrote a few lines to Araminta, begging her, as a favour, not to attempt to palliate her conduct, but to rail against her incessantly, as it would be the surest method of bringing affairs to an amicable settlement.

To her father she wrote only these few words :—

"MY DEAR PAPA,—You will be glad to hear that I am married. Augustus says that, if I behave well, he will come and see you soon.—Dear papa, your dutiful child,

"MELISSA SPIKEMAN."

That the letters of Spikeman and Melissa put the old gentleman in no small degree of rage, may be conceived; but nothing could be more judicious than the plan Spikeman had acted upon. It is useless to plead to a man who is irritated with constant gout; he only becomes more despotic and more unyielding. Had Araminta attempted to soften his indignation, it would have been equally fruitless; but the compliance with the request of her cousin of continually railing against her, had the effect intended. The vituperation of Araminta left him nothing to say; there was no opposition to direct his anathemas against; there was no coaxing or wheedling on the part of the offenders for him to repulse; and when Araminta pressed the old gentleman to vow that Melissa should never enter the doors again, he accused her of being influenced by interested motives, threw a basin at her head, and wrote an epistle requesting Melissa to come and take his blessing. Araminta refused to attend her uncle after this insult, and the old gentleman became still more anxious for the return of his daughter, as he was now left entirely to the caprice of his servants. Araminta gave Melissa an account of what had passed, and entreated her to come at once. She did so, and a general reconciliation took place. Mr. Mathews, finding his new son-in-law very indifferent to pecuniary matters, insisted upon making over to his wife an estate in Herefordshire, which, with Melissa's own fortune, rendered them in most affluent circumstances. Spikeman requested Joey to write to him now and then, and that, if he required assistance, he would apply for it; but still advised him to follow up the profession of travelling tinker as being the most independent.

Our hero had hardly time to digest the contents of Spikeman's letter when he received a large packet from Mary, accounting for her not having replied to him before, in consequence of her absence from the Hall. She had, three weeks before, received a letter written for Mrs. Chopper, acquainting her that Mrs. Chopper was so very ill that it was not thought possible that she could recover, having an abscess in the liver which threatened to break internally, and requesting Mary to obtain leave to come to Gravesend, if she possibly could, as Mrs. Chopper wished to see her before she died. Great as was Mary's repugnance to revisit Gravesend, she felt that the obligations she was under to Mrs. Chopper were too great for her to hesitate; and showing the letter to Mrs. Austin, and stating at the same time that she considered Mrs. Chopper as more than a mother to her, she obtained the leave which she requested, and set off for Gravesend.

It was with feelings of deep shame and humiliation that poor Mary walked down the main street of the town, casting her eyes up fearfully to the scenes of her former life. She was very plainly attired, and had a thick veil over her face, so that nobody recognised her; she arrived at the door of Mrs. Chopper's abode, ascended the stairs, and was once more in the room out of which she had quitted Gravesend to lead a new life ; and most conscientiously had she fulfilled her resolution, as the reader must be aware. Mrs. Chopper was in bed and slumbering when Mary softly opened the door; the signs of approaching death were on her countenance—her large, round form had wasted away—her fingers were now taper and bloodless ; Mary would not have recognised her had she fallen in with her under other circumstances. An old woman was in attendance ; she rose up when Mary entered, imagining that it was some kind lady come to visit the sick woman. Mary sat down by the side of the bed, and motioned to the old woman that she might go out, and then she raised her veil and waited till the sufferer roused. Mary had snuffed the candle twice, that she might see sufficiently to read the Prayerbook which she had taken up, when Mrs. Chopper opened her eyes.

" How very kind of you, ma'am ! " said Mrs. Chopper ; " and where is Miss—— ? My eyes are dimmer every day."

" It is me, Mary—Nancy that was ! "

" And so it is ! O Nancy, now I shall die in peace ! I thought at first it was the kind lady who comes every day to read and to pray with me. Dear Nancy, how glad I am to see you ! And how do you do ? And how is poor Peter ? "

" Quite well when I heard from him last, my dear Mrs. Chopper."

" You don't know, Nancy, what a comfort it is to me to see you looking as you do, so good and so innocent; and when I think it was by my humble means that you were put in the way of becoming so, I feel as if I had done one good act, and that perhaps my sins may be forgiven me."

" God will reward you, Mrs. Chopper ; I said so at the time, and I feel it now," replied Mary, the tears rolling down her cheeks; " I trust by your means, and with strength from above, I shall continue in the same path, so that one sinner may be saved."

" Bless you, Nancy !—You never were a bad girl in heart; I always said so. And where is Peter now ? "

" Going about the country earning his bread ; poor, but happy."

" Well, Nancy, it will soon be over with me ; I may die in a second, they tell me, or I may live for three or four days; but I sent for you that I might put my house in order. There are only two people that I care for upon earth—that is you and my poor Peter; and all I have I mean to leave between you. I have signed a paper already, in case you could not come, but now that you are come I will tell you all I wish; but give me some of that drink first."

Mary having read the directions on the label, poured out a wine-glass of the mixture and gave it to Mrs. Chopper, who swallowed it, and then proceeded, taking a paper from under her pillow—

"Nancy! this is the paper I told you of. I have about £700 in the bank, which is all that I have saved in twenty-two years; but it has been honestly made. I have, perhaps, much more owing to me, but I do not want it to be collected. Poor sailors have no money to spare, and I release them all. You will see me buried, Nancy, and tell poor Peter how I loved him, and I have left my account books, with my bad debts and good debts, to him. I am sure he would like to have them, for he knows the history of every sum-total, and he will look over them and think of me. You can sell this furniture, but the wherry you must give to William; he is not very honest, but he has a large family to keep. Do what you like, dearest, about what is here; perhaps my clothes would be useful to his wife; they are not fit for you. There's a good deal of money in the upper drawer; it will pay for my funeral and the doctor. I believe that is all now; but do tell poor Peter how I loved him. Poor fellow, I have been cheated ever since he left; but that's no matter. Now, Nancy dear, read to me a little. I have so longed to have you by my bedside to read to me, and pray for me! I want to hear you pray before I die. It will make me happy to hear you pray, and see that kind face looking up to heaven, as it was always meant to do."

Poor Mary burst into tears. After a few minutes she became more composed, and dropping down on her knees by the side of the bed, she opened the Prayer-book, and complied with the request of Mrs. Chopper; and as she fervently poured forth her supplication, occasionally her voice faltered, and she would stop to brush away the tears which dimmed her sight. She was still so occupied when the door of the room was gently opened, and a lady, with a girl about

203

fourteen or fifteen years old, quietly entered the room. Mary did not perceive them until they also had knelt down. She finished the prayer, rose, and with a short curtsey, retired from the side of the bed.

Although not recognised herself by the lady, Mary immediately remembered Mrs. Phillips and her daughter Emma, having, as we have before observed, been at one time in Mrs. Phillips' service.

"This is the young woman whom you so wished to see, Mrs. Chopper, is it not?" said Mrs. Phillips. "I am not surprised at your longing for her, for she appears well suited for a companion in such an hour; and, alas! how few there are! Sit down, I request," continued Mrs. Phillips, turning to Mary. "How do you find yourself to-day, Mrs. Chopper?"

"Sinking fast, dear madam, but not unwilling to go, since I have seen Nancy, and heard of my poor Peter; he wrote to Nancy a short time ago. Nancy, don't forget my love to Peter."

Emma Phillips, who had now grown tall and thin, immediately went up to Mary, and said, "Peter was the little boy who was with Mrs. Chopper; I met him on the road when he first came to Gravesend, did I not?"

"Yes, miss, you did," replied Mary.

"He used to come to our house sometimes, and very often to meet me as I walked home from school. I never could imagine what became of him, for he disappeared all at once without saying good-bye."

"He was obliged to go away, miss. It was not his fault; he was a very good boy, and is so still."

"Then pray remember me to him, and tell him that I often think of him."

"I will, Miss Phillips, and he will be very happy to hear that you have said so."

"How did you know that my name was Phillips? Oh, I suppose poor Mrs. Chopper told you before we came."

Mrs. Phillips had now read some time to Mrs. Chopper, and this put an end to the conversation between Mary and Emma Phillips. It was not resumed. As soon as the reading was over Mrs. Phillips and her daughter took their leave.

Mary made up a bed for herself by the side of Mrs.

204

Chopper's. About the middle of the night she was roused
by a gurgling kind of noise ; she hastened to the bedside, and
found that Mrs. Chopper was suffocating. Mary called in the
old woman to her aid, but it was useless, the abscess had burst,
and in a few seconds all was over ; and Mary, struggling with
emotion, closed the eyes of her old friend, and offered up a
prayer for her departed spirit.

The remainder of the night was passed in solemn medita-
tion, and a renewal of those vows which the poor girl had
hitherto so scrupulously adhered to, and which the death-bed
scene was so well fitted to encourage ; but Mary felt that
she had her duties towards others to discharge, and did not
give way to useless and unavailing sorrow. It was her duty
to return as soon as possible to her indulgent mistress, and
the next morning she was busy in making the necessary
arrangements. On the third day Mary attended the funeral
of her old friend, the bills were all paid, and having selected
some articles which she wished to retain as a remembrance,
she resolved to make over to William, the waterman, not
only the wherry, but all the stock in hand, furniture, and
clothes of Mrs. Chopper. This would enable him and his
wife to set up in business themselves, and provide for their
family. Mary knew that she had no right to do so without
Joey's consent, but of this she felt she was sure ; having so
done, she had nothing more to do but to see the lawyer who
had drawn up the will, and having gone through the necessary forms, she received an order on the county bank nearest
to the Hall for the money, which, with what was left in the
drawers, after paying every demand, amounted to more than
£700. She thought it was her duty to call upon Mrs. Phillips
before she went away, out of gratitude for her kindness to
Mrs. Chopper ; and as she had not been recognised, she had
no scruple in so doing. She was kindly received, and blushed
at the praise bestowed upon her. As she was going away,
Emma Phillips followed her out, and putting into her hand a
silver pencil-case, requested she would " give it to Peter as a
remembrance of his little friend, Emma." The next day
Mary arrived at the Hall, first communicated to Mrs. Austin
what had occurred, and then, having received our hero's two
last epistles, sat down to write the packet containing all the
intelligence we have made known, and ended by requesting
205

Joey to set off with his knife-grinder's wheel, and come to the village near to the Hall, that he might receive his share of Mrs. Chopper's money, the silver pencil-case, and the warm greeting of his adopted sister. Joey was not long in deciding. He resolved that he would go to Mary; and, having locked up his apartments, he once more resumed his wheel, and was soon on his way to Hampshire.

CHAPTER XXXV

A retrospect, that the parties may all start fair again.

W E must now leave our hero on his way to the Hall, while we acquaint our readers with the movements of other parties connected with our history. A correspondence had been kept up between O'Donahue and M'Shane. O'Donahue had succeeded in obtaining the pardon of the emperor, and employment in the Russian army, in which he had rapidly risen to the rank of general. Five or six years had elapsed since he had married, and both O'Donahue and his wife were anxious to visit England; a letter at last came, announcing that he had obtained leave of absence from the emperor, and would in all probability arrive in the ensuing spring.

During this period M'Shane had continued at his old quarters, Mrs. M'Shane still carrying on the business, which every year became more lucrative; so much so, indeed, that her husband had for some time thought very seriously of retiring altogether, as they had already amassed a large sum, when M'Shane received the letter from O'Donahue, announcing that in a few months he would arrive in England. Major M'Shane, who was very far from being satisfied with his negative position in society, pressed the matter more earnestly to his wife, who, although she was perfectly content with her own position, did not oppose his entreaties. M'Shane found that after disposing of the goodwill of the business, and of the house, they would have a clear £30,000, which he considered more than enough for their wants, uncumbered as they were with children.

Let it not be supposed that M'Shane had ceased in his in-

quiries after our hero ; on the contrary, he had resorted to all
that his invention could suggest to trace him out, but, as the
reader must be aware, without success. Both M'Shane and
his wife mourned his loss, as if they had been bereaved of their
own child; they still indulged the idea that some day he would
reappear, but when, they could not surmise. M'Shane had not
only searched for our hero, but had traced his father with as
little success; and he had now made up his mind that he
should see no more of Joey, if he ever did see him again,
until after the death of his father, when there would no
longer be any occasion for secrecy. Our hero and his fate
were a continual source of conversation between M'Shane
and his wife ; but latterly, after not having heard of him for
more than five years, the subject had not been so often renewed. As soon as M'Shane had wound up his affairs, and
taken his leave of the eating-house, he looked out for an estate
in the country, resolving to lay out two-thirds of his money
in land, and leave the remainder in the funds. After about
three months' search he found a property which suited him,
and, as it so happened, about six miles from the domains held
by Mr. Austin. He had taken possession and furnished it.
As a retired officer in the army he was well received ; and if
Mrs. M'Shane was sometimes laughed at for her housekeeper-
like appearance, still her sweetness of temper and unassuming
behaviour soon won her friends, and M'Shane found himself
in a very short time comfortable and happy. The O'Donahues
were expected to arrive very shortly, and M'Shane had now
a domicile fit for the reception of his old friend, who had
promised to pay him a visit as soon as he arrived.

Of the Austins little more can be said that has not been
said already. Austin was a miserable, unhappy man ; his cup
of bliss—for he had every means of procuring all that this
world considers as bliss, being in possession of station, wealth,
and respect—was poisoned by the one heavy crime which
passion had urged him to commit, and which was now a source
of hourly and unavailing repentance. His son, who should
have inherited his wealth, was lost to him, and he dared not
mention that he was in existence. Every day Austin became
more nervous and irritable, more exclusive and averse to society ;
he trembled at shadows, and his strong constitution was rapidly
giving way to the heavy weight on his conscience. He could

not sleep without opiates, and he dreaded to sleep lest he should reveal anything of the past in his slumbers. Each year added to the irascibility of his temper, and the harshness with which he treated his servants and his unhappy wife. His chief amusement was hunting, and he rode in so reckless a manner that people often thought that he was anxious to break his neck. Perhaps he was. Mrs. Austin was much to be pitied ; she knew how much her husband suffered ; how the worm gnawed within ; and having that knowledge, she submitted to all his harshness, pitying him instead of condemning him ; but her life was still more embittered by the loss of her child, and many were the bitter tears which she would shed when alone, for she dared not in her husband's presence, as he would have taken them as a reproof to himself. Her whole soul yearned after our hero, and that one feeling rendered her indifferent, not only to all the worldly advantages by which she was surrounded, but to the unkindness and hard-heartedness of her husband. Mary, who had entered her service as kitchen-maid, was very soon a favourite, and had been advanced to the situation of Mrs. Austin's own attendant. Mrs. Austin considered her a treasure, and she daily became more partial to and more confidential with her. Such was the state of affairs, when one morning, as Austin was riding to cover, a gentleman of the neighbourhood said to him, in the course of conversation—

"By-the-bye, Austin, have you heard that you have a new neighbour ?"

"What !—on the Frampton estate, I suppose ; I heard that it had been sold."

"Yes ; I have seen him. He is one of your profession —a lively, amusing sort of Irish major; gentlemanlike, nevertheless. The wife not very high-bred, but very fat, and very good-humoured, and amusing from her downright simpleness of heart. You will call upon them, I presume ?"

"Oh, of course," replied Austin. "What is his name, did you say ?"

"Major M'Shane, formerly of the 53rd Regiment, I believe."

Had a bullet passed through the heart of Austin, he could not have received a more sudden shock, and the start which he made from his saddle attracted the notice of his companion.

"What's the matter, Austin? you look pale; you are not well."

"No," replied Austin, recollecting himself, "I am not; one of those twinges from an old wound in the breast came on. I shall be better directly."

Austin stopped his horse, and put his hand to his heart. His companion rode up, and remained near him.

"It is worse than usual; I thought it was coming on last night; I fear that I must go home."

"Shall I go with you?"

"Oh no; I must not spoil your sport. I am better now a great deal; it is going off fast. Come, let us proceed, or we shall be too late at cover."

Austin had resolved to conquer his feelings. His friend had no suspicion, it is true; but when we are guilty we imagine that everybody suspects us. They rode a few minutes in silence.

"Well, I am glad that you did not go home," observed his friend; "for you will meet your new neighbour; he has subscribed to the pack, and they say he is well mounted; we shall see how he rides."

Austin made no reply; but, after riding on a few yards farther, he pulled up, saying that the pain was coming on again, and that he could not proceed. His companion expressed his sorrow at Austin's indisposition, and they separated.

Austin immediately returned home, dismounted his horse, and hastened to his private sitting-room. Mrs. Austin, who had seen him return, and could not imagine the cause, went in to her husband.

"What is the matter, my dear?" said Mrs. Austin.

"Matter!" replied Austin bitterly, pacing up and down the room; "heaven and hell conspire against us!"

"Dear Austin, don't talk in that way. What has happened?"

"Something which will compel me, I expect, to remain a prisoner in my own house, or lead to something unpleasant. We must not stay here."

Austin then threw himself down on the sofa, and was

209   o

silent. At last the persuasions and endearments of his wife overcame his humour. He told her that M'Shane was the major of his regiment when he was a private; that he would inevitably recognise him; and that, if nothing else occurred from M'Shane's knowledge of his former name, at all events the general supposition of his having been an officer in the army would be contradicted, and it would lower him in the estimation of the county gentlemen.

"It is indeed a very annoying circumstance, my dear Austin; but are you sure that he would, after so long a period, recognise the private soldier in the gentleman of fortune?"

"As sure as I sit here," replied Austin gloomily; "I wish I were dead."

"Don't say so, dear Austin, it makes me miserable."

"I never am otherwise," replied Austin, clasping his hands. "God forgive me! I have sinned, but have I not been punished?"

"You have, indeed; and as repentance is availing, my dear husband, you will receive God's mercy."

"The greatest boon, the greatest mercy, would be death," replied the unhappy man; "I envy the pedlar."

Mrs. Austin wept. Her husband, irritated at tears which, to him, seemed to imply reproach, sternly ordered her to leave the room.

That Austin repented bitterly of the crime which he had committed is not to be doubted; but it was not with the subdued soul of a Christian. His pride was continually struggling within him, and was not yet conquered; this it was that made him alternately self-condemning and irascible, and it was the continual warfare in his soul which was undermining his constitution.

Austin sent for medical advice for his supposed complaint. The country practitioner, who could discover nothing, pronounced it to be an affection of the heart. He was not far wrong; and Mr. Austin's illness was generally promulgated. Cards and calls were the consequence, and Austin kept himself a close but impatient prisoner in his own house. His hunters remained in the stables, his dogs in the kennel, and every one intimated that Mr. Austin was labouring under a disease from which he would not recover. At first this was extremely irksome to Austin, and he was very impatient;

but gradually he became reconciled, and even preferred his sedentary and solitary existence. Books were his chief amusement, but nothing could minister to a mind diseased, or drive out the rooted memory of the brain. Austin became more morose and misanthropic every day, and at last would permit no one to come near him but his valet and his wife.

Such was the position of his parents, when Joey was proceeding to their abode.

CHAPTER XXXVI

Our hero falls in with an old acquaintance, and is not very much delighted.

WE left our hero rolling his knife-grinder's wheel towards his father's house. It must be confessed that he did it very unwillingly. He was never very fond of it at any time; but since he had taken possession of Spikeman's property, and had received from Mary the intelligence that he was worth £350 more, he had taken a positive aversion to it. It retarded his movements, and it was hard work when he had not to get his livelihood by it. ' More than once he thought of rolling it into a horsepond, and leaving it below low-water mark; but then he thought it a sort of protection against inquiry, and against assault, for it told of poverty and honest employment; so Joey rolled on, but not with any feelings of regard towards his companion.

How many castles did our hero build as he went along the road! The sum of money left to him appeared to be enormous. He planned and planned again; and, like most people, at the close of the day he was just as undetermined as at the commencement. Nevertheless, he was very happy, as people always are in anticipation; unfortunately, more so than when they grasp what they have been seeking. Time rolled on, as well as the grindstone, and at last Joey found himself at the ale-house where he and Mary had put up previously to her obtaining a situation at the Hall. He immediately wrote a letter to her, acquainting her with his arrival. He would have taken the letter himself, only he recollected the treat-

ment he had received, and found another messenger in the
butcher's boy, who was going up to the Hall for orders. The
answer returned by the same party was, that Mary would come
down and see him that evening. When Mary came down
Joey was astonished at the improvement in her appearance.
She looked much younger than she did when they had parted,
and her dress was so very different that our hero could with
difficulty imagine that it was the same person who had been
his companion from Gravesend. The careless air and manner
had disappeared; there was a *retenue*—a dignity about her
which astonished him; and he felt a sort of respect mingled
with his regard for her, of which he could not divest himself.
But if she looked younger (as may well be imagined) from
her change of life, she also looked more sedate, except when
she smiled, or when occasionally, but very rarely, her merry
laughter reminded him of the careless, good-tempered Nancy
of former times. That the greeting was warm need hardly
be said. It was the greeting of a sister and younger brother
who loved each other dearly.

"You are very much grown, Joey," said Mary. "Dear
boy, how happy I am to see you!"

"And you, Mary, you're younger in the face, but older in
your manners. Are you as happy in your situation as you
have told me in your letters?"

"Quite happy; more happy than ever I deserve to be, my
dear boy; and now tell me, Joey, what do you think of
doing? You have now the means of establishing yourself."

"Yes, I have been thinking of it; but I don't know what
to do."

"Well, you must look out, and do not be in too great a
hurry. Recollect, Joey, that if anything offers which you
have any reason to believe will suit you, you shall have my
money as well as your own."

"Nay, Mary, why should I take that?"

"Because, as it is of no use to me, it must be idle; besides,
you know, if you succeed, you will be able to pay me interest
for it; so I shall gain as well as you. You must not refuse
your sister, my dear boy."

"Dear Mary, how I wish we could live in the same house!"

"That cannot be now, Joey; you are above my situation at
the Hall, even allowing that you would ever enter it."

"That I never will, if I can help it; not that I feel angry now, but I like to be independent."

"Of course you do."

"And as for that grindstone, I hate the sight of it; it has made Spikeman's fortune, but it never shall make mine."

"You don't agree then with your former companion," rejoined Mary, "that a tinker's is the nearest profession to that of a gentleman which you know of?"

"I certainly do not," replied our hero; "and as soon as I can get rid of it I will; I have rolled it here, but I will not roll it much farther. I only wish I knew where to go."

"I have something in my pocket which puts me in mind of a piece of news which I received the other day, since my return. First let me give you what I have in my pocket"—and Mary pulled out the pencil-case sent to Joey by Emma Phillips. "There, you know already who that is from."

"Yes, and I shall value it very much, for she was a dear, kind little creature; and when I was very, very miserable, she comforted me."

"Well, Joey, Miss Phillips requested me to write when I came back, as she wished to hear that I had arrived safe at the Hall. It was very kind of her, and I did so, of course. Since that I have received a letter from her, stating that her grandmother is dead, and that her mother is going to quit Gravesend for Portsmouth, to reside with her brother, who is now a widower."

"I will go to Portsmouth," replied our hero.

"I was thinking that, as her brother is a navy agent, and Mrs. Phillips is interested about you, you could not do better. If anything turns up, then you will have good advice, and your money is not so likely to be thrown away. I think, therefore, you had better go to Portsmouth, and try your fortune."

"I am very glad you have mentioned this, Mary, for, till now, one place was as indifferent to me as another; but now it is otherwise, and to Portsmouth I will certainly go."

Our hero remained two or three days longer at the village, during which time Mary was with him every evening, and once she obtained leave to go to the banker's about her money. She then turned over to Joey's account the sum

213

due to him, and arrangements were made with the bank, so that Joey could draw his capital out whenever he pleased. After which our hero took leave of Mary, promising to correspond more freely than before ; and once more putting the strap of his knife-grinder's wheel over his shoulders, he set off on his journey to Portsmouth.

Joey had not gained two miles from the village when he asked himself the question, " What shall I do with my grindstone ? " He did not like to leave it on the road ; he did not know to whom he could give it away. He rolled it on for about six miles farther, and then, quite tired, he resolved to follow the plan formerly adopted by Spikeman, and repose a little upon the turf on the roadside. The sun was very warm, and after a time Joey retreated to the other side of the hedge, which was shaded ; and having taken his bundle from the side of the wheel where it hung, he first made his dinner of the provender he had brought with him, and then, laying his head on the bundle, was soon in a sound sleep, from which he was awakened by hearing voices on the other side of the hedge. He turned round, and perceived two men on the side of the road, close to his knife-grinder's wheel. They were in their shirts and trousers only, and sitting down on the turf.

" It would be a very good plan," observed one of them; " we should then travel without suspicion."

" Yes ; if we could get off with it without being discovered. Where can the owner of it be ? "

" Well, I dare say he is away upon some business or another, and has left the wheel here till he comes back. Now, suppose we were to take it—how should we manage ? "

" Why, we cannot go along this road with it. We must get over the gates and hedges till we get across the country into another road ; and then by travelling all night, we might be quite clear."

" Yes, and then we should do well ; for even if our description as deserters was sent out from Portsmouth, we should be considered as travelling tinkers, and there would be no suspicion."

" Well, I'm ready for it. If we can only get it off the road, and conceal it till night, we may then easily manage it.

But first let's see if the fellow it belongs to may not be somewhere about here."

As the man said this he rose up and turned his face
towards the hedge, and our hero immediately perceived that
it was his old acquaintance, Furness, the schoolmaster and
marine. What to do he hardly knew. At last he perceived
Furness advancing towards the gate of the field, which was
close to where he was lying, and as escape was impossible,
our hero covered his face with his arms, and pretended to be
fast asleep. He soon heard a "Hush!" given as a signal to
the other man, and after a while footsteps close to him.
Joey pretended to snore loudly, and a whispering then took
place. At last he heard Furness say—

"Do you watch by him while I wheel away the grindstone."

"But if he wakes, what shall I do?"

"Brain him with that big stone. If he does not wake up
when I am past the second field, follow me."

That our hero had no inclination to wake after this notice
may be easily imagined; he heard the gate opened, and the
wheel trundled away, much to his delight, as Furness was the
party who had it in charge; and Joey continued to snore hard,
until at last he heard the departing footsteps of Furness's
comrade, who had watched him. He thought it prudent to
continue motionless for some time longer, to give them time
to be well away from him, and then he gradually turned round
and looked in the direction in which they had gone; he could
see nothing of them, and it was not until he had risen up,
and climbed up on the gate, that he perceived them two or
three fields off, running away at a rapid pace. Thanking
Heaven that he had escaped the danger that he was in, and
delighted with the loss of his property, our hero recommenced
his journey with his bundle over his shoulder, and before night
he was safe outside one of the stages which took him to a
town, from which there was another which would carry him
to Portsmouth, at which seaport he arrived the next evening
without further adventure.

As our hero sat on the outside of the coach and reflected
upon his last adventure, the more he felt he had reason to
congratulate himself. That Furness had deserted from the
Marine Barracks at Portsmouth was evident; and if he had

not, that he would have recognised Joey some time or other was
almost certain. Now, he felt sure that he was safe at Portsmouth, as it would be the last place at which Furness would
make his appearance; and he also felt that his knife-grinder's
wheel, in supplying Furness with the ostensible means of
livelihood, and thereby preventing his being taken up as a
deserter, had proved the best friend to him, and could not
have been disposed of better. Another piece of good fortune
was his having secured his bundle and money; for had he left
it with the wheel, it would have, of course, shared its fate.
" Besides," thought Joey, "if I should chance to fall in with
Furness again, and he attempts to approach me, I can threaten
to have him taken as a deserter, and this may deter him from
so doing." It was with a grateful heart that our hero laid his
head upon his pillow, in the humble inn at which he had
taken up his quarters.

CHAPTER XXXVII

*In which our hero returns to his former employment, but on a
grander scale of operation.*

OUR hero had received from Mary the name and address
of Mrs. Phillips' brother, and, on inquiry, found that he was
known by everybody. Joey dressed himself in his best suit,
and presented himself at the door about ten o'clock in the
morning, as Joseph O'Donahue, the name which he had taken
when he went to Gravesend, and by which name he had been
known to Mrs. Phillips and her daughter Emma when he
made occasional visits to their house. He was admitted, and
found himself once more in company with his friend Emma,
who was now fast growing up into womanhood. After the
first congratulations and inquiries, he stated his intentions
in coming down to Portsmouth, and their assistance was immediately promised. They then requested a detail of his
adventures since he quitted Gravesend, of which Joey told
everything that he safely could; passing over his meeting
with Furness, by simply stating that, while he was asleep, his
knife-grinder's wheel had been stolen by two men, and that

when he awoke he dared not offer an opposition. Mrs. Phillips and her daughter both knew that there was some mystery about our hero, which had induced him to come to, and also to leave Gravesend; but, being assured by Mary and himself that he was not to blame, they did not press him to say more than he wished; and, as soon as he finished his history, they proposed introducing him to Mr. Small, the brother of Mrs. Phillips, in whose house they were then residing, and who was then in his office.

"But perhaps, mamma, it will be better to wait till to-morrow, and in the meantime you will be able to tell my uncle all about Joey," observed Emma.

"I think it will be better, my dear," replied Mrs. Phillips; "but there is Marianne's tap at the door, for the second time; she wants me downstairs, so I must leave you for a little while; but you need not go away, O'Donahue; I will be back soon."

Mrs. Phillips left the room, and our hero found himself alone with Emma.

"You have grown very much, Joey," said Emma; "and so have I, too, they tell me."

"Yes, you have indeed," replied Joey; "you are no longer the little girl who comforted me when I was so unhappy. Do you recollect that day?"

"Yes, indeed I do, as if it were but yesterday. But you have never told me why you lead so wandering a life; you won't trust me."

"I would trust you with anything but that which is not mine to trust, as I told you four years ago; it is not my secret; as soon as I can I will tell you everything, but I hope not to lead a wandering life any longer, for I have come down here to settle, if I can."

"What made you think of coming down here?" asked Emma.

"Because you were here; Mary told me so. I have not yet thanked you for your present, but I have not forgotten your kindness in thinking of a poor boy like me, when he was far away; here it is," continued Joey, taking out the pencil-case, "and I have loved it dearly," added he, kissing it, "ever since I have had it in my possession. I very often have taken it out and thought of you."

217

"Now you are so rich a man, you should give me something to keep for your sake," replied Emma; "and I will be very careful of it, for old acquaintance' sake."

"What can I offer to you? you are a young lady; I would give you all I had in the world, if I dared, but——"

"When I first saw you," rejoined Emma, "you were dressed as a young gentleman."

"Yes, I was," replied Joey, with a sigh; and as the observation of Emma recalled to his mind the kindness of the M'Shanes, he passed his hand across his eyes to brush away a tear or two that started.

"I did not mean to make you unhappy," said Emma, taking our hero's hand.

"I am sure you did not," replied Joey, smiling. "Yes, I was then as you say; but recollect that lately I have been a knife-grinder."

"Well, you know, your friend said that it was the nearest thing to a gentleman; and now I hope you will be quite a gentleman again."

"Not a gentleman, for I must turn to some business or another," replied Joey.

"I did not mean an idle gentleman; I meant a respectable profession," said Emma. "My uncle is a very odd man, but very good-hearted; you must not mind his way towards you. He is very fond of mamma and me, and I have no doubt will interest himself about you, and see that your money is not thrown away. Perhaps you would like to set up a bumboat on your own account?" added Emma, laughing.

"No, I thank you; I had enough of that. Poor Mrs. Chopper! what a kind creature she was! I'm sure I ought to be very grateful to her for thinking of me as she did."

"I believe," said Emma, "that she was a very good woman, and so does mamma. Recollect, Joey, when you speak to my uncle, you must not contradict him."

"I am sure I shall not," replied Joey; "why should I contradict a person so far my superior in years and everything else?"

"Certainly not; and as he is fond of argument, you had better give up to him at once; and, indeed," continued Emma, laughing, "everybody else does in the end. I hope you will find a nice situation, and that we shall see a great deal of you."

" I am sure I do," replied Joey, " for I have no friends that I may see, except you. How I wish that you did know everything!"

A silence ensued between the young people, which was not interrupted until by the appearance of Mrs. Phillips, who had seen Mr. Small, and had made an engagement for our hero to present himself at nine o'clock on the following morning, after which communication our hero took his leave. He amused himself during the remainder of that day in walking over the town, which at that time presented a most bustling appearance, as an expedition was fitting out; the streets were crowded with officers of the army, navy, and marines, in their uniforms; soldiers and sailors, more or less tipsy; flaunting ribbons and gaudy colours; and every variety of noise was to be heard that could be well imagined, from the quacking of a duck, with its head out of the basket in which it was confined to be taken on board, to the martial music, the rolling of the drums, and the occasional salutes of artillery, to let the world know that some great man had put his foot on board of a ship, or had again deigned to tread upon *terra firma*. All was bustle and excitement, hurrying, jostling, cursing, and swearing; and Joey found himself, by the manner in which he was shoved about right and left, to be in the way of everybody.

At the time appointed our hero made his appearance at the door, and having given his name, was asked into the counting-house of the establishment, where sat Mr. Small and his factotum, Mr. Sleek. It may be as well here to describe the persons and peculiarities of these two gentlemen.

Mr. Small certainly did not accord with his name, for he was a man full six feet high, and stout in proportion; he was in face extremely plain, with a turned-up nose; but, at the same time, there was a lurking good-humour in his countenance, and a twinkle in his eye, which immediately prepossessed you, and in a few minutes you forgot that he was not well-favoured. Mr. Small was very fond of an argument and a joke, and he had such a forcible way of maintaining his argument when he happened to be near you, that, as Emma had told our hero, few people after a time ventured to contradict him. This mode of argument was nothing more than digging the hard knuckles of his large hand into the ribs of his opponent—we should rather say gradually gimleting, as it were, a hole in your side—as he heated in his illustrations. He was the last person in the world in his disposition to inflict pain, even upon an insect—and yet, from this habit, no one perhaps gave more, or appeared to do so with more malice, as his countenance was radiant with good-humour, at the very time when his knuckles were taking away your breath. What made it worse, was, that he had a knack of seizing the coat lappet with the other hand, so that escape was difficult; and when he had exhausted all his reasoning, he would follow it up with a pressure of his knuckles under the fifth rib, saying, "Now you feel the force of my argument, don't you?" Everybody did, and no one would oppose him unless the table was between them. It was much the same with his jokes: he would utter them, and then with a loud laugh, and the insidious insertion of his knuckles, say, "Do you take that, eh?" Mr. Sleek had also his peculiarity, and was not an agreeable person to argue with, for he had learnt to argue from his many years' constant companionship with the head of the firm. Mr. Sleek was a spare man, deeply pock-marked in the face, and with a very large mouth; and, when speaking, he sputtered to such a degree, that a quarter of an hour's conversation with him was as good as a shower-bath. At long range Mr. Sleek could beat his superior out of the field; but if Mr. Small approached once to close quarters, Mr. Sleek gave in immediately. The captains of the navy used to assert that this fibbing enforcement of his *truths,* on the part of Small, was quite contrary to all the rules of modern warfare, and never would stand it, unless they required an advance of money; and then, by submitting to a certain quantity of digs in the ribs in proportion to the unreasonableness of their demand, they usually obtained their object; as they said, he "knuckled down" in the end. As for Mr. Sleek, although the best man in the world, he was their abhorrence; he was nothing but a watering-pot, and they were not plants which required his aid to add to their vigour. Mr. Sleek, even in the largest company, invariably found himself alone, and could never imagine why. Still he was an important personage; and

220

when stock is to be got on board in a hurry, officers in his Majesty's service do not care about a little spray.

Mr. Small was, as we have observed, a navy agent—that is to say, he was a general provider of the officers and captains of his Majesty's service. He obtained their agency on any captures which they might send in, or he cashed their bills, advanced them money, supplied them with their wine, and every variety of stock which might be required ; and in consequence was reported to be accumulating a fortune. As is usually the case, he kept open house for the captains who were his clients, and occasionally invited the junior officers to the hospitalities of his table, so that Mrs. Phillips and Emma were of great use to him, and had quite sufficient to do in superintending such an establishment. Having thus made our readers better acquainted with our new characters, we shall proceed.

" Well, young man, I've heard all about you from my sister. So you wish to leave off vagabondising, do you ? "

" Yes, sir," replied Joey.

" How old are you ? can you keep books ? "

" I am seventeen, and have kept books," replied our hero in innocence ; for he considered Mrs. Chopper's day-books to come under that denomination.

" And you have some money—how much ? "

Joey replied that he had so much of his own, and that his sister had so much more.

" Seven hundred pounds ; eh, youngster ? I began business with £100 less, and here I am. Money breeds money ; do you understand that ? " and here Joey received a knuckle in his ribs, which almost took his breath away, but which he bore without flinching, as he presumed it was a mark of goodwill.

" What can we do with this lad, Sleek ? " said Mr. Small ; " and what can we do with his money ? "

" Let him stay in the counting-house here for a week," replied Mr. Sleek, " and we shall see what he can do ; and as for his money, it will be as safe here as in a country bank, until we know how to employ it, and we can allow five per cent. for it." All this was said in a shower of spray, which induced Joey to wipe his face with his pocket-handkerchief.

" Yes, I think that will do for the present," rejoined Mr.

Small; "but you observe, Sleek, that this young lad has very powerful interest, and we shall be expected to do something for him, or we shall have the worst of it. You understand that?" continued he, giving Joey a knuckle again. "The ladies! no standing against them!"

Joey thought there was no standing such digs in the ribs, but he said nothing.

"I leave him to you, Sleek. I must be off to call upon Captain James. See to the lad's food and lodging. There's an order from the gun-room of the *Hecate*." So saying, Mr. Small departed.

Mr. Sleek asked our hero where he was stopping; recommended him another lodging close to the house, with directions how to proceed, and what arrangements to make; told him to haste as much as he could, and then come back to the counting-house.

In a couple of hours our hero was back again.

"Look on this list; do you understand it?" said Mr. Sleek to Joey; "it is sea-stock for the *Hecate*, which sails in a day or two. If I send a porter with you to the people we deal with, would you be able to get all these things which are marked with a cross? the wine and the others we have here."

Joey looked over it, and was quite at home; it was only bumboating on a large scale. "Oh yes; and I know the prices of all these things," replied he; "I have been used to the supplying of ships at Gravesend."

"Why then," said Mr. Sleek, "you are the very person I want; for I have no time to attend to outdoor work now."

The porter was sent for, and our hero soon executed his task, not only with a precision but with a rapidity that was highly satisfactory to Mr. Sleek. As soon as the articles were all collected, Joey asked whether he should take them on board—"I understand the work, Mr. Sleek, and not even an egg shall be broke, I promise you." The second part of the commission was executed with the same precision by our hero, who returned with a receipt of every article having been delivered safe and in good condition. Mr. Sleek was delighted with our hero, and told Mr. Small so when they met in the evening. Mr. Sleek's opinion was given in the presence of Mrs. Phillips and Emma, who exchanged glances of satisfaction at Joey's fortunate *début*.

CHAPTER XXXVIII

*In which the wheel of Fortune turns a spoke or two in favour of
our hero.*

IF we were to analyse the feelings of our hero towards
Emma Phillips, we should hardly be warranted in saying
that he was in love with her, although at seventeen years
young men are very apt to be, or so to fancy themselves.
The difference in their positions was so great, that although
our hero would, in his dreams, often fancy himself on most
intimate terms with his kind little patroness, in his waking
thoughts she was more an object of adoration and respect
—a being to whom he was most ardently and devotedly
attached—one whose friendship and kindness had so wrought
upon his best feelings, that he would have thought it no
sacrifice to die for her; but the idea of ever being closer
allied to her than he now was had not yet entered into his
imagination; all he ever thought was that, if ever he united
himself to any female for life, the party selected must be like
Emma Phillips; or, if not, he would remain single. All his
endeavours were to prove himself worthy of her patronage,
and to be rewarded by her smiles of encouragement when
they met. She was the loadstar which guided him on to
his path of duty; and stimulated by his wishes to find favour
in her sight, Joey never relaxed in his exertions. Naturally
active and methodical, he was indefatigable, and gave the
greatest satisfaction to Mr. Sleek, who found more than half
the labour taken off his hands; and, further, that if Joey once
said a thing should be done, it was not only well done, but
done to the very time that was stipulated for its completion.
Joey cared not for meals, or anything of that kind, and often
went without his dinner.

"Sleek," said Small, one day, "that poor boy will be
starved."

"It's not my fault, sir; he won't go to his dinner if there
is anything to do; and, as there is always something to do,
it's as clear as the day that he can get no dinner. I wish he
was living in the house altogether, and came to his meals

with us after the work was done; it would be very advantageous, and much time saved."

"Time is money, Sleek. Time saved is money saved; and therefore he is worthy of his food. It shall be so. Do you see to it."

Thus, in about two months after his arrival, Joey found himself installed in a nice little bedroom, and living at the table of his patron, not only constantly in company with the naval officers, but, what was of more value to him, in the company of Mrs. Phillips and Emma.

We must pass over more than a year, during which time our hero had become a person of some importance. He was a great favourite with the naval captains, as his punctuality and rapidity corresponded with their ideas of doing business; and it was constantly said to Mr. Sleek or to Mr. Small, "Let O'Donahue and I settle the matter, and all will go right." Mr. Small had already established him at a salary of £150 per annum, besides his living in the house, and our hero was comfortable and happy. He was well known to all the officers, from his being constantly on board of their ships, and was a great favourite. Joey soon discovered that Emma had a fancy for natural curiosities; and as he boarded almost every man-of-war which came into the port, he soon filled her room with a variety of shells and of birds, which he procured her. These were presents which he could make, and which she could accept, and not a week passed without our hero adding something to her museum of live and dead objects. Indeed, Emma was now grown up, and was paid such attention to by the officers who frequented her uncle's house (not only on account of her beauty, but on account of the expectation that her uncle, who was without children, would give her a handsome fortune), that some emotions of jealousy, of which he was hardly conscious, would occasionally give severe pain to our hero. Perhaps as his fortunes rose, so did his hopes; certain it is, that sometimes he was very grave.

Emma was too clear-sighted not to perceive the cause, and hastened, by her little attentions, to remove the feeling; not that she had any definite ideas upon the subject any more than Joey, but she could not bear to see him look unhappy.

Such was the state of things, when one day Mr. Small said to Joey, as he was busy copying an order into the books, " O'Donahue, I have been laying out some of your money for you."

" Indeed, sir ! I'm very much obliged to you."

" Yes ; there was a large stock of claret sold at auction to-day : it was good, and went cheap. I have purchased to the amount of £600 on your account. You may bottle and bin it here, and sell it as you can. If you don't like the bargain, I'll take it off your hands."

" I am very grateful to you, sir," replied Joey, who knew the kindness of the act, which in two months more than doubled his capital ; and, as he was permitted to continue the business on his own account, he was very soon in a position amounting to independence, the French wine business being ever afterwards considered as exclusively belonging to our hero.

One morning, as Joey happened to be in the counting-house by himself—which was rather an unusual occurrence—a midshipman came in. Joey remembered him very well, as he had been often there before. " Good morning, Mr. O'Donahue," said the midshipman ; " is Mr. Small within ? "

" No, he is not ; can I do anything for you ? "

" Yes ; if you can tell me how I am to persuade Mr. Small to advance me a little money upon my pay, you can do something for me."

" I never heard of such an application before," replied Joey, smiling.

" No, that I venture you did not, and it requires all the impudence of a midshipman to make such a one ; but the fact is, Mr. O'Donahue, I am a mate with £40 a year, and upon that I have continued to assist my poor old mother up to the present. She now requires £10 in consequence of illness, and I have not a farthing. I will repay it if I live, that is certain ; but I have little hopes of obtaining it, and nothing but my affection for the old lady would induce me to risk the mortification of a refusal. It's true enough that ' he who goes a-borrowing goes a-sorrowing.' "

" I fear it is ; but I will so far assist you as to let you know what your only chance is. State your case to Mr. Small as you have to me to-day, and then stand close to him while he answers; if he puts his knuckles into your ribs to enforce his arguments, don't shrink, and then wait the result without interrupting him."

"Well, I'd do more than that for the old lady," replied the poor midshipman, as Mr. Small made his appearance.

The midshipman told his story in very few words, and Mr. Small heard him without interruption. When he had finished, Mr. Small commenced—

"You see, my man, you ask me to do what no navy-agent ever did before—to lend upon a promise to pay, and that promise to pay from a midshipman. In the first place, I have only the promise without the security; that's one point, do you observe? (a punch with the knuckles). And then the promise to pay depends on whether you are in the country or not. Again, if you have the money, you may not have the inclination to pay; that's another point (then came another sharp impression into the ribs of the middy). Then, again, it is not even personal security, as you may be drowned, shot, blown up, or taken out of the world before any pay is due to you; and by your death you would be unable to pay, if so inclined; there's a third point (and there was a third dig, which the middy stood boldly up against). Insure your life you cannot, for you have no money; you therefore require me to lend my money upon no security whatever, for even allowing that you would pay if you could, yet your death might prevent it; there's another point (and the knuckles again penetrated into the midshipman's side, who felt the torture increasing as hope was departing). But," continued Mr. Small, who was evidently much pleased with his own ratiocination, "there is another point not yet touched upon, which is, that as good Christians we must sometimes lend money upon no security, or even give it away, for so are we commanded; and therefore, Mr. O'Donahue, you will tell Mr. Sleek to let him have the money; there's the last and best point of all, eh?" wound up Mr. Small, with a thumping blow upon the ribs of the middy, that almost took away his breath. We give this as a specimen of Mr. Small's style of practical and theoretical logic combined.

"The admiral, sir, is coming down the street," said Sleek, entering, "and I think he is coming here."

Mr. Small, who did not venture to chop logic with admirals,

but was excessively polite to such great people, went out to receive the admiral, hat in hand.

"Now, Mr. Small," said the admiral, "the counting-house for business, if you please. I have very unexpected orders to leave Portsmouth. I must save the next tide, if possible. The ships will be ready, for you know what our navy can do when required; but, as you know, I have not one atom of stock on board. The flood-tide has made almost an hour, and we must sail at the first of the ebb, as twelve hours' delay may be most serious. Now, tell me—here is the list of what is required; boats will be ready and men in plenty to get it on board—can you get it ready by that time?"

"By that time, Sir William?" replied Small, looking over the tremendous catalogue.

"It is now eleven o'clock; can it all be down by four o'clock—that is the latest I can give you?"

"Impossible, Sir William."

"It is of the greatest importance that we sail at five o'clock—the fact is, I must and will; but it's hard that I must starve for a whole cruise."

"Indeed, Sir William," said Mr. Small, "if it were possible; but two cows, so many sheep, hay, and everything to be got from the country—we never could manage it. To-morrow morning, perhaps."

"Well, Mr. Small, I have appointed no prize-agent yet; had you obliged me——"

Our hero now stepped forward and ran over the list.

"Can you inform me, sir," said he to the flag-captain, "whether the *Zenobia* or *Orestes* sail with the squadron?"

"No, they do not," was the reply.

"I beg your pardon, Mr. Small," said Joey, "but I do think we can accomplish this with a little arrangement."

"Indeed!" cried Sir William.

"Yes, Sir William; if you would immediately make the signals for two boats to come on shore, with steady crews to assist me, I promise it shall be done."

"Well said, O'Donahue!" cried the captain. "We are all right now, admiral; if he says it shall be done, it will be done."

"May I depend upon you, Mr. O'Donahue."

"Yes, Sir William; everything shall be as you wish."

"Well, Mr. Small, if your young man keeps his word, you shall be my prize-agent. Good morning to you."

"How could you promise?" cried Small, addressing our hero, when the admiral and suite had left the counting-house.

"Because I can perform, sir," replied Joey; "I have the cows and sheep for the *Zenobia* and *Orestes*, as well as the fodder, all ready in the town; we can get others for them to-morrow, and I know where to lay my hands on everything else."

"Well, that's lucky! but there is no time to be lost."

Our hero, with his usual promptitude and activity, kept his promise; and, as Mr. Small said, it was lucky, for the prize-agency, in a few months afterwards, proved worth to him nearly £5000.

It is not to be supposed that Joey neglected his correspondence either with Mary or Spikeman, although with the latter it was not so frequent. Mary wrote to him every month; she had not many subjects to enter upon, chiefly replying to Joey's communications, and congratulating him upon his success. Indeed, now that our hero had been nearly four years with Mr. Small, he might be said to be a very rising and independent person. His capital, which had increased very considerably, had been thrown into the business, and he was now a junior partner, instead of a clerk, and had long enjoyed the full confidence both of his superior and of Mr. Sleek, who now entrusted him with almost everything. In short, Joey was in the fair way to competence and distinction.

CHAPTER XXXIX

Chapter of infinite variety, containing agony, law, love, quarrelling, and suicide.

IT may be a subject of interest on the part of the reader to inquire what were the relative positions of Emma Phillips and our hero, now that four years had passed, during which time he had been continually in her company, and gradually, as he rose in importance, removing the distance that was between them. We have only to reply that the consequences natural to such a case did ensue. Every year their intimacy increased—every year added to the hopes of our hero, who now no longer looked upon an alliance with Emma as impossible ; yet he still never felt sufficient confidence in himself or his fortunes to intimate such a thought to her. Indeed, from a long habit of veneration and respect, he was in the position of a subject before a queen who feels a partiality towards him ; he dared not give vent to his thoughts, and it remained for her to have the unfeminine task of intimating to him that he might venture. But, although to outward appearance there was nothing but respect and feelings of gratitude on his part, and condescension and amiability on hers, there was a rapid adhesion going on within. Their interviews were more restrained, their words more selected, for both parties felt how strong were the feelings which they would repress ; they were both pensive, silent, and distant—would talk unconnectedly, running from one subject to another, attempting to be lively and unconcerned when they were most inclined to be otherwise, and not daring to scrutinise too minutely their own feelings when they found themselves alone. But what they would fain conceal from themselves their very attempts to conceal made known to other people who were standing by. Both Mrs. Phillips and Mr. Small perceived how matters stood, and, had they any objections, would have immediately no longer permitted them to be in contact ; but they had no objections, for our hero had long won the hearts of both mother and uncle, and they awaited quietly the time which should arrive when the young parties should no longer conceal their feelings for each other.

It was when affairs were between our hero and Emma Phillips as we have just stated, that a circumstance took place which for a time embittered all our hero's happiness. He was walking down High Street when he perceived a file of marines marching towards him, with two men between them, handcuffed, evidently deserters who had been taken up. A feeling of alarm pervaded our hero ; he had a presentiment which induced him to go into a perfumer's shop, and to remain there, so as to have a view of the faces of the deserters as they passed along, without their being able to see him. His forebodings were correct: one of them was his old enemy and persecutor, Furness the schoolmaster.

Had a dagger been plunged into Joey's bosom, the sensation could not have been more painful than what he felt when he once more found himself so near to his dreaded denouncer. For a short time he remained so transfixed, that the woman who was attending in the shop asked whether she should bring him a glass of water. This inquiry made him recollect himself, and, complaining of a sudden pain in the side, he sat down, and took the water when it was brought; but he went home in despair, quite forgetting the business which brought him out, and retired to his own room, that he might collect his thoughts. What was he to do? This man had been brought back to the barracks; he would be tried and punished, and afterwards be set at liberty. How was it possible that he could always avoid him, or escape being recognised? and how little chance had he of escape from Furness's searching eye! Could he bribe him? Yes, he could *now*, he was rich enough; but if he did, one bribe would only be followed up by a demand for another, and a threat of denouncement if he refused. Flight appeared his only chance; but to leave his present position— to leave Emma—it was impossible. Our hero did not leave his room for the remainder of the day, but retired early to bed, that he might cogitate, for sleep he could not. After a night of misery, the effects of which were too visibly marked in his countenance on the ensuing morning, Joey determined to make some inquiries relative to what the fate of Furness might be; and having made up his mind, he accosted a sergeant of marines, with whom he had a slight acquaintance, and whom he fell in with in the streets. He observed to him that he perceived they had deserters brought in yesterday, and inquired from what ship they had deserted, or from the barracks. The sergeant replied that they had deserted from the *Niobe* frigate, and had committed theft previous to desertion; that they would remain in confinement at the barracks till the *Niobe* arrived; and that then they would be tried by a court-martial, and, without doubt, for the double offence, would go through the fleet.

Joey wished the sergeant good morning, and passed on in

his way home. His altered appearance had attracted the notice of not only his partners, but of Mrs. Phillips, and had caused much distress to the latter. Our hero remained the whole day in the counting-house, apparently unconcerned, but in reality thinking and rethinking, over and over again, his former thoughts. At last he made up his mind that he would wait the issue of the court-martial before he took any decided steps; indeed, what to do he knew not.

We leave the reader to guess the state of mind in which Joey remained for a fortnight previous to the return of the *Niobe* frigate from a Channel cruise. Two days after her arrival the signal was made for a court-martial. The sentence was well known before night; it was, that the culprits were to go through the fleet on the ensuing day.

This was, however, no consolation to our hero; he did not feel animosity against Furness so much as he did dread of him; he did not want his punishment, but his absence, and security against future annoyance. It was about nine o'clock on the next morning, when the punishment was to take place, that Joey came down from his own room. He had been thinking all night, and had decided that he had no other resource but to quit Portsmouth, Emma, and his fair prospects for ever; he had resolved so to do, to make this sacrifice; it was a bitter conclusion to arrive at, but it had been come to. His haggard countenance, when he made his appearance at the breakfast-table, shocked Mrs. Phillips and Emma; but they made no remarks. The breakfast was passed over in silence, and soon afterwards our hero found himself alone with Emma, who immediately went to him, and, with tears in her eyes, said, "What is the matter with you?—you look so ill, you alarm us all, and you make me quite miserable."

"I am afraid, Miss Phillips——"

"Miss Phillips!" replied Emma.

"I beg your pardon; but, Emma, I am afraid that I must leave you."

"Leave us!"

"Yes, leave you and Portsmouth for ever, perhaps."

"Why, what has occurred?"

"I cannot, dare not tell. Will you so far oblige me to say nothing at present; but you recollect that I was obliged to leave Gravesend on a sudden."

"I recollect you did, but why I know not; only Mary said that it was not your fault."

"I trust it was not so; but it was my misfortune. Emma, I am almost distracted; I have not slept for weeks; but pray believe me, when I say that I have done no wrong; indeed——"

"We are interrupted," said Emma hurriedly; "there is somebody coming upstairs."

She had hardly time to remove a few feet from our hero, when Captain B——, of the *Niobe*, entered the room.

"Good morning, Miss Phillips, I hope you are well. I just looked in for a moment before I go to the admiral's office; we have had a catastrophe on board the *Niobe*, which I must report immediately."

"Indeed," replied Emma; "nothing very serious, I hope."

"Why, no, only rid of a blackguard not worth hanging; one of the marines, who was to have gone round the fleet this morning, when he went to the forepart of the ship under the sentry's charge, leaped overboard, and drowned himself."

"What was his name, Captain B——?" inquired Joey, seizing him by the arm.

"His name—why, how can that interest you, O'Donahue? Well, if you wish to know, it was Furness."

"I am very sorry for him," replied our hero; "I knew him once when he was in better circumstances, that is all;" and Joey, no longer daring to trust himself with others, quitted the room, and went to his own apartment. As soon as he was there he knelt down and returned thanks, not for the death of Furness, but for the removal of the load which had so oppressed his mind. In an hour his relief was so great that he felt himself sufficiently composed to go downstairs. He went into the drawing-room to find Emma, but she was not there. He longed to have some explanation with her, but it was not until the next day that he had an opportunity.

"I hardly know what to say to you," said our hero, "or how to explain my conduct of yesterday."

"It certainly appeared very strange, especially to Captain B——, who told me that he thought you were mad."

"I care little what he thinks, but I care much what you think, Emma; and I must now tell you what, perhaps, this man's death may permit me to do. That he has been most

232

strangely connected with my life is most true; he it was who knew me, and who would, if he could, have put me in a situation in which I must either have suffered myself to be thought guilty of a crime which I am incapable of, or, let it suffice to say, have done, to exculpate myself, what I trust I never would have done, or ever will do. I can say no more than that, without betraying a secret which I am bound to keep, and the keeping of which may still prove my own destruction. When you first saw me on the way-side, Emma, it was this man who forced me from a happy home to wander about the world; it was the reappearance of this man, and his recognition of me, that induced me to quit Gravesend so suddenly. I again met him, and avoided him when he was deserting; and I trusted that, as he had deserted, I could be certain of living safely in this town without meeting with him. It was his reappearance here, as a deserter taken up, which put me in that state of agony which you have seen me in for these last three weeks; and it was the knowledge that, after his punishment, he would be again free, and likely to meet with me when walking about here, which resolved me to quit Portsmouth, as I said to you yesterday morning. Can you, therefore, be surprised at my emotion when I heard that he was removed, and that there was now no necessity for my quitting my kind patrons and you?"

"Certainly, after this explanation, I cannot be surprised at your emotion; but what does surprise me, Mr. O'Donahue, is that you should have a secret of such importance that it cannot be revealed, and which has made you tremble at the recognition of that man, when at the same time you declare your innocence. Did innocence and mystery ever walk hand in hand?"

"Your addressing me as Mr. O'Donahue, Miss Phillips, has pointed out to me the impropriety I have been guilty of in making use of your Christian name. I thought that that confidence which you placed in me when, as a mere boy, I told you exactly what I now repeat, that the secret was not my own, would not have been now so cruelly withdrawn. I have never varied in my tale, and I can honestly say that I have never felt degraded when I have admitted that I have a mystery connected with me; nay, if it should please

Heaven that I have the option given me to suffer in my own person, or reveal the secret in question, I trust that I shall submit to my fate with constancy, and be supported in my misfortune by the conviction of my innocence. I feel that I was not wrong in the communication that I made to you yesterday morning that I must leave this place. I came here because you were living here—you to whom I felt so devoted for your kindness and sympathy when I was poor and friendless. Now that I am otherwise, you are pleased to withdraw not only your goodwill, but your confidence in me; and as the spell is broken which has drawn me to this spot, I repeat, that as soon as I can, with justice to my patrons, I shall withdraw myself from your presence."

Our hero's voice faltered before he had finished speaking; and then turning away slowly, without looking up, he quitted the room.

CHAPTER XL

In which our hero tries change of air.

THE reader will observe that there has been a little altercation at the end of the last chapter. Emma Phillips was guilty of letting drop a received truism, or rather a metaphor, which offended our hero. " Did innocence and mystery ever walk hand in hand?" If Emma had put that question to us, we, from our knowledge of the world, should have replied, " Yes, very often, my dear Miss Phillips." But Emma was wrong, not only in her metaphor, but in the time of her making it. Why did she do so? Ah! that is a puzzling question to answer. We can only say, at our imminent risk, when this narrative shall be perused by the other sex, that we have made the discovery that women are not perfect; that the very best of the sex are full of contradiction, and that Emma was a woman. That women very often are more endowed than the generality of men we are ready to admit; and their cause has been taken up by Lady Morgan, Mrs. Jamieson, and many others who can write much better than we can. When we say their cause, we mean the right of

equality they would claim with our sex, and not subjection to
it. Reading my Lady Morgan the other day, which, next to
conversing with her, is one of the greatest treats we know
of, we began to speculate upon what were the causes which
had subjected woman to man; in other words, how was it
that man had got the upper hand, and kept it? That
women's minds were not inferior to men's we were forced
to admit; that their aptitude for cultivation is often greater,
was not to be denied. As to the assertion that man makes
laws, or that his frame is of more robust material, it is no
argument, as a revolt on the part of the other sex would
soon do away with such advantage; and men, brought up as
nursery-maids, would soon succumb to women who were
accustomed to athletic sports from their youth upwards.
After a great deal of cogitation we came to the conclusion,
that there is a great difference between the action in the
minds of men and women; the machinery of the latter being
more complex than that of our own sex. A man's mind is
his despot: it works but by one single action; it has one
ruling principle—one propelling power to which all is subservient. This power or passion (disguised and dormant as
it may be in feeble minds) is the only one which propels him
on; this *primum mobile,* as it may be termed, is ambition, or,
in other words, self-love; everything is sacrificed to it.

Now, as in proportion as a machine is simple so is it strong
in its action, so in proportion that a machine is complex it
becomes weak; and if we analyse a woman's mind, we shall
find that her inferiority arises from the simple fact, that there
are so many wheels within wheels working in it, so many
compensating balances (if we may use the term, and we use
it to her honour), that although usually more right-minded
than man, her strength of action is lost, and has become
feeble by the time that her decision has been made. What
will a man allow to stand in the way of his ambition—love?
no—friendship? no—he will sacrifice the best qualities, and,
which is more difficult, make the worst that are in his disposition subservient to it. He moves only one great principle,
one propelling power; and the action being single, it is
strong in proportion. But will a woman's mind decide in
this way? Will she sacrifice to ambition love, or friendship,
or natural ties? No; in her mind the claims of each are,

generally speaking, fairly balanced, and the quotient, after the calculation has been worked out, although correct, is small. Our argument, after all, only goes to prove that women, abstractedly taken, have more principle, more conscience, and better regulated minds than men—which is true if—if they could always go correct as timekeepers. But the more complex the machine, the more difficult it is to keep it in order, the more likely it is to be out of repair, and its movements to be disarranged by a trifling shock, which would have no effect upon one of such simple and powerful construction as that in our own sex. Not only do they often go wrong, but sometimes the serious shocks which they are liable to in this world will put them in a state which is past all repair.

We have no doubt that by this time the reader will say, "Never mind women's minds, but mind your own business." We left Emma in the drawing-room, rather astonished at our hero's long speech, and still more by his (for the first time during their acquaintance) venturing to breathe a contrary opinion to her own sweet self.

Emma Phillips, although she pouted a little, and the colour had mounted to her temples, nevertheless looked very lovely as she pensively reclined on the sofa. Rebuked by him who had always been so attentive, so submissive—her creature as it were—she was mortified, as every pretty woman is, at any loss of power, any symptoms of rebellion on the part of a liege vassal; and then she taxed herself, had she done wrong? She had said, "Innocence and mystery did not walk hand in hand." Was not that true? She felt that it was true, and her own opinion was corroborated by others, for she had read it in some book, either in Burke, or Rochefoucauld, or some great author. Miss Phillips bit the tip of her nail and thought again. Yes, she saw how it was—our hero had risen in the world, was independent, and was well received in society; he was no longer the little Joey of Gravesend, he was now a person of some consequence, and he was a very ungrateful fellow; but the world was full of ingratitude; still she did think better of our hero, she certainly did. Well, at all events she could prove to him that—what?—she did not exactly know. Thus ended cogitation the second, after which came another series.

What had our hero said—what had he accused her of? That she no longer bestowed on him her confidence placed in him for many years. This was true ; but were not the relative positions, was not the case different? Should he now retain any secret from her ?—there should be no secrets between them. Here again there was a full stop before the sentence was complete. After a little more reflection, her own generous mind pointed out to her that she had been in the wrong, and that our hero had cause to be offended with her ; and she made up her mind to make reparation the first time that they should be alone.

Having come to this resolution, she dismissed the previous question, and began to think about the secret itself, and what it possibly could be, and how she wished she knew what it was ; all of which was very natural. In the meantime our hero had made up his mind to leave Portsmouth, for a time at all events. This quarrel with Emma, if such it might be considered, had made him very miserable, and the anxiety he had lately suffered had seriously affected his health.

We believe that there never was anybody in this world who had grown to man's or woman's estate, and had mixed with the world, who could afterwards say that they were at any time perfectly happy ; or who, having said so, did not find that the reverse was the case a moment or two after the words were out of their mouth. "There is always something," as a good lady said to us ; and so there always is, and always will be. The removal of Furness was naturally a great relief to the mind of our hero ; he then felt as if all his difficulties were surmounted, and that he had no longer any fear of the consequences which might ensue from his father's crime. He would now, he thought, be able to walk boldly through the world without recognition, and he had built castles enough to form a metropolis, when his rupture with Emma broke the magic mirror through which he had scanned futurity. When most buoyant with hope, he found the truth of the good lady's saying—"There is always something."

After remaining in his room for an hour, Joey went down to the counting-house, where he found Mr. Small and Mr. Sleek both at work, for their labours had increased since Joey had so much neglected business.

"Well, my good friend, how do you find yourself?" said Mr. Small.

"Very far from well, sir. I feel that I cannot attend to business," replied Joey, "and I am quite ashamed of myself; I was thinking that, if you had no objection to allow me a couple of months' leave of absence, change of air would be very serviceable to me. I have something to do at Dudstone, which I have put off ever since I came to Portsmouth."

"I think change of air would be very serviceable to you, my dear fellow," replied Mr. Small; "but what business you can have at Dudstone I cannot imagine."

"Simply this—I locked up my apartments, leaving my furniture, books, and linen, when I went away, more than four years ago, and have never found time to look after them."

"Well, they must want dusting by this time, O'Donahue, so look after them if you please; but I think looking after your health is of more consequence, so you have my full consent to take a holiday, and remain away three months, if necessary, till you are perfectly re-established."

"And you have mine," added Mr. Sleek, "and I will do your work while you are away."

Our hero thanked his senior partners for their kind compliance with his wishes, and stated his intention of starting the next morning by the early coach, and then left the counting-house to make preparations for his journey.

Joey joined the party, which was numerous, at dinner. It was not until they were in the drawing-room after dinner, that Mr. Small had an opportunity of communicating to Mrs. Phillips what were our hero's intentions. Mrs. Phillips considered it a very advisable measure, as Joey had evidently suffered very much lately; probably over-exertion might have been the cause, and relaxation would effect the cure.

Emma, who was sitting by her mother, turned pale; she had not imagined that our hero would have followed up his expressed intentions of the morning, and she asked Mr. Small if he knew when O'Donahue would leave Portsmouth. The reply was, that he had taken his place on the early coach of the next morning; and Emma fell back on the sofa, and did not say anything more.

When the company had all left, Mrs. Phillips rose and

lighted a chamber candlestick to go to bed, and Emma followed the motions of her mother. Mrs. Phillips shook hands with our hero, wishing him a great deal of pleasure, and that he would return quite restored in health. Emma, who found that all chance of an interview with our hero was gone, mustered up courage enough to extend her hand, and say, " I hope your absence will be productive of health and happiness to you, Mr. O'Donahue," and then followed her mother.

Joey, who was in no humour for conversation, then bade farewell to Mr. Small and Mr. Sleek, and before Emma had risen from a not very refreshing night's rest he was two stages on his way from Portsmouth.

CHAPTER XLI

In which our hero has his head turned the wrong way.

ALTHOUGH it may be very proper, when an offence has been offered us, to show that we feel the injury, it often happens that we act too much upon impulse and carry measures to extremities, and this our hero felt as the coach wheeled him along, every second increasing his distance from Emma Phillips. Twenty times he was inclined to take a postchaise and return, but the inconsistency would have been so glaring, that shame prevented him ; so he went on until he reached the metropolis, and on arriving there, having nothing better to do, he went to bed. The next·day he booked himself for the following day's coach to Manstone, and having so done, he thought he would reconnoitre the domicile of Major and Mrs. M'Shane, and, now that Furness was no longer to be dreaded, make his existence known to them. He went to Holborn accordingly, and found the shop in the same place, with the usual enticing odour sent forth from the grating which gave light and air to the kitchen; but he perceived that there was no longer the name of M'Shane on the private door, and entering the coffee-room, and looking towards the spot where Mrs. M'Shane usually stood carving the joint, he discovered a person similarly

239

employed whose face was unknown to him; in fact, it could not be Mrs. M'Shane, as it was a man. Our hero went up to him, and inquired if the M'Shanes still carried on the business, and was told that they had sold it some time back. His next inquiry, as to what had become of them, produced an "I don't know," with some symptoms of impatience at being interrupted. Under such circumstances our hero had nothing more to do but either to sit down and eat beef or to quit the premises. He preferred the latter, and was once more at the hotel, where he dedicated the remainder of the day to thinking of his old friends, as fate had debarred him from seeing them.

The next morning Joey set off by the coach, and arrived at Manstone a little before dusk. He remained at the principal inn of the village, called the Austin Arms, in honour of the property in the immediate vicinity; and having looked at the various quarterings of arms that the signboard contained, without the slightest idea that they appertained to himself, he ordered supper, and looking out of the window of the first floor, discovered, at no great distance down the one street which composed the village, the small ale-house where he had before met Mary. Our hero no longer felt the pride of poverty; he had resented the treatment he had received at the Hall when friendless, but now that he was otherwise he had overcome the feeling, and had resolved to go up to the Hall on the following day, and ask for Mary. He was now well dressed, and with all the appearance and manners of a gentleman; and, moreover, he had been so accustomed to respect from servants, that he had no idea of being treated otherwise. The next morning, therefore, he walked up to the Hall, and knocking at the door, as soon as it was opened he told the well-powdered domestics that he wished to speak a few words to Miss Atherton, if she still lived with Mrs. Austin. His appearance was considered by these gentlemen in waiting as sufficient to induce them to show him into a parlour, and to send for Mary, who in a few minutes came down to him, and embraced him tenderly. " I should hardly have known you, my dear boy," said she, as the tears glistened in her eyes; " you have grown quite a man. I cannot imagine, as you now stand before me, that you could have been the little Joey that was living at Mrs. Chopper's."

"We are indebted to that good woman for our prosperity," replied Joey. "Do you know, Mary, that your money has multiplied so fast that I almost wish that you would take it away, lest by some accident it should be lost? I have brought you an account."

"Let me have an account of yourself, my dear brother," replied Mary; "I have no want of money; I am here well and happy."

"So you must have been, for you look as young and handsome as when I last saw you, Mary. How is your mistress?"

"She is well, and would, I think, be happy, if it were not for the strange disease of Mr. Austin, who secludes himself entirely, and will not even go outside of the park gates. He has become more overbearing and haughty than ever, and several of the servants have quitted within the last few months."

"I have no wish to meet him, dear Mary, after what passed when I was here before. I will not put up with insolence from any man, even in his own house," replied our hero.

"Do not speak so loud; his study is next to us, and that door leads to it," replied Mary; "he would not say anything to you, but he would find fault with me."

"Then you had better come to see me at the Austin Arms, where I am stopping."

"I will come this evening," replied Mary.

At this moment the door which led to the study was opened, and a voice was heard—

"Mary, I wish you would take your sweethearts to a more convenient distance."

Joey heard the harsh, hollow voice, but recognised it not; he would not turn round to look at Mr. Austin, but remained with his back to him, and the door closed again with a bang.

"Well," observed Joey, "that is a pretty fair specimen of what he is, at all events. Why did you not say I was your brother?"

"Because it was better to say nothing," replied Mary; "he will not come in again."

"Well, I shall leave you now," said Joey, "and wait till the evening; you will be certain to come?"

"Oh yes, I certainly shall," replied Mary. "Hush! I hear my mistress with Mr. Austin. I wish you could see her, you would like her very much."

The outer door of the study was closed to, and then the door of the room in which they were conversing was opened, but it was shut again immediately.

"Who was that?" said our hero, who had not turned round to ascertain.

"Mrs. Austin; she just looked in, and seeing I was engaged, she only nodded to me to say that she wanted me, I presume, and then went away again," replied Mary. "You had better go now, and I will be sure to come in the evening."

Our hero quitted the Hall; he had been in the presence of his father and mother without knowing it, and all because he happened on both occasions to have his face turned in a wrong direction, and he left the house as unconscious as he went in. As soon as our hero had left the Hall, Mary repaired to her mistress.

"Do you want me, madam?" said Mary, as she went to her mistress.

"No, Mary, not particularly, but Mr. Austin sent for me; he was annoyed at your having a strange person in the house, and desired me to send him away."

"It was my brother, madam," replied Mary.

"Your brother! I am very sorry, Mary, but you know how nervous Mr. Austin is, and there is no reasoning against nerves. I should have liked to have seen your brother very much; if I recollect rightly, you told me he was doing very well at Portsmouth, is he not?"

"Yes, madam; he is now a partner in one of the first houses there."

"Why, Mary, he will soon have you to keep his own house, I presume, and I shall lose you; indeed, you are more fit for such a situation than your present one, so I must not regret it if you do."

"He has no idea of taking a house, madam," replied Mary, "nor have I any of quitting you; your place is quite good enough for me. I promised to go down and meet him this evening, with your permission, at the Austin Arms."

"Certainly," replied Mrs. Austin; and then the conversation dropped.

Our hero remained at the inn two days, a portion of which Mary passed with him, and then he set off for Dudstone; he did not make Mary a confidante of his attachment to Emma Phillips, although he imparted to her the death of Furness, and the relief it had afforded him, promising to return to see her before he went back to Portsmouth.

Joey once more set off on his travels, and without incident arrived at the good old town of Dudstone, where he put up at the Commercial Hotel; his only object was to ascertain the condition of his lodgings. For the first two years he had sent the rent of the room to the old woman to whom the house belonged, but latterly no application had been made for it, although his address had been given; and, occupied by other business more important, our hero had quite forgotten the affair, or if he did occasionally recall it to his memory, it was soon dismissed again. His key he had brought with him, and he now proceeded to the house and knocked at the door, surmising that the old woman was possibly dead, and his property probably disposed of. The first part of the surmise was disproved by the old woman coming to the door; she did not recognise our hero, and it was not until he produced the key of his room that she was convinced that he was the lawful owner of its contents. She told him she could not write herself, and that the party who had written to Portsmouth for her was dead, and that she felt sure he would come back at some time and settle with her; and, moreover, she was afraid that the furniture would be much injured by having been shut up so long, which was not only very likely, but proved to be the case when the door was opened; she also said that she could have made money for him, had he allowed her to let the lodgings furnished, as she had had several applications. Our hero walked into his apartment, which certainly had a very mothy and mouldy appearance. As soon as a fire had been lighted, he collected all that he wanted to retain for himself, the books, plate, and some other articles which he valued for Spikeman's sake, and as old reminiscences, and putting them up in a chest, requested that it might be sent to the inn; and then, upon reflection, he thought he could do no better with the remainder than to make them a present to the old woman, which he did, after paying up her arrears of rent, and by so doing made one person, for the time, superlatively happy, which is something worth doing in this chequered world of ours. Joey, as soon as he had returned to the inn, sat down to write to Spikeman, and also to Mr. Small at Portsmouth; and having posted his letters, as he did not quit Dudstone until the next morning, he resolved to pay a visit to his former acquaintances, Miss Amelia and Miss Ophelia. His knock at the door was answered by Miss Amelia, as usual, but with only one arm unoccupied, a baby being in the other, and the squalling in the little parlour gave further evidence of matrimony. Our hero was obliged to introduce himself, as he was stared at as an utter stranger; he was then immediately welcomed, and requested to walk into the parlour. In a few minutes the whole of the family history was communicated. The old lady had been dead three years, and at her death the young ladies found themselves in possession of one thousand pounds each. This thousand pounds proved to them that husbands were to be had, even at Dudstone and its vicinity. Miss Amelia had been married more than two years to a master builder, who had plenty of occupation, not so much in building new houses at Dudstone as in repairing the old ones, and they were doing well, and had two children. Her sister had married a young farmer, and she could see her money every day in the shape of bullocks and sheep upon the farm; they also were doing well. Joey remained an hour: Mrs. Potts was very anxious that he should remain longer, and give her his opinion of her husband; but this Joey declined, and, desiring to be kindly remembered to her sister, took his leave, and the next morning was on his way to London

CHAPTER XLII

Very pleasant correspondence.

AS soon as Joey arrived at the metropolis, he went to the correspondent of the house at Portsmouth to inquire for letters. He found one of the greatest interest from Mr. Small, who, after some preliminaries relative to the business and certain commissions for him to transact in town, proceeded as follows :—

" Your health has been a source of great anxiety to us all, not only in the counting-house, but in the drawing-room; the cause of your illness was ascribed to over-exertion in your duties, and it must be admitted, that until you were ill, there was no relaxation on your part; but we have reason to suppose that there have been other causes which may have occasioned your rapid change from activity and cheerfulness to such a total prostration of body and mind. You may feel grieved when I tell you that Emma has been very unwell since you left, and the cause of her illness is beyond the skill of Mr. Taylor, our medical man. She has, however, confided so much to her mother as to let us know that you are the party who has been the chief occasion of it. She has acknowledged that she has not behaved well to you, and has not done you justice; and I really believe that it is this conviction which is the chief ground of her altered state of health. I certainly have been too much in the counting-house to know what has been going on in the parlour, but I think that you ought to know us better than to suppose that we should not in every point be most anxious for your happiness, and your being constantly with us. That Emma blames herself is certain; that she is very amiable, is equally so; your return would give us the greatest satisfaction. I hardly need say I love my niece, and am anxious for her happiness; I love you, my dear friend, and am equally anxious for yours; and I do trust that any trifling disagreement between you (for surely you must be on intimate terms to quarrel, and for her to feel the quarrel so severely) will be speedily overcome. From what her mother says, I think that her affections are seriously engaged (I treat you with the confidence I am sure you deserve), and I am sure that there is no one upon whom I would so willingly bestow my niece; or, as I find by questioning, no one to whom Mrs. Phillips would so willingly entrust her daughter. If, then, I am right in my supposition, you will be received with open arms by all, not even excepting Emma—she has no coquetry in her composition. Like all the rest of us, she has her faults; but if she has her faults, she is not too proud to acknowledge them, and that you will allow when you read the enclosed, which she has requested me to send to you, and at the same time desired me to read it first. I trust this communication will accelerate your recovery, and that we shall soon see you again. At all events, answer my letter, and if I am in error let me know, that I may undeceive others."

The enclosure from Emma was then opened by our hero; it was in few words :—

" MY DEAR FRIEND,—On reflection, I consider that I have treated you unjustly; I intended to tell you so, if I had had an opportunity, before you quitted us so hastily. My fault has preyed upon my mind ever since, and I cannot lose this first opportunity of requesting your forgiveness, and hoping that when we meet we shall be on the same friendly terms that we always had been previous to my unfortunate ebullition of temper.—Yours truly,   EMMA."

That this letter was a source of unqualified delight to our hero, may be easily imagined. He was at once told by the uncle, and certainly Emma did not leave him to suppose the contrary, that he might aspire to and obtain her hand. Our hero could not reply to it by return of post. If distress had occasioned his illness, joy now prostrated him still more, and he was compelled to return to his bed; but he was happy, almost too happy, and he slept at last, and he dreamt such visions as only can be conjured up by those who have in anticipation every wish of their heart gratified. The next day he replied to Mr. Small's, acknowledging, with frankness, his feelings towards his niece, which a sense of his own humble origin and unworthiness had prevented him from venturing to disclose, and requesting him to use his influence in his favour, as he dared not speak himself, until he had received such assurance of his unmerited good fortune as might encourage him so to do. To Emma, his reply was in a few words; he thanked her for her continued good opinion of him, the idea of having lost which had made him very miserable, assuring her that he was ashamed of the petulance which he had shown, and that it was for him to have asked pardon, and not one who had behaved so kindly, and protected him for so long a period; that he felt much better already, and hoped to be able to shorten the time of absence which had been demanded by him and kindly granted by his patrons. Having concluded and despatched these epistles, our hero determined that he would take a stroll about the metropolis.

CHAPTER XLIII

A very long chapter, with a very long story, which could not well be cut in half.

A MAN may walk a long while in the city of London without having any definite object, and yet be amused, for there are few occupations more pleasant, more instructive, or more contemplative, than looking into the shop windows; you pay a shilling to see an exhibition, whereas in this instance you have the advantage of seeing many without paying a farthing, provided that you look after your pocket-handkerchief. Thus was our hero amused: at one shop he discovered that very gay shawls were to be purchased for one pound, bandanas at 3s. 9d., and soiled Irish linen remarkably cheap; at another he saw a row of watches, from humble silver at £2, 10s., to gold and enamelled at twelve or fourteen guineas, all warranted to go well; at another he discovered that furs were at half price, because nobody wore them in the summer. He proceeded further, and came to where there was a quantity of oil-paintings exposed for sale, pointing out to the passer-by that pictures of that description were those which he ought *not* to buy. A print-shop gave him an idea of the merits of composition and design shown by the various masters; and as he could not transport himself to the Vatican, it was quite as well to see what the Vatican contained; his thoughts were on Rome and her former glories. A tobacconist's transported him to the State of Virginia, where many had been transported in former days. A grocer's wafted him still farther to the West Indies and the negroes, and from these, as if by magic, to the Spice Islands and their aromatic groves. But an old curiosity shop, with bronzes, china, marqueterie, point-lace, and armour, embraced at once a few centuries; and he thought of the feudal times, the fifteenth century, the belle of former days, the amber-headed cane and snuff-box of the beaux who sought her smiles, all gone, all dust; the workmanship of the time, even portions of their dresses, still existing—everything less perishable than man.

Our hero proceeded on, his thoughts wandering as he wandered himself, when his attention was attracted by one of those placards, the breed of which appears to have been very much improved of late, as they get larger and larger every day; what they will end in there is no saying, unless it be in placards without end. This placard intimated that there was a masquerade at Vauxhall on that evening, besides fire-works, water-works, and anything but good works. Our hero had heard of Vauxhall, and his curiosity was excited, and he resolved that he would pass away the evening in what was at that time a rather fashionable resort.

It was half-past six, and time to go, so he directed his steps over Westminster Bridge, and, having only lost three minutes in peeping through the balustrades at the barges and wherries proceeding up and down the river, after asking his way three times he found himself at the entrance, and, paying his admission, walked in. There was a goodly sprinkling of company, but not many masks; there was a man clad in brass armour, who stood quite motionless, for the armour was so heavy that he could hardly bear the weight of it. He must have suffered a very great inconvenience on such a warm night, but people stared at him as they passed by, and he was more than repaid by the attention which he attracted; so he stood and suffered on. There were about twenty-five clowns in their motley dresses, seven or eight pantaloons, three devils, and perhaps forty or fifty dominoes. Joey soon found himself close to the orchestra, which was a blaze of light, and he listened very attentively to a lady in ostrich feathers, who was pouring out a bravura, which was quite unintelligible to the audience, while the gentlemen behind her, in their cocked hats, accompanied her voice. He was leaning against one of the trees, and receiving, without knowing it, the drippings of a leaky lamp upon his coat, when two men came up and stopped on the other side of the trunk of the tree, and one said to the other—" I tell you, Joseph, she is here, and with the Christian. Manasseh traced her by the driver of the coach. She will never return to her father's house if we do not discover her this night."

"What! will she become a *Meshumed*—an apostate!" exclaimed the other; " I would see her in her grave first. Holy Father! the daughter of a rabbi to bring such disgrace upon her family! Truly our sins, and the sins of our forefathers, have brought this evil upon our house. If I meet him here I will stab him to the heart!"

"*Leemaan Hashem!* for the sake of the holy name, my son, think of what you say; you must not be so rash. Alas! alas! but we are mixed with the heathens. She must be concealed in one of the Moabitish garments," continued the elder of the two personages, whom our hero had of course ascertained to be of the house of Israel. "Manasseh tells me that he has discovered from another quarter, that the Christian had procured a domino, black, with the sleeves slashed with white. That will be a distinguishing mark; and if we see that dress we must then follow, and if a female is with it, it must be thy sister Miriam."

"I will search now, and meet you here in half-an-hour," replied the younger of the two.

"Joseph, my son, we do not part; I cannot trust you in your anger, and you have weapons with you, I know; we must go together. Rooch Hakodesh! may the Holy Spirit guide us, and the daughter of our house be restored, for she is now my heart's bitterness, and my soul's sorrow!"

"Let me but discover the *Gaw*—the infidel!" replied the son, following the father; and our hero observed him put his hand into his breast and half unsheathe a poniard.

Joey easily comprehended how the matter stood : a Jewish maiden had met by assignation, or had been run away with by some young man, and the father and son were in pursuit to recover the daughter.

"That is all very well," thought our hero; "but although they may very properly wish to prevent the marriage, I do not much like the cold steel which the young Israelite had in his hand. If I do meet with the party, at all events I will give him warning;" and Joey, having made this resolution, turned away from the orchestra and went down the covered way, which led to what are usually termed the dark walks. He had just arrived at the commencement of them, when he perceived coming towards him two dominoes, the shorter hanging on the arm of the taller so as to assure him that they were male and female. When they came to within ten yards of the lighted walk they turned abruptly, and then Joey perceived that the taller had white slashed sleeves to his domino.

"There they are," thought our hero; "well, it's not safe for them to walk here, for a murder might be committed without much chance of the party being found out. I will give them a hint, at all events;" and Joey followed the couple so as to overtake them by degrees. As he walked softly, and they were in earnest conversation, his approach was not heeded until within a few feet of them, when the taller domino turned impatiently round, as if to inquire what the intruder meant.

"You are watched, and in danger, sir, if you are the party I think you are," said Joey, going up to him, and speaking in a low voice.

"Who are you," replied the domino, "that gives this notice?"

"A perfect stranger to you, even if your mask was removed, sir; but I happened to overhear a conversation relative to a person in a domino such as you wear. I may be mistaken, and if so, there is no harm done;" and our hero turned away.

"Stop him, dear Henry," said a soft female voice. "I

fear that there is danger : he can have told you but from kindness."

The person in the domino immediately followed Joey, and accosted him, apologising for his apparent rudeness at receiving his communication, which he ascribed to the suddenness with which it was given, and requested, as a favour, that our hero would inform him why he had thought it necessary.

"I will tell you, certainly ; not that I interfere with other people's concerns ; but when I saw that one of them had a poniard——"

"A poniard !" exclaimed the female, who had now joined them.

"Yes," replied Joey ; "and appeared determined to use it. In one word, madam, is your name Miriam ? If so, what I heard concerns you ; if not, it does not, and I need say no more."

"Sir, it does concern her," replied the domino ; "and I will thank you to proceed."

Our hero then stated briefly what he had overheard, and that the parties were then in pursuit of them.

"We are lost !" exclaimed the young woman. "We shall never escape from the gardens ! What must we do ? My brother in his wrath is as a lion's whelp."

"I care little for myself," replied the domino. "I could defend myself ; but, if we meet, I shall lose you. Your father would tear you away while I was engaged with your brother."

"At all events, sir, I should recommend your not remaining in these dark walks," replied our hero, "now that you are aware of what may take place."

"And yet, if we go into the lighted part of the gardens, they will soon discover us, now that they have, as it appears, gained a knowledge of my dress."

"Then put it off," said Joey.

"But they know my person even better," rejoined the domino. "Your conduct, sir, has been so kind, that perhaps you would be inclined to assist us ?"

Our hero was in love himself, and, of course, felt sympathy for others in the same predicament ; so he replied that, if he could be of service, they might command him.

"Then, Miriam, dear, what I propose is this: will you put yourself under the protection of this stranger? I think you risk nothing, for he has proved that he is kind. You may then, without fear of detection, pass through the gardens, and be conducted by him to a place of safety. I will remain here for half-an-hour; should your father and brother meet me, although they may recognise my dress, yet not having you with me, there will be no grounds for any attack being made, and I will, after a time, return home."

"And what is to become of me?" exclaimed the terrified girl.

"You must send this gentleman to my address to-morrow morning, and he will acquaint me where you are. I am giving you a great deal of trouble, sir; but at the same time I show my confidence; I trust it will not interfere with your other engagements."

"Your confidence is, I trust, not misplaced, sir," replied our hero; "and I am just now an idle man. I promise you, if this young lady will venture to trust herself with a perfect stranger, that I will do your request. I have no mask on, madam; do you think you can trust me?"

"I think I can, sir; indeed, I must do so, or there will be shedding of blood; but, Henry, they are coming; I know them; see—right up the walk!"

Joey turned round, and perceived the two persons whose conversation he had overheard. "It is they, sir," said he to the gentleman in the domino; "leave us and walk back farther into the dark part. I must take her away on my arm and pass them boldly. Come, sir, quick!"

Our hero immediately took the young Jewess on his arm, and walked towards the father and brother. He felt her trembling like an aspen as they came close to them, and was fearful that her legs would fail her. As they passed, the face of our hero was severely scrutinised by the dark eyes of the Israelites. Joey returned their stare, and proceeded on his way; and after they had separated some paces from the father and brother, he whispered to the maiden, "You are safe now." Joey conducted his charge through the gardens, and when he arrived at the entrance he called a coach, and put the lady in.

"Where shall we drive to?" inquired our hero.

" She was dressed somewhat in the Oriental style, and he was not
a little surprised at her extreme beauty."

"I don't know; say anywhere, so that we are away from this!"

Joey ordered the man to drive to the hotel where he had taken up his abode, for he knew not where else to go.

On his arrival he left the young lady in the coach, while he went in to prepare the landlady for her appearance. He stated that he had rescued her from a very perilous situation, and that he would feel much obliged to his hostess if she would take charge of the young person until she could be restored to her friends on the ensuing morning. People like to be consulted, and to appear of importance. The fat old lady, who had bridled up at the very mention of the introduction of a lady in a domino, as soon as she heard that the party was to be placed under her protection, relaxed her compressed features, and graciously consented.

Our hero having consigned over his charge, whose face he had not yet seen, immediately retired to his own apartment. The next morning, about nine o'clock, he sent to inquire after the health of his *protégée*, and was answered by a request that he would pay her a visit. When he entered the room he found her alone. She was dressed somewhat in the Oriental style, and he was not a little surprised at her extreme beauty. Her stature was rather above the middle size; she was exquisitely formed, and her hands, ankles, and feet, were models of perfection. She was indeed one of the most exquisite specimens of the Jewish nation, and that is quite sufficient for her portrait. She rose as he entered, and coloured deeply as she saluted him. Our hero, who perceived her confusion, hastened to assure her that he was ready to obey any order she might be pleased to give him, and trusted that she had not been too much annoyed with her very unpleasant position.

"I am more obliged to you, sir, than I can well express," replied she, "by your kind consideration in putting me into the charge of the landlady of the house: that one act assured me that I was in the hands of a gentleman and man of honour. All I have to request of you now is that you will call at No. — in Berkeley Square, and inform Mr. S—— of what you have kindly done for me. You will probably hear from him the cause of the strange position in which you found us and relieved us from."

As our hero had nothing to reply, he wrote down the address and took his leave, immediately proceeding to the house of Mr. S——; but as he was walking up Berkeley Street he was encountered by two men, whom he immediately recognised as the father and brother of the young Israelite. The brother fixed his keen eye upon our hero, and appeared to recognise him; at all events, as our hero passed them they turned round and followed him, and he heard the brother say, "He was with her," or something to that purport. Our hero did not, however, consider that it was advisable to wait until they were away before he knocked at the door, as he felt convinced they were on the watch, and that any delay would not obtain the end. He knocked, and was immediately admitted. He found Mr. S—— pacing the room up and down in great anxiety, the breakfast remaining on the table untouched. He warmly greeted the arrival of our hero. Joey, as soon as he had informed him of what he had done, and in whose hands he had placed the young lady, stated the circumstance of the father and brother being outside on the watch, and that he thought that they had recognised him.

"That is nothing more than what I expected," replied Mr. S——; "but I trust easily to evade them; they are not aware that the back of this house communicates with the stables belonging to it in the mews, and we can go out by that way without their perceiving us. I've so many thanks to offer you, sir, for your kind interference in our behalf, that I hardly know how to express them. To one thing you are most. certainly entitled, and I should prove but little my sincerity if I did not immediately give it you; that is my confidence, and a knowledge of the parties whom you have assisted, and the circumstances attending this strange affair. The young lady, sir, is, as you know, a Jewess by birth, and the daughter of a rabbi, a man of great wealth and high ancestry, for certainly Jews can claim the latter higher than any other nation upon earth. I am myself a man of fortune, as it is usually termed—at all events, with sufficient to indulge any woman I should take as my wife with every luxury that can be reasonably demanded. I mention this to corroborate my assertion, that it was not her father's wealth which has been my inducement. I made the acquaintance of the father and daughter when I was travelling on the Continent; he was on his way to England, when his carriage broke down in a difficult pass on the mountains, and they would have been left on the road for the night if I had not fortunately come up in time, and, being alone, was able to convey them to the next town. I have always had a great respect for the Jewish nation. I consider that every true Christian should have; but I will not enter upon that point now. It was probably my showing such a feeling, and my being well versed in their history, which was the occasion of an intercourse of two days ripening into a regard for one another; and we parted with sincere wishes that we might meet again in this country. At the time I speak of, which was about three years ago, his daughter Miriam was, comparatively speaking, a child, and certainly not at that period, or indeed for some time after our meeting again in England, did it ever come into my ideas that I should ever feel anything for her but goodwill; but circumstances, and her father's confidence in me, threw us much together. She has no mother. After a time I found myself growing attached to her, and I taxed myself, and reflected on the consequences. I was aware how very severe the Jewish laws were upon the subject of any of their family uniting themselves to a Christian. That it was not only considered that the party concerned was dishonoured before the nation, but that the whole family became vile, and were denied the usual burial rites. Perhaps you are aware that if a Jew embraces Christianity, the same disgrace is heaped upon the relations. With this knowledge, I determined to conquer my feelings for Miriam, and of course I no longer went to her father's house; it would have been cruel to put my friend (for such he certainly was) in such a position—the more so as, being a rabbi, he would have to denounce himself and his own children.

"My absence was, however, the cause of great annoyance to the father. He sought me, and I was so pressed by him to return, that I had no choice, unless I confessed my reasons, which I did not like to do. I therefore visited the house as before, although not so frequently, and continually found myself in company with Miriam, and, her father being constantly summoned away to the duties of his office, but

too often alone. I therefore resolved that I would once
more set off on my travels, as the only means by which I
could act honourably, and get rid of the feeling which was
obtaining such a mastery over me. I went to the house to
state my intention, and at the same time bid them farewell;
when, ascending the stairs, I slipped and sprained my ankle
so severely that I could not put my foot to the ground.
This decided our fate; and I was not only domiciled for a
week in the house, but, as I lay on the sofa, was continually
attended by Miriam. Her father would not hear of my removal, but declared that my accident was a judgment against
me for my rash intention.

"That Miriam showed her regard for me in every way
that a modest maiden could do, is certain. I did, however,
make one last struggle; I did not deny my feelings towards
her, but I pointed out to her the consequences which would
ensue, which it was my duty as a friend, and her duty as a
daughter, to prevent. She heard me in silence and in tears,
and then quitted the room.

"The next day she appeared to have recovered her composure, and entered freely into general conversation, and
after a time referred to the rites of their Church. By
degrees she brought up the subject of Christianity; she
demanded the reasons and authority for our belief; in short,
she induced me to enter warmly into the subject, and to
prove, to the best of my ability, that the true Messiah had
already come. This conversation she took a pleasure in
renewing during my stay in the house; and as I considered
that the subject was one that diverted our attention from
the one I wished to avoid, I was not sorry to enter upon
it, although I had not the least idea of converting her to
our faith.

"Such was the state of affairs when I quitted the house,
and again seriously thought of removing myself from so much
temptation, when her brother Joseph arrived from Madrid,
where he had been staying with an uncle for some years,
and his return was the occasion of a jubilee, at which I
could not refuse to appear. He is a fine young man, very
intelligent and well-informed, but of a very irascible disposition; and his long residence in Spain has probably given
him those ideas of retaliation which are almost unknown in

this country. He conceived a very strong friendship for me, and I certainly was equally pleased with him; for he is full of talent, although he is revengeful, proud of his lineage, and holding to the tenets of his faith with all the obstinacy of a Pharisee. Indeed, it is strange that he could ever become so partial to a Christian, respecting as he does the rabbinical doctrines held forth to the Jewish people, and which it must be admitted have been inculcated, in consequence of the unwearied and unjustifiable persecution of the tribes for centuries, by those who call themselves Christians, but whose practice has been at open variance with the precepts of the founder of their faith. However, so it was. Joseph conceived a great regard for me, was continually at my house, and compelled me but too often to visit at his father's. At last I made up my mind that I would leave the country for a time, and was actively preparing, intending to go without saying a word to them, when I found myself one morning alone with Miriam. She walked up to me as I was sitting on the couch; I motioned to her to sit by me, but she stood before me with a stately air, fixing upon me her dark gazelle-like eyes.

"'Do you,' said she, in a slow and solemn tone of voice, 'do you remember the conversation which we had upon our respective creeds? Do you recollect how you pointed out to me your authorities and your reasons for your faith, and your sincere belief that the Messiah had already come?'

"'I do, Miriam,' replied I; 'but not with any view to interfere with your non-belief; it was only to uphold by argument my own.'

"'I do not say nay to that; I believe you,' said Miriam; 'nevertheless, I have that in my vest which, if it was known to my father or brother, would cause them to dash me to the earth, and to curse me in the name of the great Jehovah;' and she pulled out of her vest a small copy of the New Testament. 'This is the book of your creed; I have searched and compared it with our own; I have found the authorities; I have read the words of the Jews who have narrated the history and the deeds of Jesus of Nazareth, and—I am a *Christian*.'

"It may appear strange, but I assure you, sir, you cannot imagine the pain I felt when Miriam thus acknowledged herself a convert to our faith; to say to her that I **was** sorry for it would have argued little for my Christian belief; but when I reflected upon the pain and disgrace it would bring upon her family, and that I should be the cause, I was dreadfully shocked. I could only reply, ' Miriam, I wish that we had never met !'

" 'I know what your feelings are but too well,' replied she; 'but we have met, and what is done cannot be undone. I, too, when I think of my relations, am torn with anxiety and distress; but what is now my duty? If I am—and I declare, not only by the great Jehovah, but by the crucified Messiah, that I am a sincere believer in your creed, must I shrink—must I conceal it on account of my father and my brother? Does not He say, "Leave all and follow Me"? Must I not add my feeble voice in acknowledgment of the truth, if I am to consider myself a Christian? Must not my avowal be public? Yes, it must be, and it shall be! Can you blame me?'

" 'Oh no! I dare not blame you,' replied I; 'I only regret that religious differences should so mar the little happiness permitted to us in this world, and that neither Jew nor Christian will admit what our Saviour has distinctly declared—that there is no difference between the Jew and the Greek, or Gentile. I see much misery in this, and I cannot help regretting deeply that I shall be considered as the cause of it, and be upbraided with ingratitude.'

" 'You did your duty,' replied Miriam. ' I have been converted by your having so done. Now I have my duty to do. I am aware of the pain it will occasion my father, my relations, and the whole of our tribe; but if they suffer, shall I not suffer more? Thrust out from my father's door; loaded with curses and execrations; not one Jew permitted to offer me an asylum, not even to give me a morsel of bread, or a drop of water; a wanderer and an outcast! Such must be my fate.'

" 'Not so, Miriam; if your tribe desert you——'

" 'Stop one moment,' interrupted Miriam; 'do you recollect the conversation you had with me before we entered into the subject of our relative creeds? Do you remember what you then said; and was it true, or was it merely as an excuse?'

"'It was as true, Miriam, as I stand here. I have loved you long and devotedly. I have tried to conquer the passion on account of the misery your marriage with a Christian would have occasioned your relations; but if you persist in avowing your new faith, the misery will be equally incurred; and, therefore, I am doubly bound, not only by my love, but because I have, by converting you, put you in such a dreadful position, to offer you not only an asylum, but, if you will accept them, my heart and hand.'

"Miriam folded her arms across her breast, and knelt down, with her eyes fixed upon the floor. 'I can only answer in the words of Ruth,' replied she, in a low voice and with trembling lips. I hardly need observe, that after this interview the affair was decided,—the great difficulty was to get her out of the house; for you must have been inside of one of the houses of a Jew of rank to be aware of their arrangements. It was impossible that Miriam could be absent an hour without being missed; and to go out by herself without being seen was equally difficult. Her cousin is married to a Jew, who keeps the masquerade paraphernalia and costumes in Tavistock Street, and she sometimes accompanies her father and brother there, and, as usual, goes up to her cousin in the women's apartment, while her male relations remain below. We therefore hit upon this plan: That on the first masquerade night at Vauxhall she should persuade her father and brother to go with her to her cousin's; that I should be close by in a coach, and, after she had gone in, I was to drive up as the other customers do, and obtain two dominoes, and then wait while she escaped from the women's apartment and came downstairs to the street door, where I was to put her in the coach and drive off to Vauxhall. You may inquire why we went to Vauxhall. Because as but few minutes would elapse before she would be missed, it would have been almost impossible to have removed her without being discovered, for I was well known to the people. You recollect that Manasseh, who was in the shop, informed them that my domino was slashed with white in the sleeves; he knew me when I obtained the dominoes. Had I not been aware of the violence of the brother, I should have cared little had he followed me to my house, or any other place he might have traced me to; but his temper is such that his

259

sister would certainly have been sacrificed to his rage and fury, as you may imagine from what you have seen and heard. I considered, therefore, that if we once became mixed with the crowd of masks and dominoes at Vauxhall, I should elude them, and all trace of us be lost. I believe now that I have made you acquainted with every circumstance, and trust that you will still afford me your valuable assistance."

" Most certainly," replied our hero; " I am in duty bound. I cannot help thinking that they have recognised me as the party conducting her out of the dark walk. Did you meet them afterwards ? "

" No," rejoined Mr. S——; " I allowed them to walk about without coming up to me for some time, and then when they were down at the farthest end, I made all haste and took a coach home, before they could possibly come up with me, allowing that they did recognise me, which I do not think they did until they perceived me hastening away at a distance."

" What, then, are your present intentions ? " inquired our hero.

" I wish you to return with me to your hotel," replied Mr. S——; " I will then take a chaise, and leave for Scotland as fast as four horses can carry us, and unite myself to Miriam, and, as soon as I can, I shall leave the country, which will be the best step to allow their rage and indignation to cool."

" I think your plan is good," replied Joey, " and I am at your service."

In a few minutes Mr. S—— and our hero went out by the back way into the mews, and, as soon as they came to a stand, took a coach and drove to the hotel.

They had not, however, been in company with Miriam more than five minutes, when the waiter entered the room in great alarm, stating that two gentlemen were forcing their way upstairs in spite of the landlord and others, who were endeavouring to prevent them. The fact was that our hero and Mr. S—— had been perceived by Joseph and his father as they came out of the mews, and they had immediately followed them, taking a coach at the same stand, and desiring the coachman to follow the one our hero and Mr. S—— had gone into.

THE POACHER

The waiter had hardly time to make the communication before the door was forced open, and the man was so terrified that he retreated behind our hero and Mr. S——, into whose arms Miriam had thrown herself for protection. The father and brother did not, however, enter without resistance on the part of the landlord and waiters, who followed, remonstrating and checking them; but Joseph broke from them with his dagger drawn; it was wrenched from him by our hero, who dashed forward. The enraged Israelite then caught up a heavy bronze clock which was on the side-board, and crying out, "This for the Gaw and Meshumed!" (the infidel and the apostate), he hurled it at them with all his strength. It missed the parties it was intended for, but striking the waiter who had retreated behind them, fractured his skull, and he fell senseless upon the floor.

Upon this outrage the landlord and his assistants rushed upon Joseph and his father; the police were sent for, and after a desperate resistance, the Israelites were taken away to the police-office, leaving Mr. S—— and Miriam at liberty. Our hero was, however, requested by the police to attend at the examination, and, of course, could not refuse. The whole party had been a quarter of an hour waiting until another case was disposed of, before the magistrate could attend to them, when the surgeon came in and acquainted them that the unfortunate waiter had expired. The depositions were taken down, and both father and son were committed, and Joey and some others bound over to appear as witnesses. In about two hours our hero was enabled to return to the hotel, where he found that Mr. S—— had left a note for him, stating that he considered it advisable to start immediately, lest they should require his attendance at the police-court, and he should be delayed, which would give time to the relations of Miriam to take up the question; he had, therefore, set off, and would write to him as soon as he possibly could.

This affair made some noise, and appeared in all the news-papers, and our hero therefore sat down and wrote a detailed account of the whole transaction (as communicated to him by Mr. S——), which he despatched to Portsmouth. He made inquiries, and found that the sessions would come on in a fortnight, and that the grand jury would sit in a few days. He therefore made up his mind that he would not think of returning to Portsmouth until the trial was over, and in his next letter he made known his intentions, and then set off for Richmond, where he had been advised to remain for a short time, as being more favourable to an invalid than the confined atmosphere of London.

Our hero found amusement in rowing about in a wherry, up and down the river, and replying to the letters received from Mary and from Portsmouth. He also received a letter from Mr. S——, informing him of his marriage, and requesting that as soon as the trial was over he would write to him. Our hero's health also was nearly re-established, when he was informed that his attendance was required at the court to give his evidence in the case of manslaughter found by the grand jury against Joseph, the brother of Miriam.

He arrived in town, and attended the court on the following day, when the trial was to take place. A short time after the cause came on he was placed in the witness-box. At the time that he gave his depositions before the magistrate he had not thought about his name having been changed; but now that he was sworn, and had declared he would tell the truth, and nothing but the truth, when the counsel asked him if his name was not Joseph O'Donahue, our hero replied that it was Joseph Rushbrook.

"Your deposition says Joseph O'Donahue. How is this? Have you an *alias*, like many others, sir?" inquired the counsel.

"My real name is Rushbrook, but I have been called O'Donahue for some time," replied our hero.

This reply was the occasion of the opposite counsel making some very severe remarks; but the evidence of our hero was taken, and was indeed considered very favourable to the prisoner, as Joey stated that he was convinced the blow was never intended for the unfortunate waiter, but for Mr. S——.

After about an hour's examination our hero was dismissed, and in case that he might be recalled, returned as directed to the room where the witnesses were assembled.

CHAPTER XLIV

In which the tide of fortune turns against our hero.

AS soon as Joey had been dismissed from the witness-box he returned to the room in which the other witnesses were assembled, with melancholy forebodings that his real name having been given in open court would lead to some disaster. He had not been there long before a peace-officer came in, and said to him—"Step this way, if you please, sir; I have something to say to you."

Joey went with him outside the door, when the peace-officer, looking at him full in the face, said, "Your name is Joseph Rushbrook; you said so in the witness-box?"

"Yes," replied Joey, "that is my true name."

"Why did you change it?" demanded the officer.

"I had reasons," replied our hero.

"Yes, and I'll tell you the reasons," rejoined the other. "You were concerned in a murder some years ago; a reward was offered for your apprehension, and you absconded from justice. I see that you are the person; your face tells me so. You are my prisoner. Now, come away quietly, sir; it is of no use for you to resist, and you will only be worse treated."

Joey's heart had almost ceased to beat when the constable addressed him; he felt that denial was useless, and that the time was now come when either he or his father must suffer; he therefore made no reply, but quietly followed the peace-officer, who, holding him by the arm, called a coach, into which he ordered Joey to enter, and following him, directed the coachman to drive to the police-office.

As soon as the magistrate had been acquainted by the officer who the party was whom he had taken into custody, he first pointed out to our hero that he had better not say anything which might criminate himself, and then asked him if his name was Joseph Rushbrook.

Joey replied that it was.

"Have you anything to say that might prevent my committing you on the charge of murder?" demanded the magistrate.

"Nothing, except that I am not guilty," replied Joey.

"I have had the warrant out against him these seven years, or thereabouts, but he escaped me," observed the peace-officer; "he was but a lad then."

"He must have been a child, to judge by his present appearance," observed the magistrate, who was making out the committal. "I now perfectly recollect the affair."

The officer received the committal, and in half-an-hour our hero was locked up with felons of every description. His blood ran cold when he found himself enclosed within the massive walls; and as soon as the gaoler had left him alone, he shuddered and covered his face with his hands. Our hero had, however, the greatest of all consolations to support him —the consciousness of his innocence; but when he called to mind how happy and prosperous he had lately been, when he thought of Emma—and that now all his fair prospects and fondest anticipations were thrown to the ground, it is not surprising that for a short time he wept in his solitude and silence. To whom should he make known his situation? Alas! it would too soon be known; and would not every one, even Emma, shrink from a supposed murderer? No! there was one who would not—one on whose truth he could depend; Mary would not desert him, even now; he would write to her and acquaint her with his situation. Our hero, having made up his mind so to do, obtained paper and ink from the gaoler when he came into his cell, which he did in about two hours after he had been locked up. Joey wrote to Mary, stating his position in few words, and that the next morning he was to be taken down to Exeter to await his trial; and expressed a wish, if possible, that she would come there to see him; and giving a guinea to the turnkey, requested him to forward the letter.

"It shall go safe enough, young master," replied the man. "Now, do you know, yours is one of the strangest cases which ever came to my knowledge?" continued the man; "we've been talking about it among ourselves; why, the first warrant for your apprehension was out more than eight years ago; and, to look at you now, you cannot be more than seventeen or eighteen."

"Yes, I am," replied Joey; "I am twenty-two."

"Then don't you tell anybody else that, and I will forget

it. You see youth goes a great way in court; and they will see that you must have been quite a child when the deed was done—for I suppose by the evidence there is no doubt of that—and it won't be a hanging matter, that you may be certain of; you'll cross the water, that's all. So keep up your spirits, and look as young as you can."

Mary received the letter on the following day, and was in the deepest distress at its contents. She was still weeping over it, her work had been thrown down at her feet, when Mrs. Austin came into the dressing-room where she was sitting.

"What is the matter, Mary?" said Mrs. Austin.

"I have received a letter from my brother, madam," replied Mary; "he is in the greatest distress; and I must beg you to let me go to him immediately."

"Your brother, Mary! what difficulty is he in?" asked Mrs. Austin.

Mary did not reply, but wept more.

"Mary, if your brother is in distress I certainly will not refuse your going to him; but you should tell me what his distress is, or how shall I be able to advise or help you? Is it very serious?"

"He is in prison, madam."

"In prison for debt, I suppose?"

"No, madam; on a charge of murder, which he is not guilty of."

"Murder!" exclaimed Mrs. Austin, "and not guilty! Why —when—and where did this murder take place?"

"Many years ago, madam, when he was quite a child."

"How very strange!" thought Mrs. Austin, panting for breath, and dropping into a chair. "But where, Mary?"

"Down in Devonshire, madam, at Grassford."

Mrs. Austin fell senseless from her chair. Mary, very much surprised, hastened to her assistance, and after a time succeeded in restoring her, and leading her to the sofa. For some time Mrs. Austin remained with her face buried in the cushions, while Mary stood over her. At last Mrs. Austin looked up, and laying her hand upon Mary's arm, said in a solemn tone—

"Mary, do not deceive me; you say that that boy is *your* brother—tell me, is not that false? I am sure that it is. Answer me, Mary."

"He is not my born brother, madam, but I love him as one," replied Mary.

"Again answer me truly, Mary, if you have any regard for me. You know his real name; what is it?"

"Joseph Rushbrook, madam," replied Mary, weeping.

"I was certain of it!" replied Mrs. Austin, bursting into tears; "I knew it! The blow has come at last! God have mercy on me! What can be done?" And again Mrs. Austin abandoned herself to bitter grief.

Mary was in amazement; how Mrs. Austin should know anything of Joey's history, and why she should be in such distress, was to her a complete mystery; she remained for some time at the side of her mistress, who gradually became more composed. Mary at last said—"May I go to him, madam?"

"Yes," replied Mrs. Austin, "most certainly. Mary, I must have no secrets now; you must tell me everything. You see that I am deeply interested about this young man as well as yourself; it is quite sufficient for you at present to know that; before I say anything more, you must be candid with me, and tell me how you became acquainted with him, and all that you know relative to his life. That I will assist you and him in every way in my power; that neither money nor interest shall be spared, you may be assured; and I think, Mary, that after this promise you will not conceal anything from me."

"Indeed I will not, madam," replied Mary, "for I love him as much as I can love." Mary then commenced by stating that she was living at Gravesend when she first met with Joey. There was a little hesitation at the commencement of her narrative, which Mrs. Austin pretended not to observe; she then continued, winding up with the information which she had obtained from Furness, the marine, their escape, and her admission into Mrs. Austin's family.

"And it was Joseph Rushbrook that came with you to this house?"

"Yes, madam," replied Mary; "but one of the men was quite rude to me, and Joey took it up. Mr. Austin, hearing a noise, sent down to inquire the cause; the servants threw all the blame upon Joey, and he was ordered out of the house immediately. He refused even to come back to the Hall after the treatment he had received, for a long while ; but it was he who was in the parlour when you opened the door, if you recollect, a few weeks ago."

Mrs. Austin clasped her hands, and then pressed them to her forehead; after a while she said—

"And what has he been doing since he came here ? "

Mary then informed her mistress of all she knew of Joey's subsequent career.

"Well, Mary," said Mrs. Austin, "you must go to him directly. You will want money ; but, Mary, promise me that you will not say a word to him about what has passed between us,—that is, for the present; by-and-by I may trust you more."

"You may trust me, madam," replied Mary, looking her mistress in the face ; "but it is too late for me to go this afternoon; I will, if you please, now wait till to-morrow morning."

"Do so, Mary; I am glad that you do not go to-night, for I wish you to stay with me ; I have many questions to ask of you. At present I wish to be alone, my good girl. Tell Mr. Austin that I am very unwell, and do not dine below."

"Shall I bring your dinner up here, madam ? " asked Mary.

"Yes, you may *bring* it, Mary," replied Mrs. Austin, with a faint smile.

Never did two people leave one another both so much wishing to be alone as Mary and Mrs. Austin. The former quitted the room, and, having first executed her commission, returned to her own apartment, that she might reflect without being disturbed. What could be the reason of Mrs. Austin's behaviour? What could she know of Joey Rushbrook? and why so interested and moved? She had heard among the servants that Mr. and Mrs. Austin were formerly in a humbler sphere of life ; that he was a half-pay officer; but there was still no clue to such interest about Joey Rushbrook. Mary thought and thought over and over again, revolved all that had passed in her mind, but could make nothing of it ; and she was still trying to solve the mystery when the housemaid came into the room, and informed her that Mrs. Austin's bell had rung twice. Mrs. Austin, on her

part, was still more bewildered; she could not regain sufficient calmness to enable her to decide how to act. Her son
in prison, to be tried for his life for a crime he had not
committed! Would he divulge the truth, and sacrifice the
father? She thought not. If he did not, would he not be
condemned? and if he were, could she remain away from
him? or ought she not to divulge what the boy would
conceal? And if he did confess the truth, would they find
out that Mr. Austin and Joseph Rushbrook were one and
the same person? Would there be any chance of his escape?
Would he not, sooner or later, be recognised? How dreadful was her situation! Then, again, should she acquaint
her husband with the position of his son? If so, would he
come forward? Yes, most certainly he would never let Joey
suffer for his crime. Ought she to tell her husband? And
then Mary, who knew so much already, who had witnessed
her distress and anguish, who was so fond of her son, could
she trust her? Could she do without trusting her? Such
were the various and conflicting ideas which passed in the
mind of Mrs. Austin. At last she resolved that she would say
nothing to her husband; that she would send Mary to her
son, and that she would that evening have more conversation
with the girl, and decide, after she had talked with her,
whether she would make her a confidante or not. Having
made up her mind so far, she rang the bell for Mary.

"Are you better, madam?" asked Mary, who had entered
the room very quietly.

"Yes, I thank you, Mary; take your work and sit down;
I wish to have some more conversation with you about this
young person, Joseph Rushbrook; you must have seen that I
am much interested about him."

"Yes, madam."

"There were some portions of your story, Mary, which I
do not quite understand. You have now lived with me for
five years, and I have had every reason to be satisfied with
your behaviour. You have conducted yourself as a well-
behaved, modest, and attentive young woman."

"I am much obliged to you, madam, for your good opinion."

"And I hope that you will admit that I have not been a
hard mistress to you, Mary, but, on the contrary, have shown
you that I have been pleased with your conduct."

"Certainly, madam, you have; and I trust I am grateful."

"I believe so," replied Mrs. Austin. "Now, Mary, I wish you to confide in me altogether. What I wish to know is how did you in so short a time become acquainted with this Furness, so as to obtain this secret from him? I may say, whom did you live with, and how did you live, when at Gravesend? for you have not mentioned that to me. It seems so odd to me that this man should have told to a person whom he had seen but for a few hours a secret of such moment."

Mary's tears fell fast, but she made no reply.

"Cannot you answer me, Mary?"

"I can, madam," said she at last; "but if I tell the truth—and I cannot tell a lie now—you will despise me, and perhaps order me to leave the house immediately; and if you do what will become of me?"

"Mary, if you think I intend to take advantage of a confession extorted from you, you do me wrong; I ask the question because it is necessary that I should know the truth—because I cannot confide in you without you first confide in me; tell me, Mary, and do not be afraid."

"Madam, I will; but pray do not forget that I have been under your roof for five years, and that I have been during that time an honest and modest girl. I was not so once, I confess it," and Mary's cheeks were red with shame, and she hung down her head.

"We are all sinful creatures, Mary," replied Mrs. Austin; "and who is there that has not fallen into error? The Scriptures say, 'Let him who is without sin cast the first stone;' nay more, Mary, 'There is more joy over one sinner that repenteth than over ninety and nine who need no repentance.' Shall I then be harsh to you, my poor girl? No, no. By trusting me you have made me your friend; you must be mine, Mary, for I want a friend now."

Poor Mary fell on her knees before Mrs. Austin, and wept over her hand as she kissed it repeatedly.

Mrs. Austin was much affected, and as the contrite girl recovered herself, Mrs. Austin leaned on her elbow, and putting her arm round Mary's neck, drew her head towards her, and gently kissed her on the brow.

"You are, indeed, a kind friend, madam," said Mary, after

a pause, "and may the Almighty reward you! You are unhappy; I know not why, but I would die to serve you. I only wish that you would let me prove it."

"First, Mary, tell me as much of your own history as you choose to tell; I wish to know it."

Mary then entered into the details of her marriage, her husband's conduct, her subsequent career, and her determination to lead a new life, which she had so sincerely proved by her late conduct.

Mary having concluded her narrative, Mrs. Austin addressed her thus :—

"Mary, if you imagine that you have fallen in my good opinion, after what you have confessed to me, you are much mistaken; you have, on the contrary, been raised. There have been few, very few, that have had the courage and fortitude that you have shown, or who could have succeeded as you have done. I was afraid to trust you before, but now I am not. I will not ask you not to betray me, for I am sure you will not. On two points only my lips are sealed; and the reason why they are sealed is that the secret is not mine alone, and I have not permission to divulge it. That I am deeply interested in that boy is certain; nay, that he is a near and very dear connection is also the case; but what his exact relationship is towards me I must not at present say. You have asserted your belief of his innocence, and I tell you that you are right; he did not do the deed; I know who did, but I dare not reveal the name."

"That is exactly what Joey said to me, madam," observed Mary, "and, moreover, that he never would reveal it, even if he were on his trial."

"I do not think that he ever will, Mary," rejoined Mrs. Austin, bursting into tears. "Poor boy! it is horrible that he should suffer for an offence that he has not committed."

"Surely, madam, if he is found guilty they will not hang him, he was such a child."

"I scarcely know."

"It's very odd that his father and mother have disappeared in the manner they did; I think it is very suspicious," observed Mary.

"You must, of course, have your own ideas from what you

270

have already heard," replied Mrs. Austin, in a calm tone; " but, as I have already said, my lips on that subject are sealed. What I wish you to do, Mary, is not at first to let him know that I am interested about him, or even that I know anything about him. Make all the inquiries you can as to what is likely to be the issue of the affair, and when you have seen him, you must then come back and tell me all that he says, and all that has taken place."

" I will, madam."

" You had better go away early to-morrow; one of the grooms shall drive you over to meet the coach which runs to Exeter. While I think of it, take my purse, and do not spare it, Mary; for money must not be thought of now. I am very unwell, and must go to bed."

" I had better bring up the tray, madam; a mouthful and a glass of wine will be of service to you."

" Do so, dear Mary; I feel very faint."

As soon as Mrs. Austin had taken some refreshment, she entered again into conversation with Mary, asking her a hundred questions about her son. Mary, who had now nothing to conceal, answered freely; and when Mary wished her good night, Mrs. Austin was more than ever convinced that her boy's rectitude of principle would have made him an ornament to society. Then came the bitter feeling that he was about to sacrifice himself; that he would be condemned as a felon, disgraced, and perhaps executed; and as she turned on her restless pillow, she exclaimed, " Thank God that he is innocent—his poor father suffers more."

CHAPTER XLV

In which Mary makes a discovery of what has been long known to the reader.

IT was hardly ten o'clock on the second morning when Mary arrived at Exeter, and proceeded to the gaol. Her eyes were directed to the outside of the massive building, and her cheeks blanched when she viewed the chains and fetters over the entrance, so truly designating the purport of the structure. There were several people at the steps and in the passage, making inquiries, and demanding permission of the turnkey to visit the prisoners; and Mary had to wait some minutes before she could make her request. Her appearance was so different to the usual class of applicants, that the turnkey looked at her with some surprise.

"Whom do you wish to see?" inquired the man, for Mary's voice had faltered.

"Joseph Rushbrook, my brother," repeated Mary.

At this moment the head gaoler came to the wicket.

"She wishes to see her brother, young Rushbrook," said the turnkey.

"Yes, certainly," replied the gaoler; "walk in, and sit down in the parlour for a little while, till I can send a man with you."

There was a gentleness and kindness of manner shown by both the men towards Mary, for they were moved with her beauty and evident distress. Mary took a seat in the gaoler's room; the gaoler's wife was there, and she was more than kind. The turnkey came to show her to the cell; and when Mary rose, the gaoler's wife said to her, "After you have seen your brother, my dear child, you had better come back again, and sit down here a little while, and then, perhaps, I can be of some use to you, in letting you know what can be done, and what is not allowed."

Mary could not speak, but she looked at the gaoler's wife, her eyes brimming over with tears. The kind woman understood her. "Go now," said she, "and mind you come back to me."

The turnkey, without speaking, led her to the cell, fitted the key to the ponderous lock, pushed back the door, and remained outside. Mary entered, and in a second was in the arms of our hero, kissing him, and bedewing his cheeks with her tears.

"I was sure that you would come, Mary," said Joey; "now sit down, and I will tell you how this has happened, while you compose yourself; you will be better able to talk to me after a while."

They sat down on the stretchers upon which the bed had been laid during the night, their hands still clasped, and as Joey entered into a narrative of all that had passed, Mary's sobs gradually diminished, and she was restored to something like composure.

"And what do you intend to do when you are brought to trial, my dear boy?" said Mary at last.

"I shall say nothing, except 'Not Guilty,' which is the truth, Mary; I shall make no defence whatever."

"But why will you not confess the truth?" replied Mary. "I have often thought of this, and have long made up my mind, Joey, that no one could act as you do if a parent's life were not concerned; you, or anybody else, would be mad to sacrifice himself in this way, unless it were to save a father."

Joey's eyes were cast down on the stone pavement; he made no reply.

"Why, then, if I am right in my supposition," continued Mary—"I do not ask you to say yes or no on that point— why should you not tell the truth? Furness told me that your father and mother had left the village, and that he had attempted to trace them, but could not; and he expressed himself sure that they were gone to America. Why, then, supposing I am right, should you sacrifice yourself for nothing?"

"Supposing you are right, Mary," replied Joey, with his eyes still cast down, "what proof is there that my parents have left the country? It was only the supposition of Furness, and it is my conviction that they have not. Where they may be, I know not; but I feel positive that my mother would not leave the country without having first found out where I was, and have taken me with her. No, Mary, my father and mother, if alive, are still in this country."

"Recollect again, my dear boy, that your father may be dead."

"And if so, my mother would have by this time found me out; she would have advertised for me—done everything— I feel that she would have—she would have returned to Grassford, and——"

"And what, Joey?"

"I must not say what, Mary," replied our hero; "I have thought a great deal since I have been shut up here, and I have taken my resolution, which is not to be changed; so let us say no more upon the subject, dear Mary. Tell me all! about yourself."

s

Mary remained another hour with Joey, and then bade him farewell; she was anxious to return to Mrs. Austin, and acquaint her with the result of her interview. With a heavy heart she walked away from the cell, and went down into the parlour of the gaoler.

"Would you like to take anything?" said the gaoler's wife, after Mary had sat down.

"A little water," replied Mary.

"And how is your brother?"

"He is innocent," replied Mary; "he is indeed; but he won't tell anything, and they will condemn him."

"Well, well; but do not be afraid; he must have been very young at the time, innocent or guilty, and he won't suffer, that I know; but he will be sent out of the country."

"Then I will go with him," replied Mary.

"Perhaps he will be pardoned, dear; keep your spirits up, and, if you have money, get a good lawyer."

"Can you tell me who would be a good lawyer to apply to?"

"Yes; Mr. Trevor. He is a very clever man, and comes the Western Circuit; if any one can save him, he can."

"I will take his name down, if you please," said Mary.

The gaoler's wife gave Mary a piece of paper and pen and ink; Mary wrote down the name and address of Mr. Trevor, and then with many thanks took her leave.

On her return to the Hall, Mary communicated to Mrs. Austin what had passed. Mrs. Austin perceived that Joey would not swerve from his resolution, and that all that could be done was to procure the best legal assistance.

"Mary, my poor girl," said Mrs. Austin, "here is money, which you will find necessary for your adopted brother's assistance. You say that you have obtained the name of the best legal person to be employed in his behalf. To-morrow you must go to London and call upon that gentleman. It may be as well not to mention my name. As his sister, you of course seek the best legal advice. You must manage all this as if from yourself."

"I will, madam."

"And, Mary, if you think it advisable, you can remain in town for two or three days; but pray write to me every day."

"I will, madam."

" Let me know your address, as I may wish to say something to you when I know what has been done."

" I will, madam."

" And now you had better go to bed, Mary, for you must
be tired; indeed, you look very fatigued, my poor girl. I
need not caution you not to say anything to any of the
servants; good night."

Mary threw herself on the bed, she was indeed worn-out
with anxiety and grief; at last she slept. The next morning
she was on her way to town, having, in reply to the curiosity
of the servants, stated that the cause of her journey was the
dangerous illness of her brother.

As soon as she arrived in London Mary drove to the
chambers of the lawyer, whose direction she had obtained
from the Exeter gaoler's wife; he was at home, and after
waiting a short time, she was ushered by the clerk into his
presence.

" What can I do for you, young lady?" inquired Mr.
Trevor, with some surprise; " it is not often that the den of
a lawyer has such a bright vision to cheer it. Do me the
favour to take a chair."

" I am not a young lady, sir," replied Mary; " I have
come to you to request that you will be so kind as to defend
my brother, who is about to be tried."

" Your brother! what is he charged with?"

" Murder," replied Mary; " but indeed, sir, he is not
guilty," she continued, as she burst into tears.

Mr. Trevor was not only a clever, but also a kind and considerate man. He remained silent for some minutes to allow
Mary time to recover herself. When she was more composed, he said—

" What is your brother's name?"

" Joseph Rushbrook."

" Rushbrook! Rushbrook! I well remember that name,"
remarked Mr. Trevor; " strange, the Christian name also the
same! it is singular certainly. The last time I was concerned for a person of that name, I was the means of his
coming into a large landed property; now I am requested to
defend one of the same name accused of murder."

Mary was astonished at this observation of Mr. Trevor's,
but made no reply.

275

"Have you the indictment? Where did the murder take place?"

"In Devonshire, sir, many years ago."

"And he is now in Exeter gaol? Come, tell me all the particulars."

Mary told all that she knew, in a very clear and concise manner.

"Now, my good girl," said Mr. Trevor, "I must see your brother. In two days I shall be down at Exeter. If you write to him, or see him before I do, you must tell him he must trust in his lawyer, and have no reservation, or I shall not be able to do him so much service. Allow me to ask you have you any relations in Yorkshire?"

"No, sir, none."

"And yet the name and Christian name are exactly the same. It's an odd coincidence! They, however, changed their name when they came into the property."

"Changed the name of Rushbrook, sir?" said Mary, who now thought that she had a clue to Joey's parents.

"Yes, changed it to Austin; they live now in Dorsetshire. I mention it because, if interest is required for your brother, and he could prove any relationship, it might be valuable. But, bless me! what is the matter? Smithers," cried Mr. Trevor, as he ran and supported Mary, "some water! quick! the girl has fainted!"

It was surprise at this astounding intelligence, her regard for Mrs. Austin, and the light now thrown upon the interest she had shown for our hero, and the conviction of what must be her suffering, which had overcome the poor girl. In a short time she recovered.

"I thank you, sir, but I have suffered so much anxiety about my poor brother," said Mary, faltering, and almost gasping for breath.

"He cannot be a very bad boy since you are so fond of him," said Mr. Trevor.

"No, indeed; I wish I was half as good," murmured Mary.

"I will do all I possibly can, and that immediately; indeed, as soon as I have the documents, and have perused them, I will go to your brother a day sooner than I intended. Do you feel yourself well enough to go now? If you do, my clerk shall procure you a coach. Do you stay in London? If so, you must leave your address."

Mary replied that she intended to set off to Exeter that evening by the mail, and would meet him there.

Mr. Trevor handed her out, put her into the coach, and she ordered the man to drive to the inn where she was stopping. Mary's senses were quite bewildered. It was late, and the mail was to start in an hour or two. She secured her place, and during her long journey she hardly knew how time passed away. On her arrival, in the morning, she hastened to the prison. She was received kindly, as before, by the gaoler and his wife, and then attended the turnkey into Joey's cell. As soon as the door was closed she threw herself down on the bedstead, and wept bitterly, quite heedless of our hero's remonstrance or attempts to soothe her.

" Oh ! it is horrible—too horrible ! " cried the almost fainting girl. " What can—what must be done ? Either way, misery—disgrace ! Lord, forgive me ! But my head is turned. That you should be here ! That you should be in this strait ! Why was it not me ? I—I have deserved all and more ! prison, death, everything is not too bad for me ; but you, my dear, dear boy ! "

" Mary, what is the reason of this ? I cannot understand. Are matters worse than they were before ? " said Joey. " And why should you talk in such a way about yourself ? If you ever did wrong, you were driven to it by the conduct of others ; but your reformation is all your own."

" Ah, Joey ! " replied Mary ; " I should think little of my repentance if I held myself absolved by a few years' good conduct. No, no ; a whole life of repentance is not sufficient for me ; I must live on, ever repenting, and must die full of penitence, and imploring for pardon. But why do I talk of myself ? "

" What has made you thus, Mary ? "

" Joey, I cannot keep it a secret from you ; it is useless to attempt it. I have discovered your father and mother ! "

" Where are they ? and do they know anything of my position ? "

" Yes ; your mother does, but not your father."

" Tell me all, Mary, and tell me quickly."

"Your father and mother are Mr. and Mrs. Austin."

Joey's utterance failed him from astonishment; he stared at Mary, but he could not utter a word. Mary again wept; and Joey for some minutes remained by her side in silence.

"Come, Mary," said Joey at last, "you can now tell me everything."

Joey sat down by her side, and Mary then communicated what had passed between herself and Mrs. Austin; her acknowledgment that he was her relation; the interest she took in him; the money she had lavished; her sufferings, which she had witnessed; and then she wound up with the conversation between her and Mr. Trevor.

"You see, my dear boy, there is no doubt of the fact. I believe I did promise Mrs. Austin to say nothing to you about it; but I forgot my promise till just this minute. Now, Joey, what is to be done?"

"Tell me something about my father, Mary," said Joey; "I wish to know how he is estimated, and how he behaves in his new position."

Mary told him all she knew, which was not a great deal: he was respected; but he was a strange man, kept himself very much aloof from others, and preferred seclusion.

"Mary," said Joey, "you know what were my intentions before; they are now still more fixed. I will take my chance; but I never will say one word. You already know and have guessed more than I could wish; I will not say that you are right, for it is not my secret."

"I thought as much," replied Mary, "and I feel how much my arguments must be weakened by the disclosures I have made. Before, I only felt for you; now I feel for all. O Joey! why are you, so innocent, to be punished this way, and I, so guilty, to be spared?"

"It is the will of God that I should be in this strait, Mary; and now let us not renew the subject."

"But, Joey, Mr. Trevor is coming here to-morrow; and he told me to tell you that you must have no reservation with your lawyer, if you wish him to be of service to you."

"You have given your message, Mary; and now you must leave me to deal with him."

"My heart is breaking," said Mary solemnly. "I wish I were in my grave if that wish is not wicked."

278

"Mary, recollect one thing; recollect it supports me, and let it support you;—I am innocent."

"You are, I'm sure; would to Heaven that I could say the same for another! But tell me, Joey, what shall I do when I meet your mother? I loved her before; but, oh! how much I love her now! What shall I do? Shall I tell her that I have discovered all? I do not know how I can keep it from her."

"Mary, I see no objection to your telling her, but tell her also that I will not see her till after my trial; whatever my fate may be, I should like to see her after that is decided."

"I will take your message the day after to-morrow," replied Mary; "now I must go and look out for lodgings, and then write to your mother. Bless you!"

Mary quitted the cell; she had suffered so much that she could hardly gain the gaoler's parlour, where she sat down to recover herself. She inquired of the gaoler's wife if she could procure apartments near the prison, and the woman requested one of the turnkeys to take her to a lodging which would be suitable. As soon as Mary was located, she wrote a letter to Mrs. Austin, informing her of her having seen the lawyer, and that his services were secured; and then, worn out with the anxiety and excitement of the three last days, she retired to bed, and in her sleep forgot her sufferings.

CHAPTER XLVI

In which our hero makes up his mind to be hanged.

OUR hero was not sorry to be left alone; for the first time he felt the absence of Mary a relief. He was almost as much bewildered as poor Mary with the strange discovery; his father a great landed proprietor, one of the first men in the county, universally respected—in the first society! his mother, as he knew by Mary's letters written long ago, courted and sought after, loved and admired! If he had made a resolution—a promise he might say—when a mere child, that he would take the onus of the deed upon his own shoulders, to protect his father, then a poacher and in

279

humble life, how much more was it his duty, now that his father would so feel any degradation—now that, being raised so high, his fall would be so bitter, his disgrace so deeply felt, and the stigma so doubly severe! "No, no," thought Joey, "were I to impeach my father now—to accuse him of a deed which would bring him to the scaffold —I should not only be considered his murderer, but it would be said I had done it to inherit his possessions; I should be considered one who had sacrificed his father to obtain his property. I should be scouted, shunned, and deservedly despised; the disgrace of my father having been hanged would be a trifle compared with the reproach of a son having condemned a parent to the gallows. Now I am doubly bound to keep to my resolution; and come what may the secret shall die with me;" and Joey slept soundly that night.

The next morning Mr. Trevor came into his cell.

"I have seen your sister, Rushbrook," said he, "and at her request have come to assist you, if it is in my power. She has been here since, I have been informed, and if so, I have no doubt that she has told you that you must have no secrets with your lawyer. Your legal friend and adviser in this case is your true friend; he is bound in honour to secrecy, and were you to declare now that you were guilty of this murder, the very confidence would only make me more earnest in your defence. I have here all the evidence at the coroner's inquest, and the verdict against you; tell me honestly what did take place, and then I shall know better how to convince the jury that it did not."

"You are very kind, sir; but I can say nothing even to you, except that, on my honour, I am not guilty."

"But tell me, then, how did it happen?"

"I have nothing more to say, and with my thanks to you, sir, I will say nothing more."

"This is very strange; the evidence was strong against you: was the evidence correct?"

"The parties were correct in their evidence, as it appeared to them."

"And yet you are not guilty?"

"I am not; I shall plead not guilty, and leave my fate to the jury."

"Are you mad? Your sister is a sweet young woman,

and has interested me greatly; but, if innocent, you are throwing away your life."

"I am doing my duty, sir; whatever you may think of my conduct, the secret dies with me."

"And for whom do you sacrifice yourself in this way, if, as you say, and as your sister declares, you are not guilty?"

Joey made no reply, but sat down on the bedstead.

"If the deed was not done by you, by whom was it done?" urged Mr. Trevor. "If you make no reply to that, I must throw up my brief."

"You said just now," returned Joey, "that if I declared myself guilty of the murder, you would still defend me; now, because I say I am not, and will not say who is, you must throw up your brief. Surely you are inconsistent."

"I must have your confidence, my good lad."

"You never will have more than you have now. I have not requested you to defend me. I care nothing about defence."

"Then you wish to be hanged?"

"No, I do not; but, rather than say anything, I will take my chance of it."

"This is very strange," said Mr. Trevor. After a pause, he continued: "I observe that you are supposed to have killed this man, Byres, when nobody else was present; you were known to go out with your father's gun, and the keeper's evidence proved that you poached. Now, as there is no evidence of intentional murder on your part, it is not impossible that the gun went off by accident, and that, mere boy as you must have been at that time, you were so frightened at what had taken place, that you absconded from fear. It appears to me that that should be our line of defence."

"I never fired at the man at all," said Joey.

"Who fired the gun, then?" asked Mr. Trevor.

Joey made no reply.

"Rushbrook," said Mr. Trevor, "I am afraid I can be of little use to you; indeed, were it not that your sister's tears have interested me, I would not take up your cause. I cannot understand your conduct, which appears to me to be absurd; your motives are inexplicable, and all I can believe is, that you have committed the crime, and will

281

not divulge the secret to any one, not even to those who
would befriend you."

"Think of me what you please, sir," rejoined our hero;
"see me condemned, and, if it should be so, executed; and
after all *that* has taken place, believe me, when I assert to
you—as I hope for salvation—I am not guilty. I thank
you, sir, thank you sincerely, for the interest you have
shown for me; I feel grateful, excessively grateful, and the
more so for what you have said of Mary; but if you were to
remain here for a month, you could gain no more from me
than you have already."

"After such an avowal it is useless my stopping here,"
said Mr. Trevor; "I must make what defence I can, for your
sister's sake."

"Many, many thanks, sir, for your kindness; I am really
grateful to you," replied Joey.

Mr. Trevor remained for a minute scanning the countenance of our hero. There was something in it so clear and
bright, so unflinching, so proclaiming innocence, and high
feeling, that he sighed deeply as he left the cell.

His subsequent interview with Mary was short; he explained to her the difficulties arising from the obstinacy of
her brother; but at the same time expressed his determination to do his best to save him.

Mary, as soon as she had seen Mr. Trevor, set off on her
return to the Hall. As soon as she went to Mrs. Austin,
Mary apprised her of Mr. Trevor's having consented to act
as counsel for our hero, and also of Joey's resolute determination not to divulge the secret.

"Madam," said Mary, after some hesitation, "it is my
duty to have no secret from you; and I hope you will not
be angry when I tell you that I have discovered that which
you would have concealed."

"What have you discovered, Mary?" asked Mrs. Austin,
looking at her with alarm.

"That Joseph Rushbrook is your own son," said Mary,
kneeling down and kissing the hand of her mistress. "The
secret is safe with me, depend upon it," she continued.

"And how have you made the discovery, Mary; for I will
not attempt to deny it?"

Mary then entered into a detail of her conversation with

282

Mr. Trevor. "He asked me," said she, "as the sister of Joey, if we had any relatives, and I replied, ' No ; ' so that he has no suspicion of the fact. I beg your pardon, madam, but I could not keep it from Joey ; I quite forgot my promise to you at the time."

"And what did my poor child say ? "

"That he would not see you until after his trial ; but, when his fate was decided, he should like to see you once more. O madam, what a painful sacrifice ! and yet, now, I do not blame him ; for it is his duty."

" My dread is not for my son, Mary ; he is innocent, and that to me is everything ; but if my husband was to hear of his being about to be tried, I know not what would be the consequence. If it can only be kept from his knowledge ! God knows that he has suffered enough ! But what am I saying ? I was talking nonsense."

" O madam ! I know the whole ; I cannot be blinded either by Joey or you. I beg your pardon, madam ; but although Joey would not reply, I told him that his father did the deed. But do not answer me, madam ; be silent, as your son has been ; and believe me when I say that my suspicion could not be wrenched from me even by torture."

" I do trust you, Mary ; and perhaps the knowledge that you have obtained is advantageous. When does the trial come on ? "

" The assizes commence to-morrow forenoon, madam, they say."

" Oh ! how I long to have him in these arms ! " exclaimed Mrs. Austin.

" It is indeed a sad trial to a mother, madam," replied Mary, " but still it must not be until after he is——"

" Yes ; until he is condemned ! God have mercy on me ! Mary, you had better return to Exeter ; but write to me every day. Stay by him and comfort him ; and may the God of comfort listen to the prayers of an unhappy and distracted mother. Leave me now. God bless you, my dear girl ! you have indeed proved a comfort. Leave me now."

CHAPTER XLVII

In which our hero proves game to the very last.

MARY returned to Exeter. The trial of our hero was expected to come on on the following day. She preferred being with Joey to witnessing the agony and distress of Mrs. Austin, to whom she could offer no comfort; indeed, her own state of suspense was so wearing, that she almost felt relief when the day of trial came on. Mr. Trevor had once more attempted to reason with Joey, but our hero continued firm in his resolution, and Mr. Trevor, when he made his appearance in the court, wore upon his countenance the marks of sorrow and discontent; he did not, nevertheless, fail in his duty. Joey was brought to the bar, and his appearance was so different from that which was to be expected in one charged with the crime of murder, that strong interest was immediately excited; the spectators anticipated a low-bred ruffian, and they beheld a fair, handsome young man, with an open brow and intelligent countenance, whose eye quailed not when it met their own, and whose demeanour was bold without being offensive. True that there were traces of sorrow on his countenance, and that his cheeks were pale; but no one who had any knowledge of human nature, or any feeling of charity in his disposition, could say that there was the least appearance of guilt. The jury were empannelled, the counts of the indictment read over, and the trial commenced, and, as the indictment was preferred, the judge caught the date of the supposed offence.

"What is the date?" said the judge; "the year, I mean?"

Upon the reply of the clerk, his lordship observed, "Eight years ago!" and then looking at the prisoner, added, "Why, he must have been a child."

"As is too often the case," replied the prosecuting counsel; "a child in years, but not in guilt, as we shall soon bring evidence to substantiate."

As the evidence brought forward was the same as we have already mentioned as given at the inquest over the body, we shall pass it over; that of Furness, as he was not to be found, was read to the court. As the trial proceeded, and as each fact came forth more condemning, people began to look with less compassion on the prisoner; they shook their heads, and compressed their lips.

As soon as the evidence for the Crown was closed, Mr. Trevor rose in our hero's defence. He commenced by ridiculing the idea of trying a mere child upon so grave a charge, for a child the prisoner must have been at the time the offence was committed. "Look at him now, gentlemen of the jury; eight years ago the murder of the pedlar, Byres, took place; why, you may judge for yourselves whether he is now more than seventeen years of age; he could scarcely have held a gun at the time referred to."

"The prisoner's age does not appear in the indictment," observed the judge.

"May we ask his age, my lord?" demanded one of the jury.

"The prisoner may answer the question if he pleases," replied the judge, "not otherwise; perhaps he may not yet be seventeen years of age. Do you wish to state your age to the jury, prisoner?"

"I have no objection, my lord," replied Joey, not regarding the shakes of the head of his counsel; "I was twenty-two last month."

Mr. Trevor bit his lips at this unfortunate regard for truth in our hero, and after a time proceeded, observing that the very candour of the prisoner, in not taking advantage of his youthful appearance to deceive the jury, ought to be a strong argument in his favour. Mr. Trevor then continued to address the jury upon the vagueness of the evidence, and, as he proceeded, observed—"Now, gentlemen of the jury, if this case had been offered to me to give an opinion upon, I should, without any previous knowledge of the prisoner, have just come to the following conclusion—I should have said (and your intelligence and good sense will, I have no doubt, bear me out in this supposition), that, allowing that the pedlar, Byres, did receive his death by the prisoner's hand—I say, gentlemen, that *allowing* such to have been the case, for I deny that it is borne out by the evidence—that it must have been that, at the sudden meeting with the pedlar, when the lad's conscience told him that what he was

doing was wrong, that the gun of the prisoner was discharged
unintentionally, and the consequence was fatal; I should
then surmise, further, that the prisoner, frightened at the
deed which he had unintentionally committed, had absconded
upon the first impulse. That, gentlemen, I believe to be
the real state of the case; and what was more natural than
that a child under such circumstances should have been
frightened, and have attempted to evade the inquiry which
must have eventually ensued?"

"You state such to be your opinion, Mr. Trevor; do you
wish me to infer that the prisoner pleads such as his defence?"
asked the judge.

"My lord," replied Mr. Trevor, in a hesitating way, "the
prisoner has pleaded not guilty to the crime imputed to
him."

"That I am aware of, but I wish to know whether you
mean to say that the prisoner's defence is, not having anything to do with the death of the pedlar, or upon the plea of
his gun going off by accident?"

"My lord, it is my duty to my client to make no admission
whatever."

"I should think that you would be safe enough, all circumstances considered, if you took the latter course," observed
the judge humanely.

Mr. Trevor was now in a dilemma; he knew not how to
move. He was fearful, if he stated positively that our hero's
gun went off by accident, that Joey would deny it; and yet
if he was permitted to assert this to be the case, he saw, from
the bearing of the judge, that the result of the trial would be
satisfactory. It hardly need be observed that both judge,
prosecuting counsel, jury, and everybody in court, were much
astonished at this hesitation on the part of the prisoner's
counsel.

"Do you mean to assert that the gun went off by accident,
Mr. Trevor?" asked the judge.

"I never fired the gun, my lord," replied Joey, in a calm
steady voice.

"The prisoner has answered for me," replied Mr. Trevor,
recovering himself; "we are perfectly aware that by making
a statement of accidental murder, we could safely have left
the prisoner in the hands of an intelligent jury; but the fact

is, my lord, that the prisoner never fired the gun, and therefore could not be guilty of the murder imputed to him."

Mr. Trevor had felt, upon our hero's assertion, that his
case was hopeless; he roused up, however, to make a strong
appeal to the jury; unfortunately, it was declamation only,
not disproof of the charges, and the reply of the prosecuting
counsel completely established the guilt of our hero upon
what is called presumptive evidence. The jury retired for a
few minutes after the summing up of the judge, and then
returned a verdict against our hero of Guilty, but recommended him to mercy. Although the time to which we
refer was one in which leniency was seldom extended, still
there was the youth of our hero, and so much mystery in the
transaction, that when the judge passed the sentence, he
distinctly stated that the royal mercy would be so far extended, that the sentence would be commuted to transportation. Our hero made no reply; he bowed, and was led back
to his place of confinement, and in a few minutes afterwards
the arms of the weeping Mary were encircled round his
neck.

"You don't blame me, Mary?" said Joey.

"No, no," sobbed Mary; "all that the world can do is
nothing when we are innocent."

"I shall soon be far from here, Mary," said Jocy, sitting
down on the bedstead; "but, thank Heaven! it is over."

The form of Emma Phillips rose up in our hero's imagination, and he covered up his face with his hands.

"Had it not been for her!" thought he. "What must
she think of me! a convicted felon! this is the hardest of all
to bear up against."

"Joey," said Mary, who had watched him in silence and
tears, "I must go now; you will see her now, will you not?"

"She never will see me! she despises me already," replied
Joey.

"Your mother despise her noble boy? Oh, never! How
can you think so?"

"I was thinking of somebody else, Mary," replied Joey.
"Yes, I wish to see my mother."

"Then I will go now; recollect what her anxiety and impatience must be. I will travel post to-night, and be there
by to-morrow morning."

"Go, dear Mary, go, and God bless you! hasten to my poor mother, and tell her that I am quite—yes, quite happy and resigned. Go now, quickly."

Mary left the cell, and Joey, whose heart was breaking at the moment that he said he was happy and resigned, for he was thinking of his eternal separation from Emma, as soon as he was alone, threw himself on the bed, and gave full vent to those feelings of bitter anguish which he could no longer repress.

CHAPTER XLVIII

In which everybody appears to be on the move except our hero.

MARY set off with post-horses and arrived at the Hall before daylight. She remained in her own room until the post came in, when her first object was to secure the newspapers before the butler had opened them, stating that her mistress was awake, and requested to see them. She took the same precaution when the other papers came in late in the day, so that Mr. Austin should not read the account of the trial; this was the more easy to accomplish, as he seldom looked at a newspaper. As soon as the usual hour had arrived, Mary presented herself to her mistress, and communicated the melancholy result of the trial. Mrs. Austin desired Mary to say to the servants that she was going to remain with a lady, a friend of hers, some miles off, who was dangerously ill; and should, in all probability, not return that night, or even the next, if her friend was not better; and, her preparations for the journey being completed, she set off with Mary a little before dark on her way to Exeter.

But if Mr. Austin did not look at the newspapers others did, and amongst the latter was Major M'Shane, who, having returned from his tour, was sitting with O'Donahue and the two ladies in the library of his own house when the post came in. The major had hardly looked at the newspapers when the name of Rushbrook caught his eye; he turned to it, read a portion, and gave a loud whistle of surprise.

"What's the matter, my dear?" asked Mrs. M'Shane.

"Murder's the matter, my jewel," returned the major; "but don't interrupt me just now, for I'm breathless with confusion."

M'Shane read the whole account of the trial and the verdict, and then without saying a word, put it into the hands of O'Donahue. As soon as O'Donahue had finished it, M'Shane beckoned him out of the room.

"I didn't like to let Mrs. M'Shane know it, as she would take it sorely to heart," said M'Shane; "but what's to be done now, O'Donahue? You see the boy has not peached upon his father, and has convicted himself. It would be poor comfort to Mrs. M'Shane, who loves the memory of that boy better than she would a dozen little M'Shanes, if it pleased Heaven to grant them to her, to know that the boy is found, when he is only found to be sent away over the water; so it is better that nothing should be said about it just now; but what is to be done?"

"Well, it appears to me that we had better be off to Exeter directly," replied O'Donahue.

"Yes, and see him," rejoined the major.

"Before I saw him, M'Shane, I would call upon the lawyer who defended him, and tell him what you know about the father, and what our suspicions, I may say, convictions, are. He would then tell us how to proceed, so as to procure his pardon, perhaps."

"That's good advice; and now what excuse are we to make for running away?"

"As for my wife," replied O'Donahue, "I may as well tell her the truth; she will keep it secret; and as for yours, she will believe anything you please to tell her."

"And so she will, the good creature, and that's why I never can bear to deceive her about anything; but, in this instance, it is all for her own sake. And therefore, suppose your wife says that you must go to town immediately, and that I had better accompany you, as it is upon a serious affair?"

"Be it so," replied O'Donahue; "do you order the horses to be put to while I settle the affair with the females."

This was soon done, and in half-an-hour the two gentlemen were on their way to Exeter; and as soon as they arrived, which was late in the evening, they established themselves at the principal hotel.

THE POACHER

In the meantime Mrs. Austin and Mary had also arrived, and had taken up their quarters at another hotel, where Mrs. Austin would be less exposed. It was, however, too late to visit our hero when they arrived, and the next morning they proceeded to the gaol, much about the same hour that M'Shane and O'Donahue paid their visit to Mr. Trevor.

Perhaps it will be better to leave to the imagination of our readers the scene which occurred between our hero and his mother, as we have had too many painful ones already in this latter portion of our narrative. The joy and grief of both at meeting again, only to part for ever—the strong conflict between duty and love—the lacerated feelings of the doting mother, the true and affectionate son, and the devoted servant and friend—may be better imagined than expressed; but their grief was raised to its climax when our hero, pressed in his mother's arms as he narrated his adventures, confessed that another pang was added to his sufferings in parting with the object of his earliest affections.

"My poor, poor boy, this is indeed a bitter cup to drink!" exclaimed Mrs. Austin. "May God, in His mercy, look down upon you, and console you!"

"He will, mother; and when far away—not before, not until you can safely do so—promise me to go to Emma, and tell her that I was not guilty. I can bear anything but that she should despise me."

"I will, my child, I will; and I will love her dearly for your sake. Now go on with your history, my dear boy."

We must leave our hero and his mother in conversation, and return to M'Shane and O'Donahue, who, as soon as they had breakfasted, repaired to the lodgings of Mr. Trevor.

M'Shane, who was spokesman, soon entered upon the business which brought them there.

Mr. Trevor stated to him the pertinacity of our hero, and the impossibility of saving him from condemnation, remarking, at the same time, that there was a mystery which he could not fathom.

M'Shane took upon himself to explain that mystery, having, as we have before observed, already been sufficiently clear-sighted to fathom it; and referred to O'Donahue to corroborate his opinion of the elder Rushbrook's character.

290

"And this father of his is totally lost sight of, you say?" observed Mr. Trevor.

"Altogether; I have never been able to trace him," replied M'Shane.

"I was observing to his sister——" said Mr. Trevor.

"He has no sister," interrupted M'Shane.

"Still there is a young woman—and a very sweet young woman, too—who came to me in London, to engage me for his defence, who represented herself as his sister."

"That is strange," rejoined M'Shane, musing.

"But, however," continued Mr. Trevor, "as I was about to say, I was observing to this young woman how strange it was, that the first time I was legally employed for the name of Rushbrook, it should be a case which, in the opinion of the world, should produce the highest gratification, and that in the second in one which has ended in misery."

"How do you mean?" inquired M'Shane.

"I put a person of the name of Rushbrook in possession of a large fortune. I asked our young friend's sister whether he could be any relation; but she said no."

"Young Rushbrook had no sister, I am sure," interrupted M'Shane.

"I now recollect," continued Mr. Trevor, "that this person who came into the fortune stated that he had formerly held a commission in the army."

"Then, depend on it, it's Rushbrook himself, who has given himself brevet rank," replied M'Shane. "Where is he now?"

"Down in Dorsetshire," said Mr. Trevor. "He succeeded to the Austin estates, and has taken the name."

"'Tis he—'tis he—I'll swear to it," cried M'Shane. "Phillaloo! Murder and Irish! the murder's out now. No wonder this gentleman wouldn't return my visit, and keeps himself entirely at home. I beg your pardon, Mr. Trevor, but what sort of a looking personage may he be, for, as I have said, I have never seen this Mr. Austin?"

"A fine, tall, soldierly man; I should say rough, but still not vulgar; dark hair and eyes, aquiline nose; if I recollect right——"

"'Tis the man!" exclaimed O'Donahue.

"And his wife—did you see her?" asked M'Shane.

"No, I did not," replied Mr. Trevor.

"Well, I have seen her very often," rejoined M'Shane; "and a very nice creature she appears to be. I have never been in their house in my life. I called and left my card, that's all; but I have met her several times. However, as you have not seen her, that proves nothing; and now, Mr. Trevor, what do you think we should do?"

"I really am not prepared to advise; it is a case of great difficulty; I think, however, it would be advisable for you to call upon young Rushbrook, and see what you can obtain from him; after that, if you come here to-morrow morning, I will be better prepared to give you an answer."

"I will do as you wish, sir; I will call upon my friend first, and my name's not M'Shane if I don't call upon his father afterwards."

"Do nothing rashly, I beg," replied Mr. Trevor; "recollect you have come to me for advice, and I think you are bound at least to hear what I have to propose before you act."

"That's the truth, Mr. Trevor; so now with many thanks, we will take our leave, and call upon you to-morrow."

M'Shane and O'Donahue then proceeded to the gaol, and demanded permission to see our hero.

"There are two ladies with him just now," said the gaoler; "they have been there these three hours, so I suppose they will not be much longer."

"We will wait, then," replied O'Donahue.

In about a quarter of an hour Mrs. Austin and Mary made their appearance; the former was closely veiled when she entered the gaoler's parlour, in which O'Donahue and M'Shane were waiting. It had not been the intention of Mrs. Austin to have gone into the parlour, but her agitation and distress had so overcome her that she could scarcely walk, and Mary had persuaded her as she came down to go in and take a glass of water. The gentlemen rose when she came in; she immediately recognised M'Shane, and the sudden rush into her memory of what might be the issue of the meeting, was so overwhelming, that she dropped into a chair and fainted.

Mary ran for some water, and while she did so, M'Shane and O'Donahue went to the assistance of Mrs. Austin. The veil was removed; and, of course, she was immediately recognised by M‘Shane, who was now fully convinced that Austin and Rushbrook were one and the same person.

Upon the first signs of returning animation, M‘Shane had the delicacy to withdraw, and making a sign to the gaoler, he and O'Donahue repaired to the cell of our hero. The greeting was warm on both sides. M‘Shane was eager to enter upon the subject; he pointed out to Joey that he knew who committed the murder—indeed, plainly told him, that it was the deed of his father. But Joey, as before, would admit nothing; he was satisfied with their belief in his innocence, but, having made up his mind to suffer, could not be persuaded to reveal the truth; and M‘Shane and O'Donahue quitted the cell, perceiving that, unless most decided steps were taken without the knowledge of our hero, there was no chance of his being extricated from his melancholy fate. Struck with admiration at his courage and self-devotion towards an unworthy parent, they bade him farewell, simply promising to use all their endeavours in his behalf.

CHAPTER XLIX

The interview.

ACCORDING to their arrangement, on the following morning M‘Shane and O'Donahue called upon Mr. Trevor, and after half-an-hour's consultation, it was at last decided that they should make an attempt to see Austin, and bide the issue of the interview, when they would again communicate with the lawyer, who was to return to town on the following day. They then set off as fast as four horses could convey them, and drove direct to the Hall, where they arrived about six o'clock in the evening.

It had so happened that Austin had the evening before inquired for his wife. The servant reported to him what Mary had told them, and Austin, who was in a fidgety humour, had sent for the coachman who had driven the carriage, to inquire whether Mrs. Austin's friend was very ill. The coachman stated that he had not driven over to the place in question, but to the nearest post-town, where

Mrs. Austin had taken a post-chaise. This mystery and concealment on the part of his wife was not very agreeable to
a man of Mr. Austin's temper; he was by turns indignant
and alarmed; and after having passed a sleepless night, had
been all the day anxiously waiting Mrs. Austin's return,
when the sound of wheels was heard, and the carriage of
M'Shane drove up to the door. On inquiry if Mr. Austin
was at home, the servants replied that they would ascertain;
and Austin, who imagined that this unusual visit might be
connected with his wife's mysterious absence, desired the
butler to show in the visitors. Austin started at the an-
nouncement of the names, but recovering himself, he remained
standing near the table, drawn up to his full height.

" Mr. Austin," said O'Donahue, " we have ventured to call
upon you upon an affair of some importance; as Mr. Austin,
we have not the pleasure of your acquaintance, but we were
formerly, if I mistake not, serving his Majesty in the same
regiment."

" I do not pretend to deny, gentlemen, that you once knew
me under different circumstances," replied Austin haughtily;
" will you please to be seated, and then probably you will
favour me with the cause of this visit."

" May I inquire of you, Mr. Austin," said M'Shane, " if
you may have happened to look over the newspapers within
these few days?"

" No! and now I recollect—which is unusual—the papers
have not been brought to me regularly."

" They were probably withheld from you in consequence
of the intelligence they would have conveyed to you."

" May I ask what that intelligence may be?" inquired
Austin, surprised.

" The trial, conviction, and sentence to transportation for
life of one Joseph Rushbrook, for the murder of a man of
the name of Byres," replied M'Shane; " Mr. Austin, you are
of course aware that he is your son."

" You have, of course, seen the party, and he has made
that statement to you?" replied Mr. Austin.

" We have seen the party, but he has not made that
statement," replied O'Donahue; " but do you pretend to
deny it?"

" I am not aware upon what grounds you have thought

proper to come here to interrogate me," replied Austin. "Supposing that I had a son, and that son has, as you say, been guilty of the deed, it certainly is no concern of yours."

"First, with your leave, Mr. Austin," said M'Shane, "let me prove that he is your son. You were living at Grassford, where the murder was committed; your son ran away in consequence, and fell into the hands of Captain (now General) O'Donahue; from him your son was made over to me, and I adopted him; but having been recognised when at school, by Furness, the schoolmaster of the village, he absconded to avoid being apprehended; and I have never seen him from that time till yesterday morning, when I called upon him, and had an interview as soon as his mother, Mrs. Austin, had quitted the cell in Exeter gaol, where he is at present confined."

Austin started—here was the cause of Mrs. Austin's absence explained; neither could he any longer refuse to admit that Joey was his son. After a silence of a minute, he replied—

"I have to thank you much for your kindness to my poor boy, Major M'Shane; and truly sorry am I that he is in such a dilemma. Now that I am acquainted with it, I shall do all in my power. There are other Rushbrooks, gentlemen, and you cannot be surprised at my not immediately admitting that such a disgrace had occurred to my own family. Of Mrs. Austin's having been with him I assure you I had not any idea; her having gone there puts it beyond a doubt, although it has been carefully concealed from me till this moment."

It must not be supposed that, because Austin replied so calmly to Major M'Shane, he was calm within. On the contrary, from the very first of the interview he had been in a state of extreme excitement, and the struggle to command his feelings was terrible; indeed, it was now so painfully expressed in his countenance, that O'Donahue said—

"Perhaps, Mr. Austin, you will allow me to ring for a little water?"

"No, sir, thank you," replied Austin, gasping for breath.

"Since you have admitted that Joseph Rushbrook is your son, Mr. Austin," continued M'Shane, "your own flesh and blood, may I inquire of you what you intend to do in his behalf? Do you intend to allow the law to take its course, and your son to be banished for life?"

"What can I do, gentlemen? He has been tried and condemned; of course if any exertion on my part can avail—but I fear that there is no chance of that."

"Mr. Austin, if he were guilty I should not have interfered; but, in my opinion, he is innocent; do you not think so?"

"I do not believe, sir, that he ever would have done such a deed; but that avails nothing, he is condemned."

"I grant it, unless the real murderer of the pedlar could be brought forward."

"Y-e-s," replied Austin, trembling.

"Shall I denounce him, Mr. Austin?"

"Do you know him?" replied Austin, starting to his feet.

"Yes, Rushbrook," replied M'Shane, in a voice of thunder, "I do know him,—'tis yourself!"

Austin could bear up no longer, he fell down on the floor as if he had been shot. O'Donahue and M'Shane went to his assistance; they raised him up, but he was insensible. They then rang the bell for assistance, the servant came in, medical advice was sent for, and M'Shane and O'Donahue, perceiving there was no chance of prosecuting their intentions in Mr. Austin's present state, quitted the Hall just as the chaise with Mrs. Austin and Mary drove up to the door.

CHAPTER L

In which it is to be hoped that the story winds up to the satisfaction of the reader.

IT was not for some time after the arrival of the medical men that Mr. Austin could be recovered from his state of insensibility, and when he was at last restored to life, it was not to reason. He raved wildly, and it was pronounced that his attack was a brain fever. As, in his incoherent exclamations, the name of Byres was frequently repeated, as soon as the medical assistants had withdrawn, Mrs. Austin desired all the servants, with the exception of Mary, to quit the room. They did so with reluctance, for their curiosity was excited, and there was shrugging of the shoulders, and whispering, and surmising, and repeating of the words which had escaped from their unconscious master's lips, and hints that all was not right, passed from one to another in the servants' hall. In the meantime, Mrs. Austin and Mary remained with him; and well it was that the servants had been sent away, if they were not to know what had taken place so long ago, for now Austin played the whole scene over again, denounced himself as a murderer, spoke of his son, and of his remorse, and then he would imagine himself in conflict with Byres—he clenched his fists—and he laughed and chuckled—and then would change again to bitter lamentations for the deed which he had done.

"O Mary, how is this to end?" exclaimed Mrs. Austin, after one of the paroxysms had subsided.

"As guilt always must end, madam," replied Mary, bursting into tears, and clasping her hands,—"in misery."

"My dear Mary, do not distress yourself in that manner; you are no longer guilty."

"Nor is my master, then, madam; for I am sure that he has repented."

"Yes, indeed, he has repented most sincerely; one hasty deed has embittered his whole life—he never has been happy since, and never will be until he is in heaven."

"Oh, what a happy relief it would be to him!" replied Mary, musing. "I wish that I was, if such wish is not sinful."

"Mary, you must not add to my distress by talking in that manner; I want your support and consolation now."

"You have a right to demand everything of me, madam," replied Mary, "and I will do my best, I will indeed. I have often felt this before, and I thank God for it; it will make me more humble."

The fever continued for many days, during which time Mr. Austin was attended solely by his wife and Mary; the latter had written to our hero, stating the cause of her absence from him in so trying a period, and she had received an answer stating that he had received from very good authority the information that he was not likely to leave the country for some weeks, and requesting that Mary would remain with his mother until his father's dangerous illness was decided one way or the other; he stated that he should be perfectly satisfied if he only saw her once before his departure, to arrange with her relative to her affairs, and to give her legal authority to act for him, previously to his removal from the country. He told her that he had perceived an advertisement in the London papers, evidently put in by his friends at Portsmouth, offering a handsome reward to any one who could give any account of him—and that he was fearful that some of those who were at the trial would read it, and make known his position; he begged Mary to write to him every day if possible, if it were only a few lines, and sent his devoted love to his mother. Mary complied with all our hero's requests, and every day a few lines were despatched; and it was now ascertained by the other domestics, and by them made generally known, that a daily correspondence was kept up with a prisoner in Exeter gaol, which added still more mystery and interest to the state of Mr. Austin. Many were the calls and cards left at the Hall, and if we were to inquire whether curiosity or condolence was the motive of those who went there, we are afraid that the cause would, in most cases, have proved to have been the former. Among others, O'Donahue and M'Shane did not fail to send every day, waiting for the time when they could persuade Austin to do justice to his own child.

The crisis, as predicted by the medical attendants, at last arrived, and Mr. Austin recovered his reason; but, at the same time, all hopes of his again rising from his bed were given over. This intelligence was communicated to his wife, who wept and wished, but dared not utter what she wished. Mary, however, took an opportunity, when Mrs. Austin had quitted the room, to tell Mr. Austin, who was in such a feeble state that he could hardly speak, that the time would soon come when he would be summoned before a higher tribunal, and conjured him, by the hopes he had of forgiveness, now that the world was fading away before his eyes, to put away all pride, and to do that justice to his son which our hero's noble conduct towards him demanded—to make a confession, either in writing or in presence of witnesses, before he died—which would prove the innocence of his only child, the heir to the property and the name.

There was a struggle, and a long one, in the proud heart of Mr. Austin before he could consent to this act of justice. Mary had pointed out the propriety of it early in the morning, and it was not until late in the evening, after having remained in silence and with his eyes closed for the whole day, that Austin made a sign to his wife to bend down to him, and desired her in a half-whisper to send for a magistrate. His request was immediately attended to; and in an hour the summons was answered by one with whom Austin had been on good terms. Austin made his deposition in few words, and was supported by Mary while he signed the paper. It was done; and when she would have removed the pen from his fingers, she found that it was still held fast, and that his head had fallen back; the conflict between his pride and this act of duty had been too overpowering for him in his weak condition, and Mr. Austin was dead before the ink of his signature had time to dry.

The gentleman who had been summoned in his capacity of magistrate, thought it advisable to remove from the scene of distress without attempting to communicate with Mrs. Austin in her present sorrow. He had been in conversation with O'Donahue and M'Shane at the time that he was summoned, and Mr. Austin's illness and the various reports abroad had been there canvassed. O'Donahue and M'Shane had reserved the secret; but when their friend was sent for, anticipating some such result would take place, they requested him to return to them from the Hall; he did so, and acquainted them with what had passed.

"There's no time to lose, then," said M'Shane; "I will, if you please, take a copy of this deposition."

O'Donahue entered into a brief narrative of the circumstances and the behaviour of our hero; and, as soon as the copy of the deposition had been attested by the magistrate, he and M'Shane ordered horses and set off for London. They knocked up Mr. Trevor at his private house in the middle of the night, and put the document into his hands.

"Well, Major M'Shane, I would gladly have risen from a sick bed to have had this paper put into my hands; we must call upon the Secretary of State to-morrow, and I have no doubt but that the poor lad will be speedily released, take possession of his property, and be an honour to the county."

"An honour to old England," replied M'Shane; "but I shall now wish you good night."

M'Shane, before he went to bed, immediately wrote a letter to Mrs. Austin, acquainting her with what he had done, and the intentions of Mr. Trevor, sending it by express; he simply stated the facts, without any comments.

But we must now return to Portsmouth. The advertisement of Mr. Small did not escape the keen eye of the police-constable who had arrested our hero. As the reader must recollect, the arrest was made so quietly that no one was aware of the circumstance, and as the reward of £100 would be a very handsome addition to the £200 which he had already received, the man immediately set off for Portsmouth on the outside of the coach, and went to Mr. Small, whom he found in the counting-house with Mr. Sleek. He soon introduced himself, and his business with them; and such was Mr. Small's impatience that he immediately signed a cheque for the amount, and handed it to the police-officer, who then bluntly told him that our hero had been tried for murder, and sentenced to transportation, his real name being Rushbrook, and not O'Donahue.

This was a heavy blow to Mr. Small; having obtained all the particulars from the police-constable, he dismissed him, and was for some time in consultation with Mr. Sleek; and as it would be impossible long to withhold the facts, it was thought advisable that Mrs. Phillips and Emma should become acquainted with them immediately, the more so as Emma had acknowledged that there was a mystery about our hero, a portion of which she was acquainted with.

Mrs. Phillips was the first party to whom the intelligence was communicated, and she was greatly distressed. It was some time before she could decide upon whether Emma, in her weak state, should be made acquainted with the melancholy tidings, but as she had suffered so much from suspense, it was at last considered advisable that the communication should be made. It was done as cautiously as possible; Emma was not so shocked as they supposed she would have been at the intelligence.

"I have been prepared for this, or something like this,"

replied she, weeping in her mother's arms, "but I cannot believe that he has done the deed; he told me that he did not, when he was a child; he has asserted it since. Mother, I must—I will go and see him."

"See him, my child? he is confined in gaol."

"Do not refuse me, mother, you know not what I feel—you know not—I never knew myself till now how much I loved him. See him I must, and will. Dearest mother, if you value my life, if you would not drive reason from its seat, do not refuse me."

Mrs. Phillips found that it was in vain to argue, and consulted with Mr. Small, who at length (after having in vain remonstrated with Emma) decided that her request should be granted, and that very day he accompanied his niece, travelling all night until they arrived at Exeter.

In the meantime, Mrs. Austin had remained in a state of great distress; her husband lay dead; she believed that he had confessed his guilt, but to what extent she did not know, for neither she nor Mary had heard what passed between him and the magistrate. She had no one but Mary to confide in or to console her, no one to advise with or to consult. She thought of sending for the magistrate, but it would appear indecorous, and she was all anxiety and doubt. The letter from M'Shane, which arrived the next afternoon, relieved her at once; she felt that her boy was safe.

"Mary, dear, read this; he is safe," exclaimed she. "God of heaven, accept a mother's grateful tears."

"Cannot you spare me, madam?" replied Mary, returning the letter.

"Spare you. Oh yes! quick, Mary, lose not a moment; go to him, and take this letter with you. My dear, dear child."

Mary did not wait a second command; she sent for post-horses, and in half-an-hour was on her way to Exeter; travelling with as much speed as Emma and her uncle, she arrived there but a few hours after them.

Our hero had been anxiously waiting for Mary's daily communication; the post time had passed, and it had not arrived. Pale and haggard from long confinement and distress of mind, he was pacing up and down when the bolts were turned, and Emma, supported by her uncle, entered the cell. At the sight of her our hero uttered a cry, and staggered against the wall; he appeared to have lost his usual self-control. "Oh," said he, "this might have been spared me; I have not deserved this punishment. Emma, hear me. As I hope for future happiness I am innocent; I am—I am, indeed——" and he fell senseless on the pavement.

Mr. Small raised him up and put him on the bed; after a time he revived, and remained where he had been laid, sobbing convulsively.

As soon as he became more composed, Emma, who had been sitting by him, the tears coursing each other down her pale cheeks, addressed him in a calm voice.

"I feel—I am sure that you are innocent, or I should not have been here."

"Bless you for that, Emma, bless you; those few words of yours have given me more consolation than you can imagine. Is it nothing to be treated as a felon, to be disgraced, to be banished to a distant country, and that at the very time that I was full of happiness, prosperous, and anticipating—? but I cannot dwell upon that. Is it not hard to bear, Emma? and what could support me but the consciousness of my own innocence, and the assurance that she whom I love so, and whom I now lose for ever, still believes me so? Yes, it is a balm, a consolation; and I will now submit to the will of Heaven."

Emma burst into tears, leaning her face on our hero's shoulder. After a time she replied, "And am I not to be pitied? Is it nothing to love tenderly, devotedly, madly— to have given my heart, my whole thoughts, my existence to one object—why should I conceal it now?—to have been dwelling upon visions of futurity so pleasing, so delightful, all passing away as a dream, and leaving a sad reality like this? Make me one promise; you will not refuse Emma— who knelt by your side when you first met her, she who is kneeling before you now?"

"I dare not, Emma, for my heart tells me that you would propose a step which must not be—you must leave me now, and for ever."

"For ever! for ever!" cried Emma, springing on her feet. "No! no!—uncle, he says I am to leave him for ever!

302

"At the sight of her, our hero uttered a cry, and staggered
against the wall."

Who is that?" continued the frantic girl, "Mary! yes 'tis!
Mary, he says I must leave him for ever!" (It was Mary
who had just come into the cell.) "Must I, Mary?"

"No—no," replied Mary, "not so! he is saved, and his
innocence is established; he is yours for ever!"

We shall not attempt to describe the scene we could not
do justice to. We must allow the day to pass away; during
which Emma and our hero, Mr. Small and Mary, were sitting
together; tears of misery wiped away—tears of joy still
flowing and glistening with the radiance of intermingled
smiles.

The next morning M'Shane and O'Donahue arrived; the
Secretary of State had given immediate orders for our hero's
release, and they had brought the document with them.

The following day they were all *en route*, Emma and her
uncle to Portsmouth, where they anxiously awaited the
arrival of our hero as soon as he had performed his duty to
his parents.

We must allow the reader to suppose the joy of Mrs.
Austin in once more holding her child in her embrace, and
the smiles and happiness of Mary at his triumphant acquittal;
the wondering of the domestics, the scandal and rumour of
the neighbourhood. Three days sufficed to make all known,
and by that time Joey was looked upon as the hero of a
novel. On the fourth day he accompanied the remains of
his father as chief mourner. The funeral was quiet without
being mean; there was no attendance, no carriages of the
neighbouring gentry followed. Our hero was quite alone
and unsupported; but when the ceremony was over, the
want of respect shown to the memory of his father was more
than atoned for by the kindness and consideration shown
towards the son, who was warmly, yet delicately, welcomed
as the future proprietor of the Hall.

Three months passed away, and there was a great crowd
before the house of Mr. Small, navy agent at Portsmouth.
There was a large company assembled, the O'Donahues, the
M'Shanes, the Spikemans, and many others. Mrs. Austin
was there, looking ten years younger; and Mary was attending her at the toilet, both of them half smiles, half tears, for
it was the morning of our hero's wedding-day. Mr. Small
strutted about in white smalls, and Mr. Sleek spluttered over

everybody. The procession went to the church, and soon after the ceremony, one couple of the party set off for the Hall; where the others went is of no consequence.

We have now wound up the history of little Joey Rushbrook, the poacher. We have only to add that the character of our hero was not the worse as he grew older, and was the father of a family. The Hall was celebrated for hospitality, for the amiability of its possessors, and the art which they possessed of making other people happy. Mary remained with them more as a confidante than as a servant; indeed, she had so much money that she received several offers of marriage, which she invariably refused, observing, with the true humbleness of a contrite heart, that she was undeserving of any honest, good man. Everybody else, even those who knew her history, thought otherwise; but Mary continued firm in her resolution. As for all the rest of the personages introduced into these pages, they passed through life with an average portion of happiness, which is all that can be expected.

In conclusion, we have only one remark to make. In this story we have shown how a young lad, who commenced his career with poaching, ultimately became a gentleman of £7000 a year; but we must remind our youthful readers, that it does not follow that every one who commences with poaching is to have the same good fortune. We advise them, therefore, not to attempt it, as they may find that instead of £7000 a year, they may stand a chance of going to where our hero very narrowly escaped from being sent; that is, to a certain portion of her Majesty's dominions beyond the seas, latterly termed Australia, but more generally known by the appellation of Botany Bay.

A RENCONTRE

A RENCONTRE

ONE evening I was sitting alone in the *salle à manger* of the *Couronne d'Or*, at Boulogne, when Colonel G——, an old acquaintance, came in. After the first greeting he took a chair, and was soon as busily occupied as I was with a cigar, which was occasionally removed from our lips as we asked and replied to questions as to what had been our pursuits subsequently to our last rencontre. After about half-an-hour's chit-chat, he observed, as he lighted a fresh cigar—

"When I was last in this room, I was in company with a very strange personage."

"Male or female?" inquired I.

"Female," replied Colonel G——. "Altogether it's a story worth telling, and, as it will pass away the time, I will relate it to you—unless you wish to retire."

As I satisfied him that I was not anxious to go to bed, and very anxious to hear his story, he narrated it, as nearly as I can recollect, in the following words :—

"I had taken my place in the diligence from Paris, and when I arrived at *Notre Dame des Victoires* it was all ready for a start; the luggage, piled up as high as an English haystack, had been covered over and buckled down, and the *conducteur* was calling out for the passengers. I took my last hasty whiff of my cigar, and unwillingly threw away more than half of a really good Havannah ; for I perceived that in the *intérieur,* for which I had booked myself, there was one female already seated ; and women and cigars are such great luxuries in their respective ways, that they are not to be indulged in at one and the same time—the world would be too happy, and happiness, we are told, is not for us here below. Not that I agree with that moral, although it comes

307

from very high authority; there is a great deal of happiness
in this world, if you knew how to extract it,—or, rather, I
should say, of pleasure; there is a pleasure in doing good;
there is a pleasure, unfortunately, in doing wrong; there is
a pleasure in looking forward, ay, and in looking backward
also; there is pleasure in loving and being loved, in eating,
and drinking, and, though last, not least, in smoking. I do
not mean to say that there are not the drawbacks of pain,
regret, and even remorse; but there is a sort of pleasure
even in them; it is pleasant to repent, because you know
that you are doing your duty; and if there is no great
pleasure in pain, it precedes an excess when it has left you.
I say again that, if you know how to extract it, there is a
great deal of pleasure and of happiness in this world, especially if you have, as I have, a very bad memory.

"'*Allons, messieurs!*' said the *conducteur*; and when I got
in I found myself the sixth person, and opposite to the lady;
for all the other passengers were of my own sex. Having
fixed our hats up to the roof, wriggled and twisted a little
so as to get rid of coat-tails, &c., all of which was effected
previously to our having cleared *Rue Notre Dame des Victoires*,
we began to scrutinise each other. Our female companion's
veil was down and doubled, so that I could not well make
her out; my other four companions were young men—all
Frenchmen,—apparently good-tempered, and inclined to be
agreeable. A few seconds were sufficient for my reconnoitre of the gentlemen, and then my eyes were naturally
turned towards the lady. She was muffled up in a winter
cloak, so that her figure was not to be made out; and the
veil still fell down before her face, so that only one cheek
and a portion of her chin could be deciphered; that fragment
of her physiognomy was very pretty, and I watched in silence
for the removal of the veil.

"I have omitted to state that, before I got into the diligence, I saw her take a very tender adieu of a very handsome
woman; but, as her back was turned to me at the time, I
did not see her face. She had now fallen back in her seat,
and seemed disposed to commune with her own thoughts;
that did not suit my views, which were to have a view of her
face. Real politeness would have induced me to leave her
to herself, but pretended politeness was resorted to that I

might gratify my curiosity; so I inquired if she wished the window up. The answer was in the negative, and in a very sweet voice; and then there was a pause, of course—so I tried again.

"'You are melancholy at parting with your handsome sister,' observed I, leaning forward with as much appearance of interest as I could put into my beautiful phiz.

"'How could you have presumed that she was my sister?' replied she.

"'From the *strong family* likeness,' replied I, 'I felt certain of it.'

"'But she is only my sister-in-law, sir,—my brother's wife.'

"'Then, I presume, he chose a wife as like his sister as he could find; nothing more natural—I should have done the same.'

"'Sir, you are very polite,' replied the lady, who lowered down the window, adding, 'I like fresh air.'

"'Perhaps you will find yourself less incommoded if you take off your veil.'

"'I will not ascribe that proposition to curiosity on your part, sir,' replied the lady, 'as you have already seen my face.'

"'You cannot, then, be surprised at my wishing to see it once more.'

"'You are very polite, sir.'

"Although her voice was soft, there was a certain quickness and decision in her manner and language which were very remarkable. The other passengers now addressed her, and the conversation became general. The veiled lady took her share in it, and showed a great deal of smartness and repartee. In an hour more we were all very intimate. As we changed horses I took down my hat to put into it my cigar-case, which I had left in my pocket, upon which the lady observed, 'You smoke, I perceive; and so, I dare say, do all the rest of the gentlemen. Now, do not mind me; I am fond of the smell of tobacco—I am used to it.'

"We hesitated.

"'Nay, more, I smoke myself, and will take a cigar with you.'

"This was decisive. I offered my cigar-case—another gentleman struck a light. Lifting up her veil so as to show a very pretty mouth, with teeth as white as snow, she put the cigar in her mouth and set us the example. In a minute both windows were down, every one had a cigar in his mouth.

"'Where did you learn to smoke, madam?' was a question put to the *incognita* by the passenger who sat next to her.

"'Where?—In the camp—Africa—everywhere. I did belong to the army—that is, my husband was the captain of the 47th. He was killed, poor man! in the last successful expedition to Constantine:—*c'était un brave homme.*'

"'Indeed! Were you at Constantine?'

"'Yes, I was; I followed the army during the whole campaign.'

"The diligence stopped for supper or dinner, whichever it might be considered, and the *conducteur* threw open the doors. 'Now,' thought I, 'we shall see her face;' and so, I believe, thought the other passengers. But we were mistaken; the lady went upstairs and had a basin of soup taken to her. When all was ready we found her in the diligence, with her veil down as before.

"This was very provoking, for she was so lively and witty in conversation, and the features of her face which had been disclosed were so perfect, that I was really quite on a fret that she would leave me without satisfying my curiosity;— they talk of woman's curiosity, but we men have as much, after all. It became dark;—the lady evidently avoided further conversation, and we all composed ourselves as well as we could. It may be as well to state in few words, that the next morning she was as cautious and reserved as ever. The diligence arrived at this hotel—the passengers separated—and I found that the lady and I were the only two who took up our quarters there. At all events, the Frenchmen who travelled with us went away just as wise as they came.

"'You remain here?' inquired I, as soon as we had got out of the diligence.

"'Yes,' replied she. 'And you——'

"'I remain here, certainly; but I hope you do not intend to remain always veiled. It is too cruel of you.'

"'I must go to my room now, and make myself a little

more comfortable; after that, Mons. l'Anglais, I will speak to you. You are going over in the packet, I presume?'

"'I am, by to-morrow's packet.'

"'I shall put myself under your protection, for I am also going to London.'

"'I shall be most delighted.'

"'*Au revoir.*'

"About an hour afterwards a message was brought to me by the *garçon*, that the lady would be happy to receive me at No. 19. I ascended to the second floor, knocked, and was told to come in.

"She was now without a veil; and what do you think was her reason for the concealment of her person?"

"By the beard of Mokhanna, how can I tell?"

"Well then, she had two of the most beautiful eyes in the world; her eyebrows were finely arched; her forehead was splendid; her mouth was tempting,—in short, she was as pretty as you could wish a woman to be, only she had *broken her nose,*—a thousand pities, for it must once have been a very handsome one. Well, to continue, I made my bow.

"'You perceive now, sir,' said she, 'why I wore my veil down.'

"'No, indeed,' replied I.

"'You are very polite, or very blind,' rejoined she; 'the latter I believe not to be the fact. I did not choose to submit to the impertinence of my own countrymen in the diligence; they would have asked me a hundred questions upon my accident. But you are an Englishman, and have respect for a female who has been unfortunate.'

"'I trust I deserve your good opinion, madam; and if I can be in any way useful to you——'

"'You can. I shall be a stranger in England. I know that in London there is a great man, one Monsieur Lis-tong, who is very clever.'

"'Very true, madam. If your nose, instead of having been slightly injured as it is, had been left behind you in Africa, Mr. Liston would have found you another.'

"'If he will only repair the old one, I ask no more. You give me hopes. But the bones are crushed completely, as you must see.'

"'That is of no consequence. Mr. Liston has put a new

eye in, to my knowledge. The party was short-sighted, and saw better with the one put in by Mr. Liston, than with the one which had been left him.'

"'*Est-il possible? Mais, quel homme extraordinaire!* Perhaps you will do me the favour to sit with me, monsieur; and, if I mistake not, you have a request to make of me—*n'est-ce pas?*'

"'I felt such interest about you, madam, that I acknowledge, if it would not be too painful to you, I should like to ask a question.'

"'Which is, how did I break my nose? Of course you want to know. And as it is the only return I can make for past or future obligations to you, you shall most certainly be gratified. I will not detain you now. I shall expect you to supper. Adieu, monsieur.'

"I did not, of course, fail in my appointment; and after supper she commenced :—

"'The question to be answered,' said she, 'is, How did you break your nose?—is it not? Well then, at least, I shall answer it after my own fashion. So, to begin at the beginning, I am now exactly twenty-two years old. My father was tambour-majeur in the Garde Impériale. I was born in the camp—brought up in the camp—and, finally, I was married in the camp, to a lieutenant of infantry at the time. So that, you observe, I am altogether *militaire*. As a child, I was wakened up with the drum and fife, and went to sleep with the bugles; as a girl, I became quite conversant with every military manœuvre; and now that I am a woman grown, I believe that I am more fit for the *bâton* than one-half of those marshals who have gained it. I have studied little else but tactics, and have, as my poor husband said, quite a genius for them; but of that hereafter. I was married at sixteen, and have ever since followed my husband. I followed him at last to his grave. He quitted my bed for the bed of honour, where he sleeps in peace. We'll drink to his memory.'

"We emptied our glasses, when she continued :—

"'My husband's regiment was not ordered to Africa until after the first disastrous attempt upon Constantine. It fell to our lot to assist in retrieving the honour of our army in the more successful expedition which took place, as you, of course, are aware, about three months ago. I will not detain you with our embarkation or voyage. We landed from a steamer at Bona, and soon afterwards my husband's company was ordered to escort a convoy of provisions to the army which was collecting at Mzez Ammar. Well, we arrived safely at our various camps of Drean, Nech Meya, and Amman Berda. We made a little *détour* to visit Ghelma. I had curiosity to see it, as formerly it was an important city. I must say that a more tenable position I never beheld. But I tire you with these details.'

" ' On the contrary, I am delighted.'

" ' You are very good. I ought to have said something about the travelling in those wild countries, which is anything but pleasant. The soil is a species of clay, hard as a flint when the weather is dry, but running into a slippery paste as soon as moistened. It is, therefore, very fatiguing, especially in wet weather, when the soldiers slip about in a very laughable manner to look at, but very distressing to themselves. I travelled either on horseback or in one of the waggons, as it happened. I was too well known, and, I hope I may add, too well liked, not to be as well provided for as possible. It is remarkable how soon a Frenchman will make himself comfortable, wherever he may chance to be. The camp of Mzez Ammar was as busy and as lively as if it was pitched in the heart of France. The followers had built up little cabins out of the branches of trees, with their leaves on, interwoven together, all in straight lines, forming streets, very commodious, and perfectly impervious to the withering sun. There were *restaurants, cafés, débis de vin et d'eau-de-vie*, sausage-sellers, butchers, grocers—in fact, there was every trade almost, and everything you required; not very cheap certainly, but you must recollect that this little town had sprung up as if by magic, in the heart of the desert.

" ' It was in the month of September that Damremont ordered a *reconnoissance* in the direction of Constantine, and a battalion of my husband's regiment, the 47th, was ordered to form a part of it. I have said nothing about my husband. He was a good little man, and a brave officer, full of honour, but very obstinate. He never would take advice, and it v as nothing but " *Tais-toi, Coralie,*" all day long—but no one is perfect. He wished me to remain in the camp, but **I made** it a rule never to be left behind. We set off, and I rode in one of the little carriages called *cacolets*, which had been provided for the wounded. It was terrible travelling, I was jolted to atoms in the ascent of the steep mountain called the Rass-el-akba; but we gained the summit without a shot being fired. When we arrived there, and looked down beneath us, the sight was very picturesque. There were about four or five thousand of the Arab cavalry awaiting our descent; their white bournous, as they term the long dresses in which they enfold themselves, waving in the wind as they galloped at speed in every direction; while the glitter of their steel arms flashed like lightning upon your eyes. We closed our ranks and descended, the Arabs, in parties of forty or fifty, charging upon our flanks every minute, not coming to close conflict, but stopping at pistol-shot distance, discharging their guns, and then wheeling off again to a distance—mere child's play, sir; nevertheless, there were some of our men wounded, and the little waggon, upon which I was riding, was ordered up in the advance to take them in. Unfortunately, to keep clear of the troops, the driver kept too much on one side of the narrow defile through which we passed; the consequence was that the waggon upset, and I was thrown out a considerable distance down the precipice——'

" 'And broke your nose,' interrupted I.

" 'No, indeed, sir, I did not. I escaped with only a few contusions about the region of the hip, which certainly lamed me for some time, and made the jolting more disagreeable than ever. Well, the *reconnoissance* succeeded. Damremont was, however, wrong altogether. I told him so when I met him; but he was an obstinate old fool, and his answer was not as polite as it might have been, considering that at that time I was a very pretty woman. We returned to the camp at Mzez Ammar; a few days afterwards we were attacked by the Arabs, who showed great spirit and determination in their desultory mode of warfare, which, however, can make no impression on such troops as the French. The attack was continued for three days, when they decamped as suddenly as they had come. But this cannot be very interesting to you, monsieur.'

314

A RENCONTRE

"'On the contrary, do not, I beg, leave out a single remark or incident.'

"'You are very good. I presume you know how we *militaires* like to fight our battles over again. Well, sir, we remained in camp until the arrival of the Duc de Nemours, —a handsome, fair lad, who smiled upon me very graciously. On the 1st of October we set off on our expedition to Constantine; that is to say, the advanced guard did, of which my husband's company formed a portion. The weather, which had been very fine, now changed, and it rained hard all the day. The whole road was one mass of mud, and there was no end to delays and accidents. However, the weather became fine again, and on the 5th we arrived within two leagues of Constantine, when the Arabs attacked us, and I was very nearly taken prisoner.'

"'Indeed?'

"'Yes; my husband, who, as I before observed to you, was very obstinate, would have me ride on a *caisson* in the rear; whereas I wished to be in the advance, where my advice might have been useful. The charge of the Arabs was very sudden; the three men who were with the *caisson* were sabred, and I was in the arms of a chieftain, who was wheeling round his horse to make off with me, when a ball took him in the neck, and he fell with me. I disengaged myself, seized the horse by the bridle, and prevented its escape; and I also took possession of the Arab's pistols and cimeter.'

"'Indeed?'

"'My husband sold the horse the next day to one of our generals, who forgot to pay for it after my husband was killed. As for the cimeter and pistols, they were stolen from me that night; but what can you expect?—our army is brave, but a little demoralised. The next day we arrived before Constantine, and we had to defile before the enemy's guns. At one portion of the road men and horses were tumbled over by their fire; the *caisson* that I was riding upon was upset by a ball, and thrown down the ravine, dragging the horses after it. I lay among the horses' legs —they kicking furiously; it was a miracle that my life was preserved: as it was——'

"'You broke your nose,' interrupted I.

315

"'No, sir, indeed I did not. I only received a kick on the arm. which obliged me to carry it in a sling for some days. The weather became very bad; we had few tents, and they were not able to resist the storms of rain and wind. We wrapped ourselves up how we could, and sat in deep pools of water, and the Arabs attacked us before we could open the fire of our batteries; we were in such a pickle that, had the bad weather lasted, we must have retreated; and happy would those have been who could have once more found themselves safe in the camp of Mzez Ammar. I don't think that I ever suffered so much as I did at that time—the weather had even overcome the natural gallantry of our nation; and so far from receiving any attention, the general remark to me was, "What the devil do *you* do here?" This to be said to a pretty woman!

"'It was not till the 10th that we could manage to open the fire of our batteries. It was mud, mud, and mud again; the men and horses were covered with mud up to their necks—the feathers of the staff were covered with mud— every ball which was fired by the enemy sent up showers of mud; even the face of the Duc de Nemours was disfigured with it. I must say that our batteries were well situated, all except the great mortar battery. This I pointed out to Damremont when he passed me, and he was very savage. Great men don't like to be told of their faults; however, he lost his life three days afterwards from not taking my advice. He was going down the hill with Rhullières when I said to him, "Mon Général, you expose yourself too much; that which is duty in a subaltern is a fault in a general." He very politely told me to go to where he may chance to be himself now; for a cannon-ball struck him a few seconds afterwards, and he was killed on the spot. General Perregaux was severely wounded almost at the same time. For four days the fighting was awful; battery answered to battery night and day; while from every quarter of the compass we were exposed to the fierce attacks of the Arab cavalry. The commander of our army sent a flag of truce to their town, commanding them to surrender; and what do you think was the reply?—"If you want powder, we'll supply you; if you are without bread, we will send it to you; but as long as there is one good Mussulman left alive, you do not enter the town."—Was not that grand? The very reply, when made known to the troops, filled them with admiration of their enemy, and they swore by their colours that if ever they overpowered them they would give them no quarter.

"'In two days, General Vallée, to whom the command fell upon the death of Damremont, considered the breach sufficiently wide for the assault, and we every hour expected that the order would be given. It came at last. My poor husband was in the second column which mounted. Strange to say, he was very melancholy on that morning, and appeared to have a presentiment of what was to take place. "Coralie," said he to me, as he was scraping the mud off his trousers with his pocket-knife, "if I fall, you will do well. I leave you as a legacy to General Vallée—he will appreciate you. Do not forget to let him know my testamentary dispositions."

"'I promised I would not. The drums beat. He kissed me on both cheeks. "Go, my Philippe," said I; "go to glory." He did; for a mine was sprung, and he with many others was blown to atoms. I had watched the advance of the column and was able to distinguish the form of my dear Philippe when the explosion with the vast column of smoke took place. When it cleared away I could see the wounded in every direction hastening back; but my husband was not among them. In the meantime the other columns entered the breach—the firing was awful, and the carnage dreadful. It was more than an hour after the assault commenced before the French tricolor waved upon the minarets of Constantine.

"'It was not until the next day that I could make up my mind to search for my husband's body; but it was my duty. I climbed up the breach, strewed with the corpses of our brave soldiers, intermingled with those of the Arabs; but I could not find my husband. At last a head which had been blown off attracted my attention. I examined it — it was my Philippe's, blackened and burnt, and terribly disfigured; but who can disguise the fragment of a husband from the keen eyes of the wife of his bosom? I leaned over it. "My poor Philippe!" exclaimed I; and the tears were bedewing my cheeks when I perceived the Duc de Nemours close to me, with all his staff attending him. "What have we here?" said he, with surprise, to those about him. "A wife looking

317

for her husband's body, mon prince," replied I. " I cannot find it; but here is his head." He said something very complimentary and kind, and then walked on. I continued my search without success, and determined to take up my quarters in the town. As I clambered along, I gained a battered wall; and putting my foot on it, it gave way with me, and I fell down several feet. Stunned with the blow, I remained for some time insensible; when I came to, I found——'

" ' That you had broken your nose.'

" ' No, indeed; I had sprained my ankle and hurt the cap of my knee, but my nose was quite perfect. You must have a little patience yet.

" ' What fragments of my husband were found were buried in a large grave, which held the bodies and the mutilated portions of the killed; and having obtained possession of an apartment in Constantine, I remained there several days, lamenting his fate. At last it occurred to me that his testamentary dispositions should be attended to, and I wrote to General Vallée, informing him of the last wishes of my husband. His reply was very short; it was, that he was excessively flattered, but press of business would not permit him to administer to the will. It was not polite.

" ' On the 26th I quitted Constantine with a convoy of wounded men. The dysentery and the cholera made fearful ravages, and I very soon had a *caisson* all to myself. The rain again came on in torrents, and it was a dreadful funeral procession. Every minute wretches, jolted to death, were thrown down into pits by the roadside, and the cries of those who survived were dreadful. Many died of cold and hunger; and after three days we arrived at the camp of Mzez Ammar, with the loss of more than one-half of our sufferers.

" ' I took possession of one of the huts built of the boughs of the trees which I formerly described, and had leisure to think over my future plans and prospects. I was young and pretty, and hope did not desert me. I had recovered my baggage, which I had left at the camp, and was now able to attend to my toilet. The young officers who were in the camp paid me great attention, and were constantly passing and repassing to have a peep at the handsome widow, as they were pleased to call me ; and now comes the history of my misfortune.

" 'The cabin built of boughs which I occupied was double ; one portion was fenced off from the other with a wattling of branches, which ran up about seven feet, but not so high as the roof. In one apartment I was located, the other was occupied by a young officer who paid me attention, but who was not to my liking. I had been walking out in the cool of the evening, and had returned, when I heard voices in the other apartment. I entered softly and they did not perceive my approach ; they were talking about me, and I must say that the expressions were very complimentary. At last one of the party observed, "Well, she is a splendid woman, and a good soldier's wife. I hope to be a general by-and-by, and she would not disgrace a marshal's bâton. I think I shall propose to her before we leave the camp."

" 'Now, sir, I did not recognise the speaker by his voice, and, flattered by the remark, I was anxious to know who it could be who was thus prepossessed in my favour. I thought that if I could climb up on the back of the only chair which was in my apartment, I should be able to see over the partition and satisfy my curiosity. I did so, and without noise ; and I was just putting my head over to take a survey of the tenants of the other apartment when the chair tilted, and down I came on the floor, and on my face. Unfortunately, I hit my nose upon the edge of the frying-pan, with which my poor Philippe and I used to cook our meat ; and now, sir, you know how it was that I broke my nose.'

" 'What a pity !' observed I.

" 'Yes ; a great pity. I had gone through the whole campaign without any serious accident, and——But, after all, it was very natural ; the two besetting evils of women are Vanity and Curiosity, and if you were to ascertain the truth, you would find that it is upon these two stumbling-blocks that most women are upset and break their noses.'

" 'Very true, madam,' replied I. 'I thank you for your narrative, and shall be most happy to be of any use to you. But I will detain you from your rest no longer, so wish you a very good night.' "

"Well, colonel," said I, as he made a sudden stop, "what occurred after that ?"

A RENCONTRE

"I took great care of her until we arrived in London, saw her safe to the hotel in Leicester Square, and then took my leave. Whether Liston replaced her nose, and she is now *flanée*-ing about Paris, as beautiful as before her accident; or whether his skill was useless to her, and she is among the *Sœurs de Charité*, or in a convent, I cannot say; I have never seen or heard of her since."

"Well, I know Liston, and I'll not forget to ask him about her the very first time that I meet him. Will you have another cigar?"

"No, I thank you. I've finished my cigar, my bottle, and my story, and so now good night!"

THE END

www.ingramcontent.com/pod-product-compliance
Lightning Source LLC
Chambersburg PA
CBHW022209010726
47493CB00002B/477